M000190160

THE UNION OF LIES

THE GODLESS TRILOGY | BOOK TWO

CHRISTOPHER MONTEAGLE

Black Rose Writing | Texas

©2021 by Christopher Monteagle
All rights reserved. No part of this book may be reproduced, stored in a
retrieval system or transmitted in any form or by any means without the
prior written permission of the publishers, except by a reviewer who may
quote brief passages in a review to be printed in a newspaper, magazine
or journal.

The author grants the final approval for this literary material.

First printing

This is a work of fiction. Names, characters, businesses, places, events, and
incidents are either the products of the author's imagination or used in a
fictitious manner. Any resemblance to actual persons, living or dead, or
actual events is purely coincidental.

ISBN: 978-1-68433-819-1
PUBLISHED BY BLACK ROSE WRITING
www.blackrosewriting.com

Printed in the United States of America
Suggested Retail Price (SRP) $20.95

The Union of Lies is printed in Calluna
Map art credited to Edwin Menzo @fantasymapshop

aAs a planet-friendly publisher, Black Rose Writing does its best to eliminate
unnecessary waste to reduce paper usage and energy costs, while never
compromising the reading experience. As a result, the final word count vs. page count
may not meet common expectations.

To Laura and Jessica.
Daughters are gods to all fathers.

Iron Union

Kovalith

Alovat

Ironhelm

Grand Duchy

of Joana

Ciro

The Shield

Dark Spires

Mac-Soldai

Fortress of Krág

Klyph
(Malene's Fall)

Arbek

Hammerfall

Rhaskitov

Greund

Barrens of Silence

Kardak

The Render

The Forge

Outland Alliance

Roy

Marfort

Clairagon

Fairhaven

Vigilsea

Freeport   Bonehall

Dynn   The Federacy   Darcliff

Ebeth   Azad

Fyrn

Stonekeep   Greenridge

Tyne   Qharg

Wheatsheaf

Outpost

Great Southern Wastes   Ashran

Fareaches

THE
UNION OF LIES
THE GODLESS TRILOGY | BOOK TWO

INTRODUCTION

The gods have left us. After centuries of leading us they simply left. Only two remained – Bythe of the Iron Union and the Blessed Mother Maelene of the Outer Wild. War between these two last gods was inevitable, and after decades of conflict, Maelene was ultimately deceived and murdered by Bythe. The Iron Union has been in ascendancy ever since that black day.

Commander Vale – the young, illegitimate daughter of Bythe – invaded the remote town of Outpost, the home of a young woman named Elyn. A chance encounter between them revealed they were identical in appearance, but before Vale could act, Elyn and her father fled to the remote town of Fairhaven. Over the following two years, Commander Vale chafed under the cruel supervision of Yvorre – Bythe's grotesque Mistress of Spies and Assassins – who dominated and controlled Vale's every move.

In Fairhaven, Elyn slowly discovered a strange mental kinship with Vale, which aroused the suspicions of the Ageless – Maelene's followers. Elyn and Vale started to communicate in secret, both unsure of the meaning of the connection and both fearful of what would happen to them if it was discovered. Fairhaven was attacked by raiders, and Elyn's father brutally murdered in front of her. In this moment of primal grief, Elyn and Vale's connection was strengthened, and both understood the truth of their existence: they were two halves of the same person – the daughter of Bythe split in two. Mistress Yvorre exploited this tragedy to discover Elyn's whereabouts and sent her fearsome servant – the unstoppable Imbatal – to retrieve the girl.

Deserting the Iron Union, Vale desperately set out in the hope of reaching Elyn. In Fairhaven, Elyn became increasingly withdrawn as the darkness of her real father, Bythe, grew within her. Rejecting the help of the Ageless and of her friends – Jason and Nadine – Elyn could feel herself becoming consumed by the god-like power growing within her. Imbatal and his army descended upon an unprepared Fairhaven, and the city was quickly overrun. As the battle raged, Vale arrived at Fairhaven and found Elyn. Together, they sought refuge with the Ageless.

Within the Temple, Vale and Elyn were confronted by the spirit of Maelene and the terrible secret of their birth was revealed. Maelene did not die as the legends said but had been captured by Bythe and forced to bear his child. Maelene had tried to flee with their daughter, but Bythe had uncovered her treachery and tried to stop her. As the parents fought, their daughter was split into two fractured godlings: Elyn and Vale. By pure accident, or whim of fate, Elyn was lost to both of them – leaving the incomplete Vale behind. Maelene was finally defeated and enslaved by Bythe. Over time, she had eventually become the corrupted and twisted Mistress Yvorre. Upon learning this truth, Vale and Elyn defied their mother and fled the Temple.

Imbatal penetrated the city and ruthlessly hunted down Bythe's daughters. In order to save Elyn from death, Vale willingly sacrificed herself. In the moments while Vale's life slipped away, Elyn realized she was finally tired of running. Elyn surrendered herself into Vale, and the two reconciled into a new god: Valeyn.

Valeyn defeated Imbatal and his army was routed. Fearing retribution from both Bythe and Valeyn, Yvorre fled into hiding. The Ageless were devastated by the revelations of Maelene's corruption, and they offered Valeyn the chance to be worshipped as a god in her place, but Valeyn decided she would no longer be manipulated. Finally happy and content with herself, Valeyn said goodbye to Jason and Nadine, and left Fairhaven behind to find her own destiny.

But deep within the Ironhelm, Bythe was troubled.

BOOK 1
RESTITUTIONS

CHAPTER 1

"Valeyn has left us. After defending the people of Fairhaven from the fallen goddess Maelene, she simply vanished, leaving us behind.

Peace held for a time. The people of Fairhaven attempted to rebuild their lives, however this proved difficult. Maelene's betrayal of her own people was an injury that would not heal easily.

Similarly, our enemies were forced to pause and reassess. Bythe of the Iron Union had discovered the existence of his daughter, Valeyn, and it seemed only the gods themselves knew how he would react. The Iron Union's campaign against the Outland Alliance paused for three years while Bythe schemed in his Ironhelm.

Throughout the known world, it seemed that a storm had paused and people were given the briefest of moments to collect the scattered pieces of their lives. For a while, we were allowed to hope that this change might finally bring a lasting peace.

Sadly, as a storm may hold its breath for a time, it cannot simply stop – and its inevitable resumption seemed all the heavier for the respite."

~Aleasea of the Ageless

The tavern reeked. The traveler immediately identified it as one of those places where a man could lie undisturbed for hours – if not days – dozing in a pool of his own fluids as long as he routinely paid for a drink. He walked across the timber floorboards, carefully skirting the various puddles of unidentified liquids as he made his way to the bar. It was dim, despite the harsh midday sun outside. Such reminders of a brighter life were unwelcome in places like this. He reached the bar and rapped his knuckles politely but firmly on the sticky benchtop. An older man emerged from the gloom and approached. He had a drawn face and wide eyes which gave him the look of a man who was constantly in a state of terror. The traveler looked at him thoughtfully and considered this might actually be true.

"What do you have to offer a weary traveler, sir?" he asked in a clear and refined voice.

The barman looked at him cautiously before answering. "Ale, I've got a bit of grapewine left if you want it?"

The traveler smiled somewhat disapprovingly and scanned the bar shelves. "Anything a little more...what's the word...civilized?"

It's possible that another barman might have taken offense at such words, no matter how politely offered. It's possible that another barman might turn his back or even reach for a weapon under the bar at such a remark – but the traveler was an excellent judge of a man's nature.

"Of course, sir." The barman eagerly turned to the top shelves and returned with a bottle thick with dust. "Grainmalt from Rhaskiton, aged ten years!"

The traveler looked at the remaining brownish liquid in the half-empty bottle and correctly judged that it couldn't have been more than two years old and was most likely watered down. Nevertheless, he offered his thin smile again.

"How much?"

The barman glanced sideways in the obvious tell of the less practiced swindler before proceeding. "Stuff like this is rare out here, sir. I'd have to ask for fourteen copper slots for a glass."

The traveler held the barman's terrified eyes for a moment, his thin smile never faltering. "Of course, a high price to pay for such a luxury, but I can imagine the dire straits of the economy this far into the Outlands." He reached into his belt and produced a small pouch laden with coins. Almost carelessly, he began tossing them onto the benchtop. The sound they made as they rolled and clattered onto the wood seemed to reverberate throughout the entire room, attracting the attention of every eye. Coin after coin was tossed onto the bar, almost disdainfully, until they began to pile and roll over the edge. When the well-groomed traveler was finished, he rolled up his purse and returned it to his belt.

"I believe you now have roughly a hundred and fifty slots, perhaps a few more have wound up down by your boots there, I wasn't keeping track. May I take the bottle, if you would be so kind?"

The barman stared at the traveler mutely for a moment before slowly pushing the half empty bottle across the benchtop. The traveler smiled but raised an eyebrow.

"You're disappointing me, barman."

The barman's permanently frightened expression seemed to deepen, and he took an involuntary step backward, seemingly convinced something very bad was about to happen to him. The traveler closed his eyes and shook his head patiently.

"Relax, sir, I merely wondered if you expected me to drink this from the bottle, like a savage?"

The barman chuckled in obvious relief and rushed to place a grimy glass next to the bottle. The traveler picked it up, inspecting its myriad fingermarks against the light with curiosity, before also taking the bottle and turning to the room. Every eye was on him.

To be fair, the traveler would look out of place even without the ostentatious display of wealth. Tall and slender, he looked to be a well-groomed man in his early middle years. He wore a black frock coat of shimmering silk with a matching waistcoat. His black hair was slicked back against his head, revealing a slim face with dark eyes and a high forehead. He scanned the figures seated at the tables and seemed to appraise each man in turn.

The room was hardly full. As remote as Ashran was, it wasn't busy enough to sustain the usual retinue of drunks and degenerates that a larger town would support. The Royal Inquisitor looked over the face of every man in the room then addressed the gathering in a clear voice.

"Good afternoon, gentlemen. My name is Exedor, and I've travelled far to come here. I'm looking for someone, a stranger to this town. I have reason to believe this someone has passed through here recently."

The room was predictably silent. It was as if the Inquisitor hadn't even spoken. Unperturbed, he continued. "The stranger is a woman. Actually, she's little more than a girl, but tall and fit with a man's bearing. She's really quite impressive. Her name is Valeyn, and I am told she passed through this town no more than two months past."

Again, the room was silent. Some of the drinkers were still watching him, others had returned to their thoughts or quiet conversations. The Inquisitor smiled again and, with a slow but deliberate gesture, opened his coat to reveal the purse hanging at his belt.

"I am, of course, willing to compensate any man who might offer me his...expert knowledge in this matter."

Shuffles and murmurs began punctuating the silence, as if the room itself were now waking from a slumber. The Inquisitor was patient.

"Here!" A swarthy-looking, middle-aged man with greying hair and a rough beard gestured from his table at the back of the room. Two men sat at the table. Sallow looking creatures with their misspent youths long lost to them.

The Inquisitor nodded in reply and walked over to join them. He glanced at their faces and judged them both before taking the empty chair offered to him.

"Good afternoon, gentlemen," said Exedor, placing the bottle on the table and gesturing to the barman for more glasses. When they were delivered, Exedor poured three serves and offered a quick toast before downing his drink in one swift movement. The other men followed his example, and the Inquisitor quickly refilled the glasses with a grimace. "By all the gods, I'm a long way from home, but that must be the worst grainmalt I've ever tasted. Does he make it in his bedpan?"

The bearded man seated in the center of the table – clearly the alpha of the two – answered directly. "You're looking for that bitch?"

If the Inquisitor was offended by the vulgarity, he certainly showed none of it. "I'm searching for Valeyn, formerly of Fairhaven, yes. I take it you've seen her?"

The bearded man glanced at his large, brutish companion and nodded. "Yeah, she was here, about a couple of months back like you said, but before we go any further with that, let's talk terms of compensation."

"Of course," Exedor replied and reached for his pouch. He removed a small disc of black metal and placed it on the table. Both men looked at it as if not quite believing it was real.

"Is that an Iron Union marc?" the bearded man asked.

"Yes. Pure Darkiron, sell it or melt it down if you like. I'd imagine with the current state of the Outland economies you could probably buy half this tavern with it, if you felt so inclined."

The bearded man glanced again at his companion, greed evident on his face. "And what if I felt like buyin' the whole tavern, not half?"

The Inquisitor poured another round of drinks. "Why don't you let me assess the value of your information? Then we'll see what sort of arrangement we can come to."

The bearded man stared at the Inquisitor for a moment, clearly sizing him up, then nodded. "She came through town a couple of months back, like I said. All alone, just a girl and with a big damn sword on her back like she was playin' at bein' some kind of warrior. Stopped at the traders across the way to get some supplies, I think."

Exedor nodded and downed another glass of the putrid drink, gesturing for his companions to do the same. Once this was done, he refilled their glasses again. "Please continue."

"Well, like I said, she was just this woman all alone out here in the Outer Wild, so a few of the boys thought they'd offer her some protection, y'know, from bandits and the like."

"Extremely thoughtful of them," the Inquisitor replied with only a touch of sarcasm.

"I know it was – that's what gentleman like us do – but it turns out little miss high-and-mighty didn't want any of our help. In fact, she was downright rude to one of them – a friend of mine with nothing but the noblest of intentions."

"Shocking manners," the Inquisitor agreed.

"Exactly! You can't let these women walk around disrespecting us like that. You need to keep social order in a civilized society. I mean, we're not savages."

"Certainly not, sir!" the Inquisitor toasted his miserable companions and drank again.

"But the bitch wouldn't have it – just turned her back on us like we weren't even worth her time. Disgraceful behavior. So a few of the boys followed her out of town to give her a talkin' to and...well...that's when she turned on us."

The Inquisitor's playful demeanor seemed to drop and his eyes hardened. "Go on."

"Well, I was only at the back of the group, but she wasn't like anythin' I ever seen before. She just turned on us, didn't even bother to draw her weapon, and before we knew what'd happened, she'd broken Braw's arm and sent Jerdyn flying into the trees somehow. Well, after she attacked us, all unprovoked and the like, then we had to defend ourselves, right, for protection?" The bearded man looked to the Inquisitor for confirmation. Exedor didn't reply.

"Well..." the bearded man continued, slightly uncomfortable now, "well, two of the men...defended themselves...with knives and...well, I guess she didn't take too kindly to that. I'm not too sure what happened – maybe I'd been drinkin' more than I thought – but it seemed like I just blinked and then she was standin' over both of them. They were lyin' in the dirt. One had his neck broke somehow. The other had his own knife in his chest."

"And what happened next?" the Inquisitor pressed.

"Next?" The bearded man's large companion spoke for the first time. "We ran, that's what happened next. We all did. We figured out later when the other one came through, that she must've been some kinda witch or somethin'. Either way, we weren't hanging around to get cursed."

The Inquisitor's head snapped around to look at the new speaker. "Who was the other one?"

The bearded man shot his companion a black look. "Why you go runnin' off your mouth for? That's new information he never asked about. He has to buy that too, if he wants it."

The Inquisitor reached over and carefully re-stoppered the bottle. "Tell me about the other one."

The sallow-faced, bearded man looked at Exedor, and for a moment they simply stared at each other. Eventually, something in the bearded man seemed to relent and he spoke. "A few weeks later, another woman came through. This one was old, ugly, some kinda witch. We all kept away from her, especially after what her friend did to us."

"And how did you conclude that she was linked with Valeyn?" the Inquisitor asked.

"She was asking for her, same as you, only she wasn't offering no coin as payment. Most of us stayed away from her, but somehow she still managed to find out what she wanted to know."

The Inquisitor nodded. "Yes, she usually does. Very interesting. And which way did they leave?"

"Along the south road," the large companion answered quickly. It seemed as if he suddenly wanted the Inquisitor to leave the same way.

"Indeed," Exedor answered thoughtfully and slowly rose to his feet.

"Hey, where do you think you're goin'?" the bearded man asked, also rising. "We still gotta negotiate the terms of our settlement."

The Inquisitor looked at him, and all pretense at a friendly demeanor had now vanished – replaced with a cold and unforgiving stare. The large man also got to his feet but instead of confronting the Inquisitor, he turned to his companion.

"C'mon, Cane, forget him. We don't want any more part in this business, do we?"

"Shut up," Cane snapped at his friend. "This liar promised us fair compensation even before we gave him the extra information on the witch. He owes us a settlement."

"The terms of our settlement," the Inquisitor replied, "are that you may keep the coin already given and whatever remains in the bottle of that disgusting excuse for a drink. It's far more than you can ever hope to earn in a rathole like this."

A sick leer spread across Cane's weathered face. "I don't think that's true – not when we got that purse of yours right in front of us. Yeah, we may not be as civilized as you prissy folk in the Iron Union, but we sure know how to handle an arrogant fop like you." The room fell deathly still as Cane produced a large and cruel looking knife from wherever he'd been concealing it.

Exedor did not react. For a moment they all stood in place, staring at each other again, only this time it was the Inquisitor who broke the silence. "No, I think I'm right. I think it was all you could've hoped for. After all, you really don't have anything much left in your life do you, Cane?" Cane frowned slightly as the Inquisitor's eyes turned a dark shade of red and his skin seemed to pale slightly.

"Your best years are far behind you. You do nothing but drink in this wretched tavern and dream of bedding the cheapest whores you can't even afford anymore. This will be your life now, day after day, bleeding on and on until the liquor poisons your body and you die here alone." The Inquisitor's voice had become soft now, almost seductive as he leaned across the table looking into Cane's eyes. "Why prolong this existence, Cane? Why delay the inevitable decline into death? Every day is only going to get worse. Why not just end it now?"

Tears were slowly welling in Cane's eyes. He looked thoughtfully at the Inquisitor for a moment, then he raised the dagger to his own neck and started sawing into his throat as if it were meat. The tavern exploded within seconds. People began overturning chairs and looking to escape from the murderous scene before them. Exedor merely stood where he was, and watched Cane complete his own brutal suicide with genuine curiosity. Cane's large friend recovered from his shock and made a futile effort to remove the blade from his friend's neck, but it was far too late.

"Cane! Cane! What are you doing? What did you do to him?" he screamed at Exedor.

The Inquisitor shrugged. "I only told him who he really was. Is it my fault he didn't like what he heard?"

The patrons threw open the tavern doors to make their escape but stopped in terror. Figures blocked the exit. They stood tall and silent, dressed in robes of deep crimson. On their heads, they wore helms of dark scarlet metal, any human features lost to darkness but for a labored breathing that emanated from somewhere within.

"I'm sorry," the Inquisitor said in a voice that carried across the din. "I neglected to introduce my associates to you all. Quite rude of me to leave them lingering outside in the street. Please, do come in."

The patrons of the tavern screamed again but gave way as the crimson figures slowly entered in single file. The door slammed closed and six of the creatures stood facing the terrified drinkers.

"It's a shame it has to come to this – it honestly is," the Inquisitor soberly declared. "But there's a reason people like me exist, and it's because people like you exist. If you could only help yourselves, if you could only behave in a civilized way, all this simply wouldn't be necessary."

The Inquisitor watched as his associates reached up to their crimson helmets and, one by one, unlatched their faceplates. The screams in the room were abruptly silenced and Exedor felt the temperature drop – as it always did. The truth was, he was never entirely comfortable with what was about to happen. He certainly didn't fully understand it, in much the same way he didn't fully understand the new gifts Bythe had given him, but he never questioned it. Bythe was never to be questioned. Bythe's High Constable and Royal Inquisitor knew this was the difference between himself and Yvorre – between himself and Valeyn.

Although he had seen the Faede perform their work countless times, it still managed to discomfort him on some vaguely human level. There were sounds of bodies falling limp to the floor. There were muffled noises and distant moans – strange guttural sounds. He watched a young woman turn away from the Faede and walk as if in a daze. She stumbled on an overturned chair and fell to the floor without a sound – it was impossible for her to make a sound. The Inquisitor glanced down at her upturned face as it thrashed left and right. Her face was smooth with only her nose as its single feature – her eyes and mouth were gone. Exedor knew she was still conscious inside her mind, but she'd never be able to communicate again. The thought gave him a chill as he watched her start to thrash about with dull moans from within a throat with no mouth, and he looked away. He'd always thought this was the worst possible result from the Faede's work.

Another man fell to the floor and this one did scream. His arms and legs were gone, leaving nothing more than a squat torso under a head with a terrified face. The Inquisitor vaguely wondered how the Faede decided which part of their victims to take when they left people un-whole. Was there some level of deeper insight or judgment at work? Was it malicious pleasure, or just pure chance? Within a minute it was done. Everyone in the tavern had been taken. He looked at the bodies as they rolled on the floor, either in silence or screaming in fear and panic. None of them would ever be whole again. If the gods were still merciful, then hopefully most of the wretches would be dead within days.

The Inquisitor sighed, and walked back to the table where Cane still lay spurting blood onto the floor. He was surprised to find the man was still breathing, although his face was deathly white and he surely had no more than minutes of wretched life left.

"I'm glad you were able to watch," Exedor said as he gently leaned over to retrieve the coin. "You see, I'm not at all a bad person, Cane. I gave you the merciful option, but for these poor souls...?"

The Inquisitor gestured over his shoulder and shook his head gravely. He sighed and then – as if catching himself in a moment of pity – abruptly straightened and turned for the door.

"You people bring this on yourselves," he called back as he stepped over the body of a man twitching violently on the floor. He turned to the nearest of the Faede.

"Retrieve the money."

The creature turned without a word and walked over to where the barman lay with his terrified eyes now erased from his face. Exedor didn't wait. He gestured to the remaining creatures and walked to the door. He now had two quarries: Valeyn the fugitive godling, and a surprise target – Yvorre the Betrayer.

The Inquisitor wondered what reward Bythe would bestow upon him if he returned with that traitorous witch in chains. What new opportunities might open to him and how might he use these to further his own plans?

The Inquisitor looked over his retinue of Faede and wondered how they would react toward their old mistress. Would they even recognize her? He shrugged. Once he'd doggedly served Yvorre. Now, by some twist of the fates, he was to hunt her down. Justice was very satisfying. The Inquisitor knew that Bythe – the world's last true god – was smiling on him.

CHAPTER 2

"Kovalith – also known as the Forge – had been created from the energies of the gods – their kai. *It was proposed by Nishindra the Wanderer as a novelty to his brothers and sisters. It was a place where the gods could take physical form and enjoy a life constrained by rules and laws of their choosing.*

Maelene led the creation of nature and used her kai *to ensure the continuing flow of water from the oceans and mountains. Legends tells us of strange attempts to create a self-sustaining cycle of life with rain – water that falls from the sky. However these efforts were abandoned as the gods moved on to other interests.*

We were taught that many of the gods eventually grew tired of the Forge and chose to leave, but I have learned there may have been other motives for their departure. Gods are not well suited to a mortal existence."

~Aleasea of the Ageless

"Fairhaven is no longer whole! She is broken!" The voice was tired and impatient, and it echoed across the empty Council chamber. Councilor Jonas was on his feet pleading with the rest of the Council. He was a short, middle-aged man known for his wide girth and a wider grin. However, on this occasion his smile was nowhere to be seen.

"We know, Councilor, that's why it's imperative for you to stay. You're a leader of this community. How can we expect to maintain stability if we can't even set the example?" The person who replied was a well-groomed gentleman with a fine moustache and greying hair at his temples.

"Paeter," said Jonas wearily, "you know I don't want this, but what choice do we have? My business is ruined, my fields were destroyed in the siege, and they've never grown back. I need to start again somewhere safer."

"Safer?" snorted Councilor Morag, an older lady with a thin face and silver hair. "Where-ever do you think that might be? Do you intend to travel east to Azad or one of those colonies in the Fareaches? I think you'll find bigger problems than nomad raids out there. Tell us the truth. Why are you running away?"

Jonas glared at her. "What do you care, Morag? I'll finally be out of your way and you can realize your dream of running this Council – whatever's left of it." Jonas gestured to the chamber around them. The walls and ceiling were high and lined with dark wood, all engraved with intricate images of trees, leaves, and other elements of nature. The Councilors sat on a large, raised platform, with twelve high-backed chairs arranged in a semicircle facing an audience of wooden pews. Almost half the chairs were empty.

"Please, Jonas." A young woman with blonde hair rose to her feet. "The next generation of this town looks to men like you to guide them. We don't look to you for your financial means. We need people of honor and hard work to show the children of today who they should strive to become tomorrow. We need you."

Jonas looked at the young lady and smiled. "Councilor Paeter, you've trained your daughter too well. She almost makes me reconsider."

Paeter shrugged. "I haven't taught Nadine a thing. She's always known how to twist me around her finger. Now you just know what I've been dealing with for the past twenty years."

"You should listen to the young lady, Jonas. She has more sense than you do." Morag's words were harsh, but there was a sense of regretful acceptance in them.

Jonas sighed. "I apologize to all of you – I really do – but my decision is made."

He removed the gold chain, which marked him as a member of the Council, gently placed it on the table, and left the chamber. The other members watched him leave in silence.

"Well then," Paeter continued after the door had closed, "what's that? The third in as many months?"

"Who's going to replace Jonas? We haven't even been able to fill the other positions, and now we've got another vacancy," said Denethin, a short, balding man at the far end of the table.

For a moment nobody spoke.

"Perhaps I could speak to my friends again? We could start another search among the younger people," Nadine ventured quietly.

Morag sighed. "Thank you, Nadine, but while your generation supplies willingness, it lacks wisdom. You are the rare exception, of course," Morag added the last phrase with a tone of respect that sounded unusual coming from her. Nadine nodded in acknowledgment.

"He's right though. You have to admit it," Paeter added, wearily gesturing to a small pile of reports before him. "Fairhaven's broken. We've never been the same since the siege. The population falls almost every month, there aren't enough harvests to keep supplies stocked, people are going hungry, and now crime has started to rise. I can't say I really blame him for leaving."

"Father!" Nadine scolded.

"Don't worry, Nadine, we're not going anywhere. But the first step in solving a problem is to admit it exists."

"The war is taking a toll on most of the Outland colonies. We've all had to send forces to Stonekeep or Darcliff," Denethin answered.

"Yes, but none of them had been attacked like we were," Paeter replied with anger in his voice. "We are supposed to send troops and supplies to other colonies after the Northmen almost broke this town? I hope the gods curse those feral nomads."

"The gods didn't curse them, Father. In fact, it was a god who sent them. It was our god," Nadine added.

"Yes, you're right, Nadine," Paeter continued in a quieter tone, "and that only adds to our problems. The Blessed Mother Maelene was turned and corrupted by Bythe and then made Fairhaven the target of her vengeance. Not Darcliff or Ebeth, but here."

"Do not call her Blessed Mother!" snapped Morag. "She is no longer worthy of such a title. She is Yvorre. She has fallen into darkness, and she is our enemy. I will not have her referred to by any other name within these chambers!"

Paeter nodded.

"The town has lost faith," Morag continued. It seemed she was talking more to herself than to the others. "But you're right, Paeter, we cannot really blame them, can we? The Ageless themselves were powerless to stop her. They've been exposed. Even now the Temple remains a ruin, and they haven't deigned to communicate with the Council in months. Where are they in all of this?"

Nadine answered hesitantly. "I believe they're helping in their own way. They must be."

Morag's face formed a patronizing smile. "Please, girl, you need to leave your childish views behind you. We expect you and your generation to lead these people when your time comes. As part of that education you need to accept the harsh truth about our protectors. The Ageless are just like the rest of us – they are broken and afraid."

.   .   .

The unseen figure standing at the rear of the chamber listened to the words and considered them. The criticisms were harsh, but were they entirely unjustified? So much had befallen Fairhaven in recent years. So much had befallen the people – mortal and Ageless alike.

Aleasea unconsciously pulled her green robe closer around her midriff, where it still hung looser than she was used to. She had lost her right arm to Imbatal during the siege, and while she never admitted it to anyone, she was constantly aware of the loss. Small reminders like the unnatural fall of her clothes would tug on her mind. She could imagine how the broken Temple in the center of Fairhaven would also serve as a similar reminder to every man and woman who passed by. A reminder of their failed and now crippled protectors. A reminder of their failure to see the truth of Maelene until it was too late. A reminder of their failure to embrace and accept Maelene's daughter when they had the chance. The Ageless had made too many poor choices.

No, Morag's words were entirely justified.

Aleasea closed her eyes and turned her focus inward, searching for the hour. Her natural sense told her it was moments from midday, which meant that another council was about to convene, a council she dearly wanted to attend. She turned away from the meeting and silently retreated into a dark alcove behind her. It housed one of the many hidden doors that were scattered throughout Fairhaven, doors that led into the passageways of Sanctuary. She stepped through into the dim opening as the door slid quietly back into place behind her. The passageway was dark and sparsely lit by the occasional light fixed into the wall. Cracked columns lined the halls, and intricate markings were engraved into walls now marred by deep fractures. The lights were dim – most of them had failed – and Aleasea tried not to notice. She tried to focus her mind on the moment. She tried to avoid reflecting on the past, when these halls were lit with a steady, warm glow and the floors weren't uneven and rent with cracks. Now, most of the tunnels only led to the dead ends of collapsed passageways or drowned chambers flooded with water.

She instinctively navigated her way through the passageways she had known for centuries, and automatically altered her path to circumvent blocked routes that greatly outnumbered the functional ones. At a juncture where several passageways intersected, she paused and, after a moment, chose a pathway that climbed upward. She followed it for a long time as it wound ever higher in a tight spiral before leading her to a doorway. Aleasea activated the hidden mechanism and emerged onto a small balcony overlooking the town of Fairhaven.

The town spread out before her in the midday sun. She had beheld it this way for centuries and yet she never tired of the ritual. The passageway had led her to a stone tower, which was ostensibly a disused observation post mounted onto the wall of the Old City. In reality, it had been appropriated by the Ageless as a means of monitoring the town. Standing here, one could view not only Fairhaven, but much of the surrounding countryside. Standing here, one could take in the beauty of the mountains that surrounded most of the city. Standing here, one could appreciate just how broken the town had become.

Fairhaven had always been a town divided in two parts – the labyrinth of streets within the inner circle of the Old City and the more orderly roads that formed the outer circle of the New City. Aleasea always appreciated the structure of the town. From this view she could see how it had grown from a disorganized village into the Fairhaven of today. Most called it a city, but they were being generous – it was a town at heart. An intimate town. And at the heart of it, next to the river Claiream, stood the Temple of Maelene.

The ruin of the Temple.

Aleasea's eyes lingered over the structure. Its once shimmering bricks of grey and blue hues were now dull and lifeless. It stood cracked and skewed as if it had collapsed from within, its walls leaning inward and its roof now partially collapsed. It had sunken into a small crater, and it seemed fitting the building, which had served as Fairhaven's heart for so long, should now be utterly broken. It seemed honest, if nothing else.

Aleasea sighed and raised her eyes to the horizon. While the ruin of the Temple always stole her attention, it was not the reason she had felt compelled to climb the tower today. Something else was tugging at the edges of her mind. A dark feeling she couldn't quite place. She closed her eyes and breathed deeply, reaching within herself to grasp the warm glow of strength she felt there. She touched it with her mind and felt it spread throughout her body. Her limbs, toes, and scalp all tingled with the familiar sensation as it flooded her. It was a strength gifted to all Ageless. Outsiders would call it magic. Aleasea smiled as she thought of the word. What was magic?

Breathing deeply once again, she opened her eyes and let them lose focus. The strength flowed through her body and mind as one. She let her mind drift as she scanned the town before her, drinking in its feelings and sensations. There was nothing unusual in Fairhaven today.

Then she lifted her attention and scanned the fields and woods around the town. Again, there were the usual scents and feelings from the life that lingered there and again there was nothing unusual in any of this. She sighed and closed her eyes.

"*Focus,*" she mentally scolded herself.

Drawing another breath, she opened her eyes and this time it was there. Faint, like the scent of rain on the wind. It was very distant, but it was there. She tightened her attention and found her eyes drawn to the horizon. There was a feeling of darkness, a feeling of someone, or something, that shouldn't be there. A sense of disquiet mocking any attempt at comfort. It gnawed at her, and she needed to find the source. It wasn't close – she knew that now. It was far away, beyond the horizon, beyond the mountains, somewhere in the south. She closed her eyes and pressed for minutes, but nothing further came to her.

She sighed and opened her eyes. She was late. Retreating from the balcony, she retraced her steps down the spiraling passageway and resumed her journey into the depths of Sanctuary. Within minutes, she emerged into a large chamber. It was an immense cavern that had been hollowed out by Maelene and her followers centuries ago. A reflecting pool cast light upward from the depths of the water. The light rebounded from the hundreds of small crystals embedded in the cavern's high ceiling, the illusion intended to be that of a field of stars. However, the lights of the cavern were now muted and irregular, as if a shadow were creeping across them. This caused Aleasea to feel unsettled whenever she looked upward, which was why she had started training herself to consciously stop doing so.

However, the most unsettling part of the chamber was the statue of Maelene. Once, her image had dominated the space – a giant statue of a beautiful woman with outstretched arms. Water had cascaded out of each palm into the pool several dozen feet below. Now her form was cracked. Her statue had shattered during the explosion unleashed when Yvorre tried to destroy Sanctuary. It had listed in place, and the head and right arm had broken free and toppled into the depths of the pool below. They could still be seen, grotesquely illuminated under the surface. What remained of the headless statue now leaned perilously over the pool, with water no longer serenely pouring out of her palms but gushing spasmodically out of the multiple cracks throughout her edifice. It was telling that nobody had attempted to repair or even destroy the statue. Instead, it had just been left alone, as if the act of addressing the problem would open wounds still too fresh to acknowledge.

"Aleasea, you are late again."

The gravelly voice of Veroulle cut through the darkness.

"Forgive me, master," Aleasea answered as she quickened her pace and mounted the stone steps leading to a raised dais. Upon this platform stood three other robed figures. One of them dressed in the purple colors of the

Violari, and another garbed in the same emerald green as her own cloak – the cloak of the Entarion. It was the third cloak that made Aleasea unsettled. The cloak was black – a color never before assumed by any member of the Ageless – but one that had now been chosen by Ferehain, the leader of the Violari. He had chosen it almost immediately following the events of the siege and in the wake of Yvorre's brutal revelations. Ferehain had only once acknowledged the change and succinctly dismissed it as an expression of mourning for their fallen mother, but Aleasea suspected there was far more to it than simple grief. He turned his impassive face to her and greeted her with a simple nod of his head.

"My apologies to all of you," Aleasea said, as she assumed her place in the small circle they formed. E'mar stood next to Veroulle. He was another member of the Entarion, and one of the few of the *Ishantir* now remaining in Sanctuary. The elder generations of the Ageless had become disturbingly uncommon these days. Like most of the Ageless, his slender and unlined face belied his ancient years.

"This is now the third council you have failed to attend as scheduled. Is there something else that commands your attention, Aleasea?" Veroulle's obsidian face glared at her from within his robes, and his red eyes burned in the gloom of the chamber.

Although she had known Veroulle her entire life, serving alongside and then under him, she had never become accustomed to his manner. She knew that he preferred it this way, of course. He was an ancient being, one of the very first awoken by Maelene when Kovalith was young, and as such, he had certain abilities none of the others possessed. This had always set him apart and it was no surprise the Ageless had turned to him for leadership when Maelene left them – the first time.

"I observed the Fairhaven Council today. Councilor Jonas has now also resigned his position and intends to leave us," Aleasea replied.

"That is regrettable," said E'mar. "It would seem the leaders of this town lose hope by the day."

Veroulle hadn't removed his eyes from Aleasea. "While it is regrettable, he is simply one man, in one town, in a corner of the Outlands. You should all remember there are far larger concerns that occupy us. You should remain focused on that which is important, Aleasea."

She nodded but knew that Veroulle wasn't yet done with her.

"I sense it is more than the simple departure of a Councilor that troubles you today. You did not come directly here, did you?"

Aleasea knew better than to ask Veroulle how he knew these things. "I felt it again as I journeyed here today, so I climbed the stairway of the Kalve to try find the source."

"And did you find it?" asked Veroulle.

She sighed. "No, but I did sense something. It is not here, not in the town nor even among the mountains. I suspect it lies in wait for us further distant...to the south."

"Is it Yvorre?"

The sound of Ferehain's voice breaking into the conversation momentarily surprised her. She looked at him for a moment before answering. "I cannot say. Whatever it is, it is something grim and unnatural and it means us great ill."

Ferehain looked away, but Veroulle nodded slowly.

"I have felt it also, and it troubles me greatly," Veroulle said.

"As I have said before, many of us sense nothing. It is entirely possible you both suffer unclear feelings," E'mar remarked.

Veroulle's rock-like face did not often convey emotion, yet now his red eyes burned with an intensity that betrayed his mood. "And as I have said before, the fact that you do not share our feelings does not invalidate them."

E'mar nodded in submission and fell silent.

Aleasea looked at Veroulle and realized something was different. "You know something more, master," she said. It was a statement of fact, not a question.

Veroulle paused for a moment, then spoke. "I *know* nothing more, but I have been gifted an insight – a name and a premonition, little more than this."

"What name?" Aleasea asked.

"The young Lieutenant Jason, friend of Valeyn."

Aleasea raised her eyebrows. She remembered Jason well. The brash young cadet who had risked the gravest of punishments by lowering her hood to help her when she was injured. The young man who had stood alongside Vale and Elyn to face the unstoppable clockwork demon Imbatal. His bravery that day had earned him a series of rapid promotions in the years that followed, and he was now serving as Captain Lewis's right hand at Darcliff. "What role does Lieutenant Jason play in this?" she asked.

"I cannot say with certainty. However my arts have delivered a vision to me – little more than a premonition – but I am certain he is linked to the peril you and I sense, Aleasea."

"Very well," Aleasea said. "We should send for him immediately."

Veroulle shook his head. "I must go to him, and I must go now."

Even Ferehain seemed surprised by this announcement, and Veroulle suddenly had his full attention. "This is unnecessary, Veroulle. Send for the boy. He cannot be so important that you must leave us." Ferehain said with his usual candor. He was one of the few members of the Ageless who seemed to be completely unintimidated by Veroulle. When Maelene had led them, Veroulle had commanded the Violari with Ferehain acting as his close disciple. Now that Veroulle led the Ageless, Ferehain had risen to Veroulle's vacated station.

"I have also received more conventional intelligence," continued Veroulle. "The Helmsguard have begun their advances. The scouts reported they were amassing east of Outpost two weeks ago, with the intent of advancing on Stonekeep."

Aleasea nodded. "That was in line with our expectations. Have you received an update from Stonekeep?"

"This is the source of my concern. By my estimates, the Helmsguard may have arrived there as early as two days ago, yet no couriers have brought news."

E'mar frowned. "Can we not dispatch agents from Fyrn to tell us what has happened?"

Veroulle shook his head. "I have sent word to Stonekeep and Fyrn, and I have received no reply. Only Darcliff has responded to me. They dispatched riders to Stonekeep two days ago. They have also had neither message nor traveler from either town."

All four of them were silent for a moment.

"I do not understand, Veroulle," said Aleasea. "Are you suggesting the Helmsguard have not only taken Stonekeep but have already advanced as far as Fyrn?"

"That cannot be possible, Veroulle. As respected as the Helmsguard might be, they cannot simply sweep aside our defenses that easily," agreed E'mar.

Veroulle's face was as impassive and as unreadable as always. "Aleasea, you and I have felt a strong premonition of danger. I have sensed a connection to the young Lieutenant Jason, and we have lost communications with all places except for Darcliff – the fortress where Jason is assigned. I cannot dismiss this as coincidence."

"Then bring him to us and use your crafts to get your answers, Veroulle," Ferehain repeated.

"I cannot take that risk. I know that Lieutenant Jason is intrinsically linked to the peril I sense, but I know little more than this. Recalling him to Fairhaven may be the act that triggers that peril. I cannot make decisions based on supposition and guesswork, so I must go to him quickly."

"Veroulle, we need you here," Aleasea interrupted.

"The Outland Alliance needs leadership. They need all of us." Veroulle's tone had taken on an edge of irritation. "Bythe is moving toward us again and this time his fury will be unlike any force we have yet seen. Already the Cavalry of Marfort have started to reconsider their commitment. Many of their people believe they should withdraw from the alliance and protect their own. They are not the only ones who think this way. Do you also agree with them, Aleasea? Should the Ageless hide here in Fairhaven to protect what remains of our *kai* and let the others fend for themselves while we guide them from a safe distance?"

Aleasea felt abashed, as if she were an acolyte before her master once again. "It is just...this place has been the heart of the alliance for centuries. It feels wrong for so many of the Ageless to leave it."

"Look around you, Aleasea," Ferehain cut in. "You told us yourself that Fairhaven's people have all but given up hope. This town is no longer the secret heart of the Outer Wild. This Sanctuary is now just the last vestige of Maelene's *kai*. We are guarding the life force of a god who has abandoned us. Do not cling to the past out of a sense of false romanticism."

Aleasea felt a surge of irritation at his comments. She turned to him with a cool expression. "You need not lecture me on sentiment, Ferehain. I am well aware of your feelings on such matters." Ferehain didn't reply but merely returned her dispassionate stare.

"Maelene's *kai* is not to be underestimated. It is still a powerful force," E'mar added, but nobody seemed to be listening to him.

"Aleasea, I have worked hard to find an answer to our peril, and I believe I may have found a glimmer of hope in Lieutenant Jason. It is no guarantee, but he may hold the key to helping us avert danger. I must follow this through." Veroulle waited a moment before continuing. "Do you offer an alternative?"

Aleasea knew where Veroulle was leading, but she refused to indulge him. They had had this argument many times over the past three years. She wouldn't get drawn into it again. "She made her choice, Veroulle, we must respect that," Aleasea answered.

"And choices beget choices," he replied. "I have made my choice as a response to her choice. You must now respect that," Veroulle replied.

"What do you want from me, Veroulle?" she snapped, finally letting her frustration break through. "I will not apologize for my decisions that day. I acted as I judged to be just. I will not compromise what we value for the convenient opportunisms of power. I will not follow the same path our Mother walked. We all saw where that leads."

Ferehain's low voice cut through the chamber. "Noble sentiments, Aleasea, however that does not change the fact that you allowed Valeyn to walk free of us. You undertook that decision alone."

"Valeyn left of her own free will. I did not conceal this from you."

"Nor did you volunteer it until long after she had left!" Ferehain's raised voice was like a whip. Aleasea was surprised to find that she had to stop herself from flinching. "A lie of omission is still a lie. We could have acted to keep her here, had you warned us."

"You mean we could have imprisoned her?"

"I say again, Aleasea, look around you," said Ferehain. "Look at what has become of us since that day. You speak of values? What good are your ideals if we have no people to follow them? Now we are forced to spread ourselves too thin, all because we have no other options before us. Look at what your nobility has cost us. Look at what we have had to sacrifice."

Aleasea looked down at where her right arm used to be then looked back at her accuser. "Many of us made sacrifices that day, Ferehain, some more than others. Do not presume to lecture me on loss."

"Aleasea is correct, Ferehain," said Veroulle. "She exercised her judgment, and I cannot fault her dedication or her principles."

"Yet, you do not agree with my decision," she answered. It was half a question, half a statement.

"Ferehain is also correct in his assertion that Valeyn would be a most powerful ally in these times. When she left us, a significant opportunity also left with her. It would have been helpful to have explored that opportunity further, at the very least."

"Explore the opportunity?" Aleasea was almost incredulous. "How long was Elyn with us here in Sanctuary? How many opportunities did the gods give us to nurture her and give her the acceptance she desperately needed? We had a new god in our midst, and how did we treat her?" She turned to Ferehain. "You conspired to win her trust and then betrayed her. You almost killed her! And now you admonish *me* for letting her leave?"

Ferehain's face hardened yet he didn't reply. Aleasea turned back to face Veroulle. "Even you did little to help her. Instead, you played games to undermine her confidence and test her resolve. We were so smug and self-assured of our own superiority that we failed to recognize a daughter of gods when she stood alongside us. Face the truth, Veroulle, we were arrogant!"

All of them were silent for a moment. When Veroulle eventually spoke, his voice had an edge of weariness. "What you say is true. In hindsight, we all could have made better choices."

"And yet, here we are," said E'mar. Aleasea had all but forgotten he was there.

"And what of Yvorre?" asked Ferehain. "Are we to let her slip through our fingers as well?"

"Have you any new intelligence on her whereabouts?" asked Veroulle.

Ferehain hesitated for a moment before answering. "We know that she is no longer in the Iron Union..."

"We knew that some time ago," observed E'mar.

Ferehain shot him a dark look. "We believe that she has fled to the east. My Violari are continuing to search, but there is simply too much ground to cover. We need support from the Entarion if we are to locate Yvorre quickly."

"Out of the question," answered E'mar. "There are too few of us left to cover the defense of the Outlands as it is. We cannot divert more of our brethren to hunt down someone who may already be dead."

"She is not dead," said Ferehain with grim certainty. "She laughs at us from hiding and plots our destruction. Heed me, E'mar. She is a greater threat to us than all the armies of Bythe."

"I agree with E'mar," said Veroulle. "We cannot spare any more of the Entarion to aid you, especially now that we have lost contact with Stonekeep."

Ferehain shook his head derisively. "We lament missed opportunities, and yet we continue to make the same mistakes with the next breath. I will continue without your help, even if I have to search for her myself."

"Be careful not to try my patience, Ferehain." Veroulle's voice was suddenly very low. Very dangerous. "Be thankful I continue to indulge your vendetta and do not reassign your Violari to where they are truly needed."

They stared at each other in silence and the tension between them was momentarily exposed for all to see. Eventually, Ferehain lowered his eyes to the ground, but Aleasea noticed the fire within them remained strong.

"Our fight against the Iron Union must surpass all other concerns. I leave for Darcliff immediately. I will send word once I have found Lieutenant Jason," said Veroulle.

"And who will take charge in your absence?" asked Ferehain.

Veroulle seemed to consider this before answering. "I will place E'mar in charge. While you are all more than capable Ageless, at the moment I find his judgment to be the most...consistent."

All three of them nodded to Veroulle.

"Farewell. Stay united and strong. These people depend on you. I will send word once I have arrived at Darcliff."

This time all four of them bowed to each other. Veroulle left the platform first, followed by E'mar. Aleasea turned to follow, but before she mounted the first step, she glanced at Ferehain and paused. She had known him for a long time. She had known him as a comrade, and she had once known him far more intimately. Yet the man who now stood before her seemed far removed from that memory. As she glanced at him for that briefest moment, she realized it wasn't the change in the color of robes that bothered her – it was the changes in the man within them.

Ferehain stood on the platform seemingly oblivious to her, oblivious to the others, oblivious even to the chamber around him. He wore the expression of a man whose thoughts were fixed somewhere far distant. Somewhere far darker. She looked at this face and understood that, while she may have been wearing her injuries for all to see, Ferehain's scars might run far deeper than any suspected.

"Ferehain?" she asked.

His dark eyes immediately broke free of their distant focus and snapped onto hers. "Yes?"

She found she didn't know what she wanted to ask. A strange silence took hold of the space between them. She took a step forward and waited until the others had left the chamber. Ferehain stood silently, an image of discipline. After a moment, Aleasea realized it was the simplest of questions that was appropriate. "Ferehain, what is wrong?"

He looked at her for a moment as if deciding how to answer. Next to Veroulle, Ferehain was the most enigmatic and aloof of all of the Ageless. The fact that he bore a man's face seemed to make his manner even more unnerving. Aleasea had loved him once. They had shared something truly beautiful and unique, and the price they paid had changed them both. He was a very different person now. She had once been the only Ageless who could reach him – but that had been a very long time ago.

"Why do you do this, Aleasea?" he asked in reply.

"Do what? I do not understand."

"Why do you play at being the idealistic fool? We both know better than that."

Caught off guard by the backhanded compliment, she wasn't sure how to reply. Ferehain stepped forward and continued in a quieter voice. "Look at what she has done to you." He gestured to her ruined arm. "You have paid one of the highest prices of all of us. You, of all people, should understand what I am trying to do."

It took Aleasea a moment to follow his meaning. "Maelene?" she asked.

"Yvorre!" he snapped through gritted teeth. "Do not call her by any other name. Our Blessed Mother is dead. She died a hundred years ago when Bythe took her from us. Yvorre is nothing more than a mockery of our Mother."

"Ferehain, she is gone now. She was defeated and she has fled."

"She is still free."

"Is she?" Aleasea asked. "We hunt her. Bythe and his entire Iron Union also hunt her. No doubt Valeyn also hunts her. Yvorre's only power lay in her deceptions. Now that she has been exposed, she is weakened. All she can do now is run, for she can no longer hide from us – nor from Bythe."

"I don't want Bythe to find her. I want to be the one to find her."

His lapse into informal, contracted speech surprised her, but she reciprocated. "Has she hurt you so deeply that you'll let her control you with anger and vengeance? Don't let anger drive you. You've overcome worse than this, remember?"

"This isn't the same. She betrayed us Aleasea. Again." His voice was almost a plea. "Bythe has long been our enemy. His actions I can respect, but Mae—." He paused and corrected himself. "But Yvorre was our Mother. She was our guide and our virtue. How could she do this?"

"She was corrupted."

"She failed us again. She was weak."

Aleasea sighed. "You're strong, Ferehain. Maybe stronger than any of us." She paused and chose her words delicately. "What happened long ago...it wasn't her fault. She didn't know. Perhaps you place your high standards on everybody. Learn understanding and forgiveness."

Ferehain smiled. It was a thin and cold thing. "There you are again. You play the idealistic fool, and we both know it is a lie."

"That's not my intent."

"She is the real threat, Aleasea." He turned and paced about the platform. "I can feel it, and it sends me to a madness that others can't understand."

"She's gone Ferehain. She can't hurt us now."

"Yes, she can. She's the only one who can truly hurt us." He turned and walked back toward her. "Do you think she's forgotten about us? Do you think she'll just fade away or lose interest like the other gods did?"

Aleasea shrugged. "It matters little. Her power is gone. She tried to destroy Sanctuary out of spite, and now she has cut herself off from her own *kai*. You know the gods aren't all-powerful. Their strength is drawn from the power they have placed in this world. She's ruined herself in vengeance. I don't want you to follow her mistakes."

If Ferehain heard the offered intimacy, he didn't react to it. "Incorrect. She does have a base of power. You are wrong now and you were wrong then. You should not have let her go."

At first Aleasea opened her mouth to protest – then she realized what he was saying. She realized what had been troubling him. She looked at Ferehain strangely. "You don't believe that Valeyn hunts Yvorre. You think that Yvorre hunts Valeyn."

He glanced at her with a look of faint approval. "Finally, you show some sense."

"Why would she do that?"

"You said so yourself. Yvorre has ruined herself, cut herself off from her own *kai*. But you – like everyone else – refuse to see the truth she has no doubt realized. She has access to the greatest power of all. Her own daughter."

Aleasea shook her head. "That's madness. Suicide. Valeyn is more than a match for her now. Yvorre should run as far as she can from her daughter, not seek her out."

"Stop it, Aleasea! You know our Mother. You've seen what she can do to her own children. She is ruthless and manipulative and conniving. Valeyn is innocent and powerful and unsure of herself. If Yvorre finds her, she will be raw meat thrown before a prowling bear."

She paused and considered his words. While she had always accepted her brethren's disappointment at her decision to let Valeyn leave, she had never doubted that it had been the right decision. Until now.

Subconsciously imitating Ferehain, Aleasea turned and paced the platform, lost in her own thoughts. She'd been so preoccupied with Bythe over recent months that she hadn't really stopped to seriously consider Yvorre. Now that Ferehain laid out the facts before her, she realized his logic was disturbingly sound. Elyn had always been an insecure girl, while Yvorre had proven herself to be deceit's mistress. Even if Valeyn was now a stronger woman than Elyn, that seed of doubt would still be part of her, and Yvorre would be able to find it. "What are you suggesting we do?" she asked quietly.

"What I have been insisting we do. We find Yvorre or we find Valeyn before it is too late."

Aleasea smiled at the simplicity of the suggestion. It was logical of course. It was typical of Ferehain – brutally simple. It had only one flaw.

No word of Valeyn had reached them in three years. Nobody – absolutely nobody – knew where she had gone.

CHAPTER 3

"It has always been difficult to hold the Outland Alliance together. While Bythe was very effective in imposing order by decree, Maelene sought to gain consensus by respecting the freedoms of the different peoples in the east. The Ageless always acted as the leaders of this alliance, and the memory of Maelene's murder had been a powerful surrogate in her absence.

But now that Yvorre's treachery has been revealed, the Ageless no longer hold the influence we once did. Old rivalries between Marfort and Greenridge have arisen, and the Federacy talk of retreating back into isolation. I have no doubt it is this new weakness that Bythe intends to exploit."

~Aleasea of the Ageless

Tiet was beautiful. It was the most beautiful place Valeyn had seen throughout all of her shared memories with Elyn and Vale. This might not have been particularly surprising given Elyn's limited exposure to the world, but even Vale – who had been moderately well travelled – had never seen a place quite like it.

She'd stumbled across the town completely by accident, like most people seemed to. It had only been a year ago, but now it seemed like it was a vague memory from so long ago.

She stood on the narrow stone jetty that protruded into the Ocean, helping two elderly men unload their fishing nets from a small skiff. She still enjoyed this. The sun warmed her back and legs as she bent to take the load of nets from the boat. The two men had the dark-skinned complexion of most of Tiet's inhabitants. Their elderly faces were lined deeply with the emotions of a lifetime, but were frequently broken by the white flashes of the broadest grins.

"Slowing down today, pumpkin? C'mon hurry it up. We want to get to the Hava sometime before it ends tonight, don't we?" joked the taller of the two men with a smile.

Valeyn liked these two fishermen. In all the time she'd lived in Tiet they'd never once asked her any questions. Such a respect for the sanctity of one's past is only earned with age – and then not always.

"And please explain why I should do all the lifting, old man?" Valeyn answered, as she gathered up the last of the nets and placed them on the jetty. "What did you both do without me before I wandered into this place?"

"Well, whatever we did, we did it very poorly compared to you," said Anok, the shorter man.

"That's the gods' truth," said Valeyn with a smile of her own. She shot them both a warm look before returning to tie their skiff to the mooring. When she was done, she stood up and stretched her muscles in the afternoon sun.

Valeyn was tall – over six feet in height, which meant that she towered over all women and even most men. Her long, blonde hair was tied neatly into a ponytail, and she wore the practical homespun tunic and pants of a local. The sun reflected off the water and danced across her face – smooth and unlined, with pale blue eyes. She moved with a graceful presence that seemed to command attention, even as she bent to shoulder the pile of nets.

"Come on, then," she called over her shoulder. "Let's get these to the sheds so you can buy me a drink as a thank you and keep me company at the Hava."

Kayta laughed as he fell in step beside her. Despite being tall, he still only equaled Valeyn's height. "Oh, I don't think you need the company of two old men tonight, princess. There's gonna be plenty of young stallions wantin' to buy you a drink."

Valeyn's face brightened with a mischievous grin. "Now why would I want to spend the evening away from two charming gentlemen like you?

Besides, I'm sure you can teach the young stallions a thing or two about how to politely entertain a lady."

"Oh, she's a charmer, isn't she?" Kayta asked Anok.

"We dreamed for many years that a lady like you would walk into our town, my dear," said Anok.

"Unfortunately, you turned up about thirty years too late for the two of us," joined Kayta with an air of mock tragedy.

"Well then, we should find you both a couple of older ladies to charm. I think Aliae is going to be there, and surely she has a friend?" Valeyn replied as they walked down the jetty toward the shore.

"Oh, stop it, we're too old for matchmaking" replied Anok. "You just go and do your thing tonight, and try not to break any hearts this time, alright?"

She gave a noncommittal shrug in reply, despite the temptation she could feel starting to stir within. As a distraction, she turned away to look over the village as they approached it. It was still beautiful. Still idyllic.

She tried to recall the first time she saw it. She'd been travelling steadily eastward back then, hoping to strike the Ocean – or anything that might give her hope. Her recent experiences of the world had left her in need of some hope. People in Vauna had first told her about the Ocean when she'd passed through the town. This wasn't some large lake like the one Elyn had seen at Wheatsheaf or even the cold and unwelcoming water of the Northern Seas, which Vale had seen. This was the Ocean of the Fareaches. Back in the Iron Union, people spoke of it like a children's tale. In fact, parents would sing rhymes to their children about the great blue Ocean of the Fareaches. Occasionally, a traveler would claim to have seen it, or a troupe would set up a performance to tell stories of its beauty. While they may have been paid well for their entertainment, their stories were always treated with skepticism. So when Valeyn crested another rise in the road one morning and unexpectedly beheld the vast expanse of blue before her, she was completely unprepared for the experience.

It was magnificent. The water covered the landscape before her, its light blue surface reflected the sun in hundreds of distinct sparkles. It was like glass, like the smooth surface of the lake that Vale had often visualized to calm her wild mind. Where the tropical blue water casually lapped ashore, it met sand so white that Valeyn almost thought it was snow. She had no idea how long she'd stood there on that crest just staring at the Ocean.

She found the town quite by chance. After making her way to the shore and bathing in surprisingly warm waters, she'd walked down the beach until she caught sight of a collection of wooden structures and huts all gathered around a stone jetty. It was her first sight of Tiet, and even at that moment, Valeyn somehow had a feeling that she'd be staying.

She broke away from the memory as the three of them arrived at one of the fishing sheds that lined Tiet's shore. Valeyn loaded the nets into the shed then promised to see both the fishermen at the Hava before turning for home.

Although Tiet was a very simple town, Valeyn knew the state of her present clothing would be seen as inappropriate for an event such as the Hava. It was a unique custom, but one she had grown to enjoy. Every month when Kalte's star was at its peak, the townspeople of Tiet would gather on the beach. All manner of stalls, tables, and tents would be erected, and any and all people were welcome. Food would be cooked, and spiced wine and ales would be shared. Those who couldn't bring their own were welcome to donate copper – the local currency of the Fareaches. It was a simple custom, but Valeyn had learned it was the warmth of the people that made it so welcoming.

So why was it all starting to grate on her?

She walked up the dirt road that served as the village's main thoroughfare. Tiet had several wooden shopfronts dotted throughout the green foliage that seemed to saturate every other space. Valeyn saw it was unusually busy this afternoon. While Tiet was a quiet village positioned out of the way of any roads, the people who dwelt around the Fareaches often made the trek to find it – particularly in the warmer season. It wasn't uncommon for travelers, traders, and wanderers to seek out the town. Some – like Valeyn – would sometimes choose to stay, but that meant one needed to be accepted by the community. And Valeyn had learned that while the people of Tiet may be very friendly, they were also very discriminating. Valeyn liked that about them. She liked it very much.

As she approached the crowds, she walked off the main path and took up a position in a laneway between the tannery and the butcher's buildings. From there, she stood motionless as she scanned the people moving up and down the street. This now felt like it was an old habit, although she'd only picked it up no more than twelve months earlier. She knew she had her freedom, but she also knew she was never really safe. The long journey from Fairhaven had taught her that lesson.

She focused hard on the crowd of people, taking in every detail. Roughly half of them had the dark-skinned complexion of locals, and most of them she knew by sight. However, there were also a lot of outsiders today, which meant she had to be careful.

Ever since leaving Fairhaven, Valeyn had been pursued in some form. At first, it had been the Northmen, as she moved through their territory, but they'd quickly learned to leave her alone after two extremely decisive encounters.

Then it was Ferehain. Once she'd passed eastward through the mountains of the Outer Wild and started to move south toward the Fareaches, she'd begun to sense his Violari. She wasn't sure how she was able to do it – doubtless this was part of her connection with Maelene – but she realized she could feel them when they drew near. This became invaluable as Ferehain proved to be both surprisingly tenacious and surprisingly accurate when tracking her. Once she'd even seen one of the Violari. The purple-robed figure with the impenetrably dark hood stood watch on an outcrop over the road south. She never understood how the Ageless were able to move across country so quickly – even in her reconciled state, she still knew nothing more of their abilities. Fortunately, they seemed to be incapable of sensing her the way she could now sense them, and Valeyn was able to backtrack and find a very inconvenient detour to avoid detection. With time and patience, she had eventually been able to lose the Violari entirely.

Then it was everyone else who pursued her. The further south Valeyn travelled, the less civilized the world seemed to become, and it seemed that a woman travelling alone was a thing to be questioned – if not openly exploited. Valeyn found herself the subject of offers of assistance with increasing frequency and increasing persistence.

She'd been polite at first, graciously turning men away with a warm smile and congenial excuse when they approached her. But then she realized this only worked on a certain type of man – the type who were genuinely looking out for her welfare. The rest of them required her message to be expressed in a somewhat firmer fashion. Eventually she realized – to her disappointment – that the only way to discourage some was with force.

There was the grain farmer near Azad, offering her a place to stay with a slightly desperate look in his eye. Then there had been William at Qharg. She pushed that thought away; it still hurt her. Then the drunks on the road south who wouldn't accept the word no. They needed a firmer answer, and Valeyn was forced to provide it. She'd left them nursing broken wrists and bleeding mouths.

Then the innkeeper at Ashran, who was so kind when he handed her the key to her room. But that sycophantic smile was still etched onto his face when he woke her after letting himself into her room that night. There were his clumsy attempts to cover her mouth with one hand while he fumbled with the drawstring of her pants with the other. That smile had still been there when she'd twisted his face so far away from hers that his neck popped and snapped.

It had shocked her the first time she was forced to take a man's life – that had been the natural reaction of Elyn – but then she remembered that as Vale she'd done this countless times before. She stopped feeling guilt and instead, let the feeling give way to resentment then to anger.

It hadn't been her fault. All she'd wanted was to be left alone. Yet people just wouldn't let her be – unless she made them. It was this necessity that made her angry above all else. It seemed the further south she walked, the darker her moods became. One day she understood that she'd left Fairhaven to discover who she was and now the world itself was taking that choice from her. She had seethed at the injustice of it.

Then she had felt Bythe. It was a distant feeling, a tug at the edge of her mind. He was searching for her, calling to her. It was a strangely familiar feeling, and it terrified her.

She had wanted to turn back, but she knew she couldn't. Where would she go? Back to the Ageless? She was deep in the Fareaches with no idea what to do. She had turned east without a clear purpose, looking for some place far away where nobody would find her, where her father would never find her. She wanted to run to the edge of the world. And then – quite by accident – she did.

A young woman called her name and snapped Valeyn out of her memories. She turned to see Naya standing with her fruit cart at the opposite side of the road. A warm smile lit her face as she waved. Valeyn reassured herself that no one on the road seemed particularly unusual and walked over to the young woman.

"Hello, Naya, how's business?" Valeyn asked and couldn't help returning a smile as bright as the one she'd been given. Naya was one of those rare people who seemed to be gifted with an infectious form of happiness. She was sixteen years old and already very beautiful. She had smooth, dark skin and even darker eyes that were wide and round and framed in a slender face. Valeyn had no doubt that she would grow into a most alluring woman, but for now she was still a shy and awkward girl. Naya looked up at Valeyn with the adoration of a younger sister.

"Good. Lots of people in town today for the Hava and lots of people who haven't come prepared." She winked and gave the box a small shake, betraying a healthy number of coins within. "How'd Anok do out there?"

Valeyn shrugged. "Not as well as you, I'm afraid. They caught a few crayfish, which should go down well tonight, but it looks like you're the most successful negotiator in town today."

Naya gave her a serious look. "And you say that like you're surprised?"

"Forgive me, Naya," Valeyn said submissively. "I forgot who I was talking to."

Naya offered her smile in reply. "So, what were you doing over there hiding in the alleyway? Are you spying on people again?"

"Of course not. I'm just looking at the boys in town for tonight. See anyone cute?" Valeyn asked with a wink.

Naya giggled and color flushed her cheeks.

"You have, haven't you?" Valeyn pressed, the chance of gossip piquing a mild interest. "C'mon tell me."

Naya looked away. "Just a boy. He asked me if I was going to the Hava tonight, that's all."

"Who is he? Anyone I know?"

"He told me his name's Chen. He's travelling with a couple of friends."

"A foreigner?" Valeyn raised an eyebrow. "Exotic. You'll have to point him out to me tonight."

Naya paused and looked at the ground for a moment as if unsure of what to say.

"What's the matter?" asked Valeyn.

"Papa isn't well today, and I don't think he's going to want to go."

Naya's mother had died a few years earlier, and her father had never seemed interested in taking another wife, which meant the two of them lived alone, tending their orchard on the outskirts of town.

Valeyn gave her a knowing look. "And he doesn't want his beautiful daughter at the Hava without him? Especially not if he finds out that some exotic young foreigner's been making eyes at her."

"I'm sixteen, Valeyn! I'm almost of age," Naya sighed in frustration. "I'm not sure why he's so worried about me."

Valeyn reflected briefly on her own fathers: Leon and Bythe. "Well, in my experience, the best fathers are the ones who are sometimes overprotective of their daughters. You should probably be grateful."

"But..." Naya drew out the word, and Valeyn knew exactly where she was leading. "...he respects you. Everyone here respects you. If you promised you'd watch over me, then I'm sure he'd let me go."

Valeyn sighed and shook her head in disbelief. "I was serious when I said you were the best negotiator in town."

"Please, Valeyn," Naya's voice was playful but sincere. Valeyn weighed the options. Her words to Anok and Kayta had been authentic – she really had no interest in seeking out any romantic company tonight – but she knew her mood would change. Once she was comfortably seated with the fire warming her face and the ale warming her stomach, she'd feel differently. The men would appear. The thrill of seduction would take hold and she'd surrender to it. Why not?

But lately, she was beginning to tire of the predictability of impulsive behavior. She was beginning to realize that seemingly spontaneous actions had a paradoxical way of always leading to the same result the next day. Still, she wasn't sure what the night would bring.

"Look, I'll speak to your father," Valeyn answered. Naya's face broke into a broad smile but Valeyn wasn't finished. "But I need you to promise me that you'll behave yourself. I don't want to be stuck as your wet nurse tonight, alright?"

"Of course not! Thank you so much," gushed Naya as she rounded the fruit cart and thumped into Valeyn with an awkward hug.

Valeyn returned the embrace then extracted herself from it. "Alright, I'd better get going now that I have to see your father as well as make myself beautiful for tonight. I'll be there at sunset. Come find me as soon as you arrive?"

Naya nodded enthusiastically, and Valeyn continued on her journey up the thoroughfare. Already she found herself anticipating the first drink, and she knew the evening was going to be fun.

She decided that flowers were called for. The pale pink lilies that grew in the Fareaches looked beautiful in her hair, and the first of the evening's impulses urged her to buy some.

Valeyn turned and searched the street. Drela's flower stall was positioned further up the road today, no doubt taking advantage of the visitors coming into Tiet. The older, local woman was busy with a group of customers, so Valeyn made her way over and waited her turn. She stood patiently while Drela haggled with a family from out of town, an apparently simple group of four, with two young boys no older than ten. The mother – a stern-looking lady with a sharp face – seemed to be the natural leader of the family, and her large husband stood by as she politely, but firmly, stood her ground on the price for a bunch of Coffee Orchids.

Valeyn smiled to herself. Drela always doubled – if not tripled – her prices on Hava, so no matter how hard this lady bargained, Drela would still win out. She looked over the different arrays of flowers in their wild splashes of color, searching for the perfect shade of pink that would complement her hair.

She hadn't noticed the people behind her until one of them spoke. "Which one do you fancy?"

She turned to see a small group – two girls on the cusp of womanhood and four young men. No, men wasn't the right word. These were still boys, probably not yet twenty years old. While Valeyn wasn't actually that much older in physical terms, her mind now felt immeasurably older than her body appeared.

Valeyn recognized the two young women as locals: Feali and Bealdra. They were both of that age where a girl discovers how to become a woman – and in some cases how not to. Given the way they were both fawning over their respective males, Valeyn guessed that the latter was most likely the case here. They both gave Valeyn sharp glances, seemingly threatened by the tall, fair-haired lady who might try to steal their hard-won partners.

As for the males, the two who appeared surgically attached to the girls had dark complexions, but she didn't recognize either of them. The other two were fair-skinned with dark hair. One of them stood taller than the others, he almost matched Valeyn in height. He wore a handsome, youthful face and the air of a person who knew it.

"I'm sorry?" she asked neutrally.

"Which flowers do you fancy? How about you tell me your favorite and I'll buy them for you."

He smiled confidently at her. It was no doubt a smile that had peeled the clothes off more than one farmer's daughter. While Valeyn admired the confidence, she'd discovered, much to her dissatisfaction, that the younger and prouder the male was, the greater the chance of sexual disappointment. It wasn't a prejudice; it was just that they always over-promised so much.

"You're very sweet, but I'll pass. Thanks all the same."

"Oh, c'mon," he persisted. "Pick some – any color you like. Their beauty pales in comparison to your fair face."

Valeyn gave an involuntary wince. "Does that line work?"

The young man seemed momentarily taken aback by the confidence of her reply. Clearly, most young women in his limited experience were impressed with speech like that. Valeyn remembered that, to his eyes, she was probably of a similar age; to her eyes, he was juvenile.

"It works most of the time," he replied with a nervous smile, desperate to salvage some face in front of the others.

Valeyn shrugged with a sympathetic smile. "Sorry, not this time."

"Don't waste your time with her," Bealdra called over. "She's from the north. No one really understands what she's doing here."

Feali giggled and whispered something to the young man on her arm, who barked a short laugh.

Valeyn levelled a cool stare at Bealdra but didn't reply. They were girls engaging in hurtful, girlish things. And Valeyn was beyond that now.

But that wasn't true. Bealdra's words did hurt. Valeyn knew she was an outsider, and no matter how many people befriended her, she also knew she wasn't really considered one of them.

"North or south, who really cares, right?" the young man persisted. "Beauty is beauty. What's your name?"

Bealdra said something to Feali, who laughed too hard at the private joke. Valeyn had seen cats mark out territory in a similar way.

The family at the head of the queue had concluded their bargaining and moved on. Valeyn shot the girls another hard look then turned her back to them.

"Valeyn, my dear, always a pleasure. What can I get for you today? Let me guess, some lilies for tonight?" asked Drela.

Valeyn opened her mouth to answer but heard another ripple of spiteful giggling from behind her. She remembered Nathan and how he used to make her feel. A rage started to boil within her, and she struggled hard to resist the urge to turn and unleash a stream of fury at them.

No. Don't go with the anger. Don't let go of yourself.

She breathed deeply and let her emotions out in her breath the way Vale used to do... and felt herself go cold within.

"Valeyn?" Drela asked again.

"Never mind," Valeyn answered and left without another word. She refused to acknowledge the renewed burst of laughter from the group behind her as she left. She'd lost her taste for flowers.

CHAPTER 4

"The Outland Alliance was formed more from necessity than from any set of common values. One hundred fifty years ago, the free people of The Federacy, Greenridge, and Marfort all began to understand the threat posed by the Iron Union. It was the skilled diplomacy and grace of Maelene that first brought them all together, and it was the threat of Bythe's retribution that kept the alliance together after she fell.

In the three years following the Siege of Fairhaven – when the forces of Fairhaven had defeated the Northmen against overwhelming odds – Captain Lewis and the army of Fairhaven had risen considerably in the esteem of the Outland Alliance. After the new god Valeyn had appeared and then vanished, the invasion from the Iron Union had paused, allowing the Outland Alliance time to regroup. Captain Lewis had been summoned to Darcliff for a council of war and remained there as a respected leader.

However, once the full fury of Bythe's vengeance was felt, the Alliance was truly tested – from without and from within."

~Aleasea of the Ageless

Jason knew little about horses, but he knew that his mount had been pushed as hard as he dared. Sweat glistened all over the creature, and he could feel the animal start to tremble from time to time. Even using the spare horses as remounts, the nine remaining soldiers in Jason's unit had still managed to exhaust their rides as they raced back to Darcliff. He was also exhausted, but they had made good time – they were approaching Darcliff less than a week after the Helmsguard had ambushed them. How had the Iron Union passed the defenses of Stonekeep? They weren't supposed to be this far north.

Jason tried not to think about it. Four Iron Union soldiers had killed over half of his unit of twenty men in the ambush. It was only through desperation and sheer luck that they had managed to survive.

"An officer is always under orders to accept the luck the gods choose to give him – both the good and the bad," Captain Lewis had always said. The words were little comfort to Jason now. He needed to get back to Darcliff and warn his captain. He pressed a hand to his pouch and reassured himself the stolen Helmsguard message was still there – the dire warning that he needed to deliver to Captain Lewis without delay. He had pushed his men hard, and they were almost within sight of their fortress.

Then someone had noticed the smoke on the horizon. It was to the north, in the direction of Darcliff, and the sight of it gripped the entire unit. They silently quickened their pace, and within a few hours, began to hear a low rumbling. The sound grew louder as they neared Darcliff, and the agitation of the men seemed to grow with it. Mutterings of the name Bythe became more frequent, and Jason had needed to silence them on more than one occasion. His men were starting to believe the rumors – that Bythe had come to the Outlands.

Assuming the Helmsguard would also approach from the south, he headed northeast once they were on the open land. After the encounter with the Helmsguard messengers, the last thing he wanted was a full patrol of enemy soldiers finding them. They moved in a broad arc, scything around to the northern side of Darcliff – an exercise made easier by the smoke marking the position of their target. Jason had steered his men through the hollows in a slow zigzag of maneuvers designed to keep them off the ridges and crests. He knew that just because they couldn't see the enemy, it didn't mean the enemy couldn't see them.

Seemingly endless hours passed this way as the fields became greener and mountains began to take shape in the east. Only when the mountains were clear and the smoke was south of them, did Jason judge they were as safe as they could possibly be under the circumstances. He rested his unit for no more than ten minutes before turning them south and beginning this final dash toward the rising smoke of Darcliff.

The fortress was built on the crest of a ridgeline. This served as an excellent defensive position, but it also meant the massive stone citadel now blocked Jason's view of the enemy to the south. He took some consolation from the fact that he could now see that the black smoke was rising from somewhere beyond Darcliff, not from within, but even this relief was subdued by the noise. The dull rumbling they had all heard earlier in the day had grown stronger, and now it was a distinctive roar in the distance. Not the usual sounds of an army – even Jason remembered that sound from the siege of Fairhaven – this was something entirely different. It was a shrill, metallic roar. It rose and fell in pitch and volume, and with it came a distant rumble, as if a giant hammer was striking the land.

Jason glanced back at his men and the expressions on their haggard faces told him what he needed to do. They were already exhausted and now they were on the verge of panic – convinced that Bythe had come to Darcliff. Jason was no longer sure they were wrong, but he wasn't going to give them – or himself – another moment to consider it. Throwing caution aside, he nudged his horse into a trot and then a gallop, as he led the unit racing across the final miles of their journey in the fading daylight.

Darcliff loomed above them like a stone curtain. Its walls ran the line of the ridge in a solid testament to pure endurance, every brick in its grey edifice defying time, erosion, and decay. Its towers were broad and squat in their sheer girth, and the fortress gave the appearance of a thing entirely immovable.

Jason hoped that was still true as he closed within a mile of it. Motioning for a halt, he reined in his horse and paused. He waited for a few moments until he was sure he'd given the watchtowers time enough to see him, then began closing the final distance at a brisk trot – his sword extended over his head as a signal that he was an ally returning home under attack.

The shrill, undulating roar and unnatural pounding was now so loud and so constant that it drowned the sounds of their own horses. Jason forced himself to ignore it as he watched a dozen men dressed in grey leather armor emerge from a sally port within the wall. Most of them spread out in anticipation of an ambush, and almost all weapons were drawn. It was a standard custom under the circumstances, but it was also entirely redundant. Jason could see there were no fewer than twenty archers taking aim at them from the wall as they approached. He mused that if he were stupid enough to try to spring a deception, there was no doubt that he and his few remaining men would all be killed within seconds. He kept his sword raised above his head and his face somber as a grey-clad soldier approached.

"Who approaches our stone under claim of friendship?" the man asked formally. He was middle aged but wore a weathered face. Jason knew the Darcliff unit leader by sight if not by name, and he had no doubt the recognition was mutual. Still, this was wartime and there were rules to be obeyed.

"Lieutenant Jason of Fairhaven," he replied. "We've been attacked by the Helmsguard. We were taken by surprise and lost over half our men."

The older man looked over the ragged unit, his eyes impassive, his face carved from rock.

"C'mon, get inside."

The unit leader nodded in the direction of the door, and Jason ordered his men to go through, while he dismounted and remained behind, lingering next to the older soldier.

"What else?" the older man asked gruffly, apparently sensing that Jason had something on his mind. Jason was a lieutenant and was technically a higher rank than the unit leader within the rough structure of the Outland Alliance, but somehow the men of Darcliff always managed to maintain an air of superiority. It wasn't arrogance or hubris that set them apart. It was well-earned pride in who they were and what they did. Every taut muscle and fiber in their bodies was bred for duty and for combat. Jason couldn't help but feel a little like a cadet when he stood shoulder to shoulder with them. He removed the Helmsguard's message from his pouch.

"We intercepted a message. I need to get it to Captain Lewis. It's urgent."

The older man looked at him impassively for a moment longer. His expression seemed to radiate a silent disdain for the younger lieutenant. He nodded as another dull roar rent the air beyond the walls. "Very well," he replied. He motioned toward the sally port. "I'll take you to your captain."

"Thank you," Jason added with a touch of sarcasm. The unit leader ignored the tone and led Jason through the door into the fortress grounds. With a rush of orders, both men assigned duties to their charges and then set off into the heart of Darcliff.

Behind the stoic grey walls, Darcliff was a mass of activity and barely concealed chaos. Soldiers hurried this way and that, carrying messenger pouches or bundles of arrows or blankets or any other item that was needed somewhere. The unit leader led Jason to a broad stone staircase built into the western wall. As they ascended, Jason could see that the entire fortress was a hive of activity.

The grey stone keep sat in the center of the grounds reaching no higher than the walls that surrounded it. Ranks of solders were amassing within the eastern courtyard, while the western stables now housed a makeshift shanty town of farmers and refugees who had sought protection.

Protection from what?

Another shrill sound overran the noise, and the unit leader halted on the steps. Jason instinctively did the same, and a second later, the stones underfoot shook as a mighty explosion roared from the other side of the wall.

"What in the gods' names was that?" he asked. The unit leader didn't seem to hear him and simply continued walking up the steps, shouldering past other soldiers hurrying in the other direction.

When they crested the parapet of the wall, Jason's questions were answered.

The sun was descending, bleeding a deepening shade of orange across the western landscape. Arranged before the walls of the fortress were lines of soldiers grouped together in various colors. The light-blue of Fairhaven lined up next to the grey hues of Bonehall and Darcliff, with the mounted riders of Marfort in dark-green cavalry formations alongside. Yet it was the sight beyond them that captured Jason's attention.

Not half a mile distant, the rolling green fields were broken into smoldering patches of shattered ground. Smoke rose from jagged pits where a molten fire seemed to burn. Beyond this nightmarish landscape, lay the recognizable black vista of a carapace of iron men. The Helmsguard.

And yet even this sight did not concern Jason. He had seen the Helmsguard three years earlier. What he now stared at was something he had never seen before.

Five iron constructs towered over the men on the battlefield. They were each different and yet all of them looked as if they been birthed in a hellfire pit of melted steel. They loomed tall and black and terrible, like a twisted metal tower clawing at the sky, with tendrils of thick, black smoke curling upward from their bodies.

Jason tried to make sense of the sight before him. He opened his mouth to question the unit leader, but his words were drowned out by the shrill scream he had heard earlier. One of the constructs shook and then seemed to blaze with the light of the sun, before a searing white flare shot from the top of its tower into the sky. The flare shrieked as if in protest before it descended in a broad arc and slammed into the ground half a mile from Darcliff. Dirt and rocks were thrown into the sky, and a wound some fifty feet in diameter now joined the others in the ruined ground.

Jason stood frozen against the parapet. As he watched, the closest tower shuddered, and Jason braced himself for another flare. Only this time the tower gradually listed off balance and then violently tilted forward, toppling toward the ground in a spasmodic lurch. However, as Jason stared in horror at the doomed Helmsguard soldiers standing beneath the collapsing tower, the construct arrested its fall and slowly restored its balance with a grinding sound of metal against metal. It took Jason a moment before he understood what he was watching

"They're moving," Jason whispered in horror to himself. "They're moving toward us."

He could now see the metal legs that gave the war engine its locomotion, like some twisted insect of black metal. The constructs were dispersed across the plain, some closer and some further behind as if lumbering to catch up.

Jason felt a presence at his shoulder and realized the unit leader had come back to join him. "What are they?" Jason asked.

"I have duties to return to. I'm taking you to your commander, not briefing you," the unit leader replied coldly then turned away to resume his escort. Jason nodded in vague comprehension, then tore his eyes away from the field and hurried after the older man.

They walked along the parapet for a few more minutes, and in that time, Jason counted twelve more flares from the war engines, each one inching closer than the last. He wondered how long before they would be in range of the walls and what would follow then. *The walls of Darcliff will resist this. They've stood for centuries.* Then he remembered the same had been said of Stonekeep, and his confidence faltered.

"Captain Lewis." The unit leader was speaking, and Jason realized they had stopped.

They were now standing on the wall's central tower, which housed the main gate below. Lewis's erect frame and bright-blue uniform stood out against the orange sky beyond. He had aged much in the three years since the Siege of Fairhaven. His hair was now grey, and although he wasn't yet fifty, he wore the face of an old man. But when he turned his gaze on Jason, those eyes were still bright and resolved.

Lewis dismissed the unit leader, then turned to Jason with a harried look. Jason had learned how to read that look. It was the look of a man who had no time for idle words. The look demanded precise information delivered as succinctly as language would permit. Any extraneous word would be judged, and too many of them would be swiftly punished.

Jason allowed himself the luxury of a breath before launching into the most concise, yet detailed summary of the events of the past week he could manage. How he had been leading his men on a routine patrol to Fyrn when they had been ambushed by chance encounter with four Helmsguard soldiers. How they had barely managed to defeat their attackers, at great cost to his own men. How he had discovered the Helmsguard soldiers had been couriers carrying a message to another Iron Union commander in the east. A commander who was under orders to attack Fairhaven.

Lewis stood before him in silence, and even though his hard eyes moved in a constant cycle from Jason to the battlefield to his men on the tower then back to Jason, there was no doubt that Lewis was absorbing every word of the report. When Jason had finished, Lewis returned his gaze to the constructs on the battlefield while extending his hand expectantly. "The dispatch," was all he said.

Jason handed Lewis the message he'd taken from the dead Helmsguard, then stepped back as his captain scanned the page. Jason wasn't sure if Lewis could read the written language of the Iron Union, but he certainly knew better than to ask. While the verbal speech of the Iron Union and Outland Alliance was almost identical, the written forms varied greatly.

Eventually, Lewis lowered the message to his side and looked at Jason. "Are you alright?" he asked.

"I'm fine, sir. But eleven of my men can't say the same," Jason answered with a touch of bitterness.

Lewis nodded without judgment or consolation. It was a simple fact. Men died. Lewis had accepted this a long time ago.

The aging Captain sighed and looked out over the fields. "So, it's not enough for Bythe to send these things to us, he had to attack our home as well."

Jason looked at the iron towers on the battlefield and felt cold. "Sir, what are these things?"

"I really could've used you here, Jason," he muttered so quietly it seemed as if he was talking to himself.

"I'm sorry, sir. I came back as quickly as I could." Jason replied.

Lewis looked at Jason as if surprised by the comment. "That's not what I meant."

Jason had grown used to anticipating Lewis's commands over the past few years, but at this moment he had no idea what thoughts were passing through the mind of his captain.

"I'm sorry, sir, I don't understand," Jason replied.

Lewis stared hard at Jason, as if considering something. "With me, Lieutenant. You have a visitor."

Without another word, Lewis turned and marched from the tower. Jason followed as the captain walked down the steps and crossed the central courtyard toward the main keep. This journey was far quicker, with every soldier pausing to make way for Lewis as he passed through. Even the grey-clad men of Darcliff and Bonehall showed their respect, and Jason felt a twinge of frustration. Within minutes, they had entered the keep and crossed the vaulted archways of the great hall within. The room was filled with servants and soldiers going about their duties, but all made way for Lewis as if he were a ship cutting through water.

Two grey-clad guards stood before a heavy wooden door at the far end of the hall. They saluted Lewis as he approached, and one of them opened the door without a word. Lewis barely acknowledged them as he led Jason into a smaller room, and the guards closed the door behind them. Jason recognized it as the Chapel of Maelene, which had been sealed and fallen into disuse over the past few years. It was a modest sized room, designed to seat some three dozen worshippers. The rows of chairs had been replaced with a long table of dark wood that was now covered with maps. The only remaining vestige of Maelene were two stone feet on the altar at the head of the room, marking the place where her statue had been ripped from its mounting. Maelene's blessed refuge of peace was now a council of war. It seemed ironically fitting.

Two figures stood at the table. Jason recognized the other commanders of Darcliff and immediately stood at attention. Captain Haft had the look of a warrior of around sixty, but he was still stronger and fitter than most men half his age. He was bald but for a curve of cropped silver hair around the back of his head, and his strong jawline gave his face a look of fierce determination. He had been the Captain of Darcliff for over ten years, and his face was as impassive as every other Darcliff soldier Jason had met.

"What is it, Lewis?" Haft asked, seeming to sense the troubling news that Lewis brought into the room.

In reply, Lewis handed the dispatch to Haft. "My men intercepted this message outside of Fyrn a week ago. It was intended for another army maneuvering in the east."

"What do you mean to the east?" asked Captain Dagmar of Bonehall. He looked similar to Haft in many ways. Both the same age and both with hard, warrior's expressions, but Dagmar's cropped silver hair covered his head and his scarred face was gaunt and wiry. Dagmar had the look of a man who would never surrender in a fight, no matter how strong his opponent. If Haft was a symbol of masculine strength, then Dagmar was a testament to endurance.

Haft handed the paper to Dagmar. "Read it. He's right. They're trying to get word to allies across the mountains."

Dagmar scanned the paper but, clearly struggling with the language, gave up after a few moments and returned his attention to Lewis. "Are you sure this is legitimate? How did this fall into our hands?" Dagmar asked.

"Lieutenant, report." Lewis ordered without turning his head.

Jason stepped forward and launched into the same concise account of the events of the past week. When he was done, he stepped back as if he weren't even there.

The silence of the room was broken by a distant shriek of the war engines. The rumble of the explosion that followed was ominous.

Haft looked at the map. "A flanking position?" he asked with his white eyebrows furrowed. "Are they trying to encircle us?"

"Not by crossing the mountains," Dagmar said, shaking his head.

Jason fought down the urge to offer his insight. He knew that senior men never appreciated unsolicited advice. Fortunately, he didn't need to wait long.

"Baron Ethan of the Iron Union is returning to Fairhaven," announced a gravelly voice at the end of the room.

Everyone turned to look at Veroulle. He stood taller than the others with his deep violet robes flowing around him. The face like coal was visible beneath his raised hood, and his burning red eyes swept the room with a sense of ancient power.

Haft looked at the map and then back to Veroulle. "Fairhaven? Why would the Helmsguard want to strike there?"

"I can only speculate at the motives. Perhaps events of the past now repeat themselves for a futile gain, but my heart tells me this is no coincidence," Veroulle replied.

For a moment Jason thought that Veroulle's glowing eyes locked onto him but he couldn't be sure.

"This is stupid of them," Dagmar spat. "Whatever their reasons, they gain no advantage taking Fairhaven. It's not the home of Maelene any longer. Our power is here." He punctuated his point by stabbing at the line between Darcliff and Bonehall on the map. "Here is where they need to send their strength, not up into the mountains."

"And that's my concern, Captains," Lewis spoke in a tone that was almost gentle. "This message shows they clearly feel they don't need to reinforce their army here. They seem confident we will fall. On the other hand, we don't know what they want with Fairhaven."

Another explosion rattled the table and a few scrolls rolled onto the floor.

"Bonehall has never fallen!" snapped Dagmar. Jason realized there was a defiance bordering on denial in his voice. Dagmar would fight until his very fortress collapsed onto him. Jason suddenly appreciated the shortcomings of such a leader.

"Enough!" Veroulle's voice seemed to echo throughout the small room. "I would speak with Captain Lewis and Lieutenant Jason. Give me the room."

Haft and Dagmar looked at the Ageless in surprise but quickly recovered. Murmuring assent, they signaled to their guards and moments later, the doors closed firmly behind them. Veroulle moved from behind the table and stood before Jason and Lewis.

"Lieutenant Jason, it has been a long time since we last spoke," said Veroulle.

Jason shot an uncertain glance at Lewis before replying.

"Master Veroulle. I'm surprised to see you here." Realizing his words might be taken as insolent sarcasm, he rushed to clarify them. "But I'm relieved though. It's...good that you're here. Good...to...see you," Jason amended clumsily.

Veroulle stepped forward, and Jason had to fight against an instinct to step back.

"Jason, there is little time. I arrived here four days ago to seek you out," began Veroulle.

"What have I done?" Jason blurted.

"Calm down, Lieutenant," Lewis said reassuringly. "Listen."

"I am relieved to find you safe. When I arrived here to find you had not returned from your patrol, I feared the worst. I believe that Aleasea has already told you much about of our abilities. I do not claim to hold the power of foresight, but a premonition had come to me in recent days and I traveled here to heed its warning. The premonition concerns you."

Jason's mouth felt like the deserts in the Southern Wastes.

"What about me?" he whispered.

"I do not have any details beyond a feeling. However, you now appear before me at this hour, not only safe against all odds, but also bearing ill-tidings of Fairhaven. I do not believe this to be chance. And now the existence of these war engines has explained much about my premonition, although I cannot fathom how Bythe has attained this much power."

"Perhaps he's finally killed Yvorre?" Lewis suggested, the malice in his voice unmistakable.

Veroulle shook his head slightly. "No, Captain, I believe I would know if something had befallen Yvorre. This is different. Somehow Bythe has found a way to amass great power, and he is unleashing it against us. We have not seen such power displayed so openly, even during the Anarch," Veroulle said, referring to the fifty-year war between Maelene and Bythe. He closed his glowing red eyes for a moment, and when he opened them again, they were fixed on Jason.

"Step forward, Lieutenant. I have need of you."

Jason fought down an urge to run and instead stepped dutifully before the ancient being.

"I am going to touch your mind. Do not be alarmed. This will not harm you, but it may give me some of the answers I seek," said Veroulle.

Jason closed his eyes as Veroulle extended his long, black arm and gently touched Jason's forehead. A warm glow seemed to emanate from Veroulle's rough palm. It bled through Jason's brow, seeping through his neck and spine then flowing out into his limbs. As this happened, he felt a wave of vigor pass in its wake. His entire body tingled as Veroulle poured energy into him.

He felt ready to pull away, but then the room before him dissolved. In its place was a scene of burning desolation. Thick smoke clogged the air and his eyes stung at its sudden attack. Jason spun around in surprise. The small room was gone, and he was standing in the middle of a dirt roadway in the middle of a town alight with dozens of fires. He looked about for people but there were none. No survivors fleeing the blaze nor any bodies. It was strange. He looked down and realized he was wearing a blue uniform, but it was badly stained with dirt and soot.

I've been here...in the fire?

The buildings around him burned fiercely, and the blaze tore through the town in an orange firestorm. A hot wind rushed in from behind Jason to feed the inferno with a tremendous howl. A crash in the distance heralded the collapse of a building, prompting him to stumble forward in an effort to find safety. It seemed to be night, but the lurid glow of the fire and the blanket of smoke made it difficult to be sure. He staggered down the street, wiping tears with the sleeve of his dirt-smeared blue shirt.

His boots struck a low stone wall causing him to stop. Below, he could see orange flames reflected on the rippled surface of water. A river. He rested his hands on the wall and looked up – knowing what he was about to see. Rising above the river was the ruins of a mighty stone building – partly collapsed upon itself – and burning with the ferocity of the sun. The Temple of the Ageless.

This is Fairhaven.

As the shock of the recognition hit him, the scene immediately vanished and was replaced by another. Jason now stood alone in a smoke-ridden haze, surrounded by Helmsguard. The charred ruins of a city lay scattered about him. There was someone standing in front of him, someone familiar, but he couldn't make out the face – male or female. He moved forward to get a better look, but as soon as he moved, the ground beneath him trembled and bright blue energy ripped skyward from underfoot, sending Jason crashing to the ground. More streaks of light shot upward in different colors from different places, and as they did, the ground shook with greater violence. Somehow, Jason knew the world itself was coming apart, that these lights were the lifeblood of Kovalith – and that Kovalith was bleeding to death. The realization was terrifying. He opened his mouth to scream a warning, but the scene vanished before he could make a sound.

He was once again standing before Veroulle, who now stared down at him with glowing eyes. The ancient being removed his hand from Jason's forehead and walked away. He was quiet for a long time. Only the distant shrieks of the war engines broke the silence.

"What did we just see?" Jason finally asked.

"I believe we have witnessed the *Etherian*. I have only heard of such a thing from Maelene. It is when the gods will recall their *kai* to them."

"And Kovalith will be destroyed," said Jason.

"Yes," said Veroulle. "I see that Valeyn has told you much."

"What about the fire? Fairhaven was burning. Was that part of the *Etherian* too?" Jason asked.

Veroulle thought for a long moment before answering. "I do not believe so. That pivotal point is focused squarely on you, Lieutenant. You will be present when Fairhaven burns."

"Then this is Baron Ethan's doing," said Lewis. "It can't be a coincidence."

"No, it is not," Veroulle agreed.

"I can't believe this," said Jason. "Fairhaven...and the entire world...is going to burn?"

"We do not know this with certainty, Lieutenant," replied Veroulle. "No one on Kovalith possesses true foresight. However, we know that you must return to Fairhaven immediately."

Jason glanced at Captain Lewis before answering. "With respect, Master Veroulle, my place is here, especially with these war engines bearing down on Darcliff."

Veroulle nodded. "I understand your concern, but it is misguided. The presence of these machines has given vivid form to my intuition. I now understand the peril that Fairhaven will face."

"Because Baron Ethan has the same engines," Jason finished with growing horror.

"Indeed," said Veroulle.

"What are they?" Jason asked, uncertain if he should voice the question.

"We don't know," Lewis answered. "We got the first reports about a week back, probably about the same time you were ambushed. They seem to have been built in the pits of the Ironhelm and...well, you've now seen what they can do."

Another distant shriek filled the chamber.

"Can we stop them, sir?" Jason asked.

Lewis looked at him a long time as if weighing his answer. "No," he said bluntly. "Haft ordered a raid on their lines two days ago. A thousand men and cavalry went south with orders to destroy or disable as many of the war engines as possible." He paused for a moment then looked Jason directly in the eye. "We lost almost every man. No more than a hundred came back, and most of those died from their burns yesterday."

Jason couldn't comprehend what Lewis had said. "That's not possible."

Lewis sighed and ran an old man's hand through grey hair. "A week ago, I'd have agreed with you, but we seem to be powerless against whatever magic Bythe is using. It's suicide to try and attack them, and we have no idea what to do. Nobody knows this beyond the captains. The last thing we need is a blasted panic." He shook his head as if he struggled to believe what he was saying. "After we finally accepted the truth of what'd happened and we understood the power of these engines, we quietly ordered a full retreat to Darcliff to wait for them. We're going to make our united stand here." There was a grim finality in his words that Jason couldn't accept.

"Jason," Veroulle commanded. "I believe that you must return to Fairhaven with me. Your presence is pivotal in preventing what we witnessed."

Jason thought of his father and of his young wife, then shook his head emphatically. "Stop. This doesn't make any sense. Even if Baron Ethan has only one of those machines, Fairhaven's finished. We should be evacuating everyone this instant. Why am I so important?"

"Jason!" Veroulle's voice was firm. "This is no longer about one town. You witnessed the *Etherian* – the end of all life on Kovalith. That is what is at stake here. Evacuating Fairhaven will do nothing to prevent this. You are central to the events that will unfold. You have a part to play, and it is at Fairhaven."

Jason's head swam. *The end of all life?* It couldn't come to that.

"Do you think it a coincidence that Baron Ethan is personally returning to Fairhaven?" Veroulle continued.

Jason stopped and slowly followed the thread of Veroulle's logic. "Elyn," Jason said. "I mean, Valeyn."

"Precisely," said Veroulle. "Baron Ethan has ostensibly returned to claim the daughter of Bythe, his former love. You now see how you may become central to these events."

"But Valeyn left us a long time ago. We don't even know where she is. The Helmsguard have spies. Surely Ethan must know this already," said Jason.

"Again, you are correct, Jason. Which is all the more troubling. Why is Ethan looking for Valeyn in a place where she is not?"

"He wants to draw her out of hiding," Jason replied.

Veroulle's burning red eyes were impassive. "That is one possibility. I do not know what Ethan is planning, but if he seeks Valeyn, then I can see how your presence may be a critical influence over the events that are about to transpire."

Jason dropped his eyes and turned away. He desperately wanted to return to Fairhaven. He wanted to protect his wife, his father, his hometown – but on some level, he knew he was also relieved to flee Darcliff and the war engines. Like he'd been relieved when Valeyn had ordered him away from Imbatal. Like he'd been relieved when Aleasea had ordered him to flee from the Northmen. Was he really just a coward at heart?

As if to punctuate his fear, another explosion rattled the fortress, bringing a light rain of mortar onto the table from above. "Sir," Jason turned to Lewis. "I'll stay with you if you need me. I'm not afraid."

"Lieutenant," Captain Lewis spoke with his usual sense of authority. "You seem to think this is your decision to make. It is not. Master Veroulle is ordering you to return to Fairhaven, and you will do exactly as ordered. Understood?"

Jason instinctively stiffened into a soldier's formal posture. "Yes, sir."

Lewis smiled faintly and took a step toward the younger soldier. "And I understand. I see that look in your eye. I've seen it before in a lot of men. I've even seen it in the mirror from time to time. You are not a coward, Jason."

"I know, sir—" Jason began but Lewis cut him off.

"No, you don't. Deep down, you don't believe it. I don't think any of us really do. Let me tell you something. In my experience, the men who tell themselves they're brave usually turn out to be the cowards. They cling to that belief like it's a raft in a storm, like it'll save them. The men like you – the men who aren't afraid to confront themselves – they're the ones who aren't afraid to confront anything."

For a moment, Jason said nothing, then he let his fear break through. "But I feel it, sir. I'm glad to be running from here."

Lewis laughed. "Of course you bloody well are! I would be too. That doesn't make you a coward. It just means you're not completely crazy. Remember what I always taught you?"

"An officer is always under orders to accept the luck the gods choose to give him – both the good and the bad," Jason replied as if by rote.

Lewis nodded his head, then straightened and looked at Jason as if he were an equal. "Don't ever go looking to pick a fight just to prove something to yourself or others will pay the price for your pride. Is that the sort of leader you want to be? You've never been afraid to fight. I saw that about you the first day you stepped onto my parade ground as a cadet. And I think even then, I somehow knew this day would come."

Jason looked at his Captain uncertainly. "What do you mean, sir?"

"I want you to assume command from Acting-Captain Khyran. He's a fine soldier but you're the better leader. That's why I wanted you here. But if I have to lose you as my right hand, the least I can get in return is the reassurance that you're taking care of my city for me."

Jason stood at attention and saluted formally. "Thank you, sir. I'm honored. I won't fail you."

"Of course, you won't," Lewis agreed with a glint of amusement in his eyes. "Good to see the message has finally sunk through that thick skull of yours. Master Veroulle, may I ask you to see to the arrangements with the Council when you return?"

Before Veroulle could answer, a mighty shriek filled the room and the entire fortress shook. Stones fell from the ceiling and smashed onto the tabletop.

"That one's hit the keep. We're out of time," said Lewis.

The door slammed open and Captain Haft stormed into the room.

"The Helmsguard are here!" he snapped, glaring at everyone in the room. "We're starting the dispositions. I hope this doesn't inconvenience you!"

Lewis turned to Veroulle. "You need to ride now. Take Jason to the stables and get yourselves horses from Sergeant Hanniston."

A look of pure astonishment struck Haft's rugged features. "You're leaving us, Veroulle?"

"There are greater perils facing us at this hour, Captain. We are needed elsewhere." Veroulle spoke with his usual conviction, but Jason thought the words carried a ring of contrition this time.

"Greater perils?" Haft spoke as if the words were unknown to him. "We're facing weapons the likes of which we've never seen! Weapons that slaughtered hundreds of my men in a single day. We need you here, now!"

Veroulle hesitated and for a moment, Jason understood the ancient being's own conflict. Whatever guilt Jason felt must have been absurd when compared with the choices Veroulle now faced.

"Captain," Veroulle answered slowly, "the powers I possess will not defeat these engines. Even I am not capable of such an act."

"Yeah, but you can help us. Our odds of surviving this are greater with you here alongside us, aren't they?" The truth behind the words was an accusation, and Jason inwardly winced.

"Captain Haft," Lewis commanded. "*Master* Veroulle has given us his orders. We need to carry them out."

Haft looked at Veroulle as if Lewis hadn't spoken and shook his head with quiet disbelief. "I always had faith in you Ageless, even when the others had started to question you. You're supposed to be our protectors, but now look at you. When the time comes, you only look after yourselves. In the end, you're no different from your bitch, Maelene."

Lewis shouted something at Haft, but it was drowned out by the crack of force that was unleashed from Veroulle's outstretched hand. Haft was flung against the rock wall and remained pinned in place like a tapestry fixed by nails as Veroulle slowly walked toward him.

"Go ahead, Veroulle. Why don't you kill me?" Haft laughed. "It's a lot quicker and a lot more honest than sending me to die under the fire of those engines. Just get it over with, why don't you?"

Veroulle's red eyes narrowed with rage, and for a moment, Jason thought the Ageless would do it.

"What the hells?" Dagmar cried from the doorway, and Veroulle turned to see the captain flanked by half a dozen other soldiers, all watching the grim scene with disbelief. After an eternal moment, Veroulle dropped his arm and Haft slumped to the cold stone, gasping in air as if he'd been drowning.

"The captain is correct. My place is here." Veroulle's gravelly voice was the only sound in the chamber.

"Master," Jason said. "What about the *Etherian*? You said yourself, that is more important. We need your help."

Veroulle looked at Jason and almost seemed to smile. "Young Jason, I said that *you* were most important, not I. My vision is focused solely on you – it does not involve my importance or even my whereabouts, as much as I might like it to. No, my absence from your vision supports Captain Haft's logic; that I am fated to be here, where *I* am most needed."

"Veroulle..." Lewis began but another shrill whine filled the room followed by the roar of another nearby explosion.

"There is no time for discussion. My decision is made," Veroulle snapped before turning to Captain Haft. "Go to the command post. Lewis and I will join you presently."

Haft struggled to his feet, nodded brusquely then turned for the door, ushering Dagmar out as he did so.

Lewis picked up the Helmsguard message from the table and removed a gold ring from his right hand, giving both to Jason. "There's no time to put those orders in writing, I'm afraid. This ring will give you all the authority you need." He raised himself to full height and offered a formal salute. "This is where we part ways, Captain. Look after our people. I know you'll make me proud."

Jason quickly saluted in return while Veroulle only inclined his head fractionally in acknowledgment.

Lewis strode toward the door, calling back to Jason over his shoulder as he moved. "Get down to Hanniston and find yourself a horse, then ride like Bythe himself was on your heels."

The door swung closed behind him and he was gone. Jason turned to Veroulle only to discover that the ancient sorcerer was also no longer there.

He stared down at the circle of gold in his palm while, outside, the halls of the fortress began to fill with the clamor of war.

CHAPTER 5

"Do you remember it, sister? Do you remember those early days when we all sat together and marveled at the sheer beauty of the world we were building? I think of those times often and I find that I miss them. I recently returned to the Render and laughed at what we had built there in those early days, in those days before we perfected our ideas of what Kovalith should be. I believe that would be a dangerous place for mortals now. We should ensure that none of our followers ever go into that place. They will not be prepared for what they find there."

~Romona – Goddess of Death and Regeneration

Valeyn let the mild euphoria flow through her. She couldn't really get drunk, that was one of the unexpected side-effects of her elevation to godhood, but she could feel the effects of ale and other intoxicants on a subtle level. It relaxed her to an extent, and she liked to let it lead her to interesting places in her mind.

The Hava was starting.

The sun had dipped below the trees and the beach was bathed in the glow of twilight. The start of an evening was always the best part, it was the time that held so much promise and potential – no matter how badly the night might go afterward. People had already begun to flood the beach and the air was thick with the sounds and smells of people, music, firewood, and roasting meat. It was a crowded night, possibly the most crowded Hava she'd yet seen. Not only were the usual locals present, but the number of people from the outlands was far higher than normal. She was surprised to see two people in the brown robes of the Rak'Tunga clan from the Great Southern Wastes, among several styles of dress from other Fareaches settlements she didn't even recognize. Valeyn took a sip of her drink and absently hoped Tiet's location was not becoming too widely known.

The man who had given her the drink was certainly not a local, but thankfully nor was he from the north. Tan was a well-built young man from the western fields of Karaa. Sometimes farmer, sometimes mercenary, all-times masculine and sweet. Valeyn had locked eyes with him ten minutes earlier and accepted his confident offer of a cup of leaf cider – which was a common drink in these parts of the Fareaches. The taste was sweet, and her head was already starting to feel deliciously light. Yes, this was always the best part of the evening.

Valeyn was wearing a pale pink dress – actually, the only dress she owned – and was now ruing her petulant decision against the matching flowers. Regardless, she was still a striking figure. She looked over the crowd, and her buoyant mood faltered for a moment when her eyes unexpectedly fell on Bealdra and Feali. They each held a drink in one hand and desperately clung to their partner with the other. Valeyn also noticed their handsome young friend in the same group. It seemed as if he still hadn't found himself a partner, although Valeyn suspected this was more from choice than necessity. Boys like him enjoyed keeping their options open on nights like this.

Valeyn smiled at Tan and offered him a genuine but noncommittal promise to find him later in the evening. It wasn't wise to decide too soon, and there were still so many more hours left in the night. Turning away from Tan's polite protests of heartbreak, she winked at him then melted into the crowd. She peered through the throng looking for familiar faces.

"Valeyn," Naya called out.

Valeyn turned to see Naya crossing the sand toward her. She looked radiant in a tight-fitting gown of bright blue, adorned with red and yellow patterns designed to highlight a young woman's figure.

"Well, look at you," Valeyn greeted her. "I'm surprised your father let you out of his sight looking like that."

Naya smiled and blushed. "Oh, stop it, Valeyn."

"I'm not joking, no one's going to look at me twice when I've got you standing next to me. You're serious competition."

"Well, thanks, but you don't have to worry. I was just checking in with you. I'm going to find my own friends"

"Ah, yes, the exotic Chen. Where is he? You promised to point him out to me."

Naya turned and searched through the crowd. She gave a little squeal of excitement and pointed to the confident boy who had earlier offered flowers to Valeyn.

"There he is, standing next to Feali."

Valeyn's heart sank. She looked at Naya for a moment and considered telling her the truth. What could she say that wouldn't sound condescending or even shatter Naya's confidence? *He already made a pass at me, along with probably a dozen other women? You're just a name on his list of potentials?*

Valeyn remembered Elyn's fragile feelings for Jason and the hurt she had felt when he finally chose Nadine. There are some blunt truths a sixteen-year-old doesn't want to hear, no matter how honest they might be.

"Naya..." Valeyn began, "I don't know. Perhaps he's a little old for you?"

A look hardened on Naya's face and Valeyn immediately regretted her choice of words. She had just put herself on the other side of the divide between supportive sister and overprotective parent.

"Well...I like him, and he sure likes me. I thought you wanted me to have good time. What's the problem?"

Valeyn sighed. She knew that any words were probably going to be futile. Naya had the headstrong look of a teenager determined to make the world meet her expectations. Maybe there are things in life that people just have to discover for themselves? So she gets her heart broken. Join the club like the rest of the grown-ups.

"Okay, fine. Just...take it slow tonight, alright? I've still got to answer to your father if you go home pregnant."

Naya gave a sightly shocked laugh. "Valeyn, I haven't even kissed a boy, so you don't have to worry."

"Well, there's nothing wrong with a little kissing. Have fun and don't leave the beach."

Naya flashed her beautiful smile and was gone. Valeyn watched her make her way over to where Chen stood. Gods, it seemed like it was only days ago that she had been that young and that innocent. Elyn had been so naïve, so vulnerable. Then she had become Valeyn and she was a woman overnight. Valeyn suddenly felt as if she'd missed a whole part of her life. As she watched Naya embrace her first boyfriend, she realized that her own slow journey into womanhood had been stolen from her. First kiss? She thought of William at Qharg. That had certainly been no rite of passage for her.

A sense of anger flared within her. It came from nowhere. It was sharp and bitter and for a moment it poisoned the night air. She left Naya to the arms of Chen and turned to find her own distraction.

.   .   .

Two hours later Valeyn was enjoying the pleasant buzz of wine. It washed though her thoughts in a familiar way and smothered the frustrations she felt earlier. She sat on a bench alongside Anok and Kayta watching the festivities of the Hava reach full stride. The music was louder now. Drums punctuated the night along with the whoops and cheers of drunken revelers as they danced around the massive bonfire. The night was pleasantly warm, as it usually was in Tiet, and the Hava was turning out to be the best one Valeyn had seen.

"That's true," said Kayta as Valeyn pointed this out to him. "It's been a while since I seen a party like this one. What'd you think, Anok? When's the last time we had a crowd like this?"

Anok took a sip from his cup and furrowed his brow with the kind of stern concentration only the thoroughly intoxicated are capable of. "I dunno. It's gotta be a while. Maybe six years back? When Jo and Paual were married?"

Kayta laughed. "My gods, that was a good night, wasn't it? Wasn't that the night your boy was fooling around trying to impress Shebona and managed to set his hair on fire? How the hell did he do that?"

Anok shook his head. "To this day I still don't know, and I don't wanna know. He's a disgrace to my name."

"He's his father's son." Kayta lifted his cup in a mock toast and drained it.

A smile spread across Anok's face. "Yeah, that was a good night, wasn't it? In fact, wasn't that the night that you and..." Anok's sentence trailed off as he glanced at his old friend. Kayta returned his knowing look and smiled in acknowledgment of the unspoken secret they shared.

"Yeah," said Anok as he returned his gaze to the bonfire. "Yeah, that was a good night."

Valeyn seemed to be momentarily forgotten as the two old friends enjoyed an exclusive connection to the past that no newcomer could ever truly share. She glanced around the crowd looking for Naya and found her sitting in a small circle not too far away. They were an evenly matched group of girls and boys, now all partnered into seemingly inevitable pairs. Naya's face glowed with adoration as she looked over at Chen. He was talking animatedly to the group, holding their attention with the natural abilities of the charismatic, gesturing wildly with one arm while the other arm casually draped over Naya's shoulders. For her part, Naya was clinging to that embrace as if it held all the meaning in the world. Valeyn smiled at her happiness and felt as if she were intruding. She returned her attention to her two friends.

"Yes, this is the best night we've seen in a long time. We must've really pleased Kalte this month," Kayta finished.

"He deserves a toast as well!" Anok shouted and raised his cup to the night sky. He looked about, curiosity turning from confusion to concern within moments.

"Where is he?" he asked.

"Where's who?" asked Kayta. "Who've you lost now?"

"The Kalte star. I can't see him."

"Oh, my gods! You're drunk already!" Kayta hooted, slapping his palm on the bench. "What happened to the man I used to know? He'd at least be able to keep up until midnight."

Anok grinned foolishly but kept looking around the sky. "I know, I know, that boy's long gone. Where the hell is that damn thing?"

Valeyn looked up as well. While she didn't know the stars in this part of the world all that well, she still had a broad idea how to find the Kalte star. She couldn't see it either.

"You're going to have to help us out here, Kayta, I've lost him too," Valeyn said.

"Alright fine!" Kayta replied wheeling himself around on the bench and craning his neck back a little unsteadily. After a moment, he frowned. "Well, that's just damned strange."

"So it ain't just me?" asked Anok with relief in his voice.

"I don't think so," Kayta answered. "There's the brothers, Dazh and Narak, in the east." He pointed to two stars on the horizon over the water then wheeled about and pointed to a star in the north. "And there's Romona right where she should be."

"So where's Kalte?" Valeyn asked.

"He's not there," Anok said quietly.

A silence descended on the group, as all three of them struggled with what they were seeing or not seeing.

"Do you often lose stars down here in the south?" Valeyn asked, trying to inject a little humor into what had suddenly become a very solemn atmosphere.

Anok shook his head gravely. "Never."

"This doesn't bode well for us." Kayta abruptly rose to his feet. "Kalte does not bless our Hava."

"Oh, c'mon, Kayta, don't overreact. Sit down and have another drink. It's probably just behind a cloud," Valeyn said, shaking her head.

Anok also rose. "No, he's right. This is a sign from the gods. Something displeases them."

Valeyn took another drink and laughed. "The gods have abandoned us, gentlemen. Trust me on that one."

Anok and Kayta were staring down at her.

"You speak too freely, child," Anok said. Suddenly he was not a kindly old man – he was a stern grandfather rebuking a reckless young woman. "You people from the north should know all too well how the gods still watch us."

The rebuke stung mainly because it was the second reminder in one day that she wasn't one of them. She was an outsider. And it stung because it would be far worse if they knew the truth about her.

"Well, you people from the south don't have a clue what you're talking about, on so many levels!" She spat her words, the drink giving them an edge she didn't intend. "The gods have gone. They don't care about us – they never did."

"Watch your words, Valeyn," said Kayta.

"Or what? Will Bythe strike me down where I stand? Or will Maelene come to this beach and save me?" Valeyn got to her feet. "Tell me, wise fishermen, when was the last time a god even bothered to visit this little village? You're looking at a star in the sky, that's all!"

The two men shared a look for a moment, then silently turned their backs on Valeyn and walked back toward the Hava. She watched them go. "Stupid, superstitious old men," she shouted at their retreating figures. "It's people like you who give Bythe so much power."

She glanced up at the sky again. It was strange that Kalte wasn't there. Was there meaning in this? She shook her head. The black mood had crept back upon her, and now she didn't know what to do. She looked at the empty wine cup in her hand. This, at least, was a problem that needed to be fixed immediately. She walked back along the beach toward the glow of the bonfire. Perhaps the night could still be salvaged. The evening was still young enough – there was still a chance that good prospects were available and hadn't already partnered up. Perhaps she could even track down Tan?

But then there was Naya to consider. Valeyn knew she couldn't blithely chase her own desires while she still had Naya under her care. She cursed quietly and looked about for the group she'd spied earlier. Maybe it was time to send the kids home so the grown-ups could have some real fun?

She found the group, but she couldn't see Naya among them. Nor could she see Chen. Valeyn looked around but couldn't find either of them anywhere on the beach. An uneasy feeling started to well within her. She crossed the sand to where the three remaining couples sat in a rough circle.

"Where's Naya?" she asked. Bealdra rolled her eyes but otherwise pretended Valeyn didn't exist. Following her lead, the entire group didn't look up.

"Where is she?" Valeyn repeated.

"Gods, take the hint. Go. Away." Bealdra glared up at Valeyn.

"They want to be alone," said one of the boys in a way that suggested the conversation was over. He was one of the local boys who had attached himself to Feali. Valeyn slowly turned and stepped over to where he sat on the sand. She towered over the young man, who suddenly looked very awkward.

"And I don't care what *Chen* wants," she said, pinning the boy with a cold stare. "I'm looking for Naya. Tell me where she is."

Pride warring with chivalry warring with fear all showed plainly on his face as he glanced from Feali to his friends then back to Valeyn.

"Don't let her tell you what to do, Jon," Feali ordered her partner.

Valeyn crouched down on her haunches and stared into the eyes of the intimidated boy. "You're a cute one, aren't you? I can see why Feali likes you. Tell you what, why don't you tell me where Naya's gone and then you can buy me a drink when I get back? What do you think?" Her face broke into the charming smile she'd practiced on so many men over the past year.

Jon looked utterly conflicted. For a moment Valeyn thought she could feel the mix of fear, desperation, and flattery emanating from the poor boy, as he tried to think of a way out of the situation he'd placed himself in. "Hey, look...it's all good...they've just gone for a little quiet time...over by the boat sheds. There's no problem." Jon nodded down toward the jetty.

"Jon!" said an outraged Feali.

"Thank you, sweetheart," Valeyn said to Jon with a wink. She turned to Feali and couldn't resist offering her a condescending smile. It was a petty victory, but then Feali was a very petty girl, so the smile seemed appropriate.

She rose to her feet and walked toward the boat sheds lined up by the jetty. Fun or not, Valeyn decided that Naya had enjoyed enough life experiences for one evening, and it was time to send her on her way home.

Naya's nervous and trusting smile flashed into her mind.

Valeyn slowed her pace a fraction as she felt Naya's nerves resonating deep within her. Valeyn could *feel* her smile. This was strange. The only times she had ever felt this was as Elyn, as she'd unconsciously sought out her broken twin. Valeyn hadn't felt anything like this since her reconciliation. Now the feeling was back. Emotions were bubbling across the sand toward her.

Joy. Valeyn smiled as she felt Naya's innocence touch her. She felt happiness in the arms of a first love. Trust in a strong and handsome boy. Relief that he liked her. Gratitude that he found her attractive. She'd waited a long time for this kind of validation.

Then something else. Her gratitude started to waver and melt into confusion. Why was he doing this? Why now?

Then a stab of fear. Something was wrong. Valeyn quickened her steps as more of Naya's feelings flowed into her. Fear sliding into panic. A panic that froze her in place.

Valeyn ran. She crossed the sand in seconds and flung open the timber doors to the shed. Two figures lay on a blanket next to a fishing dingy. One figure writhing in self-absorbed pleasure and completely oblivious to the rigid form of the other. Naya's face was turned toward the door, and Valeyn could see the silent terror in eyes cast downward.

A cold fury filled Valeyn. Within seconds she crossed the floor and wrenched the lecherous young man off Naya with one hand, flinging him into the boat. He screamed in shock and pain as he collided with the vessel and they both crashed onto the floor. Valeyn crouched down to pull Naya to a sitting position. Her shining blue dress was now rumpled, dirty, and hitched upward around her hips from Chen's hands.

"Naya, are you alright? Has he hurt you?" Valeyn asked.

Naya said nothing but pulled her dress down around her thighs with a look of shame and embarrassment.

"Naya, look at me."

Naya looked away toward the rear of the shed, her eyes glistening, her face a mix of emotions. Valeyn could still feel them: relief, confusion...shame.

"I'm okay," she whispered. "He didn't...*do* anything."

Valeyn rose to her feet and whirled about looking for Chen. He was slowly getting to his feet, his right hand nursing his lower back as he did so. As his eyes met Valeyn's, she could see the recognition dawning in them, melting into fear like what Naya had experienced moments before. Valeyn grabbed Chen by his shirt and flung him out the doors and onto the sand. He cried out in pain again. Somewhere a distant part of Valeyn reminded her to be careful, that she was a god and this was little more than a boy. Still, she tried her best to ignore the advice. She walked to where she'd thrown Chen and hauled him to his feet.

"Please! I'm sorry. Don't hurt me. We were just having fun."

The pathetic excuse caused another flood of rage to fill Valeyn's heart.

"Fun?" she said. "No, you mean *you* were having fun. You didn't care what she felt, did you?"

Valeyn gripped him by the throat with one hand and held him aloft above the sand. He started to gurgle, and his feet kicked the air uselessly.

"Why don't we explore that?" she whispered into a face that was growing red. "For example, I'm having a lot of fun right now. I guess that means you are too, right?"

A scream sounded from behind her. Bealdra was staring in horror at the sight of Valeyn throttling her friend. The rest of her group were running across the sand.

"Do something!" Bealdra cried to them as they approached. "Get help!"

Chen's friend stepped forward as if to challenge Valeyn, but he was quickly restrained by Jon.

"No! She's a witch from the north. She'll break you in half," said Jon.

"Help!" screamed Bealdra.

"Get people to help!" Feali commanded one of the boys.

Valeyn looked from Feali to Bealdra and back to the now-purple face of Chen. For a moment, she genuinely wondered what to do. Should she kill this young predator? He was only a man after all, and she was a god. She certainly had the right. She looked deeply into eyes that had been glazed with lust and were now glazed with terror.

"Please, don't hurt him." Naya's soft request cut through her rage. Valeyn looked around to see Naya standing at the boatshed doors. "Valeyn, please," Naya said.

Valeyn stared at her for a moment longer then relaxed her grip on Chen's throat. He fell to the sand with a gasping sound and lay there writhing like a fish on dry land. None of his friends dared move to help him. She looked at them, and for a moment, she felt her godhood swell within her. These were lecherous creatures. Lustful, spiteful, and jealous. Perhaps she should judge them also? Perhaps she should wipe them from this world.

"Thank you," said Naya.

Valeyn turned her eyes back to Naya's and felt her senses return. Everyone now stood in silence, watching Valeyn. It took her a moment to realize they were all waiting on her next action. She returned her attention to the wretched figure of Chen, who was rubbing his already-bruised throat but was otherwise frozen in fear on the sand.

"Go now, you little rapist!" she hissed at him. Valeyn heard one of the girls gasp slightly at the accusation. "Leave Tiet this instant. Don't say goodbye to anyone. Don't go running for help. And most importantly, don't ever come back. If I ever see you again, I will kill you, and nobody in this town will be able to stop me. Do you believe me?"

Chen nodded vigorously. Nobody else said a word.

"Go," ordered Valeyn. "And take your friend with you."

Chen climbed to his feet as quickly as he could and gestured to his companion. For a moment, all five in the group looked from one to the other as if searching for some kind of unspoken alternative. To Chen's credit, it took him no more than a few seconds to realize it was very much in his best interests to vacate Tiet that instant. With his friend's assistance, he hobbled away across the sand as the others watched in silence. Valeyn turned back to Naya.

"Can you walk?"

Naya nodded and Valeyn cradled one arm around her as she led them away from the shed. She walked past the remaining group without a word or even a glance. In that moment, they were completely beneath her notice. The two of them walked in silence as they slowly crossed the beach.

As Valeyn's rage subsided, it was replaced by other feelings. Remorse. Hurt. Disappointment. Fear. She understood these weren't her own feelings, they were Naya's. She glanced down at her. "What's the matter?"

"Nothing," Naya replied.

"Are you upset with me?"

"No!" Naya pleaded. The edge in her voice made it very plain she was speaking the truth. In fact, the edge in her voice made the truth very plain.

Valeyn stopped. "You're...afraid of me?" Naya stared down at the sand and said nothing. "How can you be afraid of me? I just stopped you from getting raped."

Naya's face screwed up as if she were about to be sick. "I know you did. Thank you."

"So why are you afraid of me?"

It took Naya a moment before she answered. "You were going to kill Chen, weren't you?"

Valeyn thought for a moment. "I honestly don't know."

"How could you do that?"

"How can you ask me that, Naya? He's a predator."

"I know, but killing him? That's just too much."

"For you maybe, but I've seen too many men like him in the world." Valeyn studied her young friend. "There's something else, isn't there? What is it?"

The look of shame returned again to Naya's face.

"Tell me, Naya," Valeyn repeated.

Naya summoned her courage. "I don't know how I feel, it's just...I kinda wish you hadn't sent him away. I know he was taking things too far but still...I liked him. He was sweet."

Valeyn stared at her in disbelief. "*Sweet?*" She took a step back and viewed Naya as if she were at a distance. Frustration welled once again. Naya looked horrified by her own admission and tears returned to her eyes. Valeyn could feel the hurt and confusion pouring out from the injured girl, but this time, it was washed aside by Valeyn's own rising fury.

"What the hell is wrong with you?"

Naya sobbed and covered her face with her hands. "I'm sorry Valeyn...I don't know..."

Valeyn knew Naya needed help. She needed the older sister who had been there earlier in the evening. But that woman wasn't here now. She'd been replaced by someone far colder, someone who just did not want to be kind.

"I can't believe you, Naya. Why don't you go back to them if that's what you want? Where were they when you were pinned to the floor in the boatshed? They didn't even want me to find you!"

Naya was crying now. Valeyn sighed in frustration. "Get out of here. Go back home to your father and tell him what's happened. I've done all I can tonight."

Naya turned and ran up the beach back toward the crowd. Her face was lined with streaks of tears, and her pristine dress was now similarly stained. Valeyn watched her and knew she was now a very different person from the innocent girl who had entered the party hours earlier.

Join the club like the rest of the grown-ups.

Valeyn watched her until Naya reached the safety of the Hava then turned away.

The night was sour. Valeyn stewed in black thoughts as she left the beach and made her way up the dirt track that led to her cottage. She suddenly hated this place and all of its people, but she didn't know why. She felt like she should leave. Storming up the path, Valeyn approached the timber structure that had become her home over the past year. It was a small cottage with a few rooms covered by a shingled roof, but it had been more than adequate for her needs – until now. Now, she found herself despising it.

As she approached, she noticed the door was slightly ajar, but it didn't bother her. She knew why. It was the same reason why her mood had descended into blackness. The same reason why she had treated Naya with such cruelty.

Valeyn pushed the door aside, strode into the small, dark room, and looked around expectantly. She'd been repeating behaviors she'd learned before. Behaviors Vale had seen her whole life from her mentor. Her mother.

"Where are you, Yvorre?" she asked the darkness.

A gaunt figure shuffled out from the shadows and stood in the light cast from the doorframe. The stooped and wretched form was covered in a faded grey traveling cloak. The arms of the figure hung at its sides and stretched down far too long for its body. A diseased odor filled the room as the old woman shuffled further into the grey light.

"My daughter," Yvorre croaked in a withered voice. "It's so good to see you again."

CHAPTER 6

"When the gods created Kovalith they infused their energies – their kai *– into all things, and it was the combination of these energies that gave us this world. The kai of each god manifested itself in different ways and in different colors: the bright gold of Kalte, the shining green of Maelene, or the dazzling blue of Nishindra. Each power could only be wielded by the disciples of each god – outside of the Render. Within the Render, many things are possible."*

~Aleasea of the Ageless

"Why shouldn't I kill you, Mother?"

The sunken features of Yvorre twisted into a leer as she turned away from her daughter and crossed to the darkened fireplace on the far side of the room.

"I hear Vale's harsh words from a pretty new face," Yvorre croaked as she bent over the logs stacked neatly in the hearth. Extending her palm, the old woman blew over it and a gentle wisp of flame danced into life. It carried on her breath and curled across the space into the fireplace, where the logs immediately flared.

"I mean it, Yvorre. Why have you come to me? Are you looking to finally die?"

Yvorre's expression was one of complete indifference as she shuffled over to a faded leather armchair and settled into it. When she had finally made herself comfortable, she returned her attention to Valeyn and gave her an appraising look.

"My, my...you certainly have developed, haven't you? I haven't had a chance to get a good look at you. Yes...this is good." Yvorre nodded to herself in approval, as if Valeyn hadn't even spoken.

"Are you trying to provoke me? It's not a good idea. I've already come close to killing someone tonight," said Valeyn.

"Yes, I know. I could feel it," Yvorre replied, addressing Valeyn directly for the first time. "Your restraint was impressive, if unnecessary. Such an animal has no right to draw the breath of the air we've created."

"So is that why you've come? To judge the crimes of lustful boys?"

"No, I've come to behold my creation in the flesh."

Anger flooded back to Valeyn's chest. She crossed the room and stood over Yvorre. "I am not your creation."

Yvorre looked up at her impassively. "Yes, you are, Valeyn. You are my child. You are the result of the union between myself and Bythe. This is a fact you cannot ignore."

"That doesn't mean you own me."

Yvorre raised her eyebrows slightly. "Whenever did I claim ownership of you? Creation does not necessarily imply ownership, my child."

Valeyn hesitated. For a moment, she was Vale again. The dutiful student caught out by her clever teacher's word games. Yvorre's sunken eyes glittered with amusement at the reaction. Valeyn recovered quickly.

"You certainly claimed ownership of me back in Fairhaven – or rather you tried to. Or have you forgotten how you sent your clockwork demon to bring me back to you in chains?"

"Well, I sent Imbatal to secure Elyn and Vale. Yes, that is true. And yes, perhaps I was a little overzealous in my enthusiasm to help you reconcile into the magnificent god who stands before me. But I have only ever claimed control over your broken halves, Valeyn, I only wanted to reconcile you."

Valeyn took a step backward.

"Help me? Is that what you just said? Your desire was to *help* me?"

"Yes, Valeyn. I only ever wanted my daughter back as she was meant to be. I never wanted to control her."

"You're a liar," Valeyn said.

"Search for the lie in my words, Daughter. We're kindred now. You can sense that as well as I."

Valeyn paused. Was this strange resurgence in her empathy now a reaction to Yvorre's presence? She reached out with her feelings the way Elyn used to and found she could sense her mother in the chair before her. It was like a weight in her mind, something oily and unpleasant. She pulled away quickly.

"I always knew there was something wrong with Vale," Yvorre continued. "I knew she needed help. Now, perhaps I could have shown a little more compassion but..." Yvorre shrugged and let her words trail off.

Valeyn looked at her mother in silence for a moment. Part of her wanted to throw Yvorre out of the cottage, a smaller part even wanted to kill her, but another voice urged caution. It was Vale. The logical, tactical instincts of Vale warning her not to surrender any options just yet. To hear her mother out, no matter how unpleasant the experience might be. And there'd been no lie in Yvorre's words so far. "Don't sit there and pretend you had my best interests at heart. You wanted to use me as a weapon against Bythe."

Yvorre barked a short laugh. "Once again, I never said I had your best interests at heart. I worked toward our *mutual* best interests. Yes, I wanted to use you as a weapon, the same way I used the Ageless as my weapon, the same way I use myself as a weapon. Your father is evil and must be stopped. I saw a great opportunity in your existence. I always did. Ever since I first saw you in The Tower's vision."

"I'm tired of these games, Yvorre, and I'm not your student anymore. How did you find me?"

The old goddess smiled again. "How did I find you? I think a better question would be how could anyone miss you? You're a singular individual, and to add to that, you have the most peculiar habit of leaving people in various states of injury in your wake."

Vale glared at her mother. "Those people attacked me."

"Of course they did, my child." Yvorre shook her head, and for a moment, sadness seemed to touch her sunken expression. "When are you going to learn? They're animals. All of them."

Valeyn opened her mouth to argue but stopped. She remembered what Yvorre had shown her in Sanctuary. Yvorre had once been the beautiful goddess Maelene, before Bythe had imprisoned her. For over one hundred years, Maelene had slowly become twisted by Bythe. She was a broken shell of the goddess she used to be. Valeyn knew that arguing against such an experience would be futile.

"And of course," Yvorre continued, "we can now sense the bond between us, can't we? Once I was close enough, I no longer needed to seek out signs of your passing in the form of injured fools – I was guided by instinct."

"I know," Valeyn answered, anxious to regain some form of initiative in the conversation. "I could feel something within me. I wasn't sure it was you until I stood outside that door tonight."

"This is unsurprising, Valeyn. All the gods could feel a kinship with their bastard offspring. But you are different. Our brethren sired bastards from the mortals of this world. You, on the other hand, are the first union of two gods in the history of Kovalith. Did you know that?"

Valeyn glanced away. She hadn't known that, but she'd be damned if she was going to give Yvorre yet another small victory in this conversation. "For the last time, Mother, tell me what you want or I'll throw you out of here myself."

"I need help, Valeyn. I am in great danger."

The blunt honesty of the response caught Valeyn off guard. She was expecting more riddles, not a direct plea. She struggled with the order of questions as they came to her.

"Bythe?" Valeyn asked – the most obvious answer coming to mind.

"Not Bythe personally, but his proxy. His Royal Inquisitor. He was a former apprentice of mine; now he hunts me like a dog."

"Good. You deserve it. You gambled and you lost. Now you deal with the consequences. This has nothing to do with me."

"That's where you're mistaken, Valeyn. The Inquisitor is only hunting me because he stumbled across my trail while following yours. You're his main prize. I am just a bonus to him."

Valeyn eyed her mother carefully before turning away and crossing to a small cabinet on the far side of the room. She withdrew a bottle filled with grapewine and poured a small glass. She swilled the red liquid in the glass thoughtfully before taking a drink and turning back to Yvorre, who had remained silently watchful.

"Bythe is hunting both of us?" Valeyn asked. Yvorre nodded. "And this Inquisitor wants to bring both of us back to the Ironhelm, is that it?"

"It's doubtful he wants to kill you – me, I'm not so sure about. We have a...history."

Valeyn raised her eyebrows and took another sip of grapewine. "Why am I not surprised?"

"I admit I was stern with him. He was a limited student, nothing like the student Vale was."

This time it was Valeyn who laughed, and the sound had a genuine glow of amusement. "I don't remember you lavishing such praises on Vale. Do you realize I share all of her memories? The way I recall it, you were a condescending bitch to her."

Yvorre looked down at the floor, and for a moment, Valeyn thought she actually sensed remorse. It was a brief sensation, but for a moment it had been there.

"I won't apologize, Valeyn. I was the strong woman I needed to be. I still am. Your father brought out the worst parts of me. You can't claim to know what it's like to be held prisoner for decades, to be forced to bear a child with someone you despise. Judge me all you like child, but be careful. One day, life might visit such judgment on you, and you might look back at this moment and realize you weren't as wise as you thought yourself to be."

Valeyn pushed her conflicted feelings aside and moved the conversation away from them. "So, this Inquisitor is hunting me? Has he found me?"

"I don't know. He doesn't have my ability to sense you, if that's what you mean, but he certainly has several other gifts he can make use of. I suspect it will only be a matter of time."

Valeyn shrugged and drained the last of her glass before setting it atop the cabinet.

"Well, once he gets here, he's going to be disappointed he wasted the journey. Hasn't he heard about what I did to your last employee?" Valeyn gestured casually to a massive sword that was mounted on hooks above the door. It was a truly magnificent weapon, roughly five feet in length and heavy enough that no man could lift it – at least no natural man. This had been the weapon of Imbatal, Yvorre's clockwork demon that Valeyn had smashed to pieces three years earlier. Yvorre ignored the weapon and kept her eyes fixed on her daughter.

"You are strong, my daughter, I grant you that. Your preternatural gifts were a perfect match for Imbatal, but of course you know why that is, don't you?"

Valeyn hesitated. She knew Yvorre was playing another game, but she didn't know the answer to her mother's question. "I reconciled," she answered simply, hoping this would be enough to save face. It wasn't. Yvorre smiled again, but this time the smile seemed to be one of pity, not condescension. She raised herself from the chair with some effort, and slowly walked over to where her daughter stood.

"Not all gods possessed the physical abilities you have. You know this. Hasn't it occurred to you there was a reason you developed these specific gifts?"

Valeyn didn't answer. The truth was, she hadn't even considered there might be a logical reason for her specific abilities.

"When you reconciled into Valeyn it was in a moment of crisis, was it not? Imbatal had struck Vale down and was probably about to kill Elyn as well. When you reconciled, you tapped into the *kai*, the immortal energies that bind Kovalith, and you bent it to your unconscious will. You used this to craft yourself into a form that was strong, fast, and powerful. A person who could defeat Imbatal on his terms. This was no coincidence."

"I didn't do anything like that."

"Think about it, child. What are your gifts? You're strong like Imbatal? Fast like Imbatal? You can even heft his weapon like it was your own."

Valeyn looked at her, considering the words. "Are you saying I chose this power?"

Yvorre shrugged. "After a fashion. All of the gods chose their gifts when they crafted mortal forms for themselves. I suspect you had your choices forced on you by necessity – it was an unconscious choice."

Valeyn sighed irritably. "So what's your point, Mother? That you know more about the rules of being a god than I do? That you know more about me than I do? You're probably right, but I'll figure the rest out for myself, if you don't mind. I don't need your help."

"You're missing the point of the lesson, Valeyn." Yvorre's voice became harsh and Valeyn suddenly felt the conditioned pang of fear a student always feels when facing their teacher's disapproval. "You stand in your cabin drinking wine and convincing yourself of your superiority against anything that can hurt you in this world, but you haven't considered the flaw in your logic. You built yourself to defend yourself against Imbatal and you defeated Imbatal. Does this really surprise you? Do you see the problem?"

Valeyn slammed her palm onto the cabinet and the wine-stained glass fell to the floor and shattered.

"No, I don't see a problem, Yvorre. I've handled more than just Imbatal. I've handled grown men twice your size without them laying a finger on me! I won't be patronized by you."

"Mortal men!" Yvorre snorted. "You may as well boast about stealing toys from children. No, my daughter, there are creatures in this world far different from Imbatal and immeasurably greater than mortal men. Creatures with their own gifts and abilities you've never before seen. Exedor has been granted abilities from Bythe. He carries your father's *kai*. How do you expect to defend yourself against him when you've equipped yourself to defeat only Imbatal?"

Valeyn crossed to the window and stared out into the night where the glow of the Hava's fire was still visible in the sky. She didn't want to face Vale's old teacher anymore. The conversation was beginning to unsettle her.

"I think you should leave, Yvorre. We've got nothing to say to each other."

"Valeyn," Yvorre paused, as if choosing her words carefully. "There is so much you do not yet understand. How can you? You're a new god, and there are but two other gods left in this world. You're alone."

"So what? I've been alone my entire life. This is nothing new for me." Valeyn heard the slight tone of petulance creeping into her voice and she hated it.

"I know you resent me, child. You have good reason to. But it's your sense of reason I appeal to now. I can teach you. I can help you defend yourself against those who hunt you." Valeyn shook her head in disbelief, but Yvorre continued unperturbed. "Don't you see? You can use my knowledge to your own advantage. Take it as a form of payment, if you like. Think of it as revenge for all those years I treated you poorly."

"You've already taught Vale enough for a lifetime," Valeyn answered.

"No. I prepared Vale as best I could under the circumstances, but you are more than her now. You are Valeyn. A god."

"I'm not interested in your help, Yvorre."

"What do you have to fear?" Yvorre snapped. "Look at me, Valeyn! I am old. Weak. My days of youth and beauty are long behind me. I am fading from this world and soon, I'll be gone completely. You could kill me right now with barely a thought."

"I already told you not to patronize me, Mother. I get the feeling you still have plenty of tricks."

"Tricks, yes, but real power? No. My power was stripped from me over the years of my captivity. What little strength I had left was used in my failed efforts to capture you. And when I was forced to destroy Sanctuary, I lost all hope of ever restoring my former glory." She sighed and hobbled back to the chair, settling into it before continuing in a quieter voice. "However, you are right about one thing. I gambled and I lost. I have no one to blame but myself."

Valeyn looked at the ruined figure next to the glow of the fire and felt compassion touch her heart for the briefest instant. She pushed it away fiercely.

"Everything has always been a game to you, Yvorre. Are you looking for sympathy now that you've lost a round?"

"Kovalith has always been a game to our kind, albeit a game your father and I became very attached to. And so I played my final gambit and it failed. Now I have no options but to throw myself at your mercy, knowing full well how much you hate me. Do you think this is easy for me?"

Valeyn sighed in frustration and turned back to the window. The cabin was filled with silence for a moment, both mother and daughter lost within their own thoughts. The glow of the distant fire grew brighter as the Hava reached its climax.

"I only ask you to think rationally, Valeyn." Yvorre broke the silence. "Think strategically. Think for yourself. Think about your own personal advantage as I always did. I gain your protection and in exchange I submit myself to you. The positions I had in mind for us are suddenly reversed. My goals are thwarted, and you now hold the power over me that I had sought to hold over you."

"I don't trust you."

"Of course you don't, and you'd be a fool if you did – certainly not the daughter I raised. Do not trust me. Ever. Do not turn your back on me. Keep me under your control as tightly as I controlled Imbatal, and in return you'll have me as a weapon and a source of knowledge to exploit as you see fit."

There was silence as Valeyn considered the options. Yvorre spoke again. "I am at the disadvantage in this exchange, Valeyn. You have very little to lose and you have the power to terminate the arrangement at any time. You could kill me, and I doubt I could stop you."

Valeyn looked back at her old mentor. While she had no doubt that Yvorre had some plan in mind, she also couldn't dismiss the logic presented to her. This was a unique opportunity that might never come again. To gain even a measure of control over Yvorre could be immensely beneficial to anyone – especially to a godling like Valeyn. Centuries of knowledge were locked within that twisted mind. The power that could by unlocked by having such a mentor was an exciting thought.

But there was something else. Valeyn couldn't shake the memories of Maelene – the woman Yvorre has once been. This woman was also sitting before her now. Valeyn cast her mind back to those memories she had been shown in Sanctuary. Maelene had once been a beautiful woman – loved and worshipped by half a world. Maelene had once been her mother and soon her mother would be gone. This could be the last opportunity she would have to ever really know her. Could she throw that opportunity away so lightly? Her head swam slightly as the wine took effect. She decided she needed sleep. "I need you to leave. Let me think about this."

Yvorre rose to her feet again. "Where would you have me go?"

"I don't know. Surely you can keep yourself safe for one night?" Valeyn turned and faced the window again. The night sky was still lit with the orange glow of the bonfire. "If you follow the coast north for about three miles there's a small inlet with plenty of cover. I can..."

Her voice trailed off. The fire was bright in the night sky. She had never seen a Hava fire this bright. Somehow, she'd realized this while she'd been talking but she'd been ignoring it. Valeyn cursed herself.

"Valeyn..." Yvorre began.

"Quiet!" Valeyn ordered.

There were sounds in the distance. Terrible sounds. Screams of true horror. Yvorre met her eyes, and Valeyn could see the flames from the fireplace reflected in them.

"He has found us."

In an instant, Valeyn had recovered her sword from its mounting and moved toward the door. Yvorre moved to block her path.

"Don't be a fool, Valeyn."

"Step aside, Mother." Valeyn's tone left no misunderstanding that her warning would not be repeated.

"Have you heard nothing I have said? You are not ready to face this man. He will subdue you, then take you back to Bythe before the town has burned. Come with me. We must run, now."

Valeyn pushed her mother aside without effort and marched out the door. Yvorre muttered a curse as she was flung against the open door in her daughter's wake.

"Valeyn!" Yvorre's desperate voice reached across the darkness, but it couldn't touch her daughter. Valeyn simply vanished into the amber glow of the burning night leaving her mother behind.

CHAPTER 7

"The goddess Romona took an intense interest in the life the gods had created in the Forge. It is said that she was the youngest of the gods and her heart was uncorrupted. She created a great hospice in the south and named it Kardak. Over the years, thousands came to her followers for healing – or to ease their suffering.

Death was a foreign concept to the gods and Romona became fascinated by this phenomenon above all of her brethren. While the other gods chose their various interests in the life of the Forge, Romona became obsessed with the balance between life and death. Over time, a darkness fell over Kardak and many strange creatures were sighted in the surrounding lands.

Romona's fate is said to be the greatest tragedy of the gods, and a tale known by no mortal in this world."

~Aleasea of the Ageless

The screams became frantic, and Valeyn broke into a run. The night sky was now glowing, and she could see glimpses of orange flames flickering through the gaps in the trees. She gripped the sword hilt in both hands and held it aloft as she sprinted down the dirt track toward the village. As she emerged onto the main street, the full horror of what had transpired was revealed like a macabre tableau.

It wasn't one or two houses alight; the entire village was burning. Fire danced the length of the street on both sides, bathing Tiet in an orange glow, and for a moment, the illusion was almost celebratory – an illusion belied by bodies writhing on the road.

Valeyn stepped over to the nearest form with thick smoke stinging her eyes, and when she looked down, she he didn't recognize what she saw. There was the form of a man, but he was withered and shrunken to the size of a small child. The man squirmed on the road like a helpless infant, yet this face was old and wrinkled. His eyes were wide with terror, yet his mouth only opened and closed with a rasping gurgle.

She took a step back in shock and looked up the street. The second figure was now trying to drag itself along the street by its arms, as Valeyn realized it had no legs. The figure looked up and saw Valeyn through the smoke. The noise it made was supposed to be a cry for help, but the cry was a nothing more than a strangled shriek of terror. Man or woman – Valeyn couldn't tell. It started to drag itself toward Valeyn's legs, its hands reaching out to grab at her boots. She recoiled in horror and stepped back from both forms.

For a moment, Valeyn had no idea what to do. She stepped back even further and tried to understand what was happening. The street was flanked by twin curtains of fire and shrouded in smoke, making it impossible to see clearly. Bodies littered the street – some moving, others not. Further toward the beach, Valeyn could make out figures moving through the haze and a fresh scream split the thick night air. She began running toward the sound, when she saw a bright blue dress in the road before her.

It was Naya. The remains of her.

She was lying in the dirt, sobbing in racking gulps, her beautiful dress now torn and stained. Even through the smoke Valeyn could see the damage that had been done to her. The left side of her face was scarred and most of her hair was gone.

"Naya!" Valeyn knelt down and cradled her. She was so light. Too light.

"I'm sorry," Naya cried in piteous sobs. "Valeyn, I'm so sorry."

"Naya what happened to you?"

"I'm sorry, I'm sorry." Naya repeated over and over.

Valeyn hugged Naya and only then understood the horror of what had happened to her. She could feel Naya's breasts were gone, and there were empty pockets of her body everywhere under her blue dress. "Naya...my gods. Who did this to you?"

Naya clung to Valeyn even tighter at her words. "The gods, Valeyn. It was the gods – they've come back."

Valeyn gripped Naya even tighter. "It's alright, Naya, it wasn't the gods."

"Yes, it was." Naya's voice trembled, and she pulled back to look at Valeyn with blue eyes full of fear. "They caught me when I was trying to get back to father. One of them saw me and then...then..." She broke into renewed cries that increased into frantic shrieks, and Valeyn pulled her close again.

"Shhh...it's alright, you're safe now. I'm here."

Naya's breathing started to steady, and she leaned into Valeyn as if she were the only thing in the world. "I'm so sorry," Naya said again.

"Naya, I'm going to keep you safe, but I need you to try and tell me who did this to you. How many were there?"

Naya was quiet for a moment before she answered. "I don't know how many – lots of them I think. They were tall and red...they had helmets so I couldn't see their faces...until one of them looked at me..."

"That's alright," Valeyn hushed her and pulled Naya close again. "It's okay. You don't need to tell me anymore."

The Faede. Vale had known of them. She had even encountered them on occasion. Yvorre's personal guard. Unnatural creatures who would follow Yvorre wherever she travelled. Valeyn immediately suspected a trap. She picked up Naya with disturbing ease and took her to a cluster of trees, well out of the light and away from the flames.

"Naya, I'm going to leave you here for a moment..."

"Please, don't!" The cry was desperate, like a child's.

"Naya, I need to deal with them."

"Don't! They'll hurt you too."

Valeyn smiled in a reassuring way. "Naya, they can't hurt me. Trust me. I'm far more powerful than they are. Stay here a few minutes and I'll be back."

Valeyn rose to her feet.

"I'm so sorry," Naya said. "This is my fault, isn't it?"

Valeyn froze in place for a moment before staring down at the young girl with genuine confusion. "What? No, of course not. Why would you even think that?"

Naya's eyes were filling with tears and also with shame. "This is because of what I did tonight, isn't it?"

"Naya, no!"

"I was dirty. I know I shouldn't have gone with him, but I wanted to. Now I'm being punished so I can't ever do it again."

Valeyn was filled with dismay at what she was hearing. It was bad enough the Faede were tearing Tiet apart on account of Valeyn, but the thought of Naya blaming herself struck Valeyn with a sense of guilt that was suddenly unbearable.

"No, Naya. My gods, no!" She kneeled down again and gripped the young girl by the shoulders. "Naya, look at me. This is not your fault. These creatures aren't here for you, they're here for me. You've done nothing wrong!"

Naya looked back at her for a moment. "That's not true. I know it's not. You'd never hurt us, Valeyn. I'm the reason they've come. The gods are punishing me."

"No, Naya, I'd never hurt you, but these creatures are here because of me..." Her voice trailed off as she finished the sentence in her mind. The Faede were here because of her. Naya was now crippled because of her. No, Valeyn would never hurt Naya – not directly – but her thoughtlessness had wrought the same result. Naya was now looking up at her in confusion, and Valeyn started to feel sick.

"Why are they after you? Did you know they were coming?" Naya asked in a quiet voice.

Valeyn couldn't answer. She felt the choking grip of frustration melting into anger. She was a god. Did she really think she was going to be able to live a normal life? Returning to her feet, Valeyn couldn't look at the ruin of a girl lying before her.

"Stay here, please. I'm going to kill every one of them. They'll never hurt anyone again."

Naya said something but Valeyn couldn't hear it. She retrieved her sword from where she had left it on the road and walked steadily toward the beach. She rounded the flaming shopfronts and saw two of the Faede standing watch over the beach. They stood impassively – a heavy, raspy breathing emanating from within the dark grills of their faceplates. The gentle sound of a breaking wave drifted out of the darkness, and Valeyn noticed they both turned their helms to watch the water as it rode up the sand, as if they were concerned the tide would advance on them. Their red cloaks flickered in the firelight, and their shadows danced in the sand before them.

Valeyn stepped onto the sand, and they slowly turned their crimson helms in unison as they noticed her presence. She strode toward the two figures, lifting her massive sword in readiness. Both of the Faede watched her approach and then – as if acting on some unspoken command – they separated and moved to flank her on opposite sides.

She paused and eyed them both. Normally, she'd be contemptuous of such a rudimentary gambit, but today she was boiling with anger over what these creatures had done. She looked at each of them in turn before speaking.

"You might terrorize young girls and fishermen, but you have no idea who's standing before you, do you? Did your master tell you about me?"

The Faede stood immovable in the firelight. The only sounds were distant screams and their labored breathing deep within their crimson helms.

"I'm as far above you as you are above these simple people. You once bowed to my mother, and now my mother bows before me. You're nothing."

It might have been her imagination, but Valeyn thought she caught a slight reaction at the reference to Yvorre. She allowed herself the luxury of a smile before she sprang toward the Faede on her left. The creature reached up to unlatch its grilled faceplate, but the movements were lethargic to her eyes. Its hand had barely reached the latch before she swung her sword in a horizontal arc and severed its crimson helmet and right hand from the rest of its body.

As both body parts spun into the night, she turned to face the remaining Faede. Like its companion, it had also reached up to unlatch its faceplate but unlike its companion, it was now opening the grill. Valeyn then appreciated the intelligence of their tactic – by separating, they had ensured at least one of them would have time to do this. She wasted little more time admiring the cunning of these creatures and leaped at the second Faede. During the seconds she closed the distance between them, she could hear a distant scream, like a room of children wailing in unison. Shrill and high pitched, it made her stumble, and with that misstep, something unseen guided her eyes up to the void of the Faede's helmet.

Valeyn had experienced the unique feelings of death before. As Vale, she had felt a soothing numb darkness envelop her, as she lay on the ground with her life essence bleeding out of her. It had been a terrifying experience, yet it had also been strangely calming.

This was far, far worse.

As she looked into the darkness within the helmet, the shrieking voices rose in pitch and volume until they extinguished any other sound. Somehow, Valeyn knew there was a child somewhere within that figure. An innocent who had been twisted and tortured, and then turned loose on the world with all the confused hurt of the unloved. She felt a swell of grief overcome her at the thought and she staggered. The giant sword fell from her grip as her fingers went lax. The Faede seemed to be reaching out to her. It needed her. It needed her strength and her courage and her resolve. She tried to say something to the terrible child within that form, but her lips wouldn't obey, and only a mumbled sound came forth. The Faede took a step forward and the shrill noise increased within her mind. She could feel it pulling at her, trying to take parts of her very existence.

Valeyn closed her eyes against the horror, and with a swell of strength, she slowly forced herself to her feet. The Faede took a step backward. Valeyn risked opening her eyes a fraction in order to find her target. She prepared to spring, but before she could press the advantage, a second Faede emerged from the night and stood alongside the first. Valeyn clenched her eyes shut but she could now feel the second creature opening its faceplate. The shrieking increased, and she felt a black despair wash over her. She reeled back, desperate to find a way out of this trap, but she was losing all sense of direction. It seemed as if she were being pulled apart from all directions. She felt the sand beneath her palms and knew that she had somehow fallen. She wanted to scream, but she couldn't feel her mouth. In a moment of panic, it struck her that it might not even be there anymore. This thought caused her to thrash about aimlessly. She had to get away from these creatures before they took everything from her – like they did from Naya.

"That's quite enough of that, I think." The smooth voice cut through the shrieking and then all was quiet.

Valeyn could feel her equilibrium return. She knew she was crouched on her hands and knees on the sand. The heavy rasping of the Faede was still there, but the shrieking in her head had vanished. Opening her eyes, she looked up to see three red figures staring down at her from behind closed faceplates, but her attention was stolen by the man standing in front of them. He was elegantly dressed in black silk, with midnight-colored hair swept back over his high forehead. He stared down at her with a warm smile on his face.

"I'm so very sorry, my dear. I'm afraid my associates get a little carried away with their duties. I hope you are unharmed?"

Valeyn slowly got to her feet and looked about warily. There were more of the Faede emerging from the night, and they were forming a circle around her. Her eyes flickered to her sword lying in the sand between herself and the newcomer. He followed her gaze and his smile deepened.

"Oh, come now, Valeyn, please. Must we really get off to such an aggressive start? You don't even know who I am."

"I know more than you think, Exedor. I know that you're Bythe's Inquisitor, and you're here to take me back to the Ironhelm. You won't succeed."

Exedor raised his eyebrows but nodded in confirmation.

"Indeed. Forgive me. You appear to be far better informed than I gave you credit for." He seemed to look about for a moment before continuing. "I'm flattered my reputation has already made its way into the Fareaches."

Valeyn returned his smile. "Don't be flattered, you're not that important. Nobody's heard of you."

"Ah, then it could only be your mother who told you of me. Thank you." He turned to the Faede on his left and snapped a curt order. "She's here. Find her."

Three of the figures left the circle without a word, leaving several others standing in silent vigil around her. Valeyn silently cursed herself for being tricked into revealing Yvorre's presence so effortlessly. Exedor returned his attention to her.

"We'll have your mother join us presently, but Valeyn..." He paused and took her in with a warm expression. "It is truly a pleasure to finally meet you. You really have no idea how much of a fuss you've created back in the Iron Union. Your story has spread throughout the empire. I believe everyone must be talking about you by now."

"That's gratifying to hear, Exedor, but I'm not very interested in fame."

"Of course not." He chuckled and gestured to the burning town around them. "One does not exactly travel out to the back end of nowhere if one is craving attention, correct?"

Valeyn fixed him with a hard stare. "Stop the games, Inquisitor! I still have Vale's memories of the Iron Union, and I know why you're here."

Exedor shook his head, but the warm smile never left his face. "My dear girl, you do not know as much as you think. You've been talking to your mother again, haven't you?" Valeyn remained silent. "You must know by now how much she hates your father. You cannot possibly trust what she tells you."

"Just because she hates my father doesn't mean she's wrong about him."

"True," he nodded absently. "I cannot fault that logic. But surely you wouldn't make up your mind on such an important issue as your father – my immortal protector – without hearing alternative points of view?"

Valeyn shifted her balance and eyed the red-robed figures hemming her in on all sides. Her mind worked furiously for a solution. "It's a little hard to stay objective when you have these creatures threatening me," she ventured.

He nodded again, this time a little more thoughtfully. "Yes, well precautions had to be taken. It would not be prudent to introduce myself to you without any safeguards. Surely you can see my logic here?"

"Well then, now that we're acquainted, why don't you stand your Faede down, and I promise to hear you out?"

He stared at her for a long time. Finally, he motioned to his Faede, and they all took several steps backward, as if they were one. Within seconds, they had retreated into the shadows, barely visible but for the reflections cast by the flames on their crimson helms.

"Better?" Exedor asked.

She nodded and measured up the distance between them. "Alright then, give me this alternate point of view."

The smile returned to his thin face and something within that look made her uneasy. "Valeyn, you have no idea how happy your father is to know you exist. When word of you reached the Ironhelm, Bythe commanded the war to cease. Such was his happiness, he has extended peace to his enemies in your name."

"And did he name a holiday after me too?"

Exedor smiled again and took a step toward her, his palms outstretched in a conciliatory gesture. "I understand your skepticism, Valeyn. I admit, I would react much the same if I were in your position. But you have to believe me, your father wants nothing more than for you to return to him. He loves you."

This time she laughed. It was an authentic explosion of surprise and relief. "Oh please! You were doing better when you said I'd single-handedly stopped the war."

"You seem quick to judge, Valeyn, but how do you know for sure? Do you know your father?"

Anger flared within her. Within Vale. "Yes, I remember him. I remember how he threw me aside the minute he realized he had no use for me. And now that he's recognized his mistake, he wants me to come back to him?"

Exedor looked at the sand with a solemn expression on his smooth features. "Lord Bythe was worried you might feel this way. He told me to tell you he is truly sorry for his mistakes. He... regrets many of his actions over the course of his lifetime. He wants you to know that he considers his treatment of you to be paramount among these regrets."

"Just words," she snorted.

"Valeyn," Exedor began as he took another step toward her. "My god – your father – is far from a perfect being. He knows this. All the gods knew they were not perfect, but think on it, Valeyn. He is reaching out to you now. Yes, he has made mistakes. Yes, he has regrets. But are you so perfect yourself? Have you not made errors in judgment since your own ascension to godhood? Perhaps even more so because of your ascension?"

Valeyn's thoughts automatically flickered to Naya and guilt flooded her. She looked away, suddenly unable to meet his eyes.

Exedor took yet another step toward her and extended his palm. When he spoke his voice was soft, almost a whisper. "Come with me, Valeyn. I know how you're feeling. This is a terrible burden for you to bear. Let us help you through this difficult time."

Valeyn hesitated. In some distant part of her mind, she realized that Exedor knew about Naya, that he'd possibly even watched Valeyn find her. Had he deliberately targeted Naya to set up this moment?

Valeyn leaped forward, knocking aside Exedor's outstretched hand and grabbing him by the throat. In less than a heartbeat, she had him pinned in the sand with her hand around his neck.

"Keep your Faede back or I'll kill you right now!" she hissed. The Faede began to step forward out of the shadows, but Exedor stopped them with a wave of his hand.

"Good," Valeyn said, straightening herself but keeping her hand on his neck. "Now, I want you to send them away. Send them all the way back to my father. You can stay behind and we can have a little chat."

"Valeyn," Exedor croaked through a constrained windpipe. She relaxed her grip enough to let him speak. "Please be reasonable. Can't we discuss this? Your father is offering you his love. Surely this is good news?"

"That's where you're wrong, Inquisitor. I don't need my father's love. I've never needed a father!"

Exedor's eyes seemed to glow red, although Valeyn wasn't sure if this was just a trick of the firelight. For a moment, she thought she could sense Bythe's presence.

"That's not true," he whispered. "No, that's not true at all. Elyn had a father – she had a loving father. He was taken from her by her mother, wasn't he?"

Valeyn paused. She'd forgotten about Leon. How long had it been since she'd thought of him, since she'd grieved for him?

"You side with your mother and yet...isn't she the one who took away the only loving parent Elyn had ever known?"

"Shut up!" Valeyn spat.

"I think," Exedor continued, "that you may call yourself Valeyn, but you seem to be more Vale than you are Elyn. It seems that what you once feared has finally happened – the weaker Elyn has been totally consumed by her stronger twin."

"Stop talking!" Valeyn ordered, but her voice sounded weak to her own ears.

"Where is Elyn? Have you forgotten her, Vale?"

Valeyn tried to squeeze his throat, but her hand wouldn't respond.

"*Stop speaking for me, Vale!*" It was Elyn's voice within her head. A voice she hadn't heard in years.

"*Elyn...where are you?*" Vale replied. Vale's voice, not Valeyn's.

"*Why are you pushing me out, Vale? You said it wouldn't be like this!*"

"*Elyn, please! Don't do this now!*"

"Oh dear," Exedor spoke calmly as he pried Valeyn's limp hand from his neck and rose to his feet, dusting the sand from his cloak. "It would seem the great and powerful Valeyn is not as stable as she thought she was."

Valeyn was still on the sand as her twin personalities broke free within her head. She tried to speak, but instead, two distinct voices were screaming in discord. He gestured and the Faedes returned to form their circle around her.

"I wish you'd seen reason, young lady. I would have much preferred to bring you back to your father as a willing guest, but then I suppose I'm always far too trusting in the good nature of people."

Vale tried to find a steady footing within her mind, but it felt as if she were on a boat pitching about in the sea. The confidence she had felt was gone, and in its place was the deepest pit of uncertainty.

Exedor looked down at her with pity, then made a motion to one of the Faede. Valeyn saw it disappear into the night before Exedor squatted before her, his calm yet forceful expression commanding her attention.

"Do you now understand, Valeyn? Everything here is relative." He laughed for a moment, as if amused by a private joke. "What am I saying? Everything in life is relative. One day you can feel like you're the master of the world, then something happens and you feel like a hapless child again. Everything and anything can change in a heartbeat. Why, look at your mother for instance. Once she was the most beautiful goddess this land had ever seen. Now she's a wretched vagabond."

"Please, make it stop." Elyn and Vale cried out with two voices.

Exedor sighed and regarded her like a wounded pet. "It's not too late, Valeyn. We can still fix this – for everyone."

He rose to his feet as the Faede returned into the firelight carrying a bundle covered in cloth. Exedor crossed the sand and pushed back the sheet to reveal Naya's terrified face. Valeyn staggered to one knee, causing the Faedes around her to take a menacing step forward.

"No! Leave her alone!" Elyn and Vale both shouted in unison.

Exedor looked faintly surprised and stroked Naya's hair like a father.

"It's alright," he said to Naya gently. "You're safe now. It's going to be alright."

Naya's eyes became confused and flicked from Exedor to Valeyn.

"Valeyn! Help me, please."

"Don't hurt her!" Vale and Elyn cried.

Exedor shook his head. "You are misinformed about so many things, young lady. I am not here to harm children." He turned his attention to Naya and again stroked a consoling hand across her cheek. "I'm so sorry for what has happened tonight. Please believe me, I did not intend any children to be harmed."

"Stop this!" the twins demanded.

"I will," Exedor said, returning his attention to Valeyn. "In fact, I can do even better than that, I can restore her. Would you like that, Valeyn? For me to make her whole again? We can erase this whole terrible incident, you and I together."

Naya looked at Valeyn with heartbreaking hope.

"All you need to do is come with me willingly. To hear out your father. That's all I ask. After that, you're free to do what you decide, and in return, I will order my associates to undo what they have done to this poor child."

Silence gripped the beach. Valeyn slumped back to the sand, bowing her head in defeat.

"Please, Valeyn, I only ask you to be reasonable," said Exedor.

Valeyn nodded in silence and as she did, both Elyn and Vale seemed to recede within her mind.

"Splendid." Exedor smiled but this time Valeyn could see it was an expression of pure arrogance. The satisfied expression of a man who had perfectly executed a plan to the letter. The understanding infuriated her, but she could see no possible escape.

How had he trapped her so completely? So simply?

"Oh, come now, don't punish yourself," he said as if reading her thoughts. "You're still very young with much to learn, but don't worry. Your father will be able to help you there."

He gestured again and two of the Faede stepped forward, each gripping her by her wrists. Their grasp was cold as if their gauntlets were woven from ice.

"Now," Exedor looked around into the night, "all we need to do is locate your mother and we can be on our way."

"What about Naya?" Valeyn asked.

He nodded absently, his eyes scanning the night. "In time, in time. First things first. Aha! Here they are."

Valeyn saw three figures emerging from the night – two of the Faede with the stooped form of Yvorre between them. Her head was bowed as she allowed the Faede to lead her into the firelight.

"Oh, my dear Mistress Yvorre. How I've waited for this moment, above all." Exedor's look had now turned smug. He walked over to stare down at her. She remained fixated on the sand, refusing to meet his gaze.

"Oh, please, Mistress," he continued with a tone of mock offense, "don't rob me of my opportunity to confront you after all this time. This wounds me."

Yvorre still did not reply. Instead she kept her head bowed and Valeyn could now see that her eyes were closed. Exedor sighed and opened his hands in a mock gesture of helplessness.

"You really do disappoint me. I seem to remember my old teacher possessing more steel than this. I expected some steadfast defiance from you, but then I suppose this must be a difficult moment. Brought to heel by your very own Faedes?"

"Yes," Yvorre's croak was barely audible. She opened her eyes and looked at her former student. "My own Faedes. You have turned them against me."

Exedor smiled again but this time there was a wry edge to it. "I know what you're thinking, Mistress, but fear not – you've taught me very well."

Yvorre nodded slowly. "Yes, I see my commands over them are gone. You've removed them all thoroughly. They are yours now. Well done."

"I've learned from the very best." He gave a small bow. "Your commands have been removed, replaced by those of my own creation. Your Faedes are mine, like everything else that was once yours."

Yvorre closed her eyes again and said nothing. Exedor beamed in triumph. "I'm sorry, that was insensitive of me." He turned from Yvorre and motioned to the Faedes surrounding them. "It's time to go, please be gentle with your former mistress on the journey north."

"My Faedes." Yvorre opened her eyes, grimacing as if caught in a memory. "I found them in Kardak. Did you know they were wandering in the Barrens after my sister Romona had left them? I found them there."

Exedor looked back at her over his shoulder. "No, Mistress, you never told me that story."

"Romona was quite a goddess, so much better than the rest of us in so many ways. Sadly, I was never able to understand a fraction of what she had learned during her time on Kovalith, but I did learn a little."

Exedor stopped and looked at her sharply, as if he suddenly suspected a trap. He motioned to his Faedes, but they did not move.

"I only learned how to command the Faedes by copying the very basic commands created by Romona. Her commands allowed the Faedes to function at a fundamental level, and I simply built upon them. Did you know that, Exedor?"

He gestured more forcefully, but still the Faedes stood like statues.

"I don't believe you did. Otherwise, you would have removed them, wouldn't you?"

For the first time, worry broke out on the smooth features of Exedor. He glanced around at the circle of unmoving crimson figures surrounding him. Then the Faedes began moving. Again, as if they shared one mind, they moved in unison toward Exedor.

"Stop! Stay back! Seize her!" he commanded them, but they didn't obey. Valeyn's wrists were released as her captors moved toward him instead. Even the Faede carrying Naya was closing in on him, Naya's sobs becoming more frantic with every step.

As soon as the Faede had released Valeyn, Yvorre was at her side and moving with energy. "Quickly." She gripped Valeyn's arm and dragged her to her feet. Valeyn swayed uneasily and found herself leaning on her mother for support. "Can you walk?" Yvorre hissed.

Valeyn nodded vaguely and looked back to where the group of Faedes were now enveloping Exedor. Somewhere within the cluster of red she could hear Naya screaming.

"Naya..." she began, but Yvorre cut her off.

"You cannot help her. We have to go now."

"No," Valeyn mumbled as if in a drunken haze and began moving toward her screams.

With unexpected strength, Yvorre pulled Valeyn around to face her. "Valeyn we have only minutes to run. Minutes. I can only make them block his way, nothing more. He will figure out how to regain control of them in moments and then I have no more tricks to play."

Valeyn looked from her mother to the Faedes. Yvorre pulled her back sharply. "If we risk this opportunity with heroics, then he will recapture us all! I cannot carry both of you."

Valeyn felt true agony. She knew Yvorre was right, that there was nothing she could do – yet she wanted nothing more than to throw herself into that nest of creatures and let herself be torn apart by them. But she also knew that such an act would be even more selfish. A quick release she didn't deserve.

She told herself this was necessary. She told herself she would come back. She told herself whatever she needed to justify what she was about to do.

Yvorre gripped her arm and pulled her away. Valeyn mumbled a protest but it was superficial. Weak even to her own ears. She relented all too quickly, allowing Yvorre to lead her toward safety, leaving Naya to whatever grim future awaited her.

CHAPTER 8

"They are strange, these people of the Forge. How fragile their lives can be. They come to me for help, but I have found that it takes very little for them to grow sick and pass away, then they are simply no more. It is as if they never existed. Can you understand this, sister? Can you comprehend such a thing? Do you suppose they also pass back to the Etherian? Will they follow us there when we all pass? It is something that I want to understand, something that I must understand. Perhaps there is another way to help them, a more compassionate way."

~Romona – Goddess of Death and Regeneration

Jason was riding hard when he emerged out of the impossibly tall trees and swept into view of Fairhaven. He had been very cautious with his horses over the past two weeks, taking care to ensure he never rode them to exhaustion - resisting the urge to ride them to exhaustion. He had been able to secure remounts along the way, which meant that his own stamina was the only constraint. Even with Veroulle's gift of vigor, Jason had been finding himself edging dangerously toward collapse as he passed through the mountains over the last few days.

Upon seeing the walls of his hometown, the fatigue slid aside as if Veroulle had restored him again. He nudged his tired horse into a gallop and raced over the fields toward the outer gate. Entering Fairhaven was far easier than entering Darcliff had been, given that Jason was a familiar face to the watch guard who barely stopped him before allowing him to pass through the gate and into Fairhaven's outer ring.

The morning air was brisk, and mist formed on his breath as he rode past the warehouses that lined the outer streets of the town. He'd never been away so long in his life, and the sensation of returning home was a strange one. Now that he'd experienced the cold life of Darcliff, he realized he'd never before understood how much Fairhaven had molded him, how much the town was a part of him. He thought on this and, for just a moment, allowed himself a smile. It was the first time he'd smiled in weeks. It was very good to be back.

He trotted his horse as quickly as he dared without threatening the early morning shopkeepers and herders milling about the street in their half-sleeping or half-hungover states. He had been dreading this moment for days – dreading the visit to the Council chambers. Not because he was afraid to face the Council and fulfil his mission, but because he knew he would have to make a deliberate choice to prioritize them over his wife.

For a second, Jason thought about making a stop by his home on his way to the chambers, and he realized he was probably not as strong willed as he thought – that it was actually very easy to make sacrifices when he didn't have an alternative – such as being stationed miles away from her. But now, all he needed to do was to gently guide his horse left toward home instead of right toward the Council, and the willpower needed to restrain such a small movement seemed almost beyond him.

He shook his head to clear it and kicked his horse forward. His grip on the reins as he guided his horse to the right-hand path was probably much firmer than it needed to be.

It wasn't long before he arrived at the large stone building that housed the Council. Handing his horse to a bleary-eyed attendant, he strode up the steps and opened the large doors that led into the red-carpeted foyer.

"Excuse me!" came an irritated and slightly pretentious voice. "The Council is not yet open. Please vacate. Vacate!"

A portly man was bustling over from one of the alcoves, swatting away at Jason as if he were a large fly nestling on his breakfast.

"Please, I'm here..." Jason began, but the enthusiastic concierge would have none of it.

"Vacate, I say!" he cried. "City guard or not, you're filthy and smell of horse. I'll not have any of the Council members see you in my foyer."

"This is not *your* foyer," Jason snarled through gritted teeth as he fought to keep his anger in check. After everything he had endured, after all the sacrifices he'd seen, he was in no mood to bow before the pomposity of a self-important man at this hour of the morning.

"Do not speak to me in such tones!" the fat man declared with indignation as he leaned into Jason's tired face. "You may carry a sword, but that does not give you the right to bully me! I am the head supervisor of the night staff, and I will have you know that, according to the house regulations, I am indeed responsible for this foyer and every other—"

Jason hadn't meant to push him – at least he hadn't meant to push him as hard as he did – but the fat concierge went sprawling onto the plush floor where he rolled twice before coming to a stop. He lay on the ground with cheeks flushing so intensely that they almost matched the color of the carpet. Jason stood as if transfixed. The outburst of anger had been spontaneous and certainly understandable, but it had surprised him nonetheless. He opened his mouth to say something, but a wail of pain cut him off.

"My back!" the concierge shrieked. "My back is on fire. What have you done to me?"

Jason moved forward to help the round figure, but the concierge raised a chubby hand as if to ward him off.

"Stay back! Don't come any closer! I'll see you in the stocks for what you've done to me. Medic! Guards! Help!" he shrieked in a shrill pitch.

"Oh, get up, Reynold," said a feminine voice that was soft and yet commanding.

Jason turned. He knew the voice of his wife. Nadine was walking through the doors wearing a white shirt and long skirt that was typical dress for most of Fairhaven's women, but what wasn't typical was the pendant she wore around her neck, the one that marked her as a Council member. Jason was so caught between the surprise of his wife's appearance and the surprise of the pendant she wore that he was completely unprepared for the passionate kiss she proceeded to give him.

"Welcome back, husband," she whispered once it was over. A playful smile danced on her face as it always did whenever she managed to put her husband off balance.

One of the many small blessings from the gods had been his love for Nadine over these past few years. Their shared love, which had grown from a secret juvenile infatuation to something far more meaningful. It had taken some time, of course. Jason recalled those awkward first months after Elyn – after Valeyn – had left them both. He'd thought there'd no longer be any pretense needed for them to see each other. After all, they'd both related to each other through Elyn, and after Elyn left, Jason had wondered if Nadine would retreat into her higher social class and leave him to his lower one. But that hadn't happened.

At first, they'd both been subjected to endless questions about Elyn – from both the Council and Captain Lewis. Eventually, they were allowed to return to their lives, having seemingly been exonerated from any conspiracy involving the rise of a new god. After that, no one seemed to pay much attention to what they did, and Jason – suddenly finding himself with a proud career – also discovered the advantages that came with it. He was surprised to learn from his own father that Nadine's parents had begun making enquiries about him, and before long, formal introductions had been made between the two families. Afterward, things seemed to move very quickly. Not that Jason complained of course. Quite the opposite was true. Once their respective families had given their unspoken approval of the match, opportunities unexpectedly presented themselves for the young lovers to be alone in each other's company. They had been married within the year.

"Councilor Nadine," Reynold's whining voice interrupted their intimacy and her smile faded. "This is most improper. Your...husband...has trespassed on Council property and attacked me without provocation. I insist that he immediately—"

"Lieutenant Jason of Fairhaven bears orders from Captain Lewis to be delivered to the Council without delay," she interrupted Reynold with a level but strong voice. "That is why you're here, isn't it, Lieutenant?" She turned to her husband with a prompting look.

It took Jason a moment to realize she was offering him a way out of the mess he'd put himself in. Fortunately, a lie wasn't necessary, as her instincts were completely correct – which was usually the case when it came to his wife.

"That's right...Councilor," he used the title awkwardly, and she smiled again. He presented Captain Lewis's ring on his own hand, and Nadine's playful manner quickly disappeared, an expression of concern settling onto her beautiful features. She looked at Jason questioningly for a moment before turning to Reynolds.

"He bears the signet of the Captain of Fairhaven and you thought to deny him entry?"

"I...I didn't see the ring. How was I to know?"

"Did you ask?" Nadine rounded on the underling and Jason was again reminded of the nobility of his wife's blood that seemingly conditioned her for these moments of authority.

"But Councilor..."

"Lieutenant," Nadine now addressed Jason, ignoring the bewildered concierge. "What's the nature of your message?"

"Urgent intelligence for the leadership of Fairhaven, Councilor. Dire intelligence," he added pointedly.

Nadine nodded then turned back to Reynold. "It seems the only person who has violated protocols is you. You've delayed a messenger travelling under the highest of orders."

Reynold started to go pale, all importance and bluster now a distant memory.

"However," Nadine continued in a softer tone, as if controlling her temper, "I will overlook this offense under the current circumstances. Go out and summon every member of the Council now, Reynold. Not another word from you."

Reynold bowed gratefully and all but ran out the door. Nadine watched him go then turned back to her husband and fell into his arms. Their embrace was tight, and all pretenses of rank and station were lost.

"I've missed you so much," Nadine murmured into his chest. Jason nodded and stroked her hair. Her playful manner had now dissolved under the weight of his impending news. They both stood in the embrace for a long time, both silently claiming their entitlement to one moment of uncomplicated intimacy before returning to the problems they had to face.

"How did you know I was here?" he asked.

She pulled herself away from him and looked into his face.

"Perks of being a Councilor. It turns out I can ask the city watch to let me know the moment any strong and handsome lieutenants come riding into town."

Jason smiled. "Impressive. And how long have I been married to a Councilor?"

She shrugged. "Four or five months – not long after you left. My father arranged it; I think he wanted to keep me busy so I wouldn't spend all my days worrying about my husband away at war. I'm technically just acting as a replacement in a vacant role – there have been quite a few of them recently – but I think they want me to stick around."

"Well, I'm not surprised," Jason replied, gently kissing her forehead. "How's my father?"

She chuckled as she nestled back into his embrace. "Unbearable, he still won't stop talking about you to every single customer who comes to his shop, and I don't think he cares whether or not they've heard the stories before. He seems to think they need reminding."

"Oh no," groaned Jason. "He's going to go broke and it'll be my fault."

"That's right," she softly chided. "Perhaps if you'd grown up to be more of a disappointment to him, he'd be a better salesman."

Jason laughed. "Then I'll try to do worse from now on."

She took a breath as if to steady herself then stepped back to look at him.

"I know Reynold can be frustrating, but even so, it's not like you to lose your temper like that. What's wrong? What's brought you back?"

Jason sighed. "I know and I'm sorry. It's just that I've been riding for weeks now and I'm exhausted...so much has happened..." He trailed off as he realized that, despite having weeks of solitude to plan his briefing to the Council, he had no idea where to begin.

"Jason." A distorted voice called his name, causing both of them to jump. A figure stood at the far end of the foyer, its billowing green robes in sharp contrast to the red carpets.

"My lord," Nadine said quickly, bowing her head at the Ageless.

Jason was not as quick to respond. He often forgot that Nadine hadn't known the Ageless the same way he had. He had been in their Sanctuary.

He had fought alongside them more than once. And he knew this one's name.

"Hello, Aleasea," Jason greeted her calmly. Nadine gave him an uncertain look, clearly wondering if it was wise to assume one was on a first-name basis with the Ageless.

The Ageless inclined its hood and replied with its cavernous and shrieking voice. "It is good to see you again, Jason."

"Please, allow me to introduce my wife Nadine" He paused. "You probably already know who she is, don't you?"

The form of Aleasea hesitated then a slender arm reached up to lower the green hood. Her face was radiant as she glided over the carpet to greet them both.

"Yes, I know Nadine. I have watched her for some time, and I have long awaited your return. It is good to see you now reunited at this moment. I congratulate you both," she said with a warm smile.

"Uh...thanks," said Jason, caught off guard by the affection.

Aleasea turned to Nadine. "I have long wished to speak with you but waited until your husband returned. I always take such joy in the coming of new life but usually can only watch from a distance. Please tell me, Nadine, would it be acceptable to you if I—"

Aleasea abruptly stopped at the look of alarm on Nadine's face. There was silence for a moment. "Forgive me," Aleasea stammered, her face growing an unusual shade of pink. "I assumed you had..."

"He only just arrived!" Nadine blurted.

It still took Jason another moment to comprehend the painfully obvious. "You're pregnant?" he asked. Nadine nodded enthusiastically and a broad smile lit her face. Jason could feel the same expression on his own face, and she all but leaped at him, giggling with joy. They embraced again, involuntary laughter from both of them bouncing off the walls of the lobby. They broke apart, and he placed his hand on her stomach, which he now saw was larger than it had been.

"When?" he asked.

"Not exactly sure, but probably in about three or four months."

"Oh, my gods," he said. "I can't believe this. This is amazing. A baby?"

"Yes," she said with tears welling in her eyes.

Jason stood up, brushing them away, then held her close again. "I love you so much, Nadine."

"Me too," she whispered.

"Forgive me," Aleasea broke in. "It was not my place to speak that way and I have..."

Jason looked over Nadine's head at Aleasea with a broad grin. "You know, for such wise defenders of the free people, you sure have dreadful social skills."

Aleasea smiled and inclined her head. "That is true."

After Jason and Nadine had exchanged more questions and answers, Aleasea gently cleared her throat.

"I apologize again; however, I must intrude on this moment. While I am overjoyed at your news, there is another reason I have come. Do you bring word from Veroulle?"

Jason stepped back from Nadine and his joy vanished. He remembered the reason he was there. He remembered Veroulle's dark prophecy. Fairhaven would burn. The home of his newborn child would burn.

He nodded grimly.

"Then we cannot wait for the rest of the Council to be summoned, you must brief us now. Follow me, both of you," Aleasea commanded then turned to glide into the Council Chambers on the far side of the foyer. Jason and Nadine shared a look but followed quickly.

Within moments, they moved into the chamber and Jason closed the doors behind him. Two other Ageless stood on the platform at the end of the room – one in green robes and the other in black. While Jason hadn't seen Ferehain's new robes before, he somehow knew who was concealed within the darkness of the hood. He walked onto the stage with Nadine and Aleasea.

"Report," came the single command from within Ferehain's hood.

Something in the command irritated Jason.

"With respect, my lords," he began, "I have suffered a lot over the past few weeks, and I'd appreciate it if you dropped these games. I've seen your faces before. Aren't we all friends here?"

Nadine gave a sharp intake of breath at his words and silence gripped the chamber. For a second, Jason wondered if he'd stepped too far and was about to apologize when E'mar replied, "You will mind your tone, Lieutenant."

Despite the rebuke, E'mar reached up and lowered his hood to reveal his porcelain features and fair hair. After a moment, Ferehain did the same – although they both regarded Jason with a less than friendly expression.

"Are you now put at ease, Jason?" Ferehain snapped.

"Thanks," Jason murmured, feeling less sure of himself.

"Now that you are comfortable, perhaps you can deliver the report Captain Lewis entrusted you with?" E'mar asked in a voice laced with sarcasm.

Jason nodded and launched into an account of all that had happened over the previous weeks, but before he could even finish his telling of the Helmsguard messengers at Fyrn, he found himself fighting back anger at the memories. He paused as the rising emotion confused his report, rubbing a hand over his eyes as he sought to concentrate.

"Perhaps I may be able to help you, Jason," Aleasea said, stepping forward and placing her soft palm on his forehead.

He didn't pull away. A warm glow spread throughout his mind and the confusion washed away.

"Continue, Jason. Speak freely and from the heart. We will see through your mind if you allow us to."

He nodded and continued his story. As he did, the three Ageless stood as if they were statues, silently listening to his memories through Aleasea. He didn't mind. He knew it would save him from hundreds of questions later. Once it was over, the chamber again fell into silence as everyone retreated into their own thoughts.

"Do you know if Darcliff held?" asked Nadine eventually.

Jason shook his head. "They were still resisting when I passed into the mountains but...those war engines..." his voice trailed off.

"Show me the dispatch, Jason," Ferehain ordered, and Jason handed him the paper.

"Does Veroulle believe Fairhaven is going to burn?" Nadine spoke again, almost timidly this time.

"He has had a strong vision," Aleasea replied. "Strong enough that he has sent your husband back to us as a warning. Yes, Veroulle believes Fairhaven is in great peril."

Nadine put a hand to her belly and turned away quietly.

"We must discuss this with the Council and determine our next actions," said E'mar.

"There is no time for more talk," replied Ferehain as he quickly read the dispatch, clearly fluent in the lettering of the Ironhelm. "Jason's translation was largely accurate; they were certainly reaching out to another army in the east."

"Ferehain, his story cannot be completely factual," answered E'mar. "The lieutenant is exhausted, and we clearly sense his memories may be distorted by the emotion he feels."

"You think I'm making this up?" said Jason as he felt his heart start to race with anger.

"I do not doubt your sincerity, Lieutenant, merely your objectivity given what you have endured."

"You didn't see the engines, E'mar!" Jason shouted. Nadine placed a hand on his shoulder and said something to soothe him. Jason realized the angrier he became, the less rational he appeared. With a great effort he took a long breath to silence himself.

"Lieutenant," E'mar said.

The use of Jason's lower ranking title irritated him, but he forced himself to remain silent as E'mar continued.

"I can see through your mind that Veroulle was indeed concerned, but what you must understand is that concern is not fear, nor is it alarm. You are but a man with limited knowledge in the crafts of gods. What is terrifying to you is not as frightful to the Ageless, much like a child is afraid of the night – the parent does not fear, as he has knowledge of what truly lies within the shadows."

"E'mar," Jason forced his voice to remain level. "These engines razed the countryside, they levelled Fyrn, and they probably did the same to Stonekeep."

E'mar sighed with impatience. "It is simply not possible for Bythe to have amassed such strength. The gods are not all-powerful within Kovalith. They cannot conjure devastation at will. If they could, then this war would have ended generations ago."

"Yet there are...possibilities," said Ferehain.

Aleasea looked at him.

"What do you mean, Ferehain? How could Bythe have grown so powerful?" E'mar asked but Ferehain remained silent, seemingly lost in thought.

The silence was broken by Jason's low voice. "You may know Veroulle better than me, and you may know more about the gods than me, but I know my Captain – and Lewis knew he was about to die."

"I agree with Jason," Aleasea added. "While I cannot answer your question E'mar – I do not understand how Bythe has crafted this threat – the threat itself is very real. I now understand that I have been sensing this danger growing in the south for some time. This is what I have been trying to warn you about."

E'mar gaped at her. "Aleasea, please do not try and use this moment to win an argument for pride's sake."

"She is right," Ferehain's voice cut through the room, silencing everyone. "Aleasea may be frustratingly idealistic, but she is no fool. We have been the fools, E'mar. She has sensed this threat for weeks, and we have not listened to her."

Ferehain turned from where he stood at the end of the stage and strode toward the group with a sense of authority. His dark eyes swept over everybody as he spoke. "This explains the silence from the fortresses, and why it was then necessary for Veroulle to travel to Darcliff personally. It explains Aleasea's ongoing misgivings to which we gave no credence. Only a threat as grave as the one Jason has shown us could cause all this. Aleasea, you have my apologies." Aleasea nodded in acknowledgment.

"And why would the Iron Union do this, Ferehain? Why create such a force and risk it on Fairhaven?" E'mar persisted.

Ferehain looked at Jason and saw the recognition in his eyes. "Do you not see it, E'mar?" growled Ferehain. "The child soldier here understands what you do not. Aleasea, tell me, do you now truly understand what you have sensed?"

"It is Baron Ethan returning to Fairhaven," she said quietly.

"And why would Baron Ethan of the Iron Union bring war engines to Fairhaven?" asked Ferehain almost rhetorically, like a teacher driving home a lesson.

"He is coming for Valeyn," she answered.

Ferehain crossed to where she stood and leaned over, so his face was next to hers. "And tell me, Aleasea...where is she?"

"I... I don't know."

"Do not lie to me!" Ferehain roared with such unexpected fury that fear swept the room. Even Aleasea took an involuntary step backward.

"I know you, Aleasea. I know you far better than others do." Aleasea looked away, suddenly conflicted. "I do not understand your gifts completely," Ferehain continued "but I have watched you use them over centuries. You have even used them on me. I know they leave a lingering presence in your mind. You touched the minds of both Elyn and Vale when they were here. You gave them your strength, and you read them in return."

Aleasea gave him a defiant stare. "We are not compelled to disclose every mystery of our gifts with one another if we do not wish to. Maelene blessed many of us with unique crafts. Do I question the comings and goings of your dark mind?"

Ferehain smiled as if her defiance had won his argument. "My *dark mind* does not hold the key to a secret that could save this city from destruction. If it did, then I would gladly share it. Tell us the truth, Aleasea – now that you know the might of Bythe is coming to destroy us – tell me the truth at last."

"I had to respect her wishes, Ferehain," she said quietly. "I have no right to watch her like property."

"Aleasea," said Jason. "Do you know where Valeyn is?"

Aleasea looked at them each in turn, taking in all of their faces. Finally, she drew in a breath and seemed to come to a decision. "Yes," she said without hint of regret. "Yes, I have always known."

BOOK 2
REUNIFICATION

CHAPTER 1

"Like so many of the gods, we have no knowledge of the fate that ultimately befell Basalt the Crafter. Viner – an Ageless scholar long past – believed the gods had taken form in the stars above Kovalith, and that they were watching us. He believed they were judging our actions in preparation for the Etherian.

Of course, such a view was widely dismissed by the Ageless. However, I confess that I occasionally find myself glancing up at the night sky, and on those nights, I wonder if our creators are forming their immortal judgments."

~Aleasea of the Ageless

Valeyn stumbled over the loose rocks in her path. The mountain pass was starting to slope downward, but this really wasn't making the journey easier. Now a careless step could cause her to lose her footing and send her tumbling down the rough pathway – a feat she had managed to accomplish several times already.

She tried to count the number of days that had passed since leaving Tiet, but she wasn't able to. It had been several days at least, probably weeks. The pale pink dress she had been wearing that night was now so ripped and soiled from travelling that its color was little more than a distant memory. She had intentionally torn it to allow free movement of her legs, which might have reduced her modesty, but rewarded her mobility in kind.

Yvorre glanced back at her as the small trickle of rocks loosed by Valeyn's misstep clattered past her.

"Mind yourself, we are almost there. Keep down," she called back.

Valeyn didn't reply. She merely focused on the path in front of her while trying to stay as low as possible. The mountains around them were high, but unlike the familiar peaks of Fairhaven, these mountains lacked any natural magnificence. These mountains were rough stone, jutting abruptly out of the land with sheets of vertical grey cliffs. They were angular and cold, as if daring any trespasser to defy their will by trying to climb their walls. When Valeyn had first seen them, she'd thought they were completely impassable, but Yvorre had led them relentlessly toward the grey walls. Driving them day after day, as she had since they'd fled Tiet. Somehow Yvorre had known there was a single pass within the wall – a sliver of a crack within the face of the mountains.

They were now deep within the Fareaches. Valeyn guessed they had now travelled far to the south in their attempt to evade the Faede. She knew the Fareaches were largely uncharted and she knew they were said to be strange. As she glanced at the sheer walls of the cliffs lining the mountain pass, she realized the stories might have more truth than she credited them for.

A distant cry made her pause. She stopped and shrank to her haunches, wrapping her arms around her knees like a child.

"Yvorre," she called out. The old woman stopped and turned back to her daughter. "Stay there," was all she said as she began making her way back up the path as quickly as she could.

The cry slowly became louder and with it, came a sharp pain in her head. The cry was in her mind, she knew that, but it didn't make what was about to happen any less frightening.

Her vision started to dim, and the wailing rose in pitch. It was the same chilling cry of the Faede. A terrified child screaming for its life – screaming for her. Sweat broke out on her brow and her entire body began to seize up. She hated this. She hated the sheer horror of losing control of her body, but most of all, she hated the terror she couldn't escape.

Her body started to shake as the Faede's scream became louder. She felt herself start to slide down the pathway as her feet refused to respond. Then her world went black as the cry reached a climax. She could feel herself screaming even though she couldn't hear it. She lost all sense of direction as a spike of pain split her skull – then it was gone.

Valeyn opened her eyes and saw she had started to slide down the path but had come to an abrupt stop. Yvorre was holding her firmly, her long arms circling Valeyn as the trembling and spasms began to cease. She regained control of herself and gently pushed Yvorre's arms away from her.

"Is it over?" Yvorre asked. Valeyn nodded in reply.

Yvorre cast a concerned look back up the slope as if expecting something there, after a moment she returned her attention to Valeyn.

"They are getting closer. We do not have much time. Can you stand?"

Valeyn took in a deep breath and forced herself to her feet, swaying a little but otherwise remaining upright.

"Anchorwatch is near. Come, Valeyn, please. We must hurry," Yvorre said and then resumed her journey down the path.

It had been like that ever since leaving Tiet. They had barely been travelling for a day when Valeyn had first felt the spike of the Faede's cry in her mind. It hadn't been this bad at first, just a sharp pain and a distant scream. It had been so insignificant that Valeyn hadn't even mentioned it to Yvorre as they travelled along the road south east from Tiet. But then the cries became more frequent and more debilitating, and within two days she could no longer hide it. Yvorre had been angry at Valeyn when she found out – angry at her for keeping it secret – but Valeyn also sensed Yvorre had been angry with herself for not anticipating what this meant.

The Faede were now tracking her.

Those Faedes that had reached into Valeyn's being had taken something from her, and they were now using that like a lodestone to metal. Their reach had been infrequent and imprecise, but with every passing day, both qualities had slowly strengthened. During their first week of flight, Valeyn was certain the Faede only knew they had been moving south, but within days she could sense they were slowly learning her location with greater precision. And the more precise they were, the more terrifying her seizures had become.

Now she knew they were very close, possibly near the mountain pass already, and within hours they would be able to pinpoint exactly where she was. She chose not to think about what would happen if they found her.

Focus on the task at hand.

She wasn't sure whose thought that was, which memory the advice had come from. She could still feel Vale and Elyn floating in her head, but the voices were diminished now, as if the rift between her twin selves were slowly healing.

Valeyn straightened herself and took a tentative step down the path. Satisfied that she wouldn't fall straight onto her face, she felt confident taking another and continued the journey. "How much farther?" Valeyn asked.

Yvorre paused and waited for her daughter to catch up to her before answering. "It is difficult to say," Yvorre replied and then turned to resume her descent. "I have never actually been to Anchorwatch, and Kovalith becomes stranger the closer we travel to the Render, but I know we are very close."

"So how do you know we'll be safe there?"

Yvorre glanced at her in faint surprise. "You cannot sense it?"

"No," Valeyn admitted. "I haven't been able to sense much of anything since Tiet."

Yvorre nodded. "Do not worry, you will heal, and your senses will return.

"I...used to be able to feel the Constructs. I could feel The Tower deep within the Render."

Yvorre grunted a laugh. "Every god within Kovalith could sense that thing. I was surprised at Nishindra when he built it – it was an uncharacteristically boastful creation. He never courted attention in such a brazen manner."

"I was going to go there once, back when I first left Fairhaven. Why can we all feel it?" Valeyn asked.

Yvorre shrugged. "It calls all of us. Only Nishindra knows why he did this, and sadly, he has been gone for a very long time. However, I do have my suspicions."

Valeyn sighed impatiently. "I'm not going to play games with you, Mother. Either tell me or don't."

Yvorre stumbled slightly as they both stepped down a small ledge that marked the floor of the pass. The cliffs loomed on either side of them, guiding a tight winding path ahead.

"Anchorwatch is a Construct, just like The Tower," Yvorre said, apparently changing the subject as she continued to lead the way.

"Did Nishindra build it too?" Valeyn asked.

"No. Anchorwatch was built by Basalt the Wanderer. I know I taught you about him."

Valeyn smiled faintly as she recalled Vale's memories.

"Yes, haughty, arrogant, and incredibly vain?"

"Gods, yes," Yvorre shook her withered head as she walked. "You could not keep that one quiet for more than a minute. The only thing he loved more than himself was telling you about his latest magnificent adventure – which of course was just another way of telling you about himself." She smiled thinly. "Still, I admit I miss even him these days."

"What happened to him?"

Yvorre gave a shrug. "I never really found out, but he's gone...like the others. What does it matter now?"

There was silence for a moment as Yvorre withdrew into herself. Valeyn could sense a faint sadness emanating from her. Suddenly – as if realizing she had been caught in a moment of weakness – Yvorre quickened her pace and looked ahead.

"Anchorwatch served as the closest thing he had to a home when he was not wandering the land. It can protect us."

"How?"

"The Binding," Yvorre said. "Each of the gods was blessed with the gift of establishing a place of protection for ourselves. No god's power can harm another from outside a Binding."

"And Anchorwatch is a Binding?"

"It was Basalt's, yes."

Valeyn thought for a moment. "But you said he was gone. How do you know if his Binding is still working?"

"I do not," Yvorre admitted matter-of-factly. "And since you bring it up, you are right. There is every chance we will arrive at Anchorwatch and find ourselves unprotected. I simply did not wish to worry you as I have no other contingency to protect us from the Faede if this fails."

They were quiet again for a time while Valeyn pondered the implications. The path wound to the left flanked by the ever-present sheer cliff walls. Valeyn glanced up to see the thin sliver of blue sky mirroring the trail. The sun could not pierce the deep ravine and Valeyn was suddenly aware of the absence of any warmth in the valley. She thought of the Faede travelling close behind her and repressed a shiver she knew had little to do with the temperature.

"You said that a god was safe from another god within a Binding?" Valeyn asked.

"Yes."

Valeyn paused as if unsure how to broach a delicate subject. "When you held me...Elyn and Vale...captive in Sanctuary, how was Bythe able to threaten you?"

Yvorre stopped and glared at her. "You wish to mock my failures, daughter?"

Valeyn stopped also. "No, but I want to understand." She swallowed but forced herself to meet her mother's stern gaze.

After a moment Yvorre dropped her eyes and sighed. "My pride is irrelevant. You have the right to ask, and I must respect that. The truth is, while a god is protected from without, they are still vulnerable from within – if one is foolish enough to invite an enemy into a Binding. Sadly, I realized too late I had done exactly that in my haste to claim you."

Valeyn recalled the memory of Bythe's demonic form coalescing within the Arcadia and felt cold again.

"Although it brought about my ruin," Yvorre said with a distant smile, "I must concede that calling forth your father was a masterstroke, child. I did not even consider the possibility. No, despite all that happened, I cannot help but be proud of what you did. It seems on some level you are very much your mother's daughter."

Valeyn opened her mouth to argue but something unintelligible came out. She shivered again but now she was certain the cold had nothing to do with it. Shaking, she dropped to one knee as the shrieking pitched deep into her mind once again. Yvorre was immediately at her side, gripping her by the shoulders with long fingers. "Valeyn? Can you hear me?"

She tried to answer, but the pain was unlike anything she had experienced before. A deep spike of ice seemed to be driving itself straight into her mind and she gasped for breath. "They've found me," was all she could say as she began to shake violently.

Yvorre seemed to grow in height as she stepped in front of Valeyn and scanned the path behind them. Her sunken eyes shed their fatigue and blazed with the piercing energy Vale remembered from childhood. She searched the mountain pass for a moment then swung her gaze in the opposite direction and studied the path ahead. A minute passed as Yvorre stood alternating her attention in both directions as if listening for something. All was quiet but for Valeyn's muffled grunts of pain.

"I do not see anything," she said, glancing down at Valeyn. "Are you sure they are close?"

"Gods, yes!" Valeyn hissed, her eyes squeezed shut in pain. "It feels like they're right on top of us!"

Yvorre's gaze shot upward and met a bright red figure no more than a few feet from her. The Faede had been silently crawling down the sheer cliff wall like a spider – it's scarlet faceplate was now little more than an arm's reach from her own face.

Yvorre cursed in a language Valeyn didn't understand and flung her palm out to the descending creature. There was a flash of fire, and the grilled mask of the creature was instantly covered in flame. It shrieked horribly and tried to scuttle back up the cliff, only to lose its footing in its panic. It briefly scrambled for a renewed grip before tumbling down the cliff face toward them. Yvorre moved with speed and pulled Valeyn aside as the Faede landed on its back, thrashing and hissing in all directions.

For a moment, the pain subsided and Valeyn realized that Yvorre had pulled her to her feet.

"Move!" Yvorre screamed and began to pull her up the path. Valeyn shook her head clear and glanced back to see the Faede slowly rising to its feet, its crimson helm now scored black from the flames, but otherwise it seemed unharmed. Valeyn silently cursed herself for leaving her sword on the beach – as she had done every day since leaving Tiet.

She turned to Yvorre and picked her up. Carrying her mother like a child, she started to run toward the bend in the path ahead. A flash of red in the corner of her eye caught her attention and she glanced up to see another Faede crawling down the wall ahead of her. She increased her speed and began to sprint with all the unnatural energy her abilities could give her. While it still wasn't half of what she was normally capable of, it was enough to sprint past the descending creature before it could cut off their escape.

Once they cleared the bend in the narrow pass, the cliffs gave way to a broad circular valley that stretched wide before them. The sheer walls of the cliff maintained their protection in a wide circle, and it seemed the mountains existed to hide this secret from the rest of the world. A fast-running stream cut across the path ahead. Beyond this, and at the center of the valley, stood a structure that could only be Anchorwatch.

It was a tall, thin spire that stretched skyward in a beautiful display of craftsmanship. Rock and wood seemed to be melded together seamlessly in ascending spirals that curled upward before flattening into a circular plateau at the summit. There, wooden arches formed an intricate dome which gave the structure the look of an elaborate observatory. It was a scene of complete and unexpected beauty – unfortunately Valeyn had absolutely no time to appreciate it. She risked a glance back to see the second Faede was walking up the path behind them, it's lurching gate eerily determined. Valeyn hoisted Yvorre and ran into the open valley, pausing only when reaching the edge of the stream, which she guessed to be the border of Anchorwatch. While the stream was rapid, it looked no more than several feet deep.

"What are you waiting for?" Yvorre hissed.

Valeyn hesitated. "Can we enter?"

"Yes! We bear no malice. Go!" she ordered.

Holding her mother as high as her weakened arms would allow, Valeyn waded into the cold waters, which reached her chest at the lowest point before receding as she reached the safety of the other side. Once she cleared the water, Valeyn looked up at Anchorwatch to find a way in, but pain split her head again and she collapsed helplessly.

Yvorre extracted herself from Valeyn's arms and got to her feet. The Faede had now reached the other side of the stream and was standing on the bank, casting its head up and down the river as if considering something.

"I command thee to tread no further," Yvorre shouted over the water. "Thou mayest not enter under a Binding if thou intendest harm to those within."

The Faede stopped turning its head and seemed to fix its attention on Yvorre.

"Return to your new master, unclean demons!" Yvorre roared with defiance.

The Faede took a step back at her anger and seemed almost to cower, but Valeyn's hopes faltered when she saw it wasn't recoiling. It sprang forth and threw itself toward the water. As it reached the edge of the river, it launched itself high into the air and landed on the gravelly bank on the other side.

"Back!" Yvorre screamed, but the Faede didn't seem to care. It shuffled forward, completely unhindered.

"The Binding?" Valeyn asked.

Yvorre shook her head. "It is gone. I am sorry, child."

The Faede slowly walked toward them. Valeyn tried to get to her feet but the pain in her head made it impossible. This Faede had stolen something from her in Tiet, and it was now using that to cripple her. It paused before her and reached up to unlock its faceplate. Valeyn closed her eyes and tensed as she steeled herself for the onslaught that would come.

There was a shrieking cry – but it was not from the Faede.

Valeyn opened her eyes to see Yvorre now standing before her, directly in the path of the Faede's gaze. She was crying out in fear and pain, a sound Valeyn had never heard before.

Yvorre crashed to her side on the gravel as the Faede drained something from her. It curled out– oily and black – and swept into the crimson mask of the creature.

At that moment, the Faede stiffened and halted. Its labored breathing became frantic as it took an uncertain step back, looking down at its hands and body. Something black and corrosive was starting to drip out of its helmet onto the gravel. The rasping sound of its breathing became more desperate, and Valeyn thought she could almost hear it trying to speak.

Then she realized the pain in her mind had stopped with the Faede's distress. She slowly got up and staggered over to where her mother lay on the stones. The Faede was tearing at its helmet as if trying to remove it, but she didn't know how long this would last. She had no idea what was happening.

She pulled Yvorre up to a sitting position. Her ancient eyes flickered open, dull and distant.

"The water..." Yvorre croaked.

Valeyn stared at her mother in confusion.

"Use the river, Valeyn!"

Valeyn looked up at the Faede that was now half covered with a putrid black corrosion. Then she remembered how the Faede had watched the ocean at Tiet almost nervously, how this Faede had chosen to leap over the water. It hadn't gone through the water.

It couldn't go through the water?

Rallying whatever strength she had left, Valeyn shot herself forward and slammed into the creature like she was an arrow loosed from a bowstring. They both crashed onto the gravel and tumbled down the riverbank together. They rolled into the shallows of the flowing stream, and the shock of the cold water swept through her, washing away any lingering pain clouding her mind. The Faede shrieked and immediately began thrashing violently. It swung a backhanded fist to her temple, causing her to loosen her grip for a moment as her head snapped back in pain. The creature pushed itself free of Valeyn and started to scramble back up toward the shore leaving a long red trail in the water behind it. Valeyn half stumbled to a crouch then leaped at the retreating figure. Her actions were those of desperation. There was neither finesse nor skill in her movements as she crashed into the back of the Faede and sent them both into the water again.

This time, she had landed on top of the creature and summoned all her will and strength to keep it pinned to the bottom of the riverbed. The Faede writhed as if it had gone mad. It threw back its helmet, and Valeyn barely moved her own head in time to avoid the sharp metal colliding with her face. Gripping the creature by both wrists, she pressed down with all her weight and forced them both under the surface.

In the freezing chill of the water she could hear the Faede crying out, not in the childlike tone she had heard before, but in a cry of rage and fear. It struggled with her but Valeyn held her breath and her resolve. After a moment, she felt the arm of the creature snap at the shoulder and she almost lost her balance as the limb started to melt like sand in the current. She could feel chunks of the Faede starting to wash out from underneath her as if its very existence was starting to be swept away, piece by piece. The water was filling with a sickly red cloud, and she couldn't resist the urge to recoil. Breaking the surface with a mighty breath, she quickly scrambled up the bank as the Faede's corpse began to melt in a poisonous mass of dark-red fluid. It bled through the pure blue waters like a stain, and Valeyn could only watch in horror as its vaguely human form became an unrecognizable lump of twisted flesh and bone, before that, too, was slowly washed downstream.

She wanted to vomit but she could barely breathe. She turned from the river and slowly dragged herself back up the bank toward the prone form of Yvorre. She felt dizzy with nausea and exhaustion, but she forced herself to stay conscious. She staggered over to Yvorre and sank to the ground beside her. Yvorre lay still, but her eyes were open.

"Well done," was all she said.

"Are you alright? Did it hurt you?"

Before she could answer Valeyn heard something heavy hitting the dirt. She turned and immediately felt a stab of dread.

The first Faede with the scorched helm was now slowly rising to its feet from where it had landed on their side of the river.

"No..." Valeyn murmured through numb lips. She tried to rise but knew it was pointless. Before she could even lift her body, the Faede had reached into her mind with its piercing cry, sending her falling onto her back in agony.

Yvorre lay next to her, equally helpless as the figure in red slowly and deliberately walked to stand over them both. It reached up to unlatch its faceplate but stopped, raising its helm as if looking at something behind Valeyn.

A flash of black swept over Valeyn's eyes, and she heard the Faede shriek. For a moment she thought she had passed out, but the black was replaced by green. A familiar green. The green of Ageless robes.

It took her a moment to recognize Aleasea beneath the veiled green cloak, but the familiar way the Ageless wielded the kajik staves affirmed her identity.

Likewise, Valeyn knew there could be only one Ageless beneath the black cloak fighting alongside Aleasea. Only one Ageless dared wield the metal of his enemy with such cold and efficient hostility.

Valeyn watched as the green and black cloaks cut down the figure in red before it had a chance to react. Aleasea attacked with a flurry of strikes to the creature while Ferehain moved like liquid to position himself behind the Faede. Within seconds, the crimson helm was severed by Ferehain's blades, and the figure folded inward as it sank to the ground.

Valeyn wanted to say something. She wanted to voice her relief, her gratitude, her simple happiness at seeing Aleasea again. But all she could do was stare at the two figures before her as she let a swell of darkness pull her into exhaustion's embrace.

CHAPTER 2

"At first, all of the Ageless wore the green robes of the Entarion. We were united with a common focus and common methods. However, as centuries passed and the Ageless grew, Maelene decided that a more militant class of Ageless was needed, and the Violari were born. Her reasons for this decision have always remained unclear to me, but I suspect she intended to give purpose to those among us who needed it the most. My dear friend, Ferehain, was chosen as one of the founding members of the Violari after he had suffered great personal loss. I am forced to wonder what would have become of him had he not been granted an enemy to hate so completely."

~Aleasea of the Ageless

Jason entered his office, but he still wasn't comfortable doing it. He closed the heavy door behind him and looked at the large oak desk with trepidation. He'd long ago settled into a morning ritual – a coping mechanism for this awkwardness – and this morning he knew that he was going to need it. Avoiding the desk, he walked over to the one small window and looked out over Fairhaven. The sun was rising, but the morning was a bitterly cold one, so a blanket of fine mist and smoke lingered over the buildings, giving the scene a slightly magical touch. He smiled as he spent a few moments doing nothing more than appreciating the beauty of his hometown, trying to flush the problems out of his mind for just a few moments. It usually helped, but today it didn't. Today, the mere act of admiring the city only served to remind him that it was up to him to protect it – that if he was weak, this beautiful vista could be gone forever, burned to nothing. He shook his head and reminded himself that he was not about to let it happen.

Turning away from the view, he walked back to his desk. In his mind it was still the desk of Captain Lewis, but in the mind of most others, it was his: Captain Jason of Fairhaven. Nobody had challenged the appointment. Jason was held in high esteem after his assignment to Darcliff, and even the older lieutenants now obeyed him without question. Technically, he was acting-captain, but his men didn't seem to notice the slight distinction, even if the Council chose to.

The Council. They were certainly going to be his challenge today. Although none of them questioned the authenticity of his orders – certainly with his possession of the captain's ring – he knew they didn't treat him with the same deference they had granted to Captain Lewis. While they had accepted his warnings at face value, he could tell they still didn't entirely trust his objectivity. Ferehain and Aleasea had publicly recognized Jason's new authority before the Council, and leadership of the army had been transferred from a somewhat relieved Acting-Captain Khyran to Acting-Captain Jason. Once Ferehain and Aleasea had departed, however, leadership of the Ageless had fallen to E'mar, and he was not as respectful. As soon as Jason had taken his new position, he found E'mar had already begun to make decisions that should have been his. Resources and supplies of essential items were routed away from military control and placed under the authority of the Council. In recent days, E'mar had gone so far as to issue direct orders to Fairhaven troops, allocating them to civic patrols and other duties without so much as informing Jason. Yesterday, Jason finally decided this had gone far enough, and he intended to address it at the morning's Council meeting.

He looked over his desk at the piles of paperwork he had been given by the Council to review and approve. What made his job even worse was the fact that the resources to support Fairhaven's defenses were even further depleted than he'd realized. Although Lewis had controlled one of the largest bases in the Outland Alliance, most of the men and equipment had been sent to support the front lines of the conflict in the west. He now had fewer than one thousand soldiers, and almost half of them were conscripts. He scanned the reports on food supply levels and approvals of requisitions for additional bedding in the new women's barracks. He felt like an administrator instead of a Captain, and he was certain that was the Council's intent.

He pushed the bureaucratic refuse to one side and cleared a view of the city map beneath it. It now lay on his desk permanently, and it seemed like he spent every spare moment staring at it, hoping he could discover the secret that would protect Fairhaven from impending devastation. He looked over the two concentric circular walls of the city – marking the old and new settlements – and the fields beyond the city that led into the mountains to the north and the forests to the south east, but again he could see no way of using the natural surrounds against the war engines. Indeed, if the engines were capable of navigating the forests to the south, the relatively flat lands surrounding Fairhaven wouldn't pose much of a problem.

His view was interrupted by a streak of silver fur as a sleek cat leaped onto the desk and proceeded to walk across the town, eventually settling onto a position slightly to the east of the river and directly in front of Jason's view. Jason sighed and met the cat's enquiring green eyes.

"You're not helping, you know?"

The cat – clearly assuming her request for food had been understood – started to purr loudly in an effort to reward his attention.

Jason shook his head but gently collected the cat in his arms and walked to the door, quietly relishing the distraction. It seemed he had inherited Lewis's pet along with his other responsibilities. Jason would never have suspected that Captain Lewis – of all people – was a cat-person, but then he was finding he was starting to understand Lewis a lot better in so many ways. He opened the door and walked down the long hall, looking for a member of the serving staff to relieve him of at least one of his duties this morning. He had found a young boy and was calling to him, when a shout from the courtyard seized his attention. Jason distractedly handed the cat to the boy with vague instructions to feed her before hurrying down the staircase and onto the parade ground.

Three soldiers wearing the bright blue uniforms of Fairhaven were helping a grey-clad soldier down from his horse. The grey uniform was smeared with blood and dirt, and the man collapsed into the arms of one of the soldiers as soon as his feet touched the ground. Jason hurried over to them as they struggled to support the injured man.

"Another from Darcliff?" Jason asked.

"Yes, sir," a corporal replied. "Came in just on sunrise. By the look of him, he's lucky he made it."

Jason nodded. "Get him to the infirmary, Corporal. Wake the physician if he's not already up, and tell him I want a report on this man's condition on my desk within the hour."

The corporal saluted and the three of them bundled the injured man to the large medical house on the far side of the grounds. Jason watched them retreat through the early morning mist, reflecting on one important lesson he had learned from Captain Lewis: you needed to truly care for the people under your command. If you did that, they might truly follow you.

Jason heard footsteps behind him but suspected who it was. He turned to see the purple robed figure approaching him through the early morning mist. It made this Ageless look all the more mystical, even though his face was plainly visible within his hood. As Jason watched the figure approach, he remembered a time when he had once risked death to look inside the hood of one of the Ageless. It was not long ago that such an act was an unforgivable transgression. Now it seemed that all the rules were subjective. Without Maelene – or even the untarnished memory of her – to guide them, the people of Fairhaven were starting to question everything. Old rules and customs that had stood for centuries were now no longer tolerated. The Ageless themselves had fallen greatly in the esteem of the people, and they were more often than not forced to lower their hoods in public – the demand being an open act of defiance from the people they had once dominated so completely.

"Good morning, Kaler. Do you actually sleep?" Jason asked the Ageless as he approached.

The Ageless inclined his head in polite greeting. "Yes, Captain, I do sleep, but only when it is necessary." He looked at the four men now vanishing into the infirmary. "Is he another refugee from Darcliff?"

"He's the third this week. I'll get him patched up and debriefed, but I don't think he'll tell us anything the others haven't."

Survivors from Darcliff had started arriving over the past few weeks, but there were tragically few of them. The survivors had been able to confirm Jason's fears – Darcliff had fallen decisively and quickly. The defeat was so total that none of the soldiers were given clear orders on their retreat. Those who had made it to Fairhaven seemed to do so out of luck more than purpose. It was frustrating that none of them had been able to tell Jason what had happened to the command group. Jason knew the fallback position had been along the river Claiream within Marfort, but that was before they knew of the war engines. Now, only the gods knew where they had fled.

"Do you still believe the army that destroyed Darcliff will not also come for us?" Kaler asked.

Jason shrugged. "Why would they? If they smashed Darcliff as easily as we're told, they don't need to waste another army to take Fairhaven. No, I'm sure Baron Ethan has us covered all by himself."

"In that case, we need to ensure the southern defenses are better prepared," said Kaler.

"I couldn't agree more, my only problem is I need the soldiers and the resources to do it. It seems that E'mar and the Council have other priorities."

Kaler straightened within his purple robe as they both started walking back to the command building. "E'mar has always been a member of the Entarion. He does not truly understand war."

Jason glanced at the man beside him. Kaler looked young, but Jason knew he was likely to be centuries old. His skin was dark brown, and his eyes always seemed to blaze with intense concentration. Jason now recognized this look – along with the purple robes – as a hallmark of the Violari, the militant faction within the Ageless. He had been assigned to Jason as his liaison and advisor shortly after his promotion. Though Jason had recognized his name and remembered Kaler's mistreatment of Elyn three years ago, he needed to push that aside. He could not afford to hold childhood grudges, as much as he might enjoy some petty act of revenge. In addition to this, Kaler and the Violari had proven themselves to be surprisingly sympathetic allies against the dithering of the Council, and it seemed to Jason that he needed all the allies he could find.

"Well, I'm going to explain it to them this morning," Jason answered. "We need to start fortifying the fields if we're going to have any chance of stopping those engines, and I'm going to need more support from the Ageless to do it."

Kaler looked uncomfortable. "I am not certain you will receive that support."

Jason stopped walking and turned to face him.

"What are you talking about?"

"I have just come from the Temple, and E'mar has ordered more of my brethren into Marfort to aid in the fight against Bythe."

Jason felt red-hot anger rising in his chest. "What the hell is he doing? We need every weapon we can get to defend the people here!"

"He does not seem to agree with your assessment of the threats we face. I believe he feels he is better positioned to judge the situation."

"And what do you believe, Kaler?" Jason asked, barely able to keep his anger in check.

"I believe he is a fool," Kaler spoke with the blunt sincerity Jason had come to expect from him. "The Violari were created out of the necessity to fight. The Entarion will never understand this. I believe that, while you may lack experience, you understand combat far better than he does."

Jason paused and considered his options. When he spoke, he chose his words very carefully. "What if I invited you to join me at the Council today? You could act in your role as advisor and voice your own opinion?"

Kaler met his eyes and an understanding passed between them before the Ageless shook his head.

"I am sorry, Captain, but that would not be...appropriate. E'mar may be a fool, but I must respect his position as the leader of the Ageless, even if it is temporary. A schism between the Entarion and the Violari is something that my order has always been careful to avoid. Such an act on my part could spark such a divide."

Jason sighed, but he understood the dilemma Kaler faced. For a soldier, the discipline of the command structure could never be questioned. He also knew on a more practical level that he could hardly sow insurrection within the Ageless without undermining the discipline within his own army, so he let the question drop.

"For whatever it is worth," Kaler continued, almost apologetically, "I have spoken out against this decision in the Temple and used my position as leader of the Violari to keep as many in reserve here as I can. E'mar is unhappy with this, but he also must respect my position."

"Thanks, Kaler. I think I really need all the friends I can find right now," Jason replied with a smile.

Kaler nodded. "Regretfully, I believe you may be correct."

· · ·

Jason walked into the foyer of the Council Chambers and glanced around a little nervously, but the portly concierge, Reynold, was nowhere to be seen. At least that was one antagonist he didn't have to worry about this morning. Jason drew himself up to his full height and gave his uniform a quick adjustment before marching into the Chamber as confidently as he could. He hated these meetings – absolutely hated them. He'd always grown up around soldiers and active young men who understood the camaraderie and respect of the team structure. A team would have an alpha – usually the most capable of the men – and that alpha would have earned the admiration and respect of the others. The best man called the shots until he stepped down or until it was proven a better man should take over. The rest of the team would always follow his lead without question until he proved himself to be unfit. It was a simple code and it worked.

But this world was different altogether. He walked into the stuffy room and fought down the compulsion to immediately leave. The Council members all milled about the space, speaking conspiratorially in hushed tones. Here, there was no alpha. Sure, there were ranks and titles and official positions – but what did it actually mean? Who had the real authority? It seemed these discussions were more about word games and one-upmanship than they were about getting anything done. And nobody in the Council ever stepped down or declared themselves unfit. Quite the opposite. They would usually spend an incredible amount of energy proving they weren't responsible for a mistake, even if it was clear they were. He simply did not understand this world and loathed every second he was forced to enter it.

"Jason," Nadine quietly called to him, and he crossed the hall to join his now noticeably pregnant wife. She was dressed in a burgundy gown that complimented her condition very tastefully. He bent to kiss her cheek, conscious that it was probably inappropriate, given their stations – but quietly enjoying any disapproval it might stir.

"You left before I woke?" she asked him in a slightly accusing tone.

"I'm sorry," he answered. "There's just so much to do, and I wanted to go over my plans for the meeting."

Jason always prepared for these discussions meticulously. He knew he was far from the smartest person in the room, and he suspected everyone else knew it too. As a result, they seemed to enjoy critiquing his reports and exposing any error or contradiction – no matter how small. It seemed to be what they were best at.

"What did you come up with?" she asked.

"Nothing," he admitted. "They've kept me so busy with urgent requests and approvals that I just haven't had the time to focus on the strategy."

"Jason," she looked at him firmly. "That's your job now. You need to delegate these tasks to others and focus on the important issues. You're a leader."

"I know that!" he hissed back at her, but he knew she was right. He wasn't acting like a leader. The truth was he didn't know how, and he had a nagging suspicion it showed.

Nadine sighed and softened her tone. "My love, I'm trying to help you. I know you're under pressure. That's the point. They're trying to burden you with distractions so you can't focus on your job. Don't let them."

Jason smiled. "You make it sound so easy."

She returned the smile. "I didn't say it was. I can't imagine the problems you have to deal with every day, but I've come to know politics, and I can see what they're doing to you. I don't want you to play into their hands."

The sound of a wooden staff striking the table rang out across the chamber, marking the commencement of the meeting. All the members broke off from the secretive conversations and climbed the steps to the raised dais. E'mar was present in his green robes with his hood pulled back. He mounted the stage with Morag and sat alongside her, their heads bowed together in quiet conversation. Nadine's father, Paeter, took his position as the Chairman of the session – a role that was rotated among all members. Jason sat next to Nadine in one of the high-backed chairs on the stage as the members were called to order.

Paeter commenced the proceedings and called the roll. Jason immediately felt his mind start to wander. He knew he needed to pay attention, so he picked up the agenda in front of him, furrowing his brow in an effort to develop an interest in the treasury report – but it was pointless. Within seconds, his mind had drifted back to the defense of the city and the very real problems lingering outside this room.

Jason had learned that self-important people seemed to be able to make time linger interminably when given the right stage, and this stage was full of them. He sat patiently as Councilor Winton read out the inventory supplies, followed by Councilors Deana and Holmn disputing the most recent audit of the treasury report. The meeting was supposed to run for one hour, but it had already dragged on for ninety minutes, and nobody seemed interested in pointing this out. Indeed, Jason was slowly learning that, for the people around the table, this meeting was their only true place of influence – that earning recognition and validation within these walls was far more important than anything outside them. He felt a surge of revulsion and unconsciously glanced at the door.

After what seemed like hours, the Council inched their way down the agenda until they arrived at the Military Report. Jason noted its position toward the end of the agenda and wondered why it wouldn't be the top priority in a time of war. Even this seemed to be a subtle way of minimizing his role, as if he were only a functionary and the real decisions had already been made.

Paeter indicated that Jason now held the floor. Jason arranged the papers before him, cleared his throat and began reporting on the readiness of Fairhaven's defenses. He started with the latest intelligence of the enemy movements. While visual confirmation was still difficult, early reports indicated a force of roughly five hundred soldiers was moving toward Fairhaven through the forests to the southeast.

"Has there been confirmation of your war engines, Lieutenant?"

Jason noted Morag's condescension when referring to *his* war engines. They still believed he was exaggerating.

"No confirmed sightings yet, Councilor, but I believe it to be a matter of time," he replied, then added, "and my title is Captain."

She smiled thinly. "Your title is *Acting* Captain, and if you do not perform a better job, I expect that title to be very temporary."

Jason opened his mouth, but Nadine spoke first. "If it may please the Councilor, could you elaborate on the areas that could be improved?"

Morag glanced at Nadine and seemed about to say something before arresting herself. "I believe we will come to that shortly. Please continue, *Captain.*"

Jason ignored the sarcasm and tried to continue with his report, but his confidence faltered. He could sense a growing ambivalence within his audience. They all seemed preoccupied with other things while he spoke. E'mar and Morag were both reading papers spread out before them. Denethin was brazenly staring at the roof as if Jason were not even speaking. Even Paeter was glancing distractedly about the chamber. He decided to get to the point. He put down his papers and raised his voice to command what little attention he could.

"Councilors, I think the Iron Union are no more than two weeks from our gates. With this in mind, I intend to start drafting up plans to deploy soldiers into the southern fields so we can serve as a barrier against the war engines when they arrive. I intend to take direct command of all deployments, including those recently reassigned to civic duties. Do any of the Councilors have any questions or concerns about this?"

There was silence in the chamber. Jason paused, uncertain if anyone intended to speak. When the silence continued, he felt a pressing need to fill it. "So, in that case, I'll draft up the dispositions, and...present them to the Council at the next meeting," he finished uncertainly.

"At the next meeting?" E'mar now spoke. "Captain, I would have thought you would already have a detailed plan to defend this city. Are you telling us that you do not?"

Jason met his eyes for a moment. "No, I'm not saying that, I'm saying..." Jason paused for a moment to try and form his argument, but E'mar exploited his inexperience.

"I have ordered some of my Ageless to conduct their own investigations and assessment of our capabilities. They believe we are in a far worse position to defend ourselves than you are telling us, Captain," said E'mar.

"You've conducted your own assessment behind my back?" Jason was livid but forced himself to remain calm. "I've never heard of this happening before. Who authorized it?"

"Councilors Morag and Denethin made the request last week," Paeter answered, looking a little uncomfortable. "The Council has the discretion to authorize such a review, Captain. It is a standard process. Don't think of it in any other light."

"I was not aware of this, Chairman," Nadine said. The tone to her father was formal and cold.

"This was proposed to the Chairman out of sessions and is being tabled to the Council now. There is nothing inappropriate here, Councilor Nadine," Paeter countered, although to Jason's ears, he spoke with an air of shame.

Jason was confused. Morag was accusing him of exaggerating the threat, and now E'mar was accusing him of under-preparedness. In the long hours after this meeting, he would replay this moment in his mind and appreciate the deceptive manner of their maneuvering, but for now his mind was racing to keep up with the twisting conversation, and he was far from calm.

"What are you talking about, E'mar? What have I done wrong?"

Under the table, Nadine placed a hand on his arm. Nobody had accused him of doing anything wrong – except now, he had just accused himself.

"Well, now that the Captain raises the question," said Denethin, the short, balding Councilor. "There's the matter of the supply requisitions that've gone unapproved for days now. I've got traders with cartloads of grain that don't know where they're supposed to be sending them, 'cause the paperwork's held up on your desk."

Jason was dumbfounded. "You're concerned about the grain, Councilor?"

It was a genuine question, but Morag seized upon it.

"Do not be trite with us, Captain. This is not about grain; this is about governance. How can you manage the defense of this city when you cannot manage the fundamental processes of your army? You may think these processes are trivial distractions, but they are the foundations of order and stability for this city. If our supply chains fall part, then everything falls apart. How can we have faith in a man who cannot organize himself?"

"Exactly," Denethin offered his completely redundant rejoinder. "The soldiers can't fight if they can't eat."

Jason looked around the table and saw silent accusations in the faces around him. Without knowing how, he had suddenly become the cause of their problems. It was a simple trap and he'd stumbled straight into it.

"Councilors," he took a breath and then continued. "I respect the need for tactical logistics and I apologize for my administrative...oversights. I promise you I'll address them. But the biggest problem we face right now is the army that is two weeks away. I need to deal with them as the priority."

"Yes, and you intend to do this by positioning our men away from civic duties and into the fields?" E'mar asked.

"That's right. We can't afford to let the engines get within range of the city."

"Oh, please, Jason" Morag interrupted. "I think we've heard enough stories about these *engines*. We need a more rational view here."

Jason felt Nadine's grip tighten on his arm as he fought down the rage. He wondered how Captain Lewis was able to handle these closeted bureaucrats without threatening them with a military coup on a daily basis. "Councilor, I can understand that you may not trust my level of experience, but you trusted the experience of Captain Lewis, didn't you?"

She raised an eyebrow. "Indeed, I did, and I miss his rational mind greatly at this hour."

"Then I ask that you trust my honor. My captain gave me his ring and commanded me to return here with it to protect our home. That is how much he feared and respected the war engines. Master Veroulle would be standing before you now, but he chose to stay behind because of these engines. That's how much he respected them. The handful of refugees who have come back to us from Darcliff have also confirmed just how powerful these engines are. Please, Councilors, I know my story sounds fantastic – I wouldn't have believed it myself if I hadn't seen them with my own eyes – but I urge you not to underestimate this threat."

"Hmph…traumatized soldiers are hardly reliable sources of intelligence," Morag muttered, but the retort was half-hearted. Jason had scored a solid hit by referring to the credibility of Captain Lewis and Veroulle, and by referencing the trust they had placed in Jason. Attacking Jason's experience was one thing. Accusing him of lying – and therefore of treason – was quite another. Even Morag wouldn't dare go that far.

"You raise a valid point, Captain," Paeter said, seemingly eager to make amends to his son-in-law. "None of us should make judgments on something we haven't witnessed ourselves. We should trust our experiences. While I haven't seen the war engines, I was at Outpost and I can vouch for how quickly the Helmsguard can overrun a town caught unprepared."

"And you were also here at Fairhaven, when we repelled the Northmen, were you not?" E'mar asked Paeter.

"Yes, you know I was," answered Paeter, a little uncertainly.

"Then you know how effective we can be when forced to defend this city," E'mar continued. "This is not a ramshackle town. The Ageless have guarded this place for centuries, and we know how to defend it."

Jason threw Nadine a questioning look, but she only returned it. Neither of them was sure what E'mar was getting at.

"E'mar," Jason said, "Fairhaven almost fell three years ago. In fact, it was only because of the Helmsguard that we were able to defeat the Northmen."

A fire seemed to burn in E'mar's eyes at this suggestion.

"The Ageless have defended Fairhaven for centuries, Captain! Where was the Iron Union during the Northmen Raids ten years ago? Where was the Iron Union when the Paephu clan attacked us two hundred years ago? Where was the Iron Union when Dazh hammered at our gates five hundred years ago? Where were you?"

E'mar's tone had become increasingly heated as his speech mounted. It was never comforting to see an Ageless lose his temper.

"E'mar," Nadine interjected, "we all recognize the protection the Ageless have given us. I don't think the Captain meant to imply—"

"Do not leap to the defense of your husband, Councilor, I am addressing him," E'mar growled. Nadine was momentarily stunned at the rebuke, and before she could reply, E'mar resumed his attack. "Where were you during the Siege of Fairhaven three years ago, Captain? Were you at your post?"

"I was facing Imbatal!" Jason raised his own voice in reply.

"Exactly!" E'mar answered, seemingly ready for the answer. "While Captain Lewis commanded his troops responsibly, you ran off to play the hero alongside the traitorous daughter of Bythe."

Jason couldn't believe what he was hearing. "Traitorous? Elyn saved Fairhaven, if it hadn't been for her, Imbatal would've destroyed us."

"Do not be naïve! Valeyn saved no one but herself. Imbatal came for her and her alone. He was not interested in razing Fairhaven to the ground. That is an emotional exaggeration – much like your war engines. Fairhaven was not saved by Valeyn's actions. Our home was defended by the loyal and dependable work of Captain Lewis and the Ageless, both following the plans that had been in place for centuries."

Jason was speechless. How could they twist history this way?

"Fairhaven needs a captain who can defend her people selflessly," said Morag, "not someone who rushes off to chase glory with improvised plans and heroics. While your little skirmish with Yvorre's demon may have won you the adulation of your peers, it did not impress us anywhere near as much. Quite the opposite, it proved to us that you are reckless and inexperienced. You do not follow any strategy or process."

"Fights are not won by *process*, Morag." Jason's patience was almost exhausted.

"Order!" Paeter admonished Jason's breach in protocol by using Morag's name, but Morag ignored it.

"*Fights* may not be won by process. Fights can be won by ego or by sheer dumb luck. But this is a war, not some tavern brawl. You simply have not shown us that you have the mature mind required for this job."

"We cannot endorse your plan to disperse men into the fields," E'mar added.

"Endorse?" Jason questioned through gritted teeth. "With all due respect, Councilors, I was under the impression that I was informing you all of my decisions, not seeking permission for them."

"Under normal circumstances, that would be true," Morag answered. "But these are not normal times. While I respect the decision of Captain

Lewis to place you in charge of our army, I do not agree with it, and there are provisions within our bylaws to deal with such a situation."

"And what are these provisions?" asked Nadine.

"The Council may invoke emergency powers in a time of crisis. This requires a majority vote by those present," said Paeter.

"You're going to try and remove Captain Jason from command of his own men?" The unspoken warning in Nadine's voice was clear.

"Not remove him," said Denethin, "just provide an additional level of oversight to support him. After all, we just want the best outcome here. This isn't about individuals, is it?"

"And who is going to provide that oversight?" Jason asked, already knowing the answer.

Morag gestured to E'mar. "The Ageless have defended this city for generations. I, for one, would sleep much sounder knowing that the defense of my home was supervised by a man who had done this countless times before."

"E'mar is not one of the Violari," Jason shot back. "Even Ferehain supported my appointment."

"Do not presume to understand the Ageless, Jason, nor to speak on our behalf. I am the leader of the Ageless, and I concur with Councilor Morag on this point."

It was a brilliant move. By deferring to the opaque history of the Ageless, E'mar could tacitly claim credit for any number of achievements that were not his own. Jason understood his current line of attack would get him nowhere.

"And why do you question my use of soldiers on the plain?" Jason asked.

"Because it is a reckless and untested strategy. The Ageless designed Fairhaven with many protections, all based around the principle of defending the city from within. If you place soldiers in the open, we will lose this advantage."

"If we sit and wait within these walls, we'll lose everything!" Jason felt his temper start to fray, and he pulled his arm away from Nadine's grip as he rose to his feet. "Bythe knows what our advantage is, and he's overcome it. Can't you see that? For the gods' sakes, he just wiped Darcliff off the map! Do you think our walls are stronger than theirs?"

Expressions of pride and anger competed on E'mar's face. "And I do not believe Bythe has amassed the power you seek to terrify us with. I think Fairhaven will need more than your conjecture if we are going to see our way through this."

"What about the Ageless?" Jason was shouting now. "Where the hell are they? You've sent them everywhere but here, where we need them! Veroulle would never do this!"

"The Ageless aren't your concern, Captain." Morag's cold voice seemed rational by comparison. "But the fact that you seem to need their support only adds to our argument."

"That's not what I meant!" Jason yelled back but it was too late, already several heads around the table were nodding in quiet affirmation of her words. Sensing that she had managed to swing the mood of the room to her favor, she leaned forward and clasped her hands together, assuming the appearance of a reasonable arbiter.

"We're only asking for supervision, Jason. We're not removing you from your position. Please understand that we're trying to help."

Jason raged inwardly. *Supervision?* It was a humiliating undermining of his authority. He knew it would be only a matter of time before decisions were made around him, separating him from his soldiers, then he would be quietly removed from any meaningful part of command.

Paeter cleared his throat. "Councilors, we should bring this to a vote. Councilor Morag, do you propose the Ageless assume oversight of Fairhaven's defenses?"

"I do," Morag replied.

"Does anyone second the proposition?"

Denethin raised his hand with a self-important smile.

Jason had finally taken enough. He wheeled about, throwing his chair aside with a crash, and stormed off the stage toward the exit.

"This is a joke," he roared. "Cast your damned votes. I don't have to stand here while you do it!"

The image of a burning Fairhaven was vivid in his mind as he slammed the double doors behind him.

CHAPTER 3

"The work I do with Nishindra is truly wonderful, sister, and I thank you deeply for your encouragement in these difficult times. I implore you to come to Kardak and see it for yourself. I believe we have surpassed even your achievements with your Ageless. Nishindra has crafted wonders that seem to defy the limitations of the Forge. I believe he will be remembered as the greatest of us all. It is what he desires above all else. We have found a way to help these people at last. I truly believe this. They do not seem to understand, but I can comprehend things they cannot. I believe they will come to thank us in time."

~Romona – Goddess of Death and Regeneration

Valeyn opened her eyes and had no idea where she was.

The bed she lay in was unlike any bed she'd ever seen. It was intricately carved from oak and spread wide enough to sleep at least three people – maybe more. She rested atop a soft mattress that felt like it was curving around every inch of her body like a cloud of mist. She stared vapidly at the timber ceiling above her and noticed that light was streaming in from a window to her left and splashing golden hues onto the wood. Vaguely she realized it was morning light. She had been sleeping for some time.

She sat up gingerly but, to her surprise, found that – beyond a little stiffness – her body felt more or less normal. The pains that had been splitting through her head over the past few days were no longer there. In fact, her head felt good – well rested.

She looked down at herself. Her soiled pink dress was gone and had been replaced by clean practical clothes. Dark pants and a sturdy white shirt that looked more suited to a man but appeared to fit her quite well.

Slowly, she swung her legs off the bed and walked over to the window. Beyond dirty and weathered glass lay a vast panorama of magnificent grey mountains cast into gold by the light of the rising sun behind them. Looking down, Valeyn could see a river winding along the valley floor before it vanished a few miles distant.

She was in Anchorwatch, atop Anchorwatch.

The door opened behind Valeyn, and she turned quickly to face the intruder, relaxing when she was greeted by Aleasea's warm smile. She was dressed in her green robe and carried a steaming bowl in her one good hand.

"Good morning, I could sense you stirring. How do you feel?"

"Fine," Valeyn replied. "In fact, I feel better than fine – I feel good. I think that I have you to thank for that."

Aleasea merely shrugged in a noncommittal way as she placed the bowl on a table next to the bed. "I aid where my skills allow me. You are a very strong person, Valeyn."

As she did this, Valeyn noticed a chair that had been pulled out from the table so it was facing the bed. Valeyn had the feeling it had been well used recently.

"How long have you been here with me?" she asked.

"It was not wise to leave you alone. I was unsure how badly the Faede had hurt you, so I have remained here these past three days and nights."

"Three!"

"A mere three days of convalesce is extraordinary after what you have endured. You are lucky to have survived at all, Valeyn, let alone to be standing before me with only three days of rest."

"But it wasn't just my doing was it? You sat next to me for three days. You worked your magic on me the whole time. You healed me."

Aleasea smiled again in her slightly self-conscious way. "Well...I apologize for leaving you. I did not mean for you to wake alone. I wanted

139

to prepare something for you to eat when you woke. I thought I had more than enough time, but it seems my old student continues to surprise me."

Valeyn stepped over to her old mentor and embraced her for the first time. "Oh, I've missed you, Aleasea. Thank you."

Aleasea returned the embrace, and a smile lit her face. "Do not thank me alone, Valeyn. Ferehain aided you as much as I did."

Valeyn pulled back suddenly.

"Ferehain?"

Aleasea nodded. "Yes, your injuries ran deep. The Faede are twisted demons and their power is great. I fear I lacked the strength to bring you back to us alone. Fortunately, Ferehain was able to lend his strength to the task, and together, we were able to undo much of the damage the Faede had wrought."

Valeyn was quiet for a moment. The thought of Ferehain sitting by her bedside helping her to heal seemed impossible. It even felt a little grotesque. Yet Aleasea would not lie to her, and the realization was a humbling one.

"Please, you have not eaten in days," Aleasea gestured to the hot bowl of soup on the table.

Valeyn sank into the chair and started to ladle the warm liquid into her mouth. As soon as she began to eat, she appreciated how hungry her body had become – it was strange that she hadn't noticed it before – but as the meal washed into her stomach, she found herself eating with greed.

"We're in Anchorwatch?" Valeyn asked between mouthfuls.

"Yes, we were able to use our crafts to gain admittance. It took some effort, but the task was not beyond us." Aleasea looked around the room. "It would seem that no one has walked these halls for some time. Fortunately Basalt was a keen acquirer of material things, and we have been able to make use of that." She gestured to the clothes Valeyn now wore.

"Thanks. It's not really the look I'd go for, but it's probably more practical than a party dress," Valeyn said with a smile between mouthfuls.

"Indeed." Aleasea smiled in return.

When she'd finished eating, Valeyn pushed back the bowl and looked squarely at her former teacher. The Ageless merely returned the stare patiently, as if waiting for the question they both knew she would ask.

"Aleasea…" she said haltingly. "Don't take this the wrong way, I'm grateful that you saved me, but I have to ask, why are you here?"

Over the next several minutes Aleasea told Valeyn all that had happened in Fairhaven. She told Valeyn about the war engines and the attack on Darcliff. She told her of Jason's return and of Veroulle's warning. Finally, she told Valeyn how she had found her.

At this last news Valeyn sat back in her chair and stared out the window thoughtfully. She was quiet for a long time before speaking.

"So, you've known where I was this whole time?" Valeyn asked.

"I did not know your exact location. I was unable to scry you from afar and know your every move, but yes, I knew enough to have long suspected where you had gone. Once I was closer to you, I was able to sense you better – when I put my mind to it."

Valeyn laughed bitterly. "So even when I think I've broken away from you, it's still always been on your terms?"

"No, Valeyn. I always respected your wishes."

"But you knew I was never far out of reach." She looked down at the empty bowl, staring at the remains of her meal as if it had revealed something to her. "And I thought I was finally in charge of my own life. I thought I was out here making my own decisions, but I was really just on a temporary reprieve until you needed me."

Aleasea sighed. "Valeyn, listen to me. I didn't plan this. I didn't know I'd be able to sense you. I'd never used my gifts on a god before, and I was surprised at the strength of our bond after you left. I wasn't trying to trick you when I let you go. Please believe that."

In all the time that Elyn had known Aleasea, she had never before heard her teacher drop the formal speech patterns of the Ageless until now. It was now a very strange thing to hear. Valeyn realized she didn't like it. Some part of her wanted to go on thinking of Aleasea as her superior, not as an equal. It was somehow unsettling to accept that her teacher knew as much and as little about the world as she did.

"You *let* me go?" Valeyn repeated the words with spite, like a petulant child refusing to let go of an argument.

"You know what I mean to say, Valeyn." Aleasea's tone became firmer. "I didn't try to stop you from leaving Fairhaven. I didn't even report your departure to my peers until it was too late – and believe me, Valeyn, I have paid much for that betrayal."

Valeyn felt a pang of guilt and fell silent again. She hadn't ever considered what her decision to leave might have cost Aleasea. Yes, it had been Valeyn's decision to make for herself, but Aleasea had made one too. Valeyn now understood that Aleasea's failure to act was also a decision – and it had been a very costly one.

"So now you want me to go back?" Valeyn asked at length.

"I wouldn't ask this of you if the need weren't so great," Aleasea again answered using informal speech.

"What do you expect me to do? Defeat my father's army single-handed? Overcome these war engines with my godly might?" Valeyn laughed to herself. "I'm strong Aleasea but I'm not *that* strong."

"Baron Ethan is leading the army and we believe he does this for personal reasons. I believe he's come back for you."

Ethan. Vale's memories of him were strong. Her second-in-command had always been a loyal man. He'd even followed her into treason against the Union without question. Valeyn had known he'd fallen in love with her a long time ago, just as she also understood that somewhere in her heart Vale had probably loved him as well. Or at least she'd tried to. That's why Valeyn's decision to stay in Fairhaven had come as such a blow to him. It had been a double betrayal and Valeyn had no idea what that would do to a man like Ethan.

"We didn't exactly part on the best of terms. I'm not sure he's come back to catch up on old times."

"No, but you know him better than anyone. If there's anyone who can help negotiate with him, it's you."

Valeyn looked at the beautifully ancient woman. "You know it's not a negotiation that he wants. He wants to take me back to the Ironhelm."

"We would not let that happen, Valeyn."

Valeyn stood up and pushed the chair back. "No, I'm sorry but I won't do this. It took a lot for me to break away from you all, and even if I wasn't as successful as I thought, I'm still not going to put myself back into the middle of that stupid war between Bythe and..." She trailed off for a moment, suddenly remembering. "Where's Yvorre? Is she alright?"

Aleasea also rose to her feet and moved toward the door. "Yvorre also recovers, although her journey has been very...different from yours."

Valeyn gave her a questioning look, but Aleasea simply opened the door for her in reply. After a moment, Valeyn crossed the room and walked through the open door into a long, wood-paneled hallway. She waited for Aleasea to lead her down the passageway, glancing into other rooms similarly decorated to the one she had occupied. The ceiling vaulted high above them, and Valeyn noticed birds that were resting on the timber beams. She wondered absently at how they got into Anchorwatch. Had Basalt deliberately allowed wildlife safe haven in his refuge, or had they found a way to defy the will of the gods?

They emerged into a large curved space. Windows to a spectacular view of mountains spread across both sides of the room and on the opposite wall another passageway continued off somewhere into the depths of Anchorwatch. The room was clearly designed as living space with a large rectangular table in the center and several sky-blue couches and armchairs scattered throughout.

Next to one of these couches stood the erect form of Ferehain. His black cloak hung loose around his thin frame and his hood was lowered, revealing his hard, angular features, which were fixed in silent concentration on a figure on the couch before him. He did not so much as glance at Valeyn when she entered, although there was no question he knew she was there. He seemed completely captivated by the person before him.

Valeyn would not have immediately recognized the figure as Yvorre had it not been for the faded grey traveling cloak she had come to know so well over the past few weeks. The form lying on the couch was not the wretched old woman Valeyn knew. She was younger – certainly not a young woman by any stretch of generosity – but her grey hair now shimmered with a slight hint of gold, and where it had hung from her head, limp and formless, it now seemed to flow with a sense of life.

Valeyn walked over to where she lay and looked upon her in confusion.

"What have you done to her?" she asked Ferehain.

"If you are referring to her appearance, Elyn, then I have done nothing. There is some other force at work here," he answered without taking his eyes from the figure on the couch.

"That's not my name anymore," Valeyn retorted, but as soon as the words left her mouth, she knew they sounded meek.

He's no longer my teacher.

"We've helped to heal her, just as we did for you," said Aleasea. "But this change in her is not our doing."

Valeyn looked at Yvorre in fascination. Her eyes were no longer sunken into her face, and her withered and pallid skin now had a glow of health. It seemed to her that Yvorre was beginning to resemble the woman she had seen in the Arcadia. She could now discern hints of Maelene within the wreckage of Yvorre.

"Do not be fooled." Ferehain's voice cut through her thoughts as though he could hear them. "Whatever Yvorre is doing, she is doing it with evil in her heart. Stay on your guard, Elyn. She is not your mother."

The words stung unexpectedly. He had crushed a hope she hadn't even known she nurtured. She turned to look at him without knowing how to reply.

"I told you, my name is Valeyn." It was all she could say in response. Again, it sounded like a concession, and she felt anger at her impotence in front of this man.

For the first time in years, Ferehain locked his dark eyes onto her, and she felt as if he was peering into her very being – like he had when they first met.

"Changing your name does not change who you are, Elyn, not to me. Life is long and has many challenges, you do not overcome them by simply giving yourself a new name and assuming you have now changed."

"And I suppose you change who you are by buying new clothes?" Valeyn gestured to Ferehain's cloak. "It's nice, by the way. Black is definitely your color."

For an instant Valeyn thought she saw a glimmer of respect – perhaps even amusement – in his eyes, but it was quickly shielded.

"This change has been thrust upon me. I did not choose it willingly. It is a mark of what Kovalith has become, what Yvorre has done to us. I no longer consider myself to be a member of the Violari, and out of respect to them, I will not wear their robes."

"Then consider my new name to be my new robes, Ferehain. I didn't ask for this either."

He looked at her for a moment but said nothing more on the subject. Instead, he looked past her toward Aleasea.

"I sense Yvorre's imminent recovery. She will awaken soon."

Aleasea nodded. "Then we must make preparations to return. Time is running short."

"What's going to happen to her?" asked Valeyn.

"She will be judged," Ferehain answered with a sense of finality that was undeniable.

"You mean she'll be executed," replied Valeyn.

Ferehain looked down at Yvorre. His face was hard with condemnation and when he spoke, it was a pronouncement. "Yvorre destroyed our Temple. She crippled the Ageless so we could no longer defend ourselves against the tyranny of Bythe. But worse than this, Yvorre betrayed her own people. She betrayed those who loved her the most, those who would willingly lay down their lives for her had she merely suggested it. She became so obsessed with her own grief and self-pity that she allowed herself to become twisted into the very thing she despised."

"She was imprisoned by Bythe." Valeyn wasn't sure why she felt the need to defend her mother.

Ferehain gave her a look that asked the same question. "Do you forget that she wanted nothing more than to capture you? To control you and use you as a weapon?"

"You all wanted the same..." Valeyn mumbled and turned away, suddenly unsure of what she was trying to accomplish.

"No," answered Ferehain, "I had no desire to use you in any way. I simply wanted you gone."

His words were hard, but they were also truthful. Valeyn found a measure of respect in that. "Fine, whatever. Just take her and go."

"Valeyn..." Aleasea spoke, but Valeyn knew what she was about to say.

"You heard me, Aleasea. Take her and go, but I'm not coming with you." She walked to the far side of the room and looked out the window, setting all of them firmly behind her. There was silence for a moment, and in that space, she quietly hoped they would leave without another word and all her choices would be lifted from her.

"We need you, Valeyn," said Aleasea.

"No, you want something from me," she shot back. "Ever since I left Fairhaven that's all I've ever found. Everybody wants something from me."

Aleasea walked over to stand next to her by the window. Together they stood in silence watching the pink glow of the sun rising over the distant mountain peaks. It reminded Valeyn of the day she left Fairhaven.

"What happened after you left?" Aleasea asked.

Valeyn laughed, but it held no humor. She gestured to the vista before them. "I wanted to see all of this, I wanted to see the world, I wanted to go the edges of it, I wanted to see The Tower, I wanted to experience it all. I wanted to dance, drink, and make love without a care."

"And didn't you do all this?"

Valeyn shrugged. "Yes...I don't know. I don't think I really knew what I wanted to do."

"What did you do?"

"I travelled. I met people. As soon as I was clear of the Violari, that is." Valeyn smiled and nodded back toward Ferehain. "I journeyed to Qharg and stayed there for weeks. I think that was the first time I ever really started to enjoy myself. I made friends and we drank every night for a week. I was introduced to William, a gorgeous man from...well, from somewhere. He was handsome and funny, and everyone listened to him when he spoke, but he'd look at me as if I was the most important person in the room. I think everyone accepted me because of him. I had his blessing. Did you know he was the first man I ever made love to?"

"And what happened to William?"

Valeyn shrugged. "What happens to all men? They lose interest in you. The next day I realized I wasn't the most important person in the room to him anymore. Something had changed and he had more time for his friends than for me. By the end of the week, he was barely speaking to me. It's funny how it happens, Aleasea. Have you ever experienced it? They don't exactly tell you that you're not important anymore. They just have a way of making you feel it. Like they're too scared to say it out loud, and they're hoping you'll just melt away."

"I experienced it once, a very long time ago."

Valeyn looked at her with genuine surprise – she hadn't expected that response. "What happened?" she asked, but Aleasea waved the question away.

"Another time. Please go on. What did you do then?"

Valeyn sighed. "I melted away. Will's treatment of me was kind of like a silent sentence. Everyone judged me after that. The girls froze me out – more out of jealousy than anything else, and the men...well they looked at me as if I was next on their list of conquests. So one day I quietly left – I didn't even say goodbye. I figured I still had the rest of the world to see, and there were plenty more people in it."

"And what happened when you met them?"

Valeyn shook her head as if trying to recall something forgotten.

"I don't know, I really don't. It was the same thing. I had fun, I really did, but...it was almost like Will followed me wherever I went. He was always there with a different face and a different name. The same thing kept happening. I don't understand it. I don't understand why I just couldn't enjoy it the same way others seemed to."

"You were trying to be somebody you're not," Aleasea answered.

"Oh, yes, because I'm a great and powerful god."

"No, because you're a kind and loving person." Aleasea took a breath and when she continued, she seemed to speak very carefully. "Valeyn, while I don't pretend to understand the woman you are today – I never knew Vale as I knew Elyn – I cannot believe you've changed into someone vastly different to the girl I trained in Fairhaven. You are trying to understand who you are and in doing this, you're going to also understand who you are not. This is the journey of any woman."

Valeyn left the window and sank into one of the empty couches. "I just wanted to be left alone," she said quietly.

"Do not delude yourself," snapped Ferehain.

Valeyn looked up at him, anger flaring in her eyes. "What are you saying?"

"You courted attention. You admitted as much yourself. You travelled Kovalith looking for experiences. These are not the actions of someone wanting to be left alone. You expected to meet the world on your terms, and when it refused, you chose to blame the world? I agree with Aleasea. You have changed little. You are still the young Elyn I remember so well."

Valeyn shot to her feet, fists clenched as anger flooded her entire being.

"And do you remember how easily I beat you, Ferehain? Do you want a reminder?" With one hand, she lifted the nearby table and flung it to the far wall where it splintered into firewood. It felt good to finally have her strength back and she reveled in it. "I don't want your judgment, I don't want your control, I don't want you hunting me. I just want to be left alone."

"That is selfish and naïve, my daughter. You are a god now. You will never be left alone." Yvorre's voice surprised everyone, and they all turned to look at her. She had risen from the couch and was now watching all of them with an expression almost akin to satisfaction.

"Ferehain is correct, I fear. Like all of us, you secretly craved adoration, the reassurance that you are special and different to those around you, and when you did not receive this you became bitter. Do not feel bad. Ferehain may be cold, but he was possibly the most perceptive student I ever trained."

Her stern gaze swept the room. Even her voice sounded stronger. For a moment nobody seemed to know what to say. She smiled – clearly enjoying the effect she had made on everyone – then turned to Ferehain.

"Good morning, Ferehain. While I thank you for your timely rescue, I also presume you have come to return me to judgment in Fairhaven?"

Ferehain stared at her and conflict seemed to war on his face for a moment. Then it was gone. "I have come to see you face justice for what you have done to us, Yvorre."

"Yvorre." It was Valeyn who spoke. "What did the Faede do to you? You look different."

Yvorre smiled and there was a touch of warmth to it that Valeyn had never seen before. "If I were to play games with you, I would feign knowledge and mystery, but the truth is, I do not know. Those demons are some of the most powerful creations to walk the Forge, but they can only take from you what you willingly relinquish, consciously or unconsciously. It is possible it took something from me that I was glad to lose."

Valeyn thought back to the moment on the riverbank when Yvorre stood between her and the Faede, remembered something oily and black passing from Yvorre to the Faede and the corrosive effect it had on the creature. Whatever it was, it had been something poisonous.

"I saw it take something from you, it was black and felt...wrong."

"It is possible that like attracts like," said Yvorre quietly.

Aleasea looked at Yvorre with a guarded expression. "Do you think that the Faede was attracted to the corruption of Bythe within you?" she asked slowly.

Ferehain barked a short laugh. Valeyn knew the sound was a rare thing and it was never an expression of amusement.

"Are you suggesting that the Faede has drained the evil from you, Yvorre, that you are now a good being again, absolved of guilt in your crimes and ready to be forgiven?"

Yvorre turned to him with an expression of unfettered calm. "No, Ferehain, it is not that simple. I am not certain what the Faede did to me on the riverbank, nor am I suggesting that I am a different person because of it. I just know that things seem...different. I have not felt this way for a long time."

Ferehain stared at her. "You will not deceive me with your tricks, Yvorre. We both know you turned from Maelene's path a long time ago. You have not been her for decades."

"But I was her...was I not?" Yvorre looked over all of them as if asking the question. "I was her and then this world forced terrible decisions on me." She turned back to Ferehain with a defiant look. "You and my daughter discussed this very subject as I lay here. We are all on our own unending journey, Ferehain. You change the color of your cloak to show this. My daughter changes her name. Why do you think I should be any different?"

"Your journey does not take you so far that you may escape what you have done," he answered.

Yvorre gave him a long appraising look before continuing. "You were always among my best, Ferehain, but I do not expect you to understand what I had to endure all those years alone. I thought you had abandoned me. I thought all of you had."

"Do not try for sympathy with me. Do you think me a fool?" he snapped.

Yvorre waved her hand distractedly. "No, Ferehain, I am not trying to deceive you. I merely try to make you see that the world is not as black and white as you have always chosen to perceive it. But that is my fault as well. I wanted you to be the strongest you could be. I should have foreseen this would also make you inflexible."

Ferehain took a step toward her and glared down into her upturned face.

"Nothing can excuse what you have done to us," he said.

She met his glare unflinchingly. "You mean to say that nothing can excuse what I have done to *you,* Ferehain," she replied softly. "And you are right. I cannot argue."

He seemed about to speak but stopped himself, and for a moment, it seemed as if he was unsure of what he should do. He looked around the room before finding Aleasea.

"Come, Aleasea, we should prepare to leave. Stop wasting your time with Elyn. She will not help us."

"Ferehain, you act as if this is your decision to make. There are other forces at work besides your will," Yvorre said.

He glanced at her with a thin smile. "Do not entertain me. I know your strength is all but spent. You would not have needed me to save you from the Faede if you still had power. You cannot challenge me."

Yvorre sighed in return. "You speak of power? What do you say, Valeyn? You have more power than anyone in this room. You realize that whatever happens here is your decision – no one else's."

"Don't try to put this on me," Valeyn growled.

"I put nothing onto anyone. I simply state the facts as they are. You have more strength than both Aleasea and Ferehain combined. Whatever happens next cannot pass without your consent – explicit or otherwise."

"Oh, no!" Valeyn pointed firmly at the older woman. "Do not try and pretend this is my decision. I'm not going to buy into your games. They can take you for all I care. In fact, that's a great idea. Why don't you all just get out? Just leave me be."

The room was silent for a moment. Aleasea looked like she was about to speak but she said nothing. Nobody moved.

"You see?" Yvorre said. "You cannot divorce yourself from this. They do not wish to leave you be. You must make a decision."

"What decision?" Valeyn eyed the Ageless as she spoke. "You said it yourself – nobody here can make me do anything. Are you going to try to hurt me if I refuse you, Aleasea?"

Aleasea shook her head. "You know I would never harm you, Valeyn."

"You? No." Valeyn gestured to Ferehain with a tight smile. "Him? I'm not so sure."

"You must make a decision because I offer you an alternative," said Yvorre. "You can go with them and return to the life you left behind you, you can leave us all and return to the empty life ahead of you, or I can take you to The Tower."

"The Tower?" Aleasea asked, the surprise on her face clear. "Ferehain is right about you, you cannot stop telling lies."

"I do not lie, daughter," Yvorre replied.

"Why do you say she's lying?" asked Valeyn.

"Because The Tower is dead, sealed by Nishindra before he left us," said Aleasea.

"Yes, Nishindra locked The Tower, but I can open it. I can reawaken it," answered Yvorre. "You can feel The Tower, Valeyn, can you not? You told me that you feel its call."

Valeyn looked at her mother but said nothing.

"You truly are desperate, Yvorre," said Ferehain before turning to Valeyn. "The Tower will yield you no secrets. It is a refuge of the gods, now ancient and dormant. If Yvorre wishes to take you there, then you can be assured it is because it will benefit her, not you."

"That is incorrect, Ferehain. It can benefit both of us," said Yvorre. "Valeyn, you feel the call of The Tower as we all do. There is a reason for this, and it is important that I show this to you. You seek a purpose in your life, daughter. That is what you have been missing. You have found that a life of pleasure is meaningless, that you are meant for far more than this. I can help you to find that purpose. We can find it together."

At the mention of The Tower, Valeyn had felt something stir deep within her. A pang of guilt like something unfinished or a job forgotten. She knew that Yvorre was right, that her idle pleasures at Tiet and every other place had been meaningless. She knew that she hadn't been brave. She hadn't made a choice to be independent.

She had been hiding.

"Be silent, Yvorre. You are trying to manipulate her," said Aleasea.

"Manipulate?" Yvorre repeated the word as if mildly offended. "I simply offer an alternative. I offer her a choice. You are the ones who wish to hide her alternatives. You are the ones who are attempting manipulation."

"Be quiet, all of you," Valeyn snapped. She sighed and looked into the eyes of her mother. The eyes were brighter now – clearer. Could she be trusted? "How can The Tower help me?" she asked.

"The Tower was Nishindra's finest creation," answered Yvorre. "It holds secrets that only the gods may be privy to. Not even my Ageless were allowed access."

"You used The Tower to foretell my birth," said Valeyn, referring to the vision Yvorre had shown Elyn and Vale in the Arcadia.

"That was but one of the secrets held within. There are many greater secrets, secrets that will answer many questions about you and what you are meant for."

Valeyn frowned. "So why do you need me? Why not just go and unlock The Tower and all of its secrets for yourself?"

Yvorre nodded in a satisfied way. "Very perceptive, Daughter. The full truth is that I cannot unlock The Tower without you. Nishindra was angered by what he saw as my misuse of his creation, and he sealed it from me and from Bythe. He wanted us to make peace, and I suppose he thought he could accomplish this by withdrawing his support from both of us. Only the presence of both myself and Bythe together will unlock The Tower now."

"And I am both of you. My presence alone will do this," said Valeyn.

"Exactly." Excitement glittered in Yvorre's eyes and, for an instant, Valeyn caught a flash of youth in them. "My daughter, you are destined to unite this world. The Tower showed this to me. If you come with me, we can work together to unlock its secrets. There is power there that can end this war forever. That is the true purpose of your life, Valeyn –not to chase fleeting pleasures but to save countless lives."

"Valeyn, please, you cannot trust her." Aleasea's plea was almost desperate.

Valeyn moved away from all of them, shaking her head as if she couldn't comprehend what she had heard. "Leave me alone, please," she muttered and walked back toward the passageway.

"Valeyn wait..." called Aleasea.

"I need to think...this is too much..."

She walked through the archway and back into a hall. She had no idea where she was going. She just felt the need to move, to put one foot in front of the other until the world began to make sense again. She felt trapped, suffocated, and the lofty vaults of Anchorwatch were suddenly claustrophobic. She drifted through beautiful rooms she barely noticed as she tried to process what she had heard.

Could Yvorre be right? Could The Tower really unlock secrets about her that could end the war with Bythe? Was she really destined to save this world?

Part of her wanted nothing more than to reject this, wanted nothing more than to retreat to the reassurance that she controlled her life, that she could define it utterly, that no rules or judgment could intercede. But it felt shallow.

She didn't want to go back to her previous life. What would she do? Find another town like Tiet? Start again? How would it be any different? And she knew she'd be hiding. Now that she'd faced that knowledge, she knew she couldn't run from it anymore.

But what were the alternatives? Yvorre was almost certainly trying to manipulate her, and while Aleasea was trying to do the right thing, Valeyn knew Aleasea's offer would place her back under the control of the Ageless and their plots against Bythe.

Bythe.

She thought of her father and again toyed with the possibility of going to him, of walking up to the gates of the Ironhelm and demanding answers. She smiled at the thought – the thought of a hundred Helmsguard warriors placing her in shackles and marching her into captivity.

Great plan, Valeyn.

Cursing to herself, she walked into another room and stopped. Something felt off. The room was larger than the other chambers she'd wandered into, and unlike the others – this one wasn't designed for sleeping. She glanced around, trying to understand what it was that was bothering her. The chamber seemed to be some kind of study, with books lining one wall and several wooden desks and work benches placed around the room. It was something intangible, like a vague smell of something unpleasant that seemed to hang in the air, and she moved around the room to find the source.

When she saw the crimson helm, she instinctively took a step back. It lay on the floor at the far end of the room, along with a stained cloak and other fragments of its putrid ruins.

"Ferehain brought the remains up here to see if he could learn anything from them," said Aleasea from the doorway.

"I can feel them...just slightly," Valeyn said, looking down at the scraps of the creature in disgust.

"I'm sorry. They violated you quite deeply. I should have realized that their presence would carry some lingering trauma for you."

"It's alright," she said as she glanced back at Aleasea. "Are you checking up on me?"

Aleasea moved into the room and settled onto one of the chairs. Her body seemed to diminish a little and for a moment, Valeyn could sense the weight of her true age.

"Ferehain is preparing to leave with Yvorre. I don't know what to tell you to do, Valeyn."

"Aren't you going to ask me to come back with you?"

Aleasea sighed. "I'd like that, but then I think that maybe I'm being selfish too. Maybe I just want you back at my side again? Maybe you're right and I just can't let go of my role as your teacher."

Valeyn felt tears pressing against her eyes. "I know you're trying to help, but I don't want to go back there. I'm scared to go back. I can feel the energy of my father. Did you know that? I can feel his *kai,* or whatever it is you call it. The closer I am to the Ironhelm, the stronger I can feel it, and it sickens me, Aleasea, like these creatures." She gestured to the ruins of the Faede. "I'm worried that I'm going to turn out like my father if I go back there. I'm afraid that his *kai* will poison me. I don't want to face him, Aleasea. Please don't make me."

Aleasea rose and walked over to her, placing her palm against Valeyn's cheek.

"I will never allow you to be hurt, Elyn."

Aleasea's use of her childhood name brought her tears. Her gentle sobs filled the room while Aleasea again comforted her. For a brief time, Valeyn was a student again and Aleasea took the burden from her shoulders and gave her a moment of peace. Eventually their embrace was interrupted by the sound of two people approaching the chamber.

"I'm sorry," Valeyn sniffed as she pulled away. "I thought I was stronger than this."

"You've been through so much and the Faede have a way of unsettling you. It was wrong of us to bring the remains up here. I'll remove them."

Ferehain entered the room and gave them both a quick glance as if he already knew what had been said between them. Yvorre lingered at the doorway several steps behind him.

"I am ready to leave. Aleasea, will you be coming with us?"

Aleasea bent over to collect the Faede's crimson robe, and as she did, something small and black tumbled to the floor. Valeyn felt a cold pang of dread.

"What's that?" asked Valeyn.

She knelt beside Aleasea and collected the item – it turned out to be a small clump of hair, long and delicate, wrapped in a scrap of fine blue silk.

"Naya," said Valeyn, staring at the small reminder of her friend with a mixture of agony and outrage. "Are they really this cruel?"

Aleasea seemed to rapidly assess the implications of the apparently insignificant item among the Faede's remains. "They're taunting you. Ignore it," said Aleasea.

"No," replied Yvorre. "Exedor does not taunt without purpose. I taught him too well for that. This will have meaning. It is a message."

"He still has her," whispered Valeyn.

Yvorre nodded and walked over to where they both knelt, extending her palm for the message. Valeyn slowly handed it to her and watched as Yvorre peered at the small bundle from all sides before delicately unwinding the blue silk of Naya's torn dress. She looked at the fabric and her face tightened into a strange smile.

"Very well played," she murmured before handing the silk to Valeyn.

On the inside of the material – written in what looked like blood – was a single word.

Kardak.

Yvorre's own refuge, granted to her by Bythe, now apparently claimed by her former protégé.

"That is where Exedor waits – with Naya. If I had to guess, I would say his first plan was to capture us with his Faedes, but if that failed, then his backup plan was to use guilt to bring you to him instead."

155

Valeyn stared at the word as if it held the significance of the world in its bloodstained letters.

"You mean she's still alive?"

Yvorre shrugged. "Who knows? He certainly wants you to believe she is. He wants you to believe you can save her."

"Do not be so gullible, Elyn. It is clearly a trap," Ferehain interrupted sharply.

Valeyn simply continued staring at the fabric.

"I agree with them," said Aleasea. "Don't be tempted by this. There's nothing you can do to help her now. They are too strong even for you."

"I have to help her," Valeyn concluded then rose to her feet.

"Do not be a fool, child!" Yvorre snapped. "We barely survived two of them, and now you wish to attack all of them alone?"

"Not alone," she answered looking to both Aleasea then Ferehain. "If you help me, we can save her."

Aleasea also got to her feet and looked at her guardedly. "Valeyn, you're asking much. We don't know if we have the power to match them, even with you at our side."

"And we simply do not have time," added Ferehain.

"Then I'll make a deal with you both," Valeyn said, pausing for a moment before plunging ahead. "Come with me to rescue Naya, and I'll return to Fairhaven with you both."

"Don't be a fool!" spat Yvorre. "You're playing directly into his hands! If you go to Kardak, he will capture you all. He knows you will come."

"He doesn't know about Aleasea and Ferehain. He can't have factored them into his plan," countered Valeyn.

Yvorre's eyes narrowed at this minor defeat, but she was not willing to surrender. "Come with me to The Tower, Valeyn. I promise you there is a weapon there that Exedor and his Faedes cannot overcome. It will allow you to free Naya easily."

"No, Mother, if Exedor thinks I'm not going to come, he'll just kill her. I don't have time to go find your Tower now."

"No," said Ferehain. "I am taking Yvorre and returning to Fairhaven. I will not be distracted from my duty and nor should you, Aleasea."

Aleasea looked from Valeyn to Ferehain, then walked over to stand before him. For a moment Valeyn realized there was an intimacy between them. Distant and forgotten – but there.

"She is a child, Ferehain, an innocent daughter. She has done nothing wrong and deserves none of what has happened to her. Are we going to do nothing to protect her?"

Ferehain glared back at her and the mask of his face broke open for an instant. "This is not my fault, Aleasea. I didn't do this to her," he hissed.

"I've never said it was. I just remember what you once told me," she replied.

A mixture of rage, hurt, and frustration all shot across his features for a second. He closed his eyes, and when he opened them again, they were cold. They locked onto Valeyn with an intensity that made her feel like she was his student again.

"You will return with us afterward?" he asked simply.

"Yes," she answered.

"I want your word," he pressed.

She looked at him for a moment and saw nothing but cold sincerity in his eyes. She understood that – for the first time – he was addressing her as a peer.

"Yes, Ferehain, you have my word. I swear to you that I'll return to Fairhaven with you once Naya is safe."

He looked at her impassively for another few moments before answering. "Very well. We will need to prepare."

Without another word he turned and left the room. Valeyn realized that Yvorre had said nothing for a very long time. She quickly turned to look at her mother, ready to expose calculation, deceit, or cunning – and instead, she found Yvorre staring at Ferehain's retreating form with the most unexpected expression – a look of pure and honest sorrow.

CHAPTER 4

"I paid many prices the day Valeyn was born. It seemed her power was destined to wax as my own would wane. While the Ageless healed my injuries, many of them would not forgive my betrayal. By allowing Valeyn the freedom to choose her fate, it would seem I also chose judgment from many of my own people. We now appear to be more divided than we ever have been. Yet I do not regret my decision."

~Aleasea of the Ageless

"This is just unfair!" Jason complained.

He was leaning against a bench in his father's workshop. It was a small space, little more than a couple of benches filled with forests of small tools lined up in their respective holders. Dust motes hung in the sunbeams that fought their way through the small gaps in the roof. Jason's father was seated at the other bench, bent over an array of gears which he scrutinized through a loupe attached to his glasses. He was an older man, thin with a bald head and the sheen of a grey beard coating his jawline.

"What have I always told you? Life's not fair," he replied, still fixated on his delicate operation.

Jason crossed his arms sullenly, conscious he had reverted to the behavior of a child in the presence of his father, but also feeling safe enough to do so.

The Council had – very predictably – voted in favor of Morag's proposition, and within twenty-four hours, Jason had found himself obligated to submit all his plans regarding the defense of Fairhaven to E'mar. In addition to this, E'mar had begun leading daily Councils of War in the Council chambers, attended by Jason, Morag, Denethin, and a smattering of other senior officers and Ageless, although the Violari were conspicuously absent. These meetings had been primarily concerned with planning the troop dispositions within the New City and the preparations for a long siege. Jason knew they were pointless. He attended them; he said the right things – he'd learned that much from his blunders at the Council – but the posturing infuriated him.

"I really don't know what to do," Jason said.

"What does Nadine say?"

"She wants me to try and work through it, but it's easy for her to say. She was born into nobility; she knows what to say and how to say it.

"Look, Jason," he swiveled around on his stool and looked at his son with bright grey eyes. "Ever since you were a child, you've always been competitive. That's why your ma and me got you into weapons training as soon as you could pick up a sword. I just knew you'd be a great soldier."

"But this is different to that," said Jason. "This isn't about fighting, it's...well it's a different sort of fighting I guess."

"Damn right. You've always been the best at whatever you do. The problem is that you've never done this before."

"I've led people before," Jason answered. "Hell, I was leading the cadets when I was thirteen. I'm good at it, most of the time."

Caydyn looked at his son thoughtfully for a moment, then nodded to the workbench Jason had chosen to lean on. "How did you go with Bannor's clock? Did you find the problem?"

Jason looked at his father for a moment, a little irritated at the change in topic, before answering the question. "Yeah, sure. It just had a problem with the mainspring, I swapped it out. It was pretty simple."

Caydyn smiled. "You were always good at finding problems, and good at fixing them. Why aren't you working here with me?"

Jason shrugged. "C'mon, Pa, we've talked about this. It just...isn't me."

"I know. You remember the times I tried to get you to build one of these?" He gestured to a beautiful, gold trimmed clock on the bench before him. "I couldn't keep you in here for more than half an hour. I'd come back to find you out in the street playin' with the other boys. That's when I knew this life wasn't for you."

"I guess," Jason said.

"You're good at taking action. You're good at findin' problems. Hell, it was you who figured out how to kill Imbatal. Nobody else. You. 'That was my son,' I tell everyone." Caydyn gave him a proud look before he continued. "But you got no damned patience, boy, you never have. To do my job, you need to sit here for hours on end and build a clock from the ground up. You have to figure it all out carefully beforehand. You don't just go rushing into doing it. And I knew that kinda patience...well, it just wasn't in you."

"I'm sorry, but you're right. This was never me."

"Don't be sorry," Caydyn laughed. "That's my whole point. I'd be a fool of a father if I'd tried to force you down this road just 'cause it's what I like to do. You found what you were good at, and you became the best at it. Only now, you're back at my workbench, aren't you? Staring at the job of a captain like you'd stare at the gears on the tablecloth, wishing you were somewhere else because you don't know if you could be the best at this."

"You think I should quit?" Jason asked.

"Nope," he said firmly. "You're not going to quit. I won't take that as an answer, but it sounds to me that you're trying to force a mainspring in place of a hairspring, then complainin' 'cause it won't do the job the same way."

Jason looked puzzled. "Pa, just spit it out. What are you trying to say?"

Caydyn sighed. "Why don't you just see if this is the job that's right for you instead of trying to see if you can do the job the way others did it? Why don't you just focus on what you're best at? Be a leader your own way. If it means that's not good enough to be a captain of Fairhaven, then so what? No shame in being the best damned lieutenant who ever slew a demon. Bet no one in the Council can write that in their memoirs!"

Jason smiled at his father. He was going to clarify that it had been Valeyn – not him – who had actually slain Imbatal, but he knew his father would never make the distinction no matter how often it was pointed out to him.

"Hello?" Nadine's voice rang out from the next room.

"Stay there, darlin'" Caydyn called out, jumping up from his stool and bustling both his son and himself out of the workshop. "C'mon, boy, you don't keep a pregnant woman waiting, especially when she's *your* pregnant woman."

They both moved into the main living area of Caydyn's house. It was a modest space, decorated by little more than a table placed up against one wall and a few chairs. A large fireplace warmed the room and a wooden staircase ran to a door on a small landing, which led to Caydyn's own private sleeping chamber. While it was certainly no manor, Jason's father had managed to do quite well for himself as a clocksmith, and he lived in relative comfort. Nadine stood on the rug, warming herself against the fire. A small basket of vegetables sat on the table alongside a loaf of bread. She turned her head when both men entered and favored them both with a smile that seemed to glow.

"I think our baby is definitely going to take after his father," she said. "He's been doing workouts in my belly the whole walk over."

Jason jogged over to where she stood and eagerly placed his palm on her swollen stomach. She met his eyes while he carefully felt around.

"There, do you feel that?" she asked.

Jason's eyes lit up with excitement as he felt the little bumps. "Yes...yes, I feel her."

"*Him*," Nadine softly chided him. "He's definitely a boy."

At some point, Nadine had convinced herself that their baby was going to be a boy. Jason wasn't sure how or why. Perhaps it was some maternal instinct that drove her, but she was adamant. So, naturally, he took the opposite position and maintained resolutely that they were having a girl. He had absolutely no idea, of course – but he loved to tease his wife with his own fatherly intuition.

"Caydyn," she called to her father-in-law, "would you like to meet your grandson?"

"Granddaughter," Jason quietly amended, but Nadine ignored him.

Caydyn made his way over and placed his hands next to Jason's. He seemed to know what to look for and within seconds, a similar smile brightened his face.

"Oh, yes, there it is. That's a boy, no doubt about it," he said to Jason.

"Why do you always take her side?" Jason asked.

"Because you never argue with a pregnant lady," Caydyn replied.

The three of them stood for a moment, enjoying the simple wonder of an unborn child before Caydyn quietly withdrew his hand.

"I hope you've actually been helping your father," Nadine told Jason.

"He has, in his own way," Caydyn answered with a smirk. "I gave him the jobs that need a lot of muscle and not too much thinking."

"Exactly," Jason agreed with a grin.

"Well, I think maybe you've been doing too much thinking lately," Nadine replied, rubbing her husband's broad shoulders affectionately.

"Just what I was telling him," said Caydyn. "He just needs to think less and trust his instincts more."

"Yes, well, my instincts tell me that we should stop talking about my problems and focus on my wife instead." Jason said.

"Good suggestion. You *are* learning useful lessons. We should come over more often," said Nadine and moved to the table to start unpacking the vegetables from the basket. "Why don't you help me with dinner while your father takes a rest in his chamber?"

"Actually," said Caydyn, "now that you're here, Nadine, I'd like to show you both something first, if that's alright?"

He led them up the small staircase to his bedchamber. Jason carefully assisted Nadine as they ascended. When they reached the landing, Caydyn opened the door and ushered them both inside. Nadine's sharp intake of breath was the first thing Jason heard, and it momentarily stole his attention before he realized what she had seen.

His father's bedroom had completely changed since the last time he'd seen it. The bedcoverings – usually drab and functional ever since Jason's mother passed – had been replaced with lavendar-colored sheets. Nadine's favorite color. A dressing table with a mirror stood against one wall, but what drew Jason's attention was the cradle placed next to the bed.

"Jason's mother didn't want him out of arm's reach for the first six months, and I figure you'll be much the same, Nadine," said Caydyn.

"Caydyn! Oh, no, you can't do this," Nadine protested.

"Of course, I can," he replied. "Do you think I'm gonna let my grandson be raised in the barracks? Nope."

Jason and Nadine had moved into the captain's lodgings a few weeks earlier, once Lewis's personal items had been removed. While it was certainly comfortable, it was comfortable according to the comparative standards of military life, which wasn't saying much. Nadine had made the best of it, but Jason knew she'd hoped for something more homely. However, with the economic downturn hitting her family hard, there had been no other real options besides moving back in with her parents – and that hardly seemed like a fitting alternative for a Captain of Fairhaven who was already under siege.

"From this day forward, this is your home," Caydyn finished.

Jason shook his head with sheer incredulity. "Pa, thank you, but this is absurd. Where are you going to live?"

Caydyn smiled conspiratorially "Well, 1 knew about your situation, so 1 asked around and 1 got me another place a few weeks back. Old Samek, the butcher, was sellin' up everythin' and leaving for Azad. He let me buy his place real cheap. My original plan was to give it to you two, but it's only one small room and probably not that much better than the barracks, so 1 figure you should have this place instead. The gods know you're going to need the room more than 1 do, especially if this is the first of many."

Jason's eyes took in the room. It had been decorated with a father's care – now a grandfather's care. He studied the cot and found that he knew it – it had been his, kept in storage all these years and now passed on.

"Pa...1 don't know what to say," Jason said.

"Just say you don't mind if 1 still come and go into the workshop as 1 need to. I'll use its back door so as not to disturb you both."

"Oh, Caydyn," Nadine wrapped her arms around her father-in-law. "You can come and go whenever you want. Thank you so much."

Caydyn winked at his son over Nadine's blonde hair. "There you go, it's settled. Remember what I said about arguing with a pregnant lady?"

Jason nodded and joined his wife in the hug, but as he closed his eyes, his happiness was buffeted by an unwanted image. An image of flames and of death. The scene of Fairhaven – and all of this – burning to the ground.

That is not going to happen.

He unconsciously gripped his family tighter.

.   .   .

Jason stared at the landscape as if it were mocking him. To the south, the mountains reared up and continued a wall that led all the way to Greenridge. This wall had long protected Fairhaven from the Iron Union, but the view to his left was a very different story. Rolling fields descended far to the southeast, where they eventually met the distant smudge of a forest line on the horizon. There had been very few times that Fairhaven had needed to defend herself from this direction. The Outer Wild had rarely been a place of war like the lands to the east. While the Northmen raids had been a constant threat, they had almost always attacked through the mountains to the north, and – with the Siege of Fairhaven aside – they had never been able to coordinate themselves into a sizeable army. No, this was very different. Within days, an army of five hundred Iron Union soldiers would occupy these open plains and Fairhaven would be exposed before them.

"It's indefensible," Jason muttered.

He was standing outside the western wall, surveying the fields in a vain attempt to formulate a plan for the impending assault. Kaler stood next to him, his purple cloak fluttering in the breeze as he scanned the landscape with his captain.

"I would not say that it is indefensible. These walls held against the Paephu attacks. I was there. It is possible they could repel the Helmsguard," Kaler observed.

"And I was here three years ago, when just one hundred of the Helmsguard tore down this very gate," Jason countered. "And I was there at Darcliff, when the war engines obliterated walls far stronger than these." He shook his head as he considered the options. "No, if they get this close to us, Fairhaven is as good as ruined."

"So what do you suggest? Are you still set on meeting them in the field? You know that E'mar will not allow it."

He was right, of course. E'mar had increased his control over the War Council every day so that now, he was effectively commanding the entire defense, and he was determined to defend the city from within. Jason had been assigned the task of ensuring the outer walls were reinforced and ready to repel the attackers when they came.

"Why is he like this, Kaler? Why won't he listen to reason?" Jason asked.

Kaler shrugged. "He may yet be correct. We do not know that Baron Ethan brings war engines to Fairhaven. Our scouts have not yet seen evidence of this. It may be that he simply brings infantry – in which case, E'mar's strategy is sound."

"That's one hell of a risk to be taking," Jason muttered.

Kaler turned to Jason and looked at him with a grave expression. "E'mar is proud. While he is not the only Ageless to be guilty of such a flaw, he is one of the few who have been in such a position of power. Back during the Hierophace, the first years of life in the Forge, the Ageless were organized by Maelene. She created us as her children and – like children – imposed a hierarchy upon us. Those who were created during the Hierophace were our leaders, we called them the *Almaer*. You are familiar with Veroulle, Ferehain and Aleasea, but there were others who fell over the years. E'mar was never one of the *Almaer*, he was created among the *Ishantir*, the generation who followed, as was I.

"Maelene never created us as leaders. We were intended to perform a different role within the Ageless, and while that sufficed while Maelene lived, things became more complex after she fell."

"I wouldn't have thought the Ageless were capable of petty politics," Jason said.

"Do not be surprised. We are living creatures like the others of this world. Our failings are not that different from yours. I do not like the Entarion, and there are many among them who feel the same toward me. I did not trust your friend when she was brought before us and I was right to feel that way. She was proven to be the daughter of Bythe."

Jason glared at him. "She also saved us all. You almost killed her."

Kaler raised his eyebrows. "You exaggerate on both counts, but I concede I let my own prejudices and ambitions cloud my judgment. I wanted to impress Ferehain, I wanted to join him as a leader of the Violari, and I was eager to prove myself. That led to some poor judgment on my part."

Poor judgment? Jason fought down the desire to rage at him. He knew this was the closest thing to an apology he could expect from Kaler, and he couldn't afford to make any more enemies.

As if sensing Jason's mood, Kaler continued in a more conciliatory tone. "The point I am trying to make is that E'mar suffers from the same ambition that infects many of the *Ishantir.* He has existed in the shadow of Veroulle and Aleasea his entire life, and he now has the opportunity to take the lead. Sadly, he does not realize that he does not possess the same qualities as Veroulle."

"Or maybe he's just afraid to look weak," Jason added.

"That is also likely," Kaler agreed. "Either way, he will not tolerate the appearance of you undermining him. He sees this as his moment of opportunity, his moment to ascend to the leadership of the Ageless. He wants this glory for himself."

"Glory?" Jason was thunderstruck. "What glory? Don't you see that all this is going to..." He stopped himself and looked around in frustration. He hadn't shared Veroulle's vision with anyone outside of the Council – he'd been ordered to keep it secret – but at times like this he felt the urge to scream it into the sky.

Kaler watched him for a moment. "What is it, Jason?" he asked.

Jason waved him into silence and stalked back toward the city wall where a small team of men were surveying the structure. Sedren – an engineer – had been supervising them. While he was not a member of the army, he'd been conscripted into service along with most of the other skilled tradespeople. These were the only real resources left under his command. Almost all troops had been taken out of his direct control and requisitioned by E'mar for dispositions within the city.

"Well? How's the wall? Will it hold?" Jason asked the engineer, eager to find a new topic of conversation.

Sedren nodded. He was a young man, not many years older than Jason, but he'd been apprenticed under his father since he was a child. "It could do with a bit of reinforcement around the foundations. There's been some erosion there this past winter, but we should be able to get some bedrock brought in by tomorrow."

"Do it," Jason agreed absently, looking at the walls with a sense of hopelessness. If Ethan had war engines, then no amount of bedrock reinforcement would be able to stop them tearing every stone to the ground.

Sedren looked at Jason uncertainly. "Captain, I know you must have better things to do than worry about construction. I can finish the inspections by myself. Why don't you focus on your soldiers?"

Jason smiled bitterly. "You're the only soldiers I have left."

Sedren looked puzzled and had opened his mouth to respond when a cry rose from the lookout above. Jason turned and shielded his eyes against the sun as he looked eastward. A lone rider in green – a Fairhaven scout – was making his way toward the town. From the pace he was setting, Jason knew he bore news. He walked out into the field, Kaler and Sedren joining him as he waved down the rider.

The scout pulled up, recognizing Jason and offering a hurried salute. He looked exhausted, as if he had ridden for days without rest. His bay horse glistened with sweat and stood in place bellowing with a raging breath.

"Woodsman, what is it?" Jason asked.

"I've sighted them, sir, the Helmsguard," he breathed almost as heavily as his horse. "They're no more than five days march to the southeast, maybe less. Been camped there for a while I think."

"Camped?" Jason asked.

"Aye, sir. It looked like they were building something, not really sure what, but there was some massive tower of metal, and it looked like they were building another one right next to it. There were men runnin' back and forth like ants carrying massive plates of metal." He fixed Jason with a slightly desperate look. "Sir, I was hearin' stories before I left. Stories about some kind of evil weapon that Bythe's got. Is it true? Is that what I saw?"

Jason's heart sank. Any hope he had secretly nourished vanished on hearing these words. "Yes, Woodsman, that's what you saw, but you repeat this to nobody, understand?"

The Woodsman looked agitated. "Begging your pardon, sir, but I got orders to go direct to the Council with my report. I was told to report to E'mar personally."

Jason shook his head. E'mar had completely eroded his authority within such a short time. He considered ordering the poor Woodsman against reporting to E'mar, but he knew it would do little more than delay the inevitable and would likely only land the Woodsman in trouble. He waved the rider on his way and stared back across the plains. Two war engines less than a week from the gates. The news would be across all of Fairhaven before nightfall.

"Well, what do you think now, Kaler? Do you still think E'mar's plan will work?" Jason asked with a cynical edge to his voice.

"I was hoping against fate itself," Kaler answered. "If Ethan has two of these, what chance do you think we have?"

Jason scanned the fields before them. "None. The engines I saw at Darcliff had a range of roughly one mile. If these are the same, then Ethan will be able to position them in the middle of the field and simply rain fire on top of us until there's nothing left. We won't be able to reach them from within the walls, and whatever traps E'mar planned won't be of any use."

"Is there anything we can do, Captain?" Sedren asked.

"No," Jason replied flatly. "Fairhaven is going to burn. There's nothing we can do."

Sedren looked alarmed, but Kaler stepped forward, his anger clear on his face.

"What gives you the right to give up so easily, Captain? You are supposed to be our leader. Are you really just looking for an easy way out?"

Jason knew why Kaler was pressing him – trying to use pride to motivate him into action – but Jason felt numb. The confirmation of the two war engines had simply drained any hope from him.

"Veroulle had a vision," Jason said as if speaking to nobody. "He shared it with me. Fairhaven will burn and I will be there to watch."

Kaler fell silent for a moment.

"What do you mean?" Sedren asked. "Are we all going to die?"

Sedren's fear snapped Jason out of his torpor. "No, that's...that's not what I meant. I just, need time to think of a plan," Jason said in a weak attempt to allay Sedren's fears.

Kaler gave Jason a probing look. "I feel you have spent far too much time trying to think. You need to act."

"What do you suggest? I've tried to convince E'mar. He won't listen."

"E'mar knows of this?" Kaler asked.

"Better than knows, he's *seen* it. I was able to share the vision with him."

"If E'mar will not change his mind after such a revelation then he is an intractable fool." Kaler considered something for a moment before continuing. "However, I command the Violari. They will follow my lead if I ask it of them."

Jason looked at him, hope suddenly blazed in his heart. "Can you do something against this?"

Kaler shook his head. "Not in the way you would like. There are too few of us and while we are militant, we are not soldiers. We could not stand alone against an army of the Iron Union in a direct test of strength. We would be slaughtered, even without this new witchcraft that Bythe has sent us. Our power lies in far subtler ways."

"We need to meet them out on the field. If we hide in these walls and let the engines get within range, the battle's over."

"Give me some bedrock and a team of strong men, and I can try getting some more barricades built out there," Sedren suggested.

Kaler nodded. "We could assist with this. Many of the Violari have some power over the land."

Jason thought of the engines he had seen at Darcliff. He recalled their black towers and their lumbering, awkward gait. For some reason he thought of the faulty mainspring in his father's workshop. Then he thought of Imbatal.

They were all mechanisms, and all mechanisms needed the right conditions to operate, or they would fail. *What if we changed those conditions?*

"Sedren," he asked, never taking his eyes from the fields, "how good an engineer are you?"

Sedren shrugged. "Good enough. I've had a hand at building a lot of the structures in town. Tell me what you need me to build, and I'll tell you if I can build it."

"Not *build* necessarily. I was thinking more along the lines of an excavation."

"A trap?" Kaler asked.

"Maybe," Jason answered. "I need you to tell me what your people can do to help, Kaler."

Kaler met his eyes. "This is more suitable to us than a straight fight, but you know that the Council will not be happy."

"To hell with them," Jason muttered. "E'mar can have my soldiers for now. He's assigned me engineers, so I'll use them as I see fit. It's your Violari I'm going to need most. Can you keep them in line if E'mar orders you against me?"

"Normally I would not agree to this," Kaler said slowly. "But if E'mar is acting against the counsel of Veroulle, then my loyalty is to Veroulle's wishes." He thought for a long time before continuing, and when he did, his voice was grave. "I will order my Violari to act independently of the Entarion, should it become necessary.

Jason reached out and took Kaler's hand. He knew what he was asking of the Ageless, and he swore we would not forget this.

To hell with E'mar. To hell with his Council.

He decided that – no matter what happened – he would accept his fate like a Captain of Fairhaven.

.   .   .

"Explain your actions!" Councilor Morag's face was taut with fury, but Jason had prepared himself for this conversation.

"I'm sorry, Councilor, you're going to have to be more specific. What actions are you referring to?" he replied, straining to keep even a hint of sarcasm from his tone.

"Don't toy with us, boy! You know exactly what we're talking about!" Denethin leaped to his feet to join the assault.

Jason stood before the seated members of the Council. They had summoned him to their chamber as soon as he had begun executing his plan in the southern fields. He wasn't even remotely surprised when he received the summons, and this time he hadn't come alone. Kaler's presence at his side had thrown the Council from smug condescension into a state of almost palpable anxiety.

"Point of order!" Nadine exclaimed. "The Council is not to refer to the Captain of Fairhaven in such a derogatory manner. Is this a fish market?"

"Agreed," declared Paeter. "Councilor Denethin, you will refer to the captain by his recognized rank and title, not as *boy.*"

Morag continued her onslaught, seemingly unaware that the others had even spoken. "You are deploying units into the field against the wishes of the War Council."

"I'm doing no such thing, Councilor. The units allocated to defend this city remain under the discretion of E'mar and the War Council. I understand the plans for the city's defense continue unchanged."

"You're doing works in the fields!" Denethin shouted.

"I'm still in charge of the defenses," Jason shot back. "I'm using engineers to improve them. There's nothing wrong with this, and frankly, I don't need to ask your permission every time I give an order."

"Captain," E'mar added in a calm voice. "Now that we know the engines are coming, we need to double our efforts within the city wall. Panic is spreading, and it is taking everything we have to keep the people calm. Hundreds want to leave, but we cannot guarantee their safety, to say nothing of the fact that we do not even know where they could go. We need every resource. Your actions in the southern fields, while well-intentioned, are a distraction from these problems."

E'mar glanced at Kaler more than once as he spoke, seemingly waiting for the purple-robed Ageless to assert his position in the debate. Kaler said nothing.

"I'm a captain. Am I to have no authority at all?" Jason asked plainly."

"You can have authority within the confines set by the War Council," Morag answered.

"Confines?" Jason repeated the word as if he'd never heard it before. "Is it the role of the Council to *confine* the captain in a time of war? I don't recall your ever confining Captain Lewis in this way."

"You are most certainly not Captain Lewis," sneered Denethin.

"No, I'm not." Jason eyed Denethin with a look of open hostility. "Captain Lewis never had to contend with a threat like this. Not long ago, some of you even refused to believe the engines were real. You thought I was hysterical and irrational. Well, now you've seen them. Now you know they're coming. Do I get an apology, Councilor Denethin? Will you admit you were wrong?"

Denethin look about to explode, but Paeter cut him off.

"Captain, the Council accepts that you were correct in your assessment of the threat. What is your point?"

Jason paused and took in the entire Council with his eyes.

"If you still think that hiding in these walls will protect us against the war engines, even after you've seen them, then I can't change your mind. I'll respect your decision, but I will not stand by and do nothing. You need to let me do my job. Let me execute this plan. I'm not risking any soldiers. If it fails then you've lost nothing."

Nadine met his eyes and for a moment he saw a silent pleading in them. It looked as if she would object as well, but she said nothing. He looked at her in silence for a moment, then forced himself to tear his eyes away from hers. It was a harder thing to do than he expected.

"We need every man, especially engineers, to rebuild Fairhaven when this is over," said Morag. "We will not risk it."

"When this is over...?" Jason muttered in disbelief, but left the comment unaddressed. "Then I will use the Violari."

"That I cannot allow. I will need them," answered E'mar in a tone that marked the end of the discussion.

"Then the Violari will act without your blessing, E'mar," Kaler spoke in a quiet but clear voice.

The words hung in the air as silence flooded the chamber. All eyes turned to E'mar, who was looking at Kaler in stunned silence.

Jason decided to exploit the moment with his own attack before they could recover. "And if you still try to stop my plans...I'll order my own soldiers to stand against you."

"You little bastard," Morag whispered, but Jason wouldn't flinch.

"I still have enough support in the barracks. We'll probably split the army between us. Is that what you all want?"

"Arrest him!" yelled Denethin.

"Shut up, Denethin!" Paeter bellowed, causing the fat man to freeze uncertainly. Paeter rubbed his palm across his face and slumped in his chair. Jason felt terrible at putting his father-in-law in this position, but he was committed now.

"Jason, you cannot seriously threaten us with a coup on the eve of battle?" Paeter asked, as if he were negotiating with a madman on the edge of a precipice.

"You've removed me from my own command. You all started this coup," Jason said, although he knew the argument was a weak one.

"The Captain answers to the Council, not the other way around, Jason. We have the right to do this," said Paeter.

"No, Lewis made me captain and he understood what needed to be done. I'll carry out his orders, not yours." Jason paused and forced his voice into a calmer tone. "Look, you can have me executed once this is over if you want, but if you try to remove me from command before then, I'll swear before Maelene, Bythe, and every other god watching that I won't step down quietly."

"What do you propose?" Paeter asked.

"Just let me take my shot. I only need the Violari and a handful of men. If I fail, then I swear I'll step down, and you can do what you will with me."

Jason heard Morag and Denethin scoff in disbelief at his assurances, but he kept his eyes on Paeter.

"You don't seem to leave us a lot of choice now, do you, Captain?" said Paeter.

"I take no pleasure in this ultimatum, Councilors, but I can't stand by and watch my home burn like Darcliff." Jason signaled to Kaler then turned to leave.

"This isn't over," called Morag as Jason reached the doors. "We'll see you executed for this once this is over, *boy.*"

"Think positive," Jason chuckled. "There's an excellent chance the Helmsguard will save you the trouble."

Jason tried to ignore the pain that flashed on his wife's face as he left the chamber.

CHAPTER 5

"The fortresses of Stonekeep and Tyne had long held as the first line of defense for the Outland Alliance. After the Siege of Fairhaven, many of our forces were rediverted to these strongholds. It was rightly believed that the strength of our soldiers should be concentrated at the critical defense points. Similarly, the Ageless agreed that many of our brethren should be positioned there to aid against the inevitable might of the Helmsguard. We did not believe there was any recklessness in this approach. Nobody believed there was a force on Kovalith capable of destroying these structures without significant effort."

~Aleasea of the Ageless

The war engine trembled for a moment, then shot a blazing ball of fire high into the air. A deafening roar swept over the assembled men and a cloud of thick, black sulphur flew in the breeze along with the noise. The hulking body of the construct violently lurched backward as it fired, and anyone who might have been unfortunate enough to be standing under it would have been killed instantly. But there were no such misfortunes; the attending Helmsguard had all been expertly trained.

Commander Ethan – Lord of Mac-Soldai – watched the flaming projectile soar quickly over the broken ground and land in green fields beyond, flinging the grass to pieces as it added one more crater to the wreckage. In the distance, he beheld the city of Fairhaven for the second time in his life. The first time he'd seen the city was three years earlier, and then it had been under different – yet strangely similar – conditions. The city had been under siege by the Northmen and now it was about to suffer the same fate at his hands. But unlike the Northmen, he would not fail.

Clad head-to-foot in thick iron plates, their faces concealed behind masks with dark, bulbous eye-glasses and air pipes that hissed in a breathing rhythm that sounded unnatural, the Cremators moved back toward the engine. Moving with expert knowledge, they prepared the engine for the next attack by releasing valves and letting a dark cloud of steam flush from the underside of the twisted monstrosity. Ethan watched as four Cremators pushed an iron cart up against the engine. Within the cart was something Ethan could not understand; it seemed to be a liquid, and yet it flamed with the intensity of white coals at the heart of a fire. Udrax – Bythe's High Priest – had called it the Godfire – a gift from Bythe himself. Some even speculated that it was Bythe's own blood, sacrificed to end the war once and for all. No matter what it was, no one could walk within six feet of the substance without succumbing to burns. Only the fully trained and fully clothed Cremators would dare handle it directly, and even they could only do so for short periods. As such, he had been assigned a small army of Cremators to support his two engines. One of them opened a hatch in the engine and the other three gently eased the cart forward, so the liquid fire could run down a spout mounted to the front of the cart, and into the bowels of the giant machine. It shook slightly – almost as if a chill had run up its black, iron spine – then it gave a shrill, grating sound as it listed forward. Two thin, metal legs protruded from the base of the engine and served to catch its massive bulk as it leaned forward, off its balance point. One of the Cremators activated some hydraulics and the base of the engine shot forward on metal tracks, the movement causing the tower to right itself once more.

It was a crude and frustratingly slow method of movement that required intense support and coordination. The iron tracks had to be removed from behind the engine and then correctly placed in front of it, in order to keep it moving on schedule. All up, Ethan estimated he needed a team of roughly thirty men to support each engine – but the engines themselves were worth a thousand times that number of men.

The Fingers of Bythe.

That's what Udrax had named them. Ten iron towers capable of levels of destruction never before seen within the Forge – and Commander Ethan had been given two of them. It was a gesture that was symbolic of the level of trust and confidence Lord Bythe placed in him. It was a symbol that had seemed unthinkable three years earlier.

When Baron Ethan had returned to the Ironhelm after his battle at Fairhaven, he had expected nothing less than a court-martial, if not an immediate execution. It had taken him several weeks to lead his men back to his army in the Great Southern Wastes, back to Morbus – the Bureaucrator who had seemed equal parts smug and flustered at recapturing Ethan but losing Commander Vale. Morbus had immediately ordered his arrest – citing authority granted by Yvorre – but then the first messenger had arrived from the Helmsguard, and Ethan remembered how Morbus had paled at reading the dispatch.

Mistress Yvorre had been declared a traitor, and all officers who had been corrupted by her influence had been recalled to the Ironhelm immediately.

The march back into the Iron Union was long. Commander Zal had met them at Outpost and immediately assumed command, ordering Ethan, Morbus, and several of the other senior officers to the Ironhelm under guard. He had passed through his homeland of Mac-Soldai with barely a thought for his parents – his only concern was the judgment that awaited him within Bythe's fortress. That judgment took the form of High Constable Exedor, the newly appointed Royal Inquisitor. And High Constable Exedor had been very eager to prove himself indeed.

The months he spent within the dungeons of the Ironhelm were the worst he had ever experienced. Ethan's nobility gave him no protection from Exedor's questioning. How long had Ethan known Yvorre was a traitor? Why did Commander Vale desert her post and go to Fairhaven? What had Commander Vale been plotting? Where did Commander Vale flee after the siege? Why did Ethan let her go instead of returning with her in chains?

Why, indeed?

For his part, Ethan knew he had done no wrong. He had never betrayed Bythe nor the Iron Union in his heart – no matter what the complex schemes of others had been. So he had answered all of Exedor's questions with unflinching honesty.

He had no idea that Mistress Yvorre had been the goddess Maelene. He had simply been following the orders of his Commander when he followed Vale to Fairhaven. He plotted nothing, Bureaucrator Morbus administered Vale's army at the request of Yvorre. He had no idea where Commander Vale had gone. She had forced him to leave her in Fairhaven. Of course, he couldn't imprison her, she was a god now and he was just a man.

He wondered if that raw honesty had saved him. After the questioning, he simply sat in his cell for months. Nobody came to speak to him, the guards brought him food in silence, and after a time, he almost longed for Exedor to return with more questions. He felt starved of all human contact and craved any form of attention.

Then he was summoned before Bythe.

Ethan snapped himself out of his reverie. It did him no good to replay the past. He could still feel Bythe's burning stare in his mind, could still relive the sheer terror he had experienced while standing in that gaze, and those feelings were not helpful. He was a Commander now, personally appointed by Lord Bythe to return to Fairhaven and bring his daughter back to him – no matter the cost.

Another ball of fire launched from the second tower. It streaked overhead in a magnificent arc before crashing into the dirt a mile distant. Ethan wondered what the people within Fairhaven must have been thinking in the face of this deliberate display of power. That was, after all, the entire point of the barrage – to break the morale of the enemy before the battle had even begun. It had seemed to work at Darcliff. The dispatches he had received over the past week confirmed that the fortress had fallen on schedule and that the Commander Gil'zurio's army had now turned west to encircle Bonehall. The Outland Alliance would collapse within months, possibly weeks, and yet even that glory was secondary to him now.

He needed to find Vale.

Not only for Bythe – although that motivation was clearly strong enough – but also for himself. He scanned the city on the horizon, the legendary home of the Ageless, now little more than a crippled shell.

Bythe's strategy had been brilliant – by sending his main forces into Marfort in the west, he had forced the diminished Ageless to dilute their power even further by scattering themselves across the Outlands. Now Fairhaven was all but undefended.

"Sir," an old soldier approached Ethan. Their armor was identical, an overlapping carapace of iron plates covering them from their necks to their boots. Yet where Ethan had gold lining on his plates, a decoration denoting his rank of Commander, this man had silver trim, indicating that Baron Salus was second in command. "There's a problem with the supply chain again."

Annoyance flittered over Ethan's smooth face. He was a handsome young man in his middle twenties, already entering the prime of his youth and now the prime of his career. Even the dungeons had done little to mar his features, but for a premature streak of grey in his temples, yet even this early insult of age merely gave him a look of distinction.

"What is it this time, Baron?" he snapped.

"The Rak'Tunga raided one of the caravans just west of Qharg. The units were able to fend them off, but it's cost them time."

"What about the Godfire?" Ethan asked. It was the only real concern. Without the Godfire, the Fingers of Bythe would cease to function.

"The mongrels didn't get any this time, but, sir, this is the second raid this week alone. They're getting bolder and I think they know what we're transporting."

"How long before the resupply can reach us?"

"They're probably a week out now, sir. That is, assuming they don't hit any more raids."

Ethan sighed. It was the one major risk in their plan. An attack from the south was going to be Fairhaven's weakness, simply because an attack from the south was a logistical nightmare for the army that was foolish enough to attempt it. It had previously been unthinkable to try to move a large army – large enough to assault the Ageless – through miles of forested foothills with the wild men of the Great Southern Wastes at your flank. But with the Fingers of Bythe, a large army was no longer needed. A smaller force of five hundred men could navigate the journey, the only problem being the supply lines of rations, equipment – and now, of the Godfire. Even with five engines, Commander Gil'zurio's supply lines were comparatively simple in the east, but Ethan's task was far more complicated.

He glanced over at the Cremators as they loaded more of the Godfire into the engine.

"How much longer until we're within range of the walls?" Ethan asked.

"At this rate, probably no more than a day, I think," Salus replied.

"Alright, let's go easy on the barrage for now," Ethan said. "If the resupply is a week away then we're going to need all the ammunition we have, and besides, I think we've made our point."

"As you wish, sir," Salus saluted, then marched off, shouting orders to the Cremators to hold fire. A flurry of protests broke out from the shrouded fanatics, but Salus was more than equal to the challenge.

It had been Ethan's idea to delay the construction of the engines until the last possible moment. The Cremators had protested then as well, transporting the individual components across the Outlands was difficult, and the Cremators had been eager to flaunt the power of their new machines. But even diminished, the Ageless were still not to be underestimated, and Ethan wanted to ensure Fairhaven was kept ignorant of her doom until it was imminent. He was not even sure that his spy on the Fairhaven Council could keep the city distracted from such an obvious threat. Since he had assembled the engines, Ethan had sent out seven Outriders to scout Fairhaven's preparations as he advanced, but none had returned. Clearly the Ageless were now taking his threat very seriously, and he dared not risk wasting the lives of any more of his men. He knew the engines would deal with the Ageless on his terms. Now he would prove that to them.

After a few forceful commands from Salus, the Cremators broke off their protests and sullenly obeyed. Salus was an excellent soldier, and Ethan had been instrumental in his promotion to Baron – despite the fact that Salus was not from the nobility. Ethan needed good officers, not fops from Bythe's court, and Salus had proven himself under Vale's command several times.

A cry went up from somewhere in the forward lines, and a commotion rippled through his men. Ethan strode forward, keen to see what was going on. He broke through his soldiers and caught sight of a lone rider galloping toward them. Commands were shouted. Helmsguard archers loaded bows and angled them toward the rider. He was dressed in green – clearly a scout of some kind – yet a bright blue saddlecloth had been draped over the horse. He was a messenger. Observing common protocols, he stopped a few hundred yards from the army. It was intended to show respect, but Ethan knew it was probably more from a fear of being riddled with arrows if he rode any closer.

A Helmsguard Squire approached Ethan and waited. After a moment's consideration, Ethan gave orders to retrieve the message and to allow the courier to return unharmed if he required no reply.

Ethan watched his men approach the rider. He was only mildly surprised when the courier wheeled his horse about and fled back toward Fairhaven as quickly as he had arrived. What message had he brought that expected no reply? Baron Salus escorted the Squire back to Ethan.

"What does it say?" Ethan asked.

"It's written in Outland script, sir," the Squire explained.

"Did you ask him to read it to you?" Ethan asked patiently. The Squire flushed and Salus rolled his eyes. Ethan extended his hand and the Squire hurriedly gave him the paper. As Ethan scanned the message, he absently considered that growing up as an educated noble had certain advantages in the military after all.

Commander Ethan.

All in Fairhaven know that you have come to conquer us. Know that you will fail in this, as you have failed before.

I know you have come to retrieve Vale and return her to Bythe the Deceiver. Know that you will also fail, as you have failed before.

I have placed Vale beyond your reach. You cannot have her.

We know of your black weapons and we are ready for them. The Ageless have found their weakness and stand ready to expose them for the world to see.

Leave now and I will grant you mercy. If you persist, my Ageless will destroy your weapons, and I will personally destroy you.

Captain Jason of Fairhaven.

Ethan stared at the paper, then carefully read it again. His officers glanced at each other uncertainly. The sheer audacity of the words caused a roil of emotions within Ethan.

Jason.

He remembered the young man. A brave cadet who had stood up to Imbatal. Now Jason was an uncertain Captain who had been effectively sidelined – Ethan's spy had kept him informed on this before losing contact a week ago.

He read the letter for the third time.

I have placed Vale beyond your reach. You cannot have her.

Cold outrage rose in his chest, blotting out reason and placing a human face on his enemy. *Jason. The upstart wants to compete with me?* He carefully folded the message and placed it in his belt-pouch.

"Sir?" Salus asked. "What does it say?"

"Nothing. It is a meaningless taunt, an empty threat."

His words were calm, but he felt his fury rising. *I have placed Vale beyond your reach. You cannot have her.* Arrogant upstart.

"Sir!" A shout of alarm seized Ethan's attention. A sweating man in black leather armor was rushing over to him, blood running from a cut on his forehead. Ethan recognized him as an Outrider – one of the Iron Union scouts. "Sir, we've sighted the enemy. They're lying in wait to ambush us."

"Where?"

"A mile east, there's a ridge and a treeline," he said, pointing off to their left. Ethan followed his direction and could see a smudge in the distance.

"They've been using some kind of magic, sir," the Outrider continued, clearly agitated. "We hadn't seen them at all. It wasn't until I lost sight of V'jara and went to find him that I got close enough to break the spell, and there's a whole unit of Ageless there waiting for us. They'd killed V'jara, sir, for getting too close, and they tried to get me too. I barely made it back!"

Clever. They were positioned out of Ethan's direct path, to the south of the city, and he would have marched his army straight past them, leaving him exposed to an ambush from behind.

"Well done, Outrider. Get yourself to a medic. We'll deal with the Ageless."

He wondered if Captain Jason was personally overseeing the trap. It would make sense. The cocky little upstart would be looking for glory. E'mar had assumed command of all defenses within the walls. This would be his only chance to prove himself. Suddenly the message made sense – it was the desperation of an inexperienced leader.

"Baron Salus!" Ethan commanded. "Rescind my previous order. Load the Godfire and prepare the engines for assault."

"Aye, sir. Same trajectory?" Salus answered.

"No." Ethan smiled. "Let's test the power of the Ageless, shall we?"

"Yes, sir." Salus saluted and left to prepare the attack.

Ethan looked back to the line of trees in the distance. Of course, he had known that Vale left Fairhaven. His spy had already informed him long ago. He knew he was not going to be able to capture her so easily. Ethan had a far different plan in mind.

And as part of this plan, he would take pleasure in showing Captain Jason of Fairhaven how meaningless and impotent his defiance was.

•   •   •

"They are coming," Kaler said.

Jason saw he was right. The massive engines were starting to turn as they lurched forward in their staccato rhythm. Two of Jason's engineers were moving the bodies of the unfortunate Helmsguard scout who had unwittingly volunteered his life as bait. Seven Violari stood silently in a semicircle behind him. Their hoods were raised to cover their features in darkness and their purple robes flowed with the unnatural movement that used to terrify him as a child.

"Have we lowered the shroud? Can they see us now?" Jason asked, earning a raised eyebrow from Kaler.

"I have lowered *my* shroud," Kaler replied, sounding almost offended at the lack of recognition of his work. "*They* are focused on maintaining the defense."

Jason glanced back toward the walls of Fairhaven. He could make out the soldiers watching along the battlements. Over the past week, Jason had refused an increasing number of requests from his lieutenants – and even from his enlisted men – to help him directly. While Jason had honored his promise to keep his army obedient to the Council, word had still managed to leak out somehow. It probably didn't help that Jason had needed to keep the Violari near him like a personal guard. Kaler had insisted that at least two of his sorcerers were always at Jason's side, and while he hated the idea, he also knew Kaler was right. E'mar and Morag would now be looking for any opportunity to quietly seize him while maintaining the peace. So he had politely, but firmly, refused the offers of assistance and ordered his men to obey the daily commands of E'mar.

Over the past week, Jason and Kaler had overseen the preparations while daily reports on Ethan's progress kept them motivated to prepare quickly. In the end, it hadn't been enough time to do half of what they wanted, but it might be enough. The biggest challenge had been keeping the Helmsguard Outriders away. If any of them reported the trap they had been preparing, then it would all be for nothing. Fortunately, there had been very few of them, and the Ageless knew how to find them. Once the Violari had ensured those initial Helmsguard scouts would never return, no more had come their way.

The minutes seemed to stretch on interminably while the distant machines lurched forward. Jason felt his heart hammering in his chest even as he tried to force himself to remain calm.

"You have done all you can, Jason," Kaler said in a quiet voice. "You have acted admirably. Whatever happens now is in the hands of the gods."

"I'm not sure threatening insurrection was admirable."

Kaler shrugged. "The times define the style of the leader. You are doing what needs to be done. Either way, it is no longer your decision. History will judge your actions now."

"Great, as if I didn't have enough pressure," Jason smiled.

"Shall I get E'mar to lead us instead, Captain?" Kaler replied with the faintest ghost of a smile on his lips.

Their banter was silenced by a flash from one of the towers.

"Look out," Jason warned.

The ball of fire screeched in the sky and landed no more than a few hundred feet from where they stood. Jason had to turn and shield his face as a hot cloud of dirt and rocks swept over him. Some of the Ageless shuffled in their trance and Kaler gave them a glance. Jason thought he could almost sense whatever it was that was passing between them. Seconds later, Kaler returned his attention to Jason. He suddenly looked tired.

"We cannot continue this for much longer," Kaler said.

Jason tried to measure the distance of the crater to where they stood. He calculated that they probably still had another few minutes, and every step closer increased his chances, but if he was wrong, then one hit from those engines would kill them all. He looked to Kaler for guidance, but Kaler was looking out at something in front of them.

"Jason, look," Kaler said. Jason turned to see two riders from the Iron Union approaching. They both stopped short of the crater and waited. Jason could see a blue sheet draped over the black armor of the horses.

"Messengers?" Jason asked Kaler.

Kaler nodded, scanning the riders with his Ageless eyes. "Not just messengers, I believe one of them is the commander. I can see the gold edging of his armor from here."

"Are you sure?" Jason asked.

Kaler nodded again. "Yes, he wears no helmet and I can see his face. I believe Commander Ethan has come to speak with you."

Jason looked at Kaler in disbelief. The letter was supposed to enrage Ethan, but now he stood patiently before them like he'd been invited over for tea. This was not part of the plan.

"Isn't he worried we could kill him?" Jason asked.

"Evidently not," Kaler answered.

Jason felt his confidence plummet. The truth was that he had no guaranteed means of killing Ethan at that moment, even if he wanted to. *Does Ethan know this? Has he seen right through my plan.* He glanced at the battlements of Fairhaven again and understood. "He's calling me out in front of my own men," Jason said grimly.

"You do not have to go," Kaler suggested.

"Yeah, I do," Jason sighed, gesturing to his soldiers. "Like you said, history is judging me now. I don't think history is going to judge me very well if I kill the noble Commander Ethan like a coward while he stands ready to talk."

"You would not be the first leader to do such a thing," Kaler pointed out.

Jason looked at him and for a moment. He actually considered the option before shaking his head. "No. It would only make matters worse. Do you think they'd just pack up and leave after I did something like that?"

Kaler nodded slightly. "You are probably correct. In which case, I will come with you. Ethan has brought an aide; you may bring me."

"Thank you," Jason said, then nodded to the Ageless. "Make sure they're ready for the signal. We may need to improvise."

Kaler glanced at his Violari for a moment, then they both stepped out onto the field and walked toward the waiting riders.

"I think the sorcerer has come close enough," Ethan called out as they approached.

"That's an impressive looking weapon," Jason said, nodding at the massive crossbow in the hands of the heavy-set soldier mounted alongside Ethan.

"Indeed, they are, aren't they?" Ethan replied as if he were making casual conversation with a fellow soldier. "You know, I probably shouldn't be telling you this, but very few of the Helmsguard are capable of even firing one of these. They're incredibly powerful. I tried once but I couldn't even hold it steady." He laughed to himself as he gestured to the hulking soldier alongside him. "But Draz here has figured out how to be a marksman. Don't know how he does it. They're designed to penetrate armor over long distances, to be honest I'm not sure what it'd do to a human body at this range, even to an Ageless body. I'm hoping we don't have to find out."

"Well, you didn't expect me to come out alone, did you?" Jason replied in the same casual manner, but to his ears it sounded very forced.

"Fair enough," Ethan replied, but Draz kept his crossbow trained on Kaler.

"You've done well for yourself, Jason," Ethan continued "The last time we met, you weren't even a full soldier. Now look at you – a captain."

"And you're now a commander," Jason answered in the same tone. "Is that why you're here? To compare our career progressions? Should we catch up and do this every three years?"

Ethan smiled. "That's clever. You're very young, aren't you?"

Jason shot him a hard look. "Don't patronize me. I'm not that much younger than you."

"That's true, but I've had a lot of training on how to lead. One of the perks of being born a noble is that they start to prepare you for that from an early age. You know all about that from your wife, don't you?"

The comment caught Jason off guard. He wasn't expecting Nadine to become part of the equation. He quickly tried to analyze the comment, eager to see if it had a deeper meaning or if it was just a distraction, but Ethan was already talking again.

"I've come to make you an offer, as one commander to another. I've come to ask you, just once, to lay down all arms and surrender to us. Your soldiers will be treated fairly as prisoners of the Iron Union, and your citizens will not be harmed under our occupation. I promise you that I will not make this offer again."

"I thought I made my position clear in my message," Jason answered.

Ethan continued smiling, but his eyes hardened. "Yes, I got your little message. But even so, I thought I'd give you one last chance to reconsider, now that you've seen what my engines can do up close." Ethan gestured to the smoldering crater a few feet beyond them.

"And like I said in my message, the Ageless can stop your machines."

This time Ethan laughed. "Come, Jason. We know that's just not true. If Veroulle and all his power couldn't stop us at Darcliff, what hope do you have? You should know, I'm told that you even saw the destruction yourself. Was it as impressive as I've been told?"

Jason couldn't hide the surprise that flashed onto his face. "How do you know this?" he blurted.

"I know a lot of things that I shouldn't know. For instance, I know that Vale isn't here, I know that she left some time ago, but I also know a more important fact – I know she's coming back."

"You're lying," Jason growled, suddenly firmly on the defensive and disliking every second of it. He had no idea what Ethan was trying to do, but his words were worrisome.

"No, I'm not. You have a traitor in your Council. Councilor Denethin has been keeping me informed on the comings and goings of your people for some time now. He's a bit of a weasel, I agree, but at least he's smart enough to see which way the wind is blowing."

Jason's head involuntarily swung back to Fairhaven, as if he could somehow warn them.

"I'm telling you this," Ethan continued, "because I want you to understand the futility of your stand here. I've managed to infiltrate your own Council and cripple them with bickering and infighting. You were right, Jason. I have to give you credit on that. The last thing they should be doing is hiding within those walls. That's exactly where I wanted them to be." He also looked at the walls of the city he was about to destroy, and his tone softened slightly. "Bureaucrats. I really don't know why they never seem to listen to reason. Maybe it's a universal curse, or maybe Bythe is just watching over me."

Jason tried to force the uncertainty from his expression as he turned back to Ethan. "So, why are you here? Are you going to try to kill me now?"

"No, Jason," Ethan said, removing the message from his belt pouch. He glanced down at the words, as if rekindling the anger. "I wanted to come and tell you this personally. I wanted to show you that you're not as clever as you think you are." He glanced over Jason's shoulder, at the semicircle of robed Ageless. "I wanted to kill your Ageless before your eyes, then send you back to your corrupt leaders to wait for us to tear your city down around you. You went out of your way to make this personal between us."

A knowing glance passed between them. *Vale.* Jason knew it had been a dangerous lever to pull, but he was committed now. "I'm sorry she never loved you," Jason said.

Dangerous. Stupid. What are you doing? He didn't know. He was improvising now, operating purely on instinct. It felt like the right thing to do, but he couldn't say why.

Fury shot across Ethan's face for a second, then it was gone. "Yes, well, we can see how she feels about you after today. I tell you what, why don't we test my plans against yours?" Ethan said matter-of-factly. He raised his hand skyward and at the signal, a ball of flame launched from one engine and seared toward them. Jason shouted a warning to the Ageless, but it was drowned out by the terrible shriek of the missile. It landed short of the Ageless, but the explosion knocked several of them to the ground.

"Oh dear, it looks like your shield isn't as strong as you hoped," Ethan mocked.

There was no shield, but Jason wasted no time explaining. He knew the injured Violari would have fallen out of the ritual and the illusion would start to collapse – earlier than he would have liked, but if the engines came any closer, the Violari would all be killed. Cracks began to appear in the ground around him as pieces of land collapsed inward.

Ethan glanced at the unstable ground and steadied his agitated horse. The cracks spread in disparate pockets across the field as the ground simply collapsed in places where the wounded Ageless had been holding them in place. Ethan peered into the nearest crack to see a rough trench, no more than six feet deep in places. He looked at Jason with a mixture of confusion and amusement.

"My gods, what did you hope to achieve by all this?" Ethan shook his head and raised his arm to signal a second shot.

Jason turned to Kaler and nodded. Kaler appeared to do nothing, yet Jason knew he was ordering the remaining Violari to stop supporting the land. Across the field, great cracks started to stretch out like fingers, revealing more of the same trenches as they cut a rough arc across the plain. It had taken Jason's engineers a week to dig as many of them as possible, while Kaler and his Violari had used their control over land to conceal them. It had taken an enormous amount of effort from both parties, but there was now a belt of uneven ground a hundred feet wide in most places.

Ethan watched the spreading trenches as they reached his army, causing a flurry of panic as men in armor leapt to safety while others fell into the shallow pits that opened under them. Within seconds, the chaos subsided, and the Helmsguard troops were rearranging themselves among the dust. The trenches had caused some chaos, and no doubt some injuries, but the troops were quickly recovering. Now, fields of trenches and broken ground stood revealed in a rough arc in front of Fairhaven.

Ethan looked at the scene with bewildered intensity – as if trying to decide whether these actions were madness or misunderstood genius. Jason held his breath. The next few moments were now truly in the hands of the gods.

Whether it had been the Helmsguard blindly executing Ethan's last order or just sheer misfortune – one of the engines fired.

It shuddered in its place and then fired its projectile skyward – violently lurching forward as the now-uneven ground gave way beneath it. The ball of fire spiraled up drunkenly and smashed into the ground close to the Helmsguard. The engine groaned terribly as its imbalanced bulk proved too much for the uneven legs to support and it started to list sideways.

"No..." Ethan whispered. The blood drained from his face as he watched the disaster unfold. The engine slowly tilted in place as if it were mocking the frantic efforts of the Cremators to save it, then it picked up momentum and started to topple onto its side. As it fell, the long turret clipped the second machine, smashing its tower and sending metal pieces flying into the air. There was a tremendous crash as the first tower collapsed in a cloud of boiling sulphur and gas, obscuring all visibility.

A mighty cheer rose from the battlements of Fairhaven, and Ethan's expression changed from shock to outright fury.

Kaler was far quicker than Ethan expected. Before the Helmsguard commander could react, Kaler extended his arm, and the mighty crossbow flew from the clutches of the distracted Draz. It sailed across the space between them and was snatched out of the air by the youthful Ageless. With surprising ease, Kaler steadied the weapon in his own hands and fired the bolt into Draz's chest. The stunned Helmsguard flew out of his saddle and landed in a clatter of metal plates some distance behind his startled horse.

Ethan quickly assessed the shift in fortunes and wheeled his horse around before Jason could react. Seconds later, he was cantering back toward his men, mocked by a second round of cheers from the battlements.

Jason turned to Kaler, who gave the crossbow a curious glance before dropping it to the ground. "Nice work," Jason said.

"I understand weapons and this one is crude," he answered dismissively, then nodded to the chaos in the distance. "That went unexpectedly well."

"Yeah, well, let's not pretend it all went according to plan. I think the gods were on our side today."

Jason had noticed the awkward locomotion of the engines at Darcliff, his plan had been to build a concealed network of broken ground that could mire the engines if he timed it right, but he had been willing to simply use the trenches as a barrier to slow them down if nothing else went his way. This outcome had been far better than anticipated. He had hoped his letter would draw Ethan into his trap, but he couldn't have expected to collapse the towers so impressively.

An officer is always under orders to accept the luck the gods choose to give him - both the good and the bad.

He smiled for a moment at Lewis's words, then remembered the Violari. It had certainly been luck. If the engines had fired a minute later, they would have probably been close enough to wipe out all of the Violari. As it was, some of them were injured, and he needed to get them back to the Temple. Jason made a mental note of his recklessness and promised he would find a way to punish himself for it later.

Jason had barely noticed the men in blue riding quickly to join them on the plain. He heard the congratulations and the cheers as the soldiers swept through to help the injured Ageless and protect their Captain.

Captain Jason of Fairhaven.

He had earned the title in front of them all. No one – not even E'mar – could strip it from him now. Jason ordered the men to return to Fairhaven with the casualties as quickly as possible, there was no telling what Ethan might try to do in reprisal, and this was no time for hubris. Within minutes, he was riding back through the western gate, the cheers of his men all but deafening him.

He glanced down at Lewis's golden ring on his finger and smiled.

CHAPTER 6

"At first, my work was beautiful. I created Anchorwatch with Basalt. I stood in the wastes while the Rak'Tunga built the Monuments of Parl at my side. I wanted to walk the breadth of this land and build wonders. I wanted to help everyone, both god and mortal. I never wanted it to end.

But it did end. It had to. The one thing the Forge has taught me is that all things must end and change. I wasn't ready for that. My brethren became bored. They started to compete, to bicker and to fight. Maelene was one of the worst. The other, of course, was Bythe.

It was then that I knew this world would not last."

~Nishindra the Crafter

Kardak lay before Valeyn, and for a moment, she was reminded of the time Vale had first seen the ramshackle town of Outpost. It gave her the same feeling – a rotting cancer spreading across the land. But while Outpost had been a diseased thing, oozing with life and decrepitude, Kardak was a cold corpse, long dead.

She'd heard stories of it when she was an officer in the Helmsguard, but they were just stories. The kind of things soldiers say to each other to amuse themselves on cold nights. It was said to be a twisted place, corrupted by its proximity to the Render and by the restless souls of the thousands of patients who had died there. Yvorre had been granted title over it as a reward for service to Bythe. Valeyn never dreamed that one day she would see it for herself.

It stretched out for miles in a seemingly random collection of buildings, annexes, and connecting pathways. A massive and sprawling complex nestled among the tranquility of nature. Or at least she could see that had been the intent of the followers of Romona, before they vanished along with their god.

Now, nature had tried to reclaim the offensive incursion upon her land, but even so, she hadn't been entirely successful. The gardens had given way to clumps of weeds – black and waist-high. It seemed that the corruption of the Render was somehow preventing the wild from fully reclaiming that which was rightfully hers.

The spaces around the buildings seemed arid and desolate and the trees inside the walls were leafless things, twisted and forbidding. Such a place would have terrified Elyn – it probably would have made Vale think twice about entering, but as she scanned the frightening visage, Valeyn harbored only one thought. *Naya is in there.*

She also knew that Exedor was in there, along with an untold number of his Faedes. The journey westward from Anchorwatch had been long, but it had also been hastened by the use of the river. Valeyn hadn't appreciated the mastery the Ageless held over the water. With her help, it had taken the Ageless less than a day to lash together a raft, but once it had been constructed it was Aleasea who had given them speed. Valeyn recalled her sitting silently in the middle of the platform, eyes closed in perfect concentration while the water around the raft bubbled and surged with a life of its own, throwing them down the river at almost dangerous speeds. Despite the apparent recklessness of the voyage, Ferehain had steered the vessel with ease, and Valeyn had come to understand this was something both he and Aleasea had done many times before. It was probably how they had managed to reach her at Anchorwatch so quickly. Water had always been a weakness of the Iron Union, it washed away the filth of the Faede – it was logical that the Ageless would hold such power over it.

But their journey had also been hastened by something else. Time itself seemed to be passing strangely the further south they travelled. The days seemed to stretch far longer than they should have, and Valeyn understood that the Render was already having its strange effect on them.

Days became weeks, and Valeyn lost track of how far they had come, but she knew they headed west, toward the twisting of the Render. The brown plains gave way to scrub and bushland with dense thickets and wild untrammeled hinterland. By some unknown sign, Aleasea had decided to abandon the raft, and the four of them then continued their journey toward Kardak on foot. It seemed that Yvorre, Ferehain, and Aleasea all knew exactly where they were going. No question of direction passed between them, and Valeyn soon gave up asking, resigning herself to simply following their lead.

Now Valeyn and Yvorre stood before the gates of the old institution. She wasn't completely comfortable with the plan, but it made sense. Exedor would expect only her and Yvorre, and they certainly couldn't afford to betray the presence of the two powerful Ageless so soon. They needed an advantage. The gods knew that – even with the help of Ferehain and Aleasea – the Faede were more than a match for her.

She glanced around the buildings one last time, hoping to find water – a canal or reservoir that she might be able to use to her advantage if the Faede overwhelmed her – not that she was even sure it would work. Yvorre seemed to read her thoughts.

"Do not waste your time, daughter. This is a trap, after all. Exedor will not make it that easy for us."

Valeyn glanced at her. "What do you suggest then?"

"I suggest we go in and avoid detection. If we fail, we will very quickly discover what he has planned for us."

With a deep inhalation, she broke the cover of the trees and walked toward the faded, white stone walls. Yvorre followed. Valeyn was surprised at how well the walls had stood up to the wearing of time and also at how moderately small they were. Given Kardak's reputation, she had expected the walls to be far better designed to keep people inside. As she approached them, she smiled ruefully – the walls only appeared small when viewed from the outside. From the other side, the ground sloped down as it approached the wall, so that twelve feet of stone loomed above anyone unfortunate enough to stand within the boundary. From outside, Kardak appeared to be nothing more than an open hospital, but from within it was a prison. It was a simple and cruel illusion.

She leapt the wall and easily landed on the ground far below. She then turned to help Yvorre, only to see that she was no longer there. With a glance to her right, Valeyn was surprised to find her mother also standing beside her at the foot of the wall.

Yvorre smiled, and the expression brought a touch of youth to her face. "Do not look so astounded, Daughter. My strength is returning."

Valeyn opened her mouth to ask the obvious questions, but Yvorre had already moved up the incline toward the complex. Pulling her grey traveling cloak around her, Valeyn followed as quietly as possible. She was grateful for the preparations Aleasea and Ferehain had made for her. While the cloak they had found at Anchorwatch held none of the properties of those worn by the Ageless, it was still better camouflage than the white shirt or pink dress that served as her alternatives.

They began slowly walking down the weed-choked pathway, scanning the pale buildings and their empty windows for any telltale flashes of red. The grounds were completely silent. Valeyn wondered if there was a single living creature within the walls of Kardak.

"Where do we start?" Valeyn whispered.

Yvorre pointed to a large, white building directly ahead of them. "That is the oldest building here. I feel it is the best place to begin while we remain undetected."

They approached the building, which seemed to have been the main structure when the hospital had first been built. It was an unassuming thing. A flat, rectangular building of white brick no more than three stories high but stretching back far into the grounds. There were windows in the façade, but they seemed too small and too far apart – the dirty white brick competing with them to block out any visual intrusion against what was within. The late afternoon sun cast a depressing glow across the building, as if the light itself were abandoning any hope of penetrating it. The wooden doors to the building – once grand – now stood partly unhinged and slightly ajar at the end of an entryway littered with dead leaves.

Valeyn glanced around again. Reassured that she could see no Faedes, she moved to the doors and slowly pressed one open. It relented under protest, and the grinding sound it made was like a siren to Valeyn's ears. She motioned for Yvorre to follow, and they quickly moved into the building. As soon as they were inside, she paused to let her eyes adjust to the dim light.

The interior was painted a pale shade of bluish-green everywhere she looked. The walls, ceiling, and floor were all stained with the same sickly color, now chipped and flaking with patches of pale brick peeking through. No doubt it had once been intended to be soothing, yet to her it seemed terrible, as if it were a silent admission that the world was now a sterile and artificial place and there was no returning to what had been normal. She stood in a foyer with a long hallway stretching before them. It seemed to run interminably with doors lining each side like guards. In the distance, a single window marked the end of the hall, and the deep orange light of the sunset glowed like a distant beacon. Yvorre placed a hand on Valeyn's shoulder.

"We should move," she said quietly.

They started to walk down the hallway, skirting the piles of rotting wood, detritus, and dried remains of animals that marked the decades of neglect and decay. The rooms to either side of the hallway were long abandoned, and Valeyn could only guess at what had transpired here. The followers of Romona had promised healing. What they had delivered here instead would never be fully known. She quickened her pace as she continued down the hall, confident that Naya wouldn't be here and conscious that Kardak was a vast place to search. They had almost reached the end of the hallway when she heard the groan of the wooden door behind her.

"Hide!" hissed Yvorre.

Instinctively, Valeyn threw herself toward the doorway on her left and landed within a small dark room. Yvorre had darted to the right and was now gone from sight. Valeyn looked about the empty room and – seeing no cover – moved behind the open door, squeezing herself between it and the wall. She waited.

Silence filled the empty spaces around her, and Valeyn tried to steady her breathing. Long moments passed and still there was no other sound.

Was it just the wind?

She shuffled within her cramped space to peer through the gap in the door frame, and when she managed to look through, she stifled a scream.

A figure in red filled her vision. It stood motionless and silent in the center of the hall, as if it were listening for her. Valeyn didn't breathe. It seemed to stand immobile for an eternity, then it slowly moved its head from left to right – as if it were smelling the stale air of the hallway. Valeyn continued to hold her breath. Somehow, she knew that she was strong, that she could probably kill this thing – she should kill this thing. She certainly shouldn't be afraid of it.

Yet she was.

She started to doubt the plan, and a sickly panic began to rise within her. This was a mistake. She had to get out. Her heart started to race as her mind began a frantic and uncontrolled reaction based on pure self-preservation. There was a window in the room. Valeyn calculated that if she slammed the door shut, she should be able to cross the room and throw herself out of the window before the Faede could react. Then she could hopefully run to the walls before it alerted the others. She could probably even draw them away from Yvorre. She involuntarily began the mental justifications that would turn cowardice into courage.

She had poised herself to push the door when she heard the rasping sound of the Faede's breathing from the hallway. She started and swung her head around, only to see the red figure shuffling further up the hall. It was moving away, seemingly convinced that it had lost the trail.

She watched the Faede reach the end of the hallway then turn left and vanish from her view. Then Valeyn breathed as well – it was shaky and uncertain. She moved out from behind the door and stood in the center of the room for a long time.

At some point, Yvorre had entered and stood beside her. Valeyn could feel her mother's eyes but didn't want to acknowledge them. She felt scared. She felt ashamed.

"We should go back, they already know we're here. This isn't going to work," Valeyn said.

Yvorre positioned herself so she now stood directly before her daughter.

"Look at me, Valeyn," she ordered, and the voice had a touch of steel.

Almost out of reflex, Valeyn looked into the stern face of her former mistress. When Yvorre spoke, it was the voice of her old teacher – stern, cold, instructive.

"Remember who you are. You are a Commander in the Iron Union. You are the heir to both Bythe and Maelene. You hold more power than any in this place. You will not be afraid."

The fear was starting to retreat with her teacher's words. Valeyn closed her eyes and forced herself into a series of deep, long breaths. She used Vale's childhood training to force herself to calm, like the unspoiled surface of a lake. Eventually, the fear settled and Valeyn opened her eyes. She knew Yvorre was right. They had to go on. Naya was somewhere in here.

"Thank you," Valeyn said.

Yvorre nodded dispassionately, yet Valeyn still caught a glimpse of feeling within her eyes. They walked out of the room and checked the hallway before continuing toward the dirt-stained window at its end. The hallway split into two opposite passageways leading toward two separate wings of the hospital. The orange glow of the afternoon sun smeared the dirt-caked window like blood, and beyond the glass, Valeyn could see the two long wings of the white building stretching into the distance. Her heart sank.

"This place is huge," Valeyn whispered. "It could take hours to search it, maybe days."

Yvorre nodded. "I can guide us through, but I had hoped we would have had more time before they discovered we were here."

Valeyn glanced out the window. "If the Faede already know we're here, there's no chance we're going to be able to wander around this place before they find us – even with you guiding us."

"There is one chance," Yvorre said. "You had a bond with her. You may be able to use this, given your current state."

Valeyn knew what Yvorre was referring to – the wound reopened by Yvorre and Exedor and the Faede. It was the uncertainty between Elyn and Vale that still persisted – even now. Perhaps it would always be there in some form? But along with it, came something else – that tendril of empathy. She had felt it when Yvorre intruded on her life, and it had grown after Exedor had stripped her of confidence.

"Do you think I can?" asked Valeyn.

"We have no choice."

Valeyn sighed. "What if they find me?"

Yvorre placed a hand on her arm. "I can help. I will not let them harm you."

It was risky and the thought of it made her stomach clench, but she knew she had to try. She closed her eyes again and reached within herself. She pushed past her bubbling fear and reached further to the pain within her. She could feel it now and this time, she latched onto it and dragged it to the surface. It hurt. It felt like old fears and forgotten nightmares suddenly remembered, but she refused to let it go. Grabbing hold of it firmly, she opened herself up to the surrounding hospital, listening for anything, searching for something pure.

Instantly, she felt polluted and wanted to recoil. The hospital reeked of corruption, death, and hate, whether it was from the Faede or Romona's work, she couldn't tell. Clenching her jaw, she refused to let go. She forced her feelings through the hallways, spread them like tree roots searching for water, but everything she touched felt soiled. The Faede were there, spread throughout the complex, and she knew they were searching for her. They turned toward her at her touch – as if the presence of such life and feeling were a beacon to their wrecked existence.

Stay calm, my child. It was the voice of Maelene – soft and warm in her head. It filled her with a sense of love. Valeyn turned her feelings back to the Faede, and, while their corruption felt like a stain, she also knew they couldn't find her. Her empathy was something they could no longer understand. She pushed through Kardak, searching for Naya. After long minutes, the sheer stink of the corruption seemed to cloud her mind. She wanted to push forward but it was becoming hard to breathe.

Relax, Valeyn. Return.

Valeyn gave one last surge toward a distant light, but it was impossible. She needed to pull herself back. As soon as Valeyn withdrew into her own body, she bent over double and was violently sick onto the pale green floor. The vomit spattered the dusty stone and yet it didn't seem out of place.

"Are you alright?" Yvorre asked.

Valeyn straightened and wiped her chin, pressing down the ugly feelings as she again forced herself to calm. There had been a faint call of purity in that sea of filth. Naya was alive.

"Did you see?" Valeyn asked.

Yvorre nodded in reply. "Yes, I know where he has taken her. Follow me."

Yvorre turned right – away from the direction the Faede had taken – and strode with purpose into the depths of the hospital. Valeyn followed. She knew the Faede were dispersed across Kardak and it was unlikely they would converge on her, even if they knew where she was. The sun was still lingering in the sky, but she was unsure how long it would last. It seemed that Kovalith's natural laws were very flexible this close to the Render. The passageway eventually led to a disused stairwell that ran both up- and downward to shadowed and unseen destinations. Here, Yvorre paused and looked at Valeyn with an unusual expression.

"I am not entirely sure what we will find down here. I do not know what Exedor has done, but this may be unpleasant for you."

Before Valeyn could reply, Yvorre mounted the downward steps and descended into the basement level of the institution.

Valeyn followed. When they reached the bottom, she realized the weak light of the sun would not follow them into the bowels of the building.

"Can you give us some light?" Valeyn asked.

"I can, but I will not," Yvorre answered. "Besides, I fear we will not need it."

Yvorre moved into the darkness without waiting for Valeyn to follow. After a moment's pause, Valeyn stepped cautiously into another long passageway that stretched into impenetrable blackness. The wall provided her only bearings, and she placed her hand on it constantly as she walked, as if it were a lifeline. After long moments of darkness, she heard something. It was a distant, rhythmic sound. A constant beat of something large and far away. It was strange and yet it reassured her that she was on the right path. Something was down there.

As she inched her way through the darkness toward the noise, she spied a distant light at the end of the corridor. It seemed to be pulsing, first brighter, then dimmer. Before long, Valeyn could make out the silhouette of Yvorre in front of her as they moved closer to the source.

They emerged into a large room, littered with an assortment of boxes and workbenches. Some of the boxes were still intact, others had been emptied and clearly looted, with various metal objects haphazardly thrown about the room. By the cleared dust on the equipment, she guessed this had happened recently. The benches were lined with tools and other strange instruments that Valeyn didn't recognize. The source of the light was a long, thin pipe that ran the length of the ceiling and continued through an alcove into the next room. It pulsed bright and dim in time with the slow, beating sound, which had become much louder now that she stood in the chamber.

"Where are we?" Valeyn asked.

"It is not important. Come, we have little time," Yvorre replied tersely and moved toward the archway that led to the next room.

There was something strangely familiar about the space, something familiar about the sound, that made her pause. Valeyn scanned the benches and the bizarre objects cast about her but couldn't place the feeling. The slow, rhythmic beating seemed to be coming from the room beyond the chamber, in the direction the lights were leading. Walking around the open boxes, she stepped over the rubbish and began to follow Yvorre.

There was a sound, and something moved in the darkness to her right. She spun, and Aleasea's kajik staves appeared in her hands as if from nowhere.

To her right was another smaller space set into the wall – almost an alcove – and something was moving within. The figure was jerking upright, over and over, as if it were pinned to a bed. After watching it move like this for a few moments, Valeyn slowly began to walk toward it. She used a Helmsguard combat stance, ready for something to launch at her at any moment. As she approached the alcove, she could see the figure was lying on a bench. It seemed to be trying to raise itself, but it couldn't. The distant beat rang in her ears as she neared the figure. The beat was echoed by another sound. A similar, quieter rhythm, but still keeping exact time with the louder sound. It was coming from the figure in front of her.

It was the sound of a clock.

Instinctively, she recoiled as the figure of Imbatal lurched upward at her from the bench – strange metallic hands grappling with the empty air in a vain attempt to throttle her. She stared at the creature in mute horror, unable to comprehend the tangible fact of its existence. It was almost identical to the monster that had almost killed Vale in Fairhaven, yet it was broken. Or rather – it was unfinished. Its head was covered in the same white cloth, betraying only two eye-slits, but its body was a grotesque assortment of twisted flesh and clockwork. Gears and pulleys seemed stitched crudely into the connective tissue of whatever the creature had originally been. While its arms were intact, Valeyn saw that it had no legs, and it lay on the table, pinned into place by a crude metal spike thrust through its abdomen. It seemed to recognize Valeyn. Or perhaps it was just conditioned to kill? Either way, it was moving mechanically in a constant loop, lurching up from the table toward her, only to fail and retreat before trying again.

"You do not need to see this," Yvorre's voice drifted over her shoulder. Valeyn almost couldn't hear it. "What is it doing here?" she asked.

"It shouldn't be here. This is Exedor's doing," Yvorre answered.

Valeyn tore her eyes away from the monster before her and looked at the room as if seeing it for the first time.

"This is where you...created Imbatal?"

"I did not create Imbatal," Yvorre admitted. "The truth is, I understood very little about the creature, despite my best efforts. What you see here is the work of my sister Romona, or of her followers no doubt. Their experiments were...cruel."

"They made Imbatal?"

A look of frustration swept Yvorre's face. "This is not the time for this conversation, Valeyn. I will answer your questions later, I promise you, but now we are in danger," she cast a glance at the figure thrashing on the bench before continuing, "possibly more danger than I foresaw."

Valeyn followed her gaze and then, her line of thought.

"What is Exedor doing here?"

"I do not know," Yvorre answered, then turned abruptly and walked toward the archway. Valeyn cast one more glance at the creature struggling to rise from the table and felt a brief stab of pity. She pushed it away fiercely and followed her mother. Yvorre had paused at the archway. Valeyn walked to join her but stopped a few feet short. She could now see the room beyond, and it momentarily stunned her.

The space was immense – carved out from the rock floor, it dropped beneath them for hundreds of feet. The area was spanned by dozens of metal walkways and stairs that crisscrossed the cavern in a complex and beautiful filigree. A giant clockwork mechanism filled the room. It arched

– stunning and elegant – with hundreds of rotating gears and arms all moving in unison. It glinted like gold in the pulsing light of the pipes which ran out from the machine in different directions. As the gears moved in flawless synchronicity, a unified sound echoed throughout the chamber in a cavernous, rhythmic beat. The pulsing light cast an eerie glow over the cavern which – combined with the beating heart of the machine – gave Valeyn the feeling the entire space was alive.

She forced herself out of her shock and stepped beside her mother. "What is this?" she asked.

"It is power, Valeyn." Yvorre said nothing more and moved carefully into the room.

As Valeyn followed, she realized she could hear a second sound over the beat of the clockwork engine. It was a male voice, coming from somewhere beneath them. Valeyn cautiously moved onto the metal walkway and peered over the edge. On a large, metal platform, a dozen feet below them, stood Exedor. He was pacing the scaffolding, still dressed elegantly in his black frock coat of shimmering silk and talking to someone in an extravagant fashion. Valeyn gave Yvorre an understanding glance, then slowly began moving toward the nearest steps.

"...worshipping Dazh or Nishindra, or whichever blasted god you people follow. What does it matter? Where are they now? Did they leap to your defense? Do you see the entire futility of how you are leading your lives?" Exedor turned and looked at someone blocked from Valeyn's vision by the walkway. "That's actually an interesting question. Which one was it, my dear? Which god did you follow?"

"Kalte," Naya replied.

Exedor shrugged. "Actually, no. I lied. That's not at all interesting." He smiled as he resumed pacing the platform. "Kalte...who was he again? The god of the dirt? No, that doesn't sound right. How did your people put it?"

"The god of bountiful harvest."

"Bountiful harvest?" Exedor stopped and faced Naya with a look of amusement. "That's really just another way of saying food, isn't it?" He paced again, now apparently talking to himself more than to Naya. "The god of *food*. Really? Of all the gods on offer, you all chose to line up behind him. That explains a lot."

All was silent for a moment, as Exedor leaned on the railing and seemed to stare into the depths of the cavern. Valeyn signaled for Yvorre to stay where she was, then started moving further down the steps, careful to keep the metal columns between her and Exedor as she closed in on him.

"They're not worth it, you know? None of them are," Exedor spoke to the blackness beneath him. "It's the one thing I've learned during all the years of my life, child. They are not worth your blind worship." He turned and gestured to the machine turning above them. "They created us just like they created these things. We're no different in their eyes. We're just tools, parts, machinery to be used and then discarded."

"And yet you still serve Bythe," Naya retorted. "How does that make you any better than us? In fact, if you believe this and yet still serve him, I think it makes you worse than us."

Exedor smiled at her defiance. "You have a sharp mind, my dear. I fear you were wasted in Tiet. You're absolutely correct. I would be a hypocrite and a fool if I stood before you as his blind servant, but I am none of those things. Would it surprise you to learn that there are many within the Iron Union who feel as I do? People who are no longer blind to the injustices that our Lord Bythe heaps upon his own people?" He walked over so that he stood closer to her. "No, there are many who feel as I do – many people in many positions throughout the entire Iron Union – and our numbers grow, slowly and quietly. Bythe is now the last true god on Kovalith, and though he thinks he has cemented his hold over the world, he is blind to see that the opposite is true. Never before have the gods been so vulnerable – now that there is only one of them left."

He paused and looked about the space theatrically before continuing in a conversational tone. "Actually, that's not entirely accurate, there are two others, but they're hardly a concern to me. I hope you don't mind me talking about you that way, Valeyn. I know it's very rude, but then, eavesdropping also shows incredibly poor manners."

Valeyn froze where she stood.

"You may come out from hiding, my dear. You too, Yvorre. We have so much to discuss."

Yvorre moved to the railing at the edge of the walkway, so that she peered down at him from above. "I have nothing that I wish to say to you,

Exedor. You were a disappointment to me before; you are an even greater disappointment to me now. You are meddling with power you do not understand. This is beyond you. This is arrogance."

Exedor's genuine laughter echoed off the walls of the cavernous space. "Arrogance? You dare lecture me on arrogance, *Mistress* Yvorre? You, who have always chased power at any cost, now admonish me for doing the same? I almost take that as high praise."

"What are you doing in Kardak?" Yvorre snapped.

"Lord Bythe bequeathed Kardak to me. It is mine now. The real question should be what are *you* doing in Kardak, but we all know the answer." He gestured to his left. "Come, my dear. We have visitors who have come a long way to see you. Don't be rude, come and greet them."

There was a sound of metal striking metal in an uneven and syncopated discord. Naya lurched into Valeyn's view.

Valeyn couldn't tell exactly what Exedor had done to her, but she was instantly reminded of the creature thrashing on the workbench. Her body looked wrong. Metal poles were lashed to the remains of her legs, causing her to walk with a terrible, lilted gait. Exedor's finishing touch had been to dress her again in a bright blue dress. The sick humor made the contrast of her deformity all the more terrible. A murderous rage filled Valeyn, and she resolved to end his life without another thought.

As if sensing her fury, Yvorre immediately spoke before Valeyn had a chance to act.

"And what do you gain by torturing this poor child? I have not taught you so poorly, so I can only surmise that you are doing this to provoke Valeyn into a rash action. Not very subtle, Exedor. You must do better."

Exedor's gloating smile slipped a fraction as he contended with the mind of his former mistress. "I was merely making good on my promise to restore her. I don't think either of you can judge me, given that you both left her behind."

"You bastard," Valeyn hissed. "You did this to her, not us."

Exedor turned to her and the smile renewed. "That is true, although it was only necessary because you put her in harm's way. There is a reason the gods never lived in fishing villages, Valeyn. That's like trying to carefully live among ants – no matter how much you may claim you care for them, it's only a matter of time before you crush innocents without even knowing you did it. At least those gods with a conscience had the decency to distance themselves from the ants they claimed to care about, but you? You lived among them. No, you hid behind them. You used them as shields."

Valeyn forced herself to stare at the metal grating of the steps before her. She could feel Exedor's words boring into her mind, even from that distance. He felt stronger somehow.

"You still have not answered me." Yvorre's voice seemed to pull his attention from her and the pressure was relieved. "What games do you play at here? Are you attempting to unlock Romona's secrets? I can assure you, that is no easy task. I tried for decades and failed."

"Yes, that is true." Exedor seemed to lose interest in Valeyn and now positioned himself on the platform to stare at Yvorre with a burning intensity. "And now I know the reason you failed, *Maelene*."

He spat the name as if it were a curse. Yvorre simply looked at him.

"I admit that I suspected, but I didn't know for certain until you betrayed yourself. Then so many things began to make sense to me. Your twisted hatred. Why you were never able to rise above your own spite and pettiness. Why you limited us, never gave us the opportunity to be all we needed to be."

"Is that what this is about?" Yvorre asked. "You want to get back at me because I was cruel to you? That is pettiness, Exedor. You were always searching for a mother to guide you. As I have always said, I am not that person."

Exedor's face hardened. "You're so smug, aren't you? All your kind are. So assured of your superiority over us. But you don't see your one failing, the one reason why you're all falling away from Kovalith, the reason you could never unlock Romona's secrets – you refuse to change."

Yvorre was silent, and a triumphant light flared in Exedor's eyes.

"You will not change, will you?" he continued. "When you enter Kovalith, you choose your mastery over one piece of the world and then that's it – you will never adapt again. That is why the work that Nishindra and Romona created here will always be foreign to you. You will never change yourself to understand it.

"We do not need change. We have power."

"No, you *had* power. You had power when you created this world and set the rules, but power is not static here. Maybe it is back where you come from, but here, power is fluid. It moves and turns like the wheels in a clock. It can be transferred."

Valeyn could hear a hidden meaning behind his words and a sense of danger grew within her.

Yvorre seemed to hear it too, and her voice became grave. "Exedor, tell me what you have done."

He turned with another theatrical flourish and paced around Naya. "I was always fascinated by this place, Maelene – the Great Institute of Kardak. Romona's followers built it to heal the sick, but we know now that they really wanted to understand death. So many people came into these walls, and so few left. Where did they go, Maelene?"

Yvorre refused to answer and the silence dragged out. Eventually, he continued. "And Nishindra the Crafter, what was his interest here?" He pointed at the massive clockwork structure above him. You never told me he had a hand in creating this place. What work was he undertaking?"

Again, Yvorre remained silent, but Valeyn sensed that she knew the answer.

"Never mind, once I was given this place as my reward, I set out to discover this for myself, and I did. Little Romona became obsessed with death, and also with the journey in between life and death. She wanted to understand the limits to which life could be extended, and Nishindra wanted to understand the reach of his crafts." Exedor paused and threw his arms wide as if to encompass the facility above them. "And here, in the Great Institute of Kardak, they worked together to meld their two ambitions."

"That is obvious," Yvorre said. "But Nishindra and Romona are both gone from this world, and they have taken their secrets with them. Their work cannot be unlocked."

"Not so!" declared Exedor. "What you mean to say is that *you* could not unlock the secrets of their work, but that is because you are inflexible. You refused to change, to adapt, but I have no such limitations, Maelene. Mortals are not afraid to change. That is how we will defeat you."

He walked over to the massive construct as it clicked with a booming, mechanical symphony of parts. "This is power. Pure, unfettered power, which Nishindra learned to transfer to flesh. To mortal flesh." He turned back to them, and when he did, Valeyn saw that he had unbuttoned his shirt. Stitched crudely into his navel was a brass socket, surrounded by bleeding and infected flesh. He touched it almost intimately and smiled at it. "You speak of my mother? I nurse at the teat of power now, Maelene. This legacy of the gods is my mother."

Valeyn had once witnessed Yvorre's fear, back in Sanctuary when Vale had summoned Bythe, so Valeyn had marked that look, which is peculiar to each person. As she glanced up at Yvorre, she sensed it again.

"Exedor, you fool," Yvorre said quietly. "You have no idea what you have done."

"Power can be transferred to flesh. You knew this. That's how you kept us in line with your enforcer, Imbatal. He was the same."

"That was never the same! This...what you have done is not meant to be," Yvorre's voice was heightened with anxiety.

"But you didn't create Imbatal. How do you know what is meant to be and what isn't? What is possible and what is not?"

Valeyn could sense that somewhere within Yvorre blossomed the heart of Maelene, and that Maelene was repulsed by the unnatural union of steel and flesh. The corruption of life by the perverse. She looked at Naya and saw the corruption he had also forced onto her, but now there was a look of hope within Naya's eyes that was heartbreaking, and Valeyn steeled herself because of it.

Valeyn knew the time had come. She leaped from the stairwell and crossed the landing in three powerful strides. Somewhere above her, Yvorre was shouting a warning, but it was too late. She was committed. Brandishing her kajik staves, she flew at Exedor as he turned to look at her. As their eyes met, her head seemed to split open and she was knocked from her trajectory, flung sideways across the platform like a limp doll. She hit the metal surface and pinwheeled across it toward the perilous ledge. Breath exploded from her lungs and all direction was lost to her. In a sickening moment, she realized the metal was no longer beneath her and that she was falling. Her mind registered that she had tumbled over the edge. She was falling. Slowly.

"Valeyn!" Ferehain's voice slapped her, and she looked up to see a figure in black reaching out. She reached back to him, but she seemed to be moving sluggishly – as if in a dream. Then she understood what was happening. Aleasea stood beyond Ferehain, her face set deep in concentration, slowing the effects of time in order to give Ferehain the opportunity to save her. Valeyn reached out and – with frustrating languor – slowly found Ferehain's iron grip.

Time instantly returned to normal, and Ferehain swung her unceremoniously back onto the platform, where she landed like a sack of rocks. Only then, did Valeyn understand the danger she had placed them in. Exedor was supposed to have been caught off guard by the two powerful Ageless – but the element of surprise had now been squandered by her reckless attack. Instead of ambushing Exedor, they had revealed themselves too early.

The look of surprise on Exedor's face was already vanishing, as he assessed the scene before him.

Ferehain wasted no time. Spinning in place, he thrust his arms forward and a violent crash echoed around the chamber. A shockwave of force slammed into Exedor and sent him crashing into the metal barrier at the far end of the platform. Ferehain moved to follow him but was stopped by two Faedes emerging from opposite ends of the platform.

"Aleasea, get the child," he ordered. "Valeyn!" He pointed to the Faede at his left, then leaped at the creature to his right.

Valeyn had completed very little combat training among the Violari at her time in Sanctuary, but she remembered enough of it to snap into action. In combat, the Ageless always acted as a tightly coordinated – almost choreographed – team, with each member performing a complementary role within the attacking unit. It was fluid and adaptive and completely alien to Vale's structured training within the Helmsguard. As Ferehain flew at his target, Valeyn lunged at hers with a supernatural gait. She had lost her kajik staves during the fall, but she still didn't hesitate. The Faede turned to meet her and was already opening its faceplate when she rammed into it. Using her left hand, she slammed the metal faceplate shut. Grabbing the robes of the creature with her right, she hauled it over her head, and flung the thrashing figure over the railing and into the blackness below.

She turned to see Ferehain battling with his own Faede. He moved with lightning speed, slashing metal blades back and forth over the body of the creature as it tried in vain to engage him. As she moved to help him, a cry from Aleasea caused her head to snap around.

Naya lay on the cold metal floor, alive but helpless. Aleasea knelt beside her, head in her hands. Exedor walked toward her, almost casually, his eyes red and his skin pale. He said something to Aleasea that was inaudible over the noise, but Valeyn knew what he was doing to her.

Valeyn rushed at Exedor again. His focus seemed to be on Aleasea, and with her increased speed, Valeyn knew that she could catch him off guard. But as she closed within a few feet, his head whipped in her direction. Again, her mind exploded in a sea of excruciating sparks. She stumbled and crashed to the floor, rolling over and over until she landed at his feet. Her mind was in agony. Whatever he had done to himself in the bowels of Kardak had increased his power immensely. Through the haze of pain, she now understood his confidence, and cursed her own stupidity.

"My sincere apologies, Valeyn," Exedor said with a smile. "I didn't mean to send you hurtling to your death. I'm afraid I don't yet know my own strength."

Exploiting his distraction, Aleasea quickly rose to her feet and lashed out with her foot, but her movements were groggy, almost drunken, and Exedor had time to step back before she struck. It almost certainly saved him. What would have been a crippling blow instead glanced off the metal plate in his stomach, sending the air out of him for a moment as he doubled over. His eyes widened in shock and anger as he understood what Aleasea had tried to do.

"You bitch!" he snarled and swung his backhanded fist at her cheek. It connected, and she fell to the floor with a cry of pain.

Nursing his stomach in a perverse way, his response was as fierce as a mother defending her unborn child. "Don't you dare try to take this from me!" He stepped over to where she lay and kicked her savagely in her own stomach. Aleasea cried out in agony. It was a terrible thing for Valeyn to hear.

It also brought Ferehain.

He swept onto Exedor like a black cloud. He was so swift and his actions so furious that even Valeyn's improved sight could barely keep up. Ferehain's blades slashed at Exedor's face in an almost elegant flourish, and he staggered backward with a scream. His gloved hand shot to cover his face and blood poured out between his fingers. Ferehain gave both Aleasea and Valeyn a quick glance to confirm they were alive, before returning his attention to Exedor. He raised his blades and advanced.

Exedor lifted his head to meet his executioner and Ferehain paused momentarily. Exedor's face was a lattice of savage red cuts. Blood streamed from eyes that were no longer there. Exedor moaned in an almost pitiful wail as he knelt on the platform.

Ferehain looked down at him as if unsure what to do next. Then his own face fell into an expression of sorrow. He stood there for a moment like a man caught between rage and heartbreak, then he looked around the cavern, an alien air of uncertainty upon him.

"Oh, Ferehain," mocked Exedor, a smile twisting his bleeding face. "Ferehain, the most legendary Ageless, who would have guessed this about you?"

"Stop this..." Ferehain murmured, but he did not move. Instead, he stood as if rooted to the spot.

"What have you done, Ferehain?" Exedor persisted, with his smooth voice made all the more horrific by the wreckage of his face.

"Get away from me," Ferehain growled, but he did little more. He seemed to be diverting all his strength to the sole act of standing.

"Your strength is just a ruse, isn't it? A shield behind which you truly cower because you simply cannot face the injustices of this world."

Exedor struggled to his feet and touched his bleeding eye sockets gingerly. "You've taken my sight," he commented, almost casually before he began walking to the corner of the platform where Naya lay. "Not long ago, that would have maimed me, but now I can see more with my mind than I ever could with my eyes."

Ferehain began visibly trembling as he struggled to remain on his feet. Valeyn thought she could see a tear run from the corner of his eye, but before she could be certain, Exedor raised the metal pole he had retrieved and struck Ferehain savagely across the head with it. He fell to the platform without a sound. Exedor stared down at him with sightless eyes. The grin that peeked through a curtain of blood had a slightly crazed tilt.

"But that doesn't mean I'm not going to miss them," he snarled as he began beating Ferehain's prone figure with the metal object. He swung the pole over and over, each strike breaking Ferehain's body with a terrible sound. Valeyn tried to struggle to her feet, but the platform seemed to be shifting under her. Exedor didn't even glance in her direction as he continued to beat Ferehain with a manic glee.

"Stop! Please!" The voice of Yvorre cut across the scene, and Exedor paused mid-strike. Breathing hard, he nonchalantly rested on the now-bloodied pole as if it were a cane, and removed a handkerchief from within his coat, casually mopping up sweat and blood from his brow before turning his ruined face toward Yvorre.

"I'm sorry, Mistress, did you speak?"

Yvorre wasn't looking at him. Instead, her eyes were fixed on Ferehain in pure horror. There was a compassion in that expression that Valeyn had never seen before, it reminded her of the woman she had met in the Arcadia – of Maelene.

"You do not need to kill him, Exedor. You have won," she called out to him with a voice that sounded close to breaking.

"Yes, I know. My victory was never in doubt. What you don't seem to understand is that I don't need him alive either. My orders were to retrieve your daughter. You are my unexpected bonus, but I certainly have no desire to take your employees back to the Ironhelm with us."

Two more Faedes had emerged on the walkways above Yvorre, blocking her exit. They were now all trapped.

"Please, do not kill them," Yvorre begged.

Exedor raised his eyebrows, which gave his blood-stained face an even more horrific look. "And so, it has finally happened. My former Mistress and great god Maelene begs before me. I thought I'd never see this day come. Now, sadly, I can't actually see it – thanks to him."

He gave Ferehain's body another brutal kick, but the figure in black made no sound.

Yvorre seemed to compose herself for a moment before continuing. "What is it that you want? Do you want to take us back to Bythe in chains?"

"That's what Bythe's Royal Inquisitor is bound to do," Exedor answered with a touch of sarcasm.

"And yet, what if I could offer you something more?"

Silence held in the cavern but for the sound of labored breathing of the Faede above them.

"Go on," Exedor said in a flat voice.

"I heard what you were saying earlier. You know I heard you. You are one of the Prodigals."

Exedor smiled. "The Prodigals are just a myth. They do not exist. If they did, then the Royal Inquisitor would seek out all of their members and have them tortured to reveal any conspirators against our great Lord Bythe."

Yvorre ignored the sarcasm and continued. "Why return us to Bythe and hand over power when you could take power for yourself? Keep us all here at Kardak, and I will be your servant. I will help guide you in your pursuits of Nishindra's secrets."

"You already admitted you couldn't unlock his secrets. I've done more with his power in three years than you accomplished in three decades. No, you're going to have to do much better than that."

"I offer you myself and my daughter in exchange for keeping us alive. What more can I offer you than that?"

Exedor fixed her with a sightless stare. "The Tower."

Yvorre hesitated for the briefest of moments before recovering, but it was a moment too long.

"I cannot help you. The Tower is sealed," she began.

"Don't lie to me," Exedor barked. "I can almost taste it. It hangs over all of you like a presence, from you most of all. You want nothing more than to flee there, and your daughter is the key. You will take me to The Tower, you will open it for me, and then I will keep your precious followers alive."

Yvorre stared back at him for a long time, as if countless options bounced back and forth in her mind, none of any use. She looked trapped.

"Very well, to Bythe it is," Exedor muttered and raised the metal bar over Ferehain's skull.

"Stop!" she cried. "I accept. Keep my Ageless alive, and I agree to your conditions."

"You will take me to The Tower?"

"Yes."

"You will unlock it for me?"

"Yes."

"And you will grant me access to the powers contained within?"

At this she paused, but finally relented. "Yes."

He considered her for a moment longer, clearly reading her with unnatural sight, then continued. "I don't believe you for a moment. I know that – even now – you scheme for an escape, but understand this. If I suspect the merest inkling of a trap, I will kill them both without hesitation, and that will be on your head. Do you understand?"

Yvorre nodded in silence as the two Faedes moved behind her. Four others now made their way onto the platform from somewhere unseen. Valeyn could only look up as one of them stopped before her.

"Then this has been a very productive day for all of us," Exedor gloated as the Faede reached up to open its faceplate. "Thank you all so much for accepting my invitation to visit. " Exedor said more but Valeyn couldn't hear. His words were obliterated by the horrific sound of a child's desperate scream.

CHAPTER 7

"Fairhaven was a small town when compared with the mighty fortresses of Darcliff and Stonekeep. It did not boast the skilled riders of Marfort nor the sailors of the Federacy – and yet Fairhaven was still considered the home of the Outland Alliance. There are many reasons for this strange contradiction, chief among these the fact that Maelene created Fairhaven and blessed it as her own sanctuary long before her war against Bythe. She created the Temple and established her Ageless over the course of centuries. When the Anarch began and the free colonies needed to defend themselves against Bythe, Fairhaven became central to the Outland Alliance. Although its strategic value may have diminished since Maelene's betrayal, the symbolism of Fairhaven remains. Should our home ever fall – the significance of such a loss would be recognized throughout all of Kovalith."

~Aleasea of the Ageless

"Marmaduke," Jason said with a grin, as he lay on the bed cradling his wife. "If it's a boy, we'll call him Marmaduke."

"Marmaduke?" Nadine answered, raising an eyebrow as she turned her face up to him.

"What's wrong with Marmaduke?" Jason asked with mock offense. "It has a...regal bearing to it." He gestured with his free hand, as if making a grand proclamation. "Lord Marmaduke the...First."

"We are not calling our son Marmaduke."

"Well, no, of course we aren't. That's because we're having a little girl, aren't we?" He leaned down to address Nadine's swollen belly directly.

"He's not listening to you," Nadine answered.

"Sure, she is." He placed his hand on her stomach and concentrated. "Hello, little Marmadine. Can you hear me?"

They both lay in silence for a moment, waiting for the tiny kicks that might signify approval in the mind of an eager parent.

"See? Nothing," said Nadine. "That's because he's a boy – a little Jason, all of my own."

"Well...maybe she just doesn't like the name."

"Oh no, that couldn't be it. Who wouldn't want to be called Marmadine?"

"Alright then..." Jason said before lapsing into thought. "I know. Morag!"

"Oh gods, do you hate our child that much?" Nadine laughed.

He kissed Nadine on the forehead. "Don't even joke about that," he chided softly. "Nothing can stop me from loving you both. It doesn't matter what we call him...or her."

"I think you're right though," Nadine admitted after a moment. "I haven't told you – I wanted it to be a surprise – but I've had a feeling she's a little girl."

"Really?" Jason asked, suddenly excited. "Can women tell?"

Nadine laughed again. "No, silly. We're not sorcerers, but sometimes mothers get a feeling, and I think I'm getting one about her." She patted her stomach.

"A girl," Jason repeated as a million possibilities now opened before him.

"If she is a girl," Nadine said tentatively, "what if we called her Elyn?"

Jason looked at Nadine for a moment, then nodded. "Yes, I'd like that."

Nadine smiled. "Me too."

There was a knock on the door, and Jason gently disengaged himself from his wife. "Time to go," he said, as he crossed to the cupboard and hurriedly threw on his blue uniform. It was strange how quickly they had become used to their new home over the past few weeks. It was the best gift his father could have given them.

Nadine struggled to sit up and swung her feet over the bed, earning a look from her husband.

"Hey, why don't you go back to sleep? You don't have to be at the Council for another couple of hours. I should be able to come back and help you by then."

Nadine waved him away. "Don't be silly. We both have a city to defend. I can take care of myself."

"Alright," Jason kissed her goodbye, then descended the stairs. As soon as he left their room, the pressures of his command seemed to descend on him from nowhere. It was as if her very presence had been keeping them at bay, and now that she was gone, the anxieties flooded in like ants finding unguarded sugar.

Were the night's missions successful? Were there more casualties while you lay there in your wife's arms? What about today? Are you ready?

He pushed them away, as he always did, reminding himself that he needed this time with his wife. If he didn't find a few hours of peace in her arms whenever he could, he just didn't think he'd make it through.

He was greeted at the door by two lieutenants who gave him a morning briefing as they walked to the base – something that had become a ritual over the past few weeks. Jason was grateful he no longer needed the Violari to guard him night and day now that he'd truly won his leadership. His first meeting was in his office with Sedren to review progress of the additional excavations Jason had ordered. The rough arc of ditches had now been extended into a far more elaborate web of trenches surrounding much of the southeastern outlook of Fairhaven, although Sedren admitted they had now dug as much as they dared. Even with the protection of the army, the Helmsguard had started refining techniques of raining arrows into the trenches as the engineers worked. In the past week, Jason had ordered them to work under the cover of night, but now even this was proving to be too dangerous – this morning Sedren reported that five engineers had fallen the previous evening.

The next meeting was to coordinate the day's orders with his lieutenants and with Kaler. Over the past three weeks, Jason had been relentless with his attacks on Ethan's men. Every day, his army had harried and hampered the efforts of the Helmsguard as they tried to repair their engines. One of the engines – the one that had fallen so spectacularly –

appeared to have been smashed beyond repair, but Ethan had been using parts from the wreckage to restore the second one. Jason was determined he would not succeed.

They reviewed the efforts of the previous day. Lieutenant Shane delivered his report. He was a brawny young man whom Jason remembered well as a fairly ruthless bully from his youth. Jason had bested him in the tournament at the Wellspring Festival, causing Shane to treat him very differently afterward. Those childish days – only a few years past – seemed long behind them now. This morning the weary young man was delivering his report on the night raids Jason had ordered. They had not gone as well this time.

"They were ready for us, sir," Shane was finishing. "Units Fey and Josslyn couldn't even pass the fourth trench before they were pinned down by archers. We lost nine soldiers, with twelve more injured. I ordered them back. I had no choice, sir."

Jason nodded. "You did the right thing, Shane. We don't have that many soldiers to spare."

"And the flanking party?" Jason turned to Lieutenant Geordine, a young woman with a hard face. Over the past week, she had been responsible for leading a unit of riders to sweep into the enemy camp at night. The ploy was to find an unguarded section of the campsite, ride in hard, and cause as much damage to the Helmsguard as was humanly possible before retreating into the night after a few minutes. It had been extremely effective, until now.

"Sorry, sir," she replied, shaking her head. "They have Outriders positioned in the field, and they're learning how to spot us better every night. We were out there almost until dawn. When I finally tried a run, the horns were blaring before we were within a hundred feet of them. We disengaged."

"So, it would seem that our raids have become less effective over time," said Kaler.

Jason sighed and leaned over the map as if it would offer up an alternative solution. "What about the supply lines?" he asked Kaler.

"Whatever it is that the Helmsguard bring from the Iron Union, they are guarding it well. We think it almost certainly fuels the engines. They have a supply train that is now roughly two days to the south. My brethren have been able to slow their progress, but we can do little more. It is well guarded."

Jason turned to the window and thought deeply for a moment. When he spoke, he tried to make his voice as passionless as possible.

"What would it cost us if we wanted to destroy that supply train, Kaler?"

"I am not certain the Violari could succeed, Captain, and if we did, the price would be high," Kaler replied in an equally dispassionate tone.

"If that supply train is fueling the engines, then the price of doing nothing could be even higher. If they repair their machine and get it fully armed, we're in trouble. These trenches will slow them down, but they won't stop them," said Jason.

"Those engines are powerful, but they seem to be a lot of work," said Lieutenant Geordine. "If we could cut off their supply, then perhaps the Helmsguard might find they're more trouble than they're worth?"

Kaler nodded. "I will work with the lieutenants on a plan."

"Good. Make sure you have a draft ready for me by sundown. That's it everyone, get to it," Jason ordered. All three officers saluted, then left his office.

He slumped into his chair and rubbed the bridge of his nose. This was not the news he wanted. He'd hoped the raids of the past few weeks would hamper the Helmsguard to the point they would be forced to retreat. They might even force the Helmsguard into abandoning the wreckage of their engine for the Ageless to study. Unfortunately, a stalemate now seemed to be looming between Jason and Ethan – each could prevent the other from advancing, but neither could make the other retreat. The last thing he wanted to do was to put Kaler's Violari in danger, but if Ethan managed to get his engine operating again, the results would be catastrophic.

There was a rap on his door and a messenger hurriedly entered. "Beggin' your pardon, sir," he said, breathlessly.

"What is it?" Jason asked, irritated at the intrusion.

"War Council, sir. They've got an emissary from the enemy. They asked for you to come immediately."

"A messenger? What did he say?"

"Don't know, sir. Councilor Morag just told me to come get you."

Jason wasted no more time. He grabbed his Captain's dress-jacket, hurriedly buttoning it up as he rushed down the steps, following the messenger out of the base. He had found that wearing the trappings of a captain made people respond to him like one – or maybe it was just in his head. Either way, he'd decided he was no longer seeking acceptance of people. He was a leader. It was time to dress accordingly.

He noticed the heavy presence of guards outside the chambers before he even entered. Once inside, he saw no fewer than twelve armed men inside the foyer. They all snapped to attention when he entered but he barely noticed as he rushed into the Council chamber, where another dozen men stood guard around a figure in black iron armor.

The need for a War Council had required some changes to the Council chambers. The rows of seats before the raised stage had all been cleared, replaced with a large, circular table on which lay several maps. Any questions over Jason's leadership of the army had been annihilated after his victory against Ethan. Even the Council had been forced to concede that his insubordination – while still completely unacceptable – must be balanced alongside his outstanding achievement. And as such, his formal disciplinary review would be suspended until the invasion was repelled. Jason had discovered that his voice at the War Council was suddenly the strongest in the room. Even E'mar quietly deferred to Jason's opinion whenever there were conflicting views on an issue.

For his part, Jason had been gracious in accepting the belated recognition, not wishing to punish his opponents or to hold grudges – he had simply set about reorganizing the War Council into a more effective group. E'mar retained his political leadership and continued to oversee the defenses within the walls, but Jason now enjoyed unquestioned authority over Fairhaven's army – and he used it.

Most of the Council were already present. Jason immediately caught sight of Nadine, as well as her father, Morag, and E'mar. He bristled as he caught sight of Denethin, but before he could say anything, the man in the black armor stopped talking and turned to face him. As soon as the soldier looked at Jason he seemed to act as if the other Councilors had suddenly vanished. He stood to attention and stuck a mailed fist across his chest in salute.

"Captain Jason of Fairhaven. I am Squire Calix of Lord Bythe's Fifth Battalion. The Helmsguard recognize you as the Respected Enemy, and I extend all rights and courtesies of parlay on behalf of my leader, Commander Ethan of Mac-Soldai."

Jason was surprised at the gesture and gave an awkward nod. "As you were...soldier," he answered. He'd barely had time to get used to ordering his own men. He had no idea what the protocol was for enemy officers.

"The courier has brought us a message. It would seem that Commander Ethan would like to negotiate," said Paeter.

"Negotiate?" Jason repeated.

"Correct, sir," Squire Calix answered. "My commander proposes he meet with you at noon tomorrow, in neutral territory in the field. He wishes to discuss terms for an armistice."

"An armistice?" Jason asked with suspicion. "Does Commander Ethan have the authority to negotiate a truce for the Iron Union?"

"Not for the Iron Union, Captain, but Commander Ethan wishes to open negotiations between our two armies."

"To what end?" Jason questioned.

"We wish to discuss potential terms of your surrender, or at the very least, terms for evacuating any civilians who may be caught up in any ongoing hostilities between our two forces."

Jason glanced at the other members of the Council. They seemed to be waiting for his opinion before voicing their own.

"When I met Commander Ethan on the field, he made it very clear to me that he would not repeat any offer of negotiation. What's changed?"

The soldier looked uncomfortable. "Sir, I haven't been given any instructions on that topic."

Jason studied the man intensely. While an offer of a brief truce with the Iron Union wasn't unheard of – there had been a few of them throughout the fifty years of the Anarch and during the battles that raged afterward – this still didn't feel right. Ethan was a proud man and Jason had baited him on a personal level; he had even admitted that Jason's insult had hit a nerve. On top of that, Jason had won a victory that had been so unexpected – even to him – that it must have been humiliating to Ethan.

And now he wants to talk?

"No," Jason replied slowly. "I don't think so. You may tell Commander Ethan that his offer is declined. I simply don't trust him."

"Captain Jason, please be reasonable. They are offering us peace," Denethin said with an impetuous tone.

"I don't want to hear a word from you, Denethin!" Jason spat. It infuriated him that he was still on the Council, despite Ethan's admission that he was their spy. Denethin had denied it, of course, and Jason had no hard evidence beyond Ethan's accusation. So Denethin had managed to convince the Council that Ethan had been lying, that it was clearly a trick intended to sow doubt within the leadership of Fairhaven. Even Jason had been forced to concede this was possible, though he didn't agree, and Denethin was permitted to remain in his position – albeit with considerably less power.

"Captain, please. I think we should discuss this," E'mar interjected. Jason sighed and motioned to his guards, instructing them to move the messenger outside. Once the doors were closed, Jason turned back to the Council.

"What is it you want to discuss, E'mar?" Jason asked.

"Councilor Denethin has a point. Perhaps we should not dismiss this opportunity."

"I don't trust Ethan, and I certainly don't trust him," Jason growled, pointing at Denethin.

"Captain, how many times are we going to go over this? I am not a traitor. Please believe me," Denethin begged.

"Either way, this is not about Denethin," said Morag. "The messenger has a point. We have hundreds of people who want to flee and no means to help them. We've heard nothing from the west. For all we know, the Iron Union has already conquered everything that side of the mountains. We need to provide our people with safety. There is no harm in hearing what Commander Ethan has to say to us."

"Captain Jason," Paeter asked, "do we have a plan to drive him off our southern plains?"

Jason shook his head and moved to the maps on the large table. "I admit, the raids aren't as effective now as they had been, but we're still working on several ideas." He pointed to a dotted line curving around the mountain range north of the Great Southern Wastes. "We know this is their supply line for the engines – they need this to fuel them. The train is heavily guarded, but if we find a way to knock it out, that engine is useless. Ethan doesn't have enough men to attack Fairhaven directly, his whole strategy was based on these machines. If we cripple them, then he'll have no choice but to retreat."

"That sounds like a risk. Would it hurt us to speak to Ethan in any case? Maybe we need a backup plan," Paeter said.

"We're still working on the strategy for this," Jason answered. "I can't make any promises that it's going to work, but it's the best option we've got."

"My Entarion tell me that this supply train is very well defended and that any assault on it will be costly," E'mar observed, measuring Jason with a cool gaze.

"It might be costly, but we're out of options. I'll review the plans this evening and make a decision," Jason snapped in a tone that left no uncertainty about his new authority over the army.

"We now have options, Captain," said Denethin. "I believe we should negotiate with the Commander. There's no harm."

"No," Jason said firmly. "I won't do it. I've made my decision."

"Then I will go instead, Captain," E'mar replied.

"Out of the question," Jason started but Morag cut him off.

"You do not give orders to the Council, Jason. I have discussed this with my fellow Councilors, and we agree that this offer should be given due consideration," Morag said.

Jason shook his head in frustration. "You can't trust him. What if it's a trap?"

"I will go to protect the Council," E'mar replied, "and I will take a retinue of my best Entarion. I will insist on an even number of delegates. Under those circumstances, no Helmsguard will be a match for us."

"Your assistance will not be needed, Captain," Denethin said with a slight sneer in his tone.

Jason opened his mouth to give Denethin a very colorful piece of his mind but Paeter spoke first.

"That's enough, Denethin!" Anger flashed in the older man's eyes as he spoke. He turned to Jason and his expression softened. "I'll go with them also. Don't worry. I'll make sure that no one makes a decision until we've discussed it in front of the whole Council."

"Father, no!" Nadine cried.

"Do not worry, Councilor Nadine," E'mar reassured her. "Your father will be well protected. I will ensure no harm comes to him."

"Alright, I'll go as well!" Jason snapped.

"I do not think that is wise. Your animosity toward one another may pollute the negotiations, and my Entarion will provide all the protection the Council needs," said E'mar.

"Perhaps it might be best if Ethan negotiates with us, Jason," said Paeter. "As you've told us, there's already a fair bit of bad blood between the two of you. Why don't you let us play as the good negotiators and you can be the threat?"

There was no doubt Paeter was a smooth diplomat, which was the reason he had continued to lead the Council. Jason met the eyes of his wife, then reluctantly nodded.

"Denethin stays here," Jason added, glowering at the man. "I don't want him anywhere near the enemy."

"That is logical under the circumstances," E'mar agreed.

Denethin looked hurt and opened his mouth to object but changed his mind after a sharp look from Paeter. After some final arrangements, the meeting dissolved, and Morag left to relay the message to the waiting squire. Jason approached Nadine and Paeter.

"Father, please. Why are you putting yourself in this position? I don't like it," said Nadine.

Paeter smiled and placed a hand on her shoulder. "I need you to focus on one thing and one thing only." He placed a hand on his daughter's swollen belly. "I want to see my grandchild fit and healthy, not worried sick because you've been teaching him bad habits before he's even born...or she's even born." He corrected himself.

"She's right, Paeter," Jason said. "Let me come, or at least send some of my own men."

Paeter looked over his shoulder to ensure they weren't overheard, then turned back to Jason. "They've already decided they don't want you anywhere near this. You've cost them a lot of pride, and they want to try and claim that back." Jason started to protest but he was forestalled by

Paeter's raised palms. "It's alright, I can be your eyes and ears. The best way you can help me is to work on this plan. We can't negotiate with Bythe's people. We need to push them back to the west." He looked down at Nadine then back at Jason. "I can't have my grandchild grow up in an occupied city. I wouldn't accept it in Outpost. I will not accept it here. Please, Jason, find a way."

Jason met Paeter's eyes and nodded. He hoped his eyes expressed confidence to his father-in-law. He hoped they didn't betray the images of flames that were always at the edge of his mind.

.   •   •

By the time Jason arrived back at his office, it was almost sunset. He rushed in, fiercely unbuttoning his jacket against the heat of the roaring fireplace. As he turned to hang it on the stand, he was startled by Kaler's voice.

"I understand we have been contacted by the Helmsguard?"

Jason turned to see Kaler seated at his table, alongside Lieutenants Shane and Geordine. He had almost forgotten he asked for a briefing on the plan.

"Yes," Jason replied. "A messenger arrived this morning. They want to discuss terms for evacuating civilians before they recommence their attack."

"Sounds like they're just trying different ways to threaten us," said Shane.

Jason smiled. Shane's simple and direct view of life was one of the reasons Jason had promoted him. He needed people who didn't overthink things the way he did.

"That's possible," answered Jason. "The Council and some of the Entarion are going to meet them at midday tomorrow. They'll hear what they have to say."

"You're not going?" Geordine asked.

"No, they think I might upset the delicate negotiations."

Shane grunted a laugh. "Yeah, you might remind Ethan how you pulled his pants down in front of his own men."

Geordine laughed as well and Jason grinned at them both. "Yes, well maybe they have a point, I'm not sure I could keep my mouth shut. Probably better we leave this to more sophisticated people than us."

Kaler rose from the table and walked to the window, deep in thought. The soldiers watched him in an awkward silence.

"What is it, Kaler?" Jason asked.

"I am not certain," Kaler responded vaguely, "but I am not comfortable with this."

"Neither was I, but the Council have made up their mind," said Jason.

Kaler turned back to face them with the look of someone trying to solve a complex puzzle. "You know I was the student of Ferehain. What you may not know is that Ferehain was present at the Fall of Maelene. He taught me the lessons of Bythe's treachery, which he had experienced firsthand."

Kaler was referring to Bythe's betrayal of Maelene at Klyph, a tragedy taught to every child in Fairhaven, although Jason knew nobody who had seen it personally.

"Bythe made a similar offering to Maelene, but he concealed his soldiers in the surrounding hills. By the time Ferehain realized the deception, it was too late. I wonder if Commander Ethan is now following the example of his master?"

"E'mar is taking a contingent of the Entarion with him. Hopefully, they should be able to spot a trap," said Jason.

Kaler nodded. "We may even be able to use this to our advantage."

"How so?" asked Jason.

"We've been working on a plan, sir," Shane added. "We think there's a way that we can lead a few units of infantry 'round the southeast to flank the shipment. If we have support from the Violari, we stand a decent chance of being able to pull this off."

"And if the Helmsguard are preoccupied with the meeting tomorrow, that may present an ideal opportunity to strike," Geordine finished, looking at Kaler.

"Can we do this in time?" Jason asked as a note of excitement crept into his voice.

"If we work through the night, we might," Kaler agreed. "If E'mar can keep the Helmsguard focused on him, then this could turn into a blessing for us."

"Then let's make sure he's ready to help," Jason said sitting at the table and giving the maps his full attention. "Show me everything, then we'll coordinate with E'mar later tonight."

Jason tried to force down the sense of hope surging in his chest as Shane started to walk him through the plan.

CHAPTER 8

"The Render was the place where the gods drafted the world. Much that we take for granted is the product of toil within that strange land. The water that gives life and runs through our land is the fruit of our Blessed Mother Maelene, and Pia – goddess of the oceans and sister of Bythe. Together, they worked their energies to provide the endless supply of water from the oceans and mountains. There are legends they tried to create an endless cycle of water from the heavens, however such miracles are even beyond the reaches of gods."

~Aleasea of the Ageless

The utter desolation of the Render stretched in all directions.

The sun – now a giant and shimmering red ball – hung in the dark grey sky tenuously, as if it might break free and fall into the land at any moment. Although it hadn't moved from its position directly above them for countless days, Valeyn still glanced up at it from time to time to reassure herself it was still there.

Days. The very concept seemed alien now. How can time be measured when the sun itself refuses to move? Time and every other perception seemed distorted in this place. It was an unnatural feeling and it filled Valeyn with disgust – as if she were in a place forbidden to her.

Another hot blast of wind assailed her face, forcing her to cover her mouth with her cloak. This time it came from the south, directly ahead of her, but she'd become used to the random nature of the elements in this place. There was no logic to the eddies of the wind, no consistency to its fury or potency. The weather changed with random frequency, and Valeyn even wondered if she might finally see water falling from the sky as she had heard from the legends. The land itself was now little more than broken rock lined with gigantic cracks that could swallow unwary horses – at least that's what it looked like in this section of the Render. Sometime ago they had been forcing their way through a desert before it ended against rolling green fields. But Valeyn had abandoned any hope of applying reasoning to the land. There was simply no stability to be found here.

She stumbled over a gap in the rocks, and the cart she was pulling shuddered with the jolt. She looked back as the wind buffeted her head, peering through the violent air to make sure Naya was alright. The young girl smiled weakly and gave a small wave to indicate that she was. Valeyn's strength aside, she was now the only member of the party capable of pulling the infirmed girl. Ferehain walked alongside her, still partially supported by Aleasea from time to time, but strong enough to walk unaided for the most part. His recovery had been difficult, and for a time, it seemed that Exedor would leave him imprisoned in Kardak, but Yvorre had ensured he would not be abandoned. In the days following his brutal beating, Yvorre had knelt beside him with her eyes closed, willing the natural energies of the Forge into his broken body, and within a week, Ferehain had been capable of free movement again.

Valeyn knew that Exedor's concession had been out of necessity more than compassion. He knew that Ferehain and Aleasea were his only leverage over Yvorre, and exhausting half of that leverage before even leaving Kardak was not wise. He would need every bargaining chip at his disposal when they finally reached The Tower, so he had waited until Ferehain was fit enough to travel – but not fit enough to fight – before ordering their departure.

Yvorre looked almost protective as she walked alongside the cart that held Naya. She looked up as Valeyn glanced back, and their eyes met for a moment. Yvorre's eyes were no longer sunken and hollow. They were the bright and clear blue eyes Valeyn remembered from the Arcadia. Of all that had happened over the past several weeks, Yvorre's transformation had been the greatest. The matted grey hair had slowly turned into flowing gold. Her weathered and lined face was now all but completed erased, leaving behind a woman of radiant beauty. Looking at her, Valeyn understood there was now little left of the woman named Yvorre. The name no longer seemed fitting. She was looking into the eyes of Maelene.

"You should be watching where you step, Valeyn. I don't want you falling into a crevice before we reach The Tower. What good would that do us?" Exedor's voice drifted back to her.

Valeyn knew he wasn't looking in her direction; he didn't need to. She didn't understand how his new sight worked, or what its limitations might be, but it was certainly a formidable skill. Valeyn looked at her mother for a moment longer before returning her attention to the perilous path before her. Exedor was striding confidently ahead of her, seemingly oblivious to her actions.

Six of the Faede walked at the edge of the party like an honor guard – although honor was the last thing these creatures seemed capable of. One of the Faede was permanently assigned to each of them, and every time they stopped to rest, that Faede would perform its work. It seemed that Exedor's instructions were to keep them weak, but not incapacitated, since they needed enough strength to make the arduous journey through the Render. So, while Valeyn had strength enough to pull Naya's cart, she was far from capable of attacking any of the Faede, let alone Exedor.

They journeyed like that for more uncountable hours before Exedor called a halt. Like so many times before, Valeyn, Aleasea, Ferehain, and Maelene set about making a camp while the Faede surrounded them watchfully.

"I don't suppose you could help this time?" Naya asked a red-cloaked figure as she struggled off the cart. Receiving no reply, she set about making a fire using wood they had collected along the way. Her walking irons were a grotesque mockery of her former limbs, but they were crudely functional enough to enable basic duties, so she had decided to leave them attached.

Ferehain slumped to the ground with a soft groan, causing Aleasea to bend over him, deep concern etched into her face. She murmured to him softly, as she began the futile attempt of making him comfortable on the unforgiving rock. Valeyn knew her well enough now to understand this was no mere act of compassion between comrades – this was something far deeper.

"She once cared for him passionately," Maelene's voice, now soft and bereft of Yvorre's former bitterness, interrupted her thoughts. "I believe she always will."

They built the fire in silence and ate a sparse meal of bread next to the lukewarm, blue flame that the Render had chosen to give them this time. Fire was like everything else in the Render, imperfect and inconsistent. Like draft copies of a final painting, the Render was usually a shallow approximation of what reality would finally be.

Exedor did not eat. Instead, he sat, as he always did, on a stool common among the travelling Helmsguard, and corrupted himself with the vile workings of Kardak. Valeyn would watch as one of the Faede brought his strange clockwork mechanism and set it in front of Exedor, before he set to work on it, adjusting it, winding it, and finally pouring a strange draught of his own blood mixed with other abominations into its mechanisms. Then he connected the machine to the horror built into his navel, and his mouth tightened into a pained grimace.

His ruined face was now hideously scarred and marked with dried blood and festering wounds – yet he made no attempt to attend to or even conceal them. It was as if he wore his injuries with pride, a silent testament to his seeming invulnerability and a daily reminder of the futility of their best efforts to harm him.

"You should not be doing this to yourself, Exedor," Maelene again argued with him. "It is unnatural. It will destroy you."

"Thank you for your concern, Mistress, but as I have told you, I am more than satisfied with my work," Exedor answered.

"There is a reason Nishindra and Romona rejected the work you now do," Maelene continued in a level voice. "Do you believe you have stumbled onto a discovery they overlooked for centuries? I know you are intelligent, so you must accept the logic of this. You cannot have become so arrogant that you ignore it."

Exedor seemed momentarily put off-balance by this question. While he may have held physical domination over her, the intellectual battle had never been yielded.

"Then tell me," he answered after a moment, "what happened to the fruits of all that work? Where did Romona's followers go? Why did Nishindra leave?"

Maelene turned away and looked back into the unsatisfying fire. "I have told you before, I found Kardak abandoned when it was bequeathed to me," she replied.

Exedor laughed. "That's another half truth, isn't it? Kardak may have been abandoned when you found it, but you already knew much of what had happened there before."

Maelene did not respond. Her gaze remained fixed on the strange flame before her.

"Did you know I found letters there? Surely you found them too. It turns out that little Romona was quite the writer."

Maelene maintained her silence but it seemed to Valeyn that her mother's posture stiffened.

"What you did to her was awful," Exedor continued in his conversational tone. "You, Bythe, and Nishindra, you all stood by and did nothing as she slowly lost her mind."

"You have no idea what you are talking about!" Maelene snapped.

"I think I do. You see, I've been thinking about what we said to each other back at Kardak about your inability to adapt within Kovalith. You all lose your grip on your sanity, don't you? You're so poisoned by your own inflexibility, it erodes your own mind. And now I think about Romona's letters and it starts to make a lot more sense."

Valeyn looked from Exedor to Maelene, but her mother remained stoic against the unspoken accusations. "What's he saying?" Valeyn finally asked.

"I'm saying," Exedor continued, "she knew Romona was losing her grip on sanity. They all knew – well, the few of them who were left, at least. They knew and they killed her."

Maelene's face darkened and she whirled to face him. "Do not lie to her. That is not what happened."

"I don't understand," Valeyn replied. "Maelene, you told me the gods decided to leave because they became bored with Kovalith."

Exedor laughed before Maelene could reply. "Bored? At the end, there were only four of them left! The rest had gone mad, killed themselves, killed each other, or allowed themselves to be killed. One by one, they had all discovered they weren't meant to be here. This mortal existence, locking you into a place where you cannot change – it destroys your sanity."

"But the legends?" Valeyn said.

"The legends are nothing more than sorry people trying to make sense of the nonsensical," Exedor continued. "There was no wisdom behind the destruction that Dazh and Narak wrought. They were driven crazy by the thrill of battle. And now the Men of the Wastes believe it was some divine example to them?" Exedor shook his head. "I suppose it's better than having to admit that two gods destroyed your village and killed your family for no good reason beyond madness and deranged amusement."

Maelene pulled her eyes from Exedor and looked at her daughter. "He is exaggerating. At the end, there were only four of us left: myself, your father, Nishindra, and Romona. One by one, all the gods had slowly changed over the centuries, sending most of them to untimely deaths in one way or another."

"So he's right?" Valeyn asked.

"He's only repeating what Romona discovered. She was the weakest of us, but she was also the most sensitive and insightful. Little Romona wanted to understand life, but over time that slowly changed to a need to understand the bridge between life and death, the limits to which life can be pressed. She was the only one of us to become aware of the change happening within her. The other gods could not. I believe her constant efforts to heal people gave her a unique insight into our own creeping madness. She thought it was a disease." Maelene smiled bitterly. "In some ways, she was right. A disease of gods. How completely fitting."

"She warned you of this," Exedor snapped. "Once she understood what was happening to her, she begged each of you to leave the Forge, but you would not. Even worse, you manipulated her into staying because of your petty war."

Maelene sighed, ignoring Exedor and talking instead to her daughter. "By that point, I was at odds with your father. Romona was helping me and I did not want her to go. I needed her."

"Why did you need her?" Valeyn asked.

"Nishindra and Romona were building terrible things at the requests of both of your parents," Exedor interrupted. "Nishindra's talent for crafting machinery combined with Romona's insane desire to heal the dead. The further she descended into madness, the more potent her creations became. She was very useful to your mother. I believe Romona was working on her greatest weapon when she died – one that would have certainly turned the tide of the war in favor of your mother."

"You were exploiting her madness to build a weapon?" Valeyn asked.

Maelene was quiet for a moment before continuing. "I had become obsessed. I did not understand how far she had fallen until it was too late. When I returned to Kardak one day, I found her body surrounded by her followers. They had stood by in useless worship as she cut her own throat in the pursuit of understanding death. I could not believe she would do that to herself. In my grief, I flew into a rage and I killed what remained of her followers – all of them."

"Be honest, mistress. Were you aggrieved by her death, or were you simply angered by the loss of your weapon?" Exedor asked.

Maelene glared at him. "Both."

"Obviously, poor little Romona couldn't make any more journal entries with a slit throat," Exedor continued, "so I'm afraid I'm not sure what happened next. I have to guess that Nishindra took her work and fled to The Tower."

"Is that true?" Valeyn asked. "Is that what we're looking for now?"

"When I followed Nishindra to The Tower, he had already hidden the weapon from me. He was horrified at what we had done and vowed to put an end to the war. We argued and I was able to use his Oraculate to search for the weapon. That is where I learned of you, Valeyn. After I left, Shin sealed The Tower, and then he too vanished," Maelene finished.

"You were looking for a weapon when you learned about your daughter, and so you merely replaced one tool with another. You're as cruel to each other as you are to your followers." Exedor smiled. "At least I have to respect your consistency."

Maelene sighed but said no more. She seemed to lose all desire to fence with Exedor, as if his words had finally hit their mark. Exedor smiled and turned his back on her – seemingly satisfied with the evening's victory.

It was becoming obvious – even to Valeyn – that Exedor was changing. The refined man she had first encountered on the beach at Tiet was slowly shifting into something different – something stronger, but also something less human. It was possible he was starting to achieve the godhood he clearly sought; however, it was also possible that he was not. Valeyn wondered if she would also change. Would the same madness slowly pollute her like the machines corrupting Exedor?

Ferehain moaned again, and Naya hobbled over to where he lay in Aleasea's lap. Bending awkwardly, she offered him bread. Recognizing her attempt to help him, Ferehain struggled to a sitting position, taking the food from her with a smile that Valeyn had never before seen.

"Thank you, little one," he murmured

Valeyn hadn't witnessed Ferehain offer such a casual kindness to anyone, and her eyes lingered on him for a moment longer as he slowly lowered himself back into Aleasea's caring embrace. Valeyn glanced at her mother to find Maelene deep within her own thoughts. Sensations of regret seem to emanate from her.

"I'm sorry," Valeyn said. "You were right. I should have listened to you at Anchorwatch. I played straight into Exedor's hands."

"Do not blame yourself," Maelene replied. "We all agreed to this plan, and it was a good plan. The four of us should have been able to overcome Exedor. He was never this powerful, even when we encountered him at Tiet."

"What has he done to himself?" Valeyn whispered.

Maelene shook her head almost sympathetically. "I honestly do not know, but I suspect he took this path after he failed at Tiet. Exactly how he combined Nishindra's work and Bythe's power is a mystery to me." She sighed before continuing. "He was right about us when he said we could never truly understand each other. That was part of the appeal of this place. The limitations of the Forge were a refreshing novelty to us. To have our wisdom and knowledge restricted by the confines of this place was a...challenge. So when I tried to uncover the secrets of Imbatal, I was thwarted by my own limitations."

"Did Nishindra and Romona create Imbatal?" Valeyn asked.

"I believe Imbatal was one of their earlier creations. I found him forgotten when I took ownership of Kardak, and I took him as my servant, like the Faede." Maelene looked thoughtful for a moment. "I am sorry, Valeyn. I have made many bad decisions."

Valeyn stared into the fire for a time before she spoke again.

"It seems like all I've done since becoming Valeyn is make bad choices, from hiding in Tiet to going after Naya. It's been one wrong decision after another."

Maelene looked at her, and when she spoke her voice was warm. "Godhood does not guarantee wisdom. Sometimes the opposite is true. Aleasea spoke wisely in Anchorwatch. Over the past few years, you were simply trying to discover who you are, which meant you also needed to discover who you are not. Besides, your desire to walk willingly into the dangers of Kardak was an act motivated by love, and that proved you far nobler than all of us."

Valeyn smiled back at her mother. "Thank you."

Maelene looked back into the fire before continuing. "Even I was motivated by selfishness when I tried to convince you to come with me to The Tower. I feel ashamed when I look back at that moment now, like so much that I have done these past years."

Valeyn didn't know what to say. Any consolation felt like it would be seen as an insincere reciprocation of Maelene's own comfort. She decided to be honest. "How did it happen?" she asked. "How did you become Yvorre?"

Maelene was silent for a long time, and it seemed as if she wasn't going to reply. "There was no sudden transformation," she said eventually. "I suppose that is one of the things I was not prepared for. Exedor was right – we are incapable of changing. Or perhaps a more accurate definition would be that we are incapable of adapting. When Bythe imprisoned me, I was full of...rage, of anger. I could not believe I had *lost*. I did not want to believe it. Perhaps if I had been more flexible, I could have altered my behavior and found a way out. Instead, I resisted Bythe for years. I did not want to give in to him, and then over time, I knew I could not win. That realization burned within me. All the years that I was imprisoned alone in the Ironhelm, it fed upon itself until it became a smoldering hatred. I wanted to do nothing more than hurt the people who had put me there. Bythe and the entire Iron Union, but also my own Ageless."

At this, Maelene looked over at Aleasea and Ferehain. "I blamed them for failing to come for me, for failing to overcome Bythe's impenetrable defenses and rescue me – even for failing to realize I was still alive. I was full of hate."

She paused for a moment and glanced at Valeyn, and for a moment she looked like she wasn't sure what to say, then guilt flooded her perfect face. "It was even out of hatred that I agreed to bear you. I was looking for leverage over Bythe, for a form of power over him. You were my only option. I agreed to bear him a child in exchange for a measure of freedom within his empire. Over time, I was able to slowly expand that freedom. However, I admit this came at a cost – I began to relish the opportunity to vent my hatred at anything and at anyone. This zeal pleased Bythe. By the time he granted me the title of Yvorre, Mistress of Spies and Assassins, the name was merely a formality. I had already forgotten who I was.

Once I was certain I had earned a measure of his trust, I struck. I stole you away with the intent of fleeing to The Tower and using you as a weapon against him, but even there I failed, and the damage we did to you was unforgivable. I fear you know the rest of the story from there."

Valeyn stared into the fire as well. She understood that both Bythe and Yvorre had broken her in ways that no parent ever should. She understood she'd been deprived of the life she deserved because of this. For a moment, she felt an old anger burn toward her mother, and she opened her mouth to accuse her, but the genuine remorse she sensed from Maelene stopped her. She looked at her mother for a moment longer, then chose her words carefully.

"My childhood was difficult, yes," Valeyn began slowly, "but I've also had a long time to think about it. What would have happened if you hadn't tried to steal me away from my father that night? I would've been raised in his image. Yes, I'd have been powerful within the Iron Union, but I'd be nothing more than a shadow of him, acting as he does, hurting people the same way he does. What you both did to me caused me years of pain. But in an unexpected way, it also gave me a chance to be free of you both. I wouldn't have been able to make my own choices had either of you been able to claim me. I'd have just been a weapon in your war against each other. I'd be hurting people even now." Valeyn held her breath for a moment as she considered a truth she had not dared give voice to. "It's kind of perverse, but what you both did to me probably gave me the best options under the circumstances – not that you intended it that way."

Maelene looked at her uncertainly. "Are you saying you have made peace with this?"

"No, I'm saying that you've placed me in the same prison that Bythe placed you. Don't you see that? I may not be locked in the Ironhelm, but my options are no different." Anger flared in her again and she fought it down. "I have two choices: I can hold onto my rage like you did, or I can accept the injustice of my life and move on. But you've shown me where the first path leads, and for that I'm genuinely grateful."

Valeyn turned and looked at Maelene squarely – as true equals for the first time. "I don't think I could forgive you for what you did. Telling you that I did would be a lie. But I can't let it poison me anymore. I need to accept your mistakes and maybe even his. I think I finally understand that I need adapt the way you couldn't. I need to be a better version of you."

Maelene nodded and tenderness shone in her blue eyes. "That would make me proud."

They both turned their eyes to the fire and sat quietly. Only Aleasea's tender reassurances broke the silence of the strange night.

CHAPTER 9

"Very little is known of the Prodigals. In fact, there is no documented record of their existence. If they are ever mentioned, it is with cautious voices and hushed tones. Within the Ironhelm, it is said that nobody mentions the word at all. If there are conspirators within Bythe's court, they are cunning and patient, for no one has ever truthfully confessed to the Inquisitors.

And yet the Prodigals persist, as a rumor, as a legend, and as a threat. We can only imagine what Bythe will do to any traitors he uncovers in his midst."

~Aleasea of the Ageless

Ethan decided that he liked Paeter, or at least that he respected the man. He supposed it was due to his noble blood. There was a measure of decency and respect about him that Ethan recognized as kindred. Paeter knew how to communicate with him on a certain level. It was almost a universal code that went unspoken and unacknowledged – when two noblemen conversed, there was a mutual understanding. These men had influence and responsibilities that set them apart from average commoners. They both shared the same problems, albeit they were problems faced on opposite sides of the war. Ethan decided that he liked him, and for a moment regretted that Paeter was going to die.

He tried to brace himself against the cold wind while Paeter formally introduced the delegation. He had decided that iron plated armor was not well suited to the chilling climate of the mountains – even in the middle of the day. They had both agreed on this position in the center of the field, out of bowshot range of either army. Ethan and his retinue of five soldiers had approached first, carefully navigating the network of trenches that were more an irritation than a hindrance. He wondered how Paeter would react if he knew the Cremators had already devised a method to get through them. For a moment he considered telling the delegation – just to see their reaction – but he reminded himself it was an unnecessary and petty indulgence.

Ethan scanned the group before him. Councilor Paeter was wrapped in a thick burgundy travelling cloak – clearly more practically dressed than Ethan – as he introduced Councilor Morag and E'mar. Three more Ageless stood silently behind them, their faces hidden behind billowing green robes.

"And where is Captain Jason?" Ethan asked. "I would have expected him as well."

"We thought it might be better if we led the negotiations, Commander," Paeter said with a reassuring smile. "I think we can both agree that Captain Jason is a very capable soldier, but perhaps he needs to work on his diplomacy."

It was a shame. Ethan hadn't really expected Jason to attend the meeting, but it would have made things simpler if he had.

"Yes, he is…young," Ethan said with obvious disdain.

"Regardless of his age," Morag announced in a stern tone, "he is our captain, and he is doing his job admirably. It is probably fortunate for you that he chose to remain behind."

Ethan noted the unexpected gesture of respect from Morag. It spoke much of Jason that even his political enemies would praise him in private.

Paeter raised his hands as if to quell an argument. "Commander Ethan, please. We have come in good faith to negotiate with you. I must make it clear from the outset that we are not going to surrender to you, but we are willing to discuss the safety of the civilians and agree to terms for their safe passage out of harm's way. I know that the Helmsguard are not barbarians like the Northmen, so you must accept that my proposition is reasonable."

Ethan looked at Paeter. The older man was right – the Iron Union was an example of civilized behavior to the rest of the world – and because of this he decided to give Paeter one final chance to live.

"Yes, it is a reasonable request, but your terms for negotiation are simply unrealistic. My engines are almost restored, and when that happens, I will destroy your city within a matter of hours." Ethan paused for a moment to allow his words to have their effect.

"But...the civilians—" Paeter began, but Ethan cut him off.

"The civilians can be spared by your unconditional surrender right here and now. You're right. We aren't like the wildmen of the Great Southern Wastes. I respect the lives of innocents just like you do, so I'm giving you the opportunity to save them. Take it."

"This is unconscionable. You come to threaten innocent lives, and now you try to lay the blame at our feet?" cried Morag.

"Rationalize how we got here however you want," Ethan fired back. "The fact remains that – right now – I am offering you the chance to save these people. If you don't take it, then you can shoulder the responsibility for what I am ordered to do next!"

Morag signaled, and E'mar stepped forward. He had lowered his hood, and his eyes shone fiercely.

"We know what you're thinking, Helmsguard. Don't think you can surprise us with an ambush," said Morag. "The Ageless have swept these fields, and they will know if a soldier comes within a hundred feet of us."

"Morag, please," Paeter interjected.

"It's alright, Councilor," Ethan replied. "She's right to be prepared. The truth is, if you do not agree to my surrender, then you're both going to die right here."

Morag smirked. "You're an arrogant little bastard. You should not have invited us here, Ethan. We know about your spy. We knew this was a trap, but we've set a trap for you!" Morag signaled to E'mar.

Both Morag and Paeter stepped backward as E'mar sank to one knee and placed his palm on the ground. He closed his eyes and began murmuring indistinctly. In an instant, the Helmsguard had their weapons drawn, but they were too far away to stop E'mar from what he was about to do. Ethan drew his own sword and took a step forward.

"No," Ethan said calmly. "I'm afraid you knew nothing of my spy."

E'mar removed his hand from the ground and clenched it in a tight fist. As he did, the three Ageless behind him staggered to the ground as if they were exhausted. E'mar flung his arm toward them and opened his fist, sending a wave of force at the three figures. They were flung backward several feet and landed heavily on the ground.

"E'mar? What are you doing?" Morag screamed, but Em'ar ignored her, instead turning to Ethan.

"Kill them quickly," E'mar barked. "They will recover at any moment."

The Helmsguard needed no further instructions. The five guards raced over to where the Ageless lay dazed in the dirt. Their emerald robes were now limp as they tried vainly to climb to their feet, but the Helmsguard fell upon them mercilessly. The cold steel of the Iron Union stabbed at the Ageless with ruthless ferocity, as if a second of respite could thwart their murder. Within seconds, the green robes were stained red, and the once-magical figures of the Ageless never moved again.

Paeter had grabbed Morag by the arm and turned to run toward Fairhaven. Ethan watched them and almost felt a stab of pity. E'mar made the slightest of gestures at them and they both cried out, stumbling to their knees as they clutched their heads in pain. E'mar started toward them both with a cold smile painting his features.

"Leave them to us!" Ethan called out. "Kaler will be raiding the Godfire by now. You need to stop them."

E'mar paused and considered Ethan for a moment before nodding and turning to face south. He kneeled and again placed his hand on the dirt, murmuring something under his breath. As he did, he reached into his cloak with one hand and brought forth a glass orb filled with green light. The light pulsed and surged, as if it were trying to escape the glass with each word E'mar chanted.

Realizing he could do nothing more, Ethan signaled to his soldiers and crossed over to where Paeter and Morag were kneeling. They both looked up at him, expressions of pain and fear warring on their faces.

"Ethan, please. For the gods' sakes!" Paeter cried.

Ethan's face was stone as he nodded to the soldiers. They raised their blades and sank them into the backs of both Morag and Paeter. Their screams were typical of those who had never expected to be killed – a cry of fear and pain in equal parts. Fortunately, Ethan's soldiers were well trained in killing, and the cries quickly faded, before they both fell silent.

"Sir?" the senior knight asked an unspoken question.

"Yes, do it," Ethan replied then walked away.

Behind him, two of the soldiers unhooked axes from their belts and began brutally hacking at the necks of the two executed Councilors. Ethan tried to block out the sound, as if fearing he would be forced to remember it for the rest of his days.

Before nightfall, Ethan would ensure those heads were delivered back to Fairhaven. The brazen display was merciless, but it was necessary. Ethan wanted everyone in the city to see what had happened. He needed them to understand exactly how doomed they were. He wanted the fear and the misery to be almost palpable.

He knew that somewhere up on that wall, Jason was watching. The thought gave him a glimmer of satisfaction.

·   ·   ·

Nadine's tears were soaking Jason's shirt as he held her face against him. The sobs wracked her body as she screamed another muffled cry into his chest, thumping her fists against Jason's thighs with despair that was indiscriminate. He gripped her head firmly and tried to weather her grief. His own eyes still stung from his dried tears, but he barely noticed.

He'd raced to Nadine at the chambers as soon he'd witnessed the betrayal. He couldn't remember how he'd gotten there; he was dazed from what he'd seen. Numb. His mind struggled to comprehend all that he'd witnessed. E'mar was a traitor. Paeter had been murdered. Jason had crashed into the Council chamber, yelling for his wife. The grim faces of the staff told him what he dreaded: she already knew. He burst into the antechamber and found her cradled in her mother's arms. Raelle looked barely capable of standing, yet the duty to console her daughter seemed to eclipse her own needs. Then Jason had taken Nadine into his own arms.

He wasn't sure how long they had all been there now – grief had a way of making time meaningless. All he knew was that he needed to be with his wife.

At some point, Lieutenant Geordine must have entered. She stood quietly by the door, her own face a mask of respectful sorrow, but Jason knew she had been waiting for him. He met her eyes silently for a moment before turning his attention back to Nadine. He had to be with her – Fairhaven could wait.

As if sensing Jason's predicament, Raelle stepped forward and gently pried her daughter away from him.

"Come with me, Nadine. Jason needs to work now," Raelle hushed.

Jason reluctantly let Raelle pull his wife away.

"I'll be back as soon as I can, I promise," Jason said.

"Why didn't you go with him? Why didn't you protect him?" Nadine sobbed at Jason, her eyes swollen and red.

The accusation was like a blow, and Jason physically reeled. He took a step backward and looked about the room like he didn't know where he was.

Why didn't I go? Was I afraid just like I was at Stonekeep? Why am I not lying there dead like them? Don't I deserve it more than they did?

He involuntarily recalled the day Aleasea had ordered him to flee from Imbatal. He remembered the shameful relief he'd felt at saving his own life.

"Nadine," Raelle's voice was consoling but disciplined, the tone of a practiced mother. "If he'd gone, then you'd be grieving for your husband now as well as for your father. Be grateful he didn't go."

"I just want him back, Mother. Make him come back!" Her pleas became muffled as she sank into her mother's embrace.

Raelle nodded at Jason as she gently eased Nadine onto the couch. Jason stood watching for a moment longer, then signaled for Geordine to come to him. She marched over immediately.

"I'm so sorry, Captain..." she began but Jason interrupted her.

"Don't worry about me, Lieutenant, just report," he replied, his eyes never leaving his wife.

"Sir, it's bad out there. Word's gotten out, and the whole city is starting to panic."

"Convene the War Council right away. I'll be there shortly," Jason ordered absently.

"It's not fair, none of this is fair, it's not my fault, I'm sorry," Nadine was crying to her mother.

"Sir, E'mar led the War Council! He's turned on us!" Geordine insisted.

"Yes, you're right," Jason answered, still watching Nadine. "Then find Kaler. I'm appointing him to lead the War Council until I arrive."

"Of course, it's not your fault. You couldn't have done anything," Raelle said to Nadine.

"Sir," Geordine pressed. "Kaler hasn't returned. We think he's dead too."

"No. It's the baby. I haven't felt her move in days... I think something's wrong," Nadine cried.

Jason went cold.

Raelle immediately went to her knees and placed her hands on Nadine's stomach. Concern weighed heavily on her face. Jason was immediately at their side.

"What is it?" he asked desperately.

"I don't know," murmured Raelle. She felt Nadine's stomach for a moment then signaled one of the attendants. "Find a midwife, now!"

The attendant paled slightly then hurried out of the room.

Nadine was sobbing quietly. "I'm sorry," Nadine repeated over and over in a tragic litany.

"Nadine," Jason kneeled beside her and tried to take her hand, but she snatched it away.

"No. Don't look at me. Go away!" she shrieked.

Raelle stood and ushered Jason away from Nadine. "It's alright, Jason. Come away. She's not herself. Leave her with me for now," Raelle said.

"But she needs me," Jason replied.

"Yes, she will, but she doesn't know it now."

"Captain," Geordine interrupted. "I'm sorry, sir, but we need you right now!"

"Well, I can't go!" Jason roared back at her.

"No, go, Jason. I'll stay with her. She'll be alright." Raelle placed a hand on his shoulder. When he still hesitated, Raelle pulled him to meet her eyes – and when she did, he saw cold fury barely contained. "I want you to make sure you get that bastard for what he's done to us."

Jason nodded. "Send someone to find me the moment you have news," he answered.

He allowed Geordine to lead him out of the antechamber, and the following hours passed in a disjointed assortment of half-remembered meetings and conversations. Jason tried to focus on the problems before him, but he could never keep his mind away from his wife for more than a few minutes.

Kaler's raiding parties had not returned. Lieutenant Shane was also missing. Jason ordered teams to search for them and then turned his attention to restoring order within Fairhaven. The Council was called, and Jason had little opposition when he declared Military Protocols. The few remaining Councilors were stunned. Even Denethin was unusually quiet. Within hours, a curfew had been declared – the first since the Northmen had raided the Wellspring Festival – and Jason ordered his men to enforce it.

At some point during the evening, Jason's duties took him to the outer walls. He checked on his men and ensured orders were understood: the city was to be completely locked down and the gates would not open for any reason, save for an order signed by him, personally. He ascended the southern watchtower and walked along the battlements. The night was quiet now. Jason turned to the east and saw that the sky had begun to lighten near the horizon. Dawn was not far away.

"Jason," Kaler's familiar voice greeted him, and Jason swung around to face him.

"Oh, thank the gods!" Jason stepped forward and visibly restrained himself from embracing the Ageless out of sheer relief. Instead, he steadied himself and tried to adopt the formal admiration that was most respectful for a soldier. He'd hoped that Kaler would be able to regain access to the city without help, but Jason had never seen him like this. He was exhausted and bleeding from a wound somewhere on his forehead. His purple robes were ripped and smeared, and he walked with a slight limp. Jason waited until he was standing before him.

"Welcome back, Kaler. Do you need medical care?" Jason knew the answer but asked anyway.

"No, Captain. I am here to report the failure of my mission."

"Then proceed," Jason replied gently.

Kaler relayed the details efficiently, as was the hallmark of the Violari. The raid had been proceeding as planned. Lieutenant Shane had led seven units to the flank of the supply train, with seven Violari standing in support. The shipments had appeared lightly guarded, as they had hoped. They had concluded that Ethan was focusing his attention on the negotiations. They did not suspect a trap until it was too late.

Shane's soldiers attacked and – with the help of the Violari – quickly overcame the Helmsguard, but something went wrong. The Violari became weak and disoriented. They broke off their attack and were unable to defend themselves.

Kaler only later understood what had happened. Somehow, E'mar had found a way to tap into the ruins of the Arcadia – and discovered the remnants of Maelene's *kai*. He had learned how to control it, and how to divorce others from it. His betrayal had been perfect. While Kaler could not say how far back the treachery ran, he knew today's slaughter had been coordinated with their enemy. With the Violari rendered helpless, the dozens of Helmsguard who had been waiting in ambush revealed themselves. Shane's attack quickly descended into a massacre of his own men.

Somehow, Kaler had survived. He was not clear how many others had been as fortunate. It had taken him long and painful hours to return to Fairhaven undetected by the Helmsguard troops searching for survivors, and he had managed to enter the city using one of the many hidden passageways from Sanctuary.

"How many Ageless are left?" Jason asked almost breathlessly.

"I do not know. I will go to the Temple now that I have reported to you."

"Do you think they can fight?"

Kaler shook his head slowly. "I am still exiled from the *kai*, and I suspect this will be true for all of my kin, save for the traitor. We may be able to undo what he has done, but this will take time I fear we do not have."

"What about the shipment?" Jason asked reluctantly.

"We were unable to get close to it. The material will have reached Ethan by now. I expect he will have his remaining engine operating within days."

Jason looked out over the fields. They were quiet and dark, but for the twinkling of distant lights dotted across the landscape – the picturesque aftermath of Ethan's perfect trap. For an absurd moment, Jason considered how peaceful the scene appeared to be. He dismissed Kaler with an absent wave of his hand and stared out into the shadows of the south. It seemed unusually dark, and Jason looked up at the black sky. There were a handful of stars puncturing the night, but they seemed too few. Jason's brow furrowed, and he found himself wondering if the gods themselves were casting a shroud over Fairhaven.

He glanced to the east and wondered if the approaching sun had chased the stars away or if perhaps his depression was poisoning his sight. He realized this might be the last time the dawn touched Fairhaven's walls.

"Sir." A messenger had approached, and he interrupted Jason's thoughts with a tone of urgency. "Please, you're needed at the Infirmary."

Jason did not move. Instead he closed his eyes and tried to force every last ounce of feeling from his being. "Is my wife alright?" he asked slowly.

"Sir, I was told to ask you to come to the Infirmary before—"

"Answer me!" Jason's voice broke in the peaceful dawn.

"No sir. It's your child. It was delivered an hour ago. I'm afraid...the baby did not survive."

Jason turned from the messenger and took a few uncertain steps before stopping. He glanced at the dawn in confusion for a moment, as if puzzled why something so beautiful had a right to exist.

"Was it a boy or a girl?" he asked weakly.

The messenger hesitated then lowered his eyes. "She was a girl, sir."

Jason nodded. Then he slowly sat down, placed his back against the cold stones of the wall, and wept.

CHAPTER 10

"The Ageless do not have a concept of youth as other races do. By definition, the Ageless are largely immune to time's destructive whims. However, while our bodies do not age, our minds are not dissimilar to those of mortal men and women. While our bodies may be ageless, our minds sometimes grow old and weary."

~Aleasea of the Ageless

The Render had forced all sense of time from Valeyn. She no longer had any sense of how long they had been travelling. One camp led to the next, followed by the next, in a never-ending ritual that was overseen by the cold, red sun always hovering above them. The ground continued to grow less accommodating the further south they travelled, with the petty inconveniences of cracks in the trail now a distant memory. Instead, the grounds to the east and west were now dropping away at perilous angles and descending into unfathomable depths of nothing. It seemed as if they were being herded along an increasingly narrow path the further south they travelled. Valeyn estimated that the belt of rocky ground before them was no more than a mile across.

A splitting noise rent the air and Naya cried out. Valeyn felt the cart in her hands lurch to one side. She gripped the beams and tried to steady it, but in her weakened state it was lurching out of her grip.

"I can't hold it," she gasped, and the cart toppled onto its side with a violent crash. Naya squealed as she was flung onto the ground.

"Oh, what is it now?" Exedor growled as he turned at the sound.

Ferehain moved to Naya quickly and crouched next to her.

"I'm alright," Naya said as Ferehain helped her to her feet. "I just got frightened."

Valeyn looked at the cart and saw the problem – weeks of travel over the broken rocks of the Render had taken their toll on the timber spokes and the entire wheel had collapsed in on itself.

"The cart is ruined, Exedor," said Maelene.

Exedor looked at the cart then shrugged. "Then it seems like this is the end of the journey for the cripple. I suggest you leave her a blanket. She might be here a while."

"We will not leave her," said Ferehain.

Exedor grunted and walked back toward the upended cart. He looked at it, pulling one of the broken spokes from the wheel and examining it thoughtfully before wheeling around and striking Ferehain across the face with the broken piece of wood. Ferehain cried out and sank to his knees. Exedor raised the stick to strike Ferehain again when Naya stepped awkwardly in between them.

"Don't hurt him!" she screamed.

For a moment, Exedor looked like he was about to hit her too, then his grotesque face broke into a smile. "The great Ferehain hiding behind the protection of a crippled child? Oh, this is too fitting."

"Exedor, stop this!" Maelene commanded.

"I have no interest in escorting your entire retinue, Maelene. She can stay behind."

"Come now," Maelene said as she walked over to him. "She is just a child. What have you to fear from her? Surely you are not suggesting we leave an innocent, crippled girl to die?"

Exedor smirked. "Don't play mind games with me. I really don't care what becomes of her."

Maelene smiled in return. "But I know that you do. You have been trying to assert moral superiority over me for weeks, reminding me how the gods abused and mistreated their own creations and how we do not deserve to rule. This point matters to you. And now you are going to do this? If you leave her here, you prove yourself no better than us, and I will remind you of this when the time comes. Do you really want to tarnish your victory over such a small thing?"

Exedor's smile did not drop but he seemed to be weighing up his options before he spoke. "I said I don't care, and I meant it. It is time for us to rest. You have one hour before we continue. If you wish her to come with us then you had better figure something out. That responsibility now rests with you. I will not wait for her to shuffle along behind us with those broken little legs." He chuckled to himself as he turned away, motioning for the Faede to form their oppressive circle around the group.

"Are you alright, Ferehain?" Aleasea asked as soon as Exedor had left.

"I am fine," he said, turning back to Naya as if the attack had never happened. "We need to leave the cart behind. Can you walk?"

"I don't think so. I think I broke these things when I fell."

Ferehain bent over Naya, first examining, then adjusting the irons on her legs, moving them back into position with a practiced ease.

"How did you learn to do this?" Naya asked.

"I have always studied the arts of my enemies, little one," he answered. "And we have been at war with the Iron Union for decades. Metal holds little mystery to me now."

Aleasea placed her hand on Ferehain's shoulder. "Come, let me first see if you are injured, please."

Ferehain shook his head. "Thank you, Aleasea, but I do not need any more care. I am no longer as weak as I was."

Aleasea sighed and relented. "Well, you are still as stubborn as you ever were," she said with a faint smile.

Naya laughed. "You two sound like you're married."

The innocence of Naya's comment caught everyone off guard – everyone but Ferehain, who simply continued working on Naya's irons as if she had asked about the weather.

"The Ageless do not marry," he answered. "There was once a time when we did, but we no longer do."

"Why not?"

Aleasea's face fell. She looked as if she were about to speak, but Ferehain continued unperturbed.

"Because our mother Maelene forbade it. We were not to be trusted with the gift of life and it was taken from us."

"Ferehain, that is not true," said Maelene.

"You can't have children?" Naya asked.

"Naya, I don't think this is any of our business," Valeyn interrupted.

"Let the child ask," Ferehain replied, never raising his face from his work. "I agree with Exedor on one point. She should know the truth of the gods she worships. Aleasea and I were among the first of the Ageless ever born into this world. We soon chose each other as *Unsul*, that is what you call betrothed or bound to one another. The truth is we wanted a child. The Ageless defend life and we wanted to understand it, and we wanted to share this with each other. Maelene did not approve of this and forbade it, but we both had strong feelings, so we disobeyed her."

"Were you in love?" Naya asked.

"Our emotions are different from yours. It is difficult to compare immortal lives with..." Ferehain trailed off for a moment as if searching for the right words, then he closed his eyes briefly and continued. "Yes, we experienced love. We had a child. She was a little girl."

"That's cute," Naya smiled. "A little Ageless baby. Where is she now?"

"She grew to be a young child. She was beautiful, like you, but one day, for no reason, she became ill and started to fade." Ferehain's voice was halting, and he spoke with an unusual level of restraint. "We took her to our mother, but she was unable to help us."

"Ferehain, I did everything I could, but she was not meant to be," Maelene answered.

"Nothing we did could save her. Aleasea and I sat by her bed day after day for almost a year, yet every day we could only watch her become weaker. Then one day, she finally passed. We understood then that the Ageless were not meant to bear children. It was not our place in this world."

Tears formed in Naya's eyes and broke down her cheek. "I'm so sorry."

"After that, our mother removed the gift of life from all of her Ageless so she would never be disobeyed again," he finished.

"That is not true," Maelene answered. "I did not know if my Ageless could bear children. It was not part of my design. I forbade this because of what you suffered. When Sa—"

"Do not say her name!" Ferehain snapped, and Maelene checked herself.

She watched Ferehain for a moment before continuing in a soft voice. "When...your daughter passed, I could not bear for any of my children to suffer that way again. I wanted to spare you all that pain. That is why I took the gift from you; it was meant to be a kindness."

Ferehain gave no indication he heard. He continued talking as he finalized the repairs to Naya's walking frames. "Afterward, our mother created the Violari and sent me to work on acts of war. It was there I learned how to repair metal. I grew to understand strength." With a final snap, he fixed the last iron rod in place and looked at Naya with a smile bereft of warmth. "There, all better."

Aleasea slowly stood and walked a short distance away from Ferehain, her face heavy with remembered grief. In that movement, Valeyn appreciated the gulf that had grown between them. She rose to go to Aleasea but felt a restraining hand on her shoulder and turned to see Maelene shaking her head.

"Valeyn, we cannot take the cart with us. Can you carry Naya?" Maelene asked.

"Of course," Valeyn answered, slightly confused.

"Then come, we must take what we can. Bring her, please," Maelene said as she turned and walked over to the ruined cart.

Valeyn obeyed and gently cradled Naya as she lifted the young girl from the ground and followed Maelene. Several moments later, she looked up to see Aleasea quietly wrapped in the arms of Ferehain and she quickly looked away – suddenly feeling guilty as if her gaze had intruded upon something very personal. Only the Faede watched them without pity.

·　　·　　·

This was a mistake.

Jason looked down at the tiny form of his daughter and his vision instantly blurred as his eyes filled with tears. He breathed in a gulping gasp of air and violently rubbed them away – forcing himself to look at her. He had to do this. He had to see her, just once.

She was so small.

"Elyn," was all he could say. He pulled the blanket up to her chin to protect her from the cold. She would have been so beautiful.

He sobbed again, and this time he felt his hands gripping the bench so hard he thought the timber would break. His arms trembled from the strain, and his entire body started to shake. A wash of hot grief and anger flooded him, and a moan came unbidden from his throat. He felt the need to strike out. He felt the desire to scream and rage – yet he only shook. He wanted to rip everything down – yet he could only weep.

"Jason, please, come away now," Caydyn said as he gently placed his hand on his shoulder. "You've said goodbye. Now you need to come away with me."

Jason shook his head like a child. "No. What if she wakes up?"

Caydyn turned Jason's head to face him, and Jason saw heartbreak on his father's face.

"She won't, Jason. I know how you're feeling, but you need to come with me now. No good will come from remaining here any longer. The longer you stay and dwell, the more you will fall into sadness and the harder it will be for you to leave. Please trust me on this."

Jason leaned over and kissed tiny Elyn on the forehead. She was cold. Then he straightened and turned from the room.

Caydyn hurried after him as he left the Infirmary.

"Jason, come with me, you need to rest for a while," he pleaded.

"I can't," Jason mumbled. "I'm sorry, but I can't. This city is going to burn, and I need to do something...I just don't know what..."

"Let the others deal with this for today. You need to grieve. You need to be with Nadine."

Jason recalled the judgment in his wife's eyes and felt a renewed flush of guilt. He'd forgotten about her father.

Paeter.

Little Elyn.

So much tragedy in such a short time. He knew if he started down that path – if he opened the door to all that pain – then it would simply overwhelm him.

"I can't...I can't deal with it now..." was all Jason could say.

"Jason, you need..."

"Go to Nadine and Raelle. Be with them, please. Tell them I'll be there as soon as I can." The words sounded weak, but they were all he could offer.

His father said something, but Jason was no longer listening. He was marching across the parade ground – ignoring the offered salutes of his men – and out into the city of Fairhaven.

The streets were filled with people rushing to and fro, pointlessly looking for some kind of escape from the impending invasion. Families were loading possessions onto carts, heedless of the warnings that the gates were already barred. Everywhere he looked, he saw the townsfolk's stinking refuse and their easily discarded lives. He pressed himself through the crowd with a sense of violent disgust. What right did they have to any of this? What value had they placed on a normal life? What freedoms had they taken for granted?

His cheeks were wet, and he dimly realized he was still crying, but it didn't seem to matter. He walked quickly over the rough cobblestones and entered the town square. Before him, the River Claiream divided the town, and the bridge was again packed with people rushing to the markets to buy the few supplies left for sale. Above this chaos, the ruins of the once-proud Temple sunk dejectedly into its crater. It all seemed very fitting.

Jason crossed the bridge and stalked up the cracked steps of the temple. He didn't even pause as he stepped over the threshold. Once, this place would have terrified him – as it terrified everyone in Fairhaven – and what he was now doing would have been unthinkable. Today, the place held no terror for him. It was just another broken keepsake from a different time.

He stood in the center of the shattered room. The pillars – once soaring columns of smooth grey stone – were fractured and slanted in precarious positions. Many had fallen and lay smashed over the broken, uneven floor.

Jason opened his mouth to shout, but before he could, the robed figure of Kaler stood before him. Even in his angered state, Jason was momentarily silenced by the surprise. Kaler appeared stronger than he had been the previous night, and his bleeding forehead was now smooth and clean, although his robes were still stained.

"Captain, you do not need to come to the Temple yourself. If you have need of me, you need only to send word," Kaler said.

"I don't want you in my office. I want to see the condition of the Ageless for myself."

Kaler's face turned grim. "E'mar's treachery was greater than we suspected."

"How so?"

Kaler paused for a moment. "I will show you. Come with me."

He turned and moved toward the broken shrine of Maelene. Jason followed him behind the monument and down a long tunnel that led to the depths of Sanctuary. Jason had been in these tunnels once before, but they were very different now. The passageways were dimly lit and half-collapsed in places. Jason could see where the Ageless had repaired some corridors but left others in a state of total disorder.

After a time, they approached the Arcadia. A wall of rocks now blocked the massive arch that marked the entrance to the room.

"This was E'mar's doing," Kaler said as they approached. "Some months ago, he quietly ordered Sanctuary to be sealed off from us. At the time, we believed it was to protect the power within, should the war go badly for us. Now, we know he had a different motive."

Jason saw that a hole had been forced through the stones, allowing both of them to pass through into the Arcadia. It was an immense room capped with a high, domed ceiling, but that was the only part of the room that looked familiar to Jason. The timber platform, the bench, and the orbs were all gone. Even the intricate carvings on the cupola had been erased by the blast three years earlier. All that remained was a pulsing ball of green light hovering in the center of the broken room. It was around the size of a grapefruit, and its beating glow seemed somehow feeble.

"This used to be the source of Maelene's power, of our power. She created this place and imbued it with her life force," Kaler said.

"I remember," answered Jason with an unconscious air of respect. "But I thought she also destroyed it?"

"She damaged it greatly, but Yvorre could not destroy her own creation when she was so far away. She had devoted too much of herself into this place. The core of her power remained in here. We were able to restore much of the room, but the *kai* needed to be controlled, lest it grow and cover the land like wildflowers. Together we were able to fashion an artefact – a Cour – strong enough to contain the flow of *kai* and to control its passage into us."

"And E'mar stole it?" Jason asked.

"He has done more than that. E'mar has discovered how to manipulate the Cour and control our source of *kai*. He must have been slowly learning this art after Veroulle left."

"Did E'mar cause Veroulle to be weakened?" Jason asked.

"It is very possible," Kaler said bitterly. "Without the Cour it is difficult to understand what he has done."

Jason cursed. How much had he undermined them?

"So what now?" asked Jason. "Can you fix it? Can you build another Cour and regain control?"

Kaler shook his head. "It would take time, even if we had full access to our *kai,* which we currently do not. There is no telling how long it would take to undo this, if indeed we could. I fear the few of us who remain will have little power to resist Ethan's army now."

"So it's over." Jason heard himself say the words, but he couldn't comprehend them. It was impossible to accept that they had lost, that they had exhausted all their options and now faced no alternative other than defeat. He turned away from the glowing ball of light and ordered Kaler to lead him back to the surface. They both retraced their steps in silence and emerged from the Temple into the morning sun. Beneath them, the people of Fairhaven were still scurrying around in a panic. Jason watched as blue-liveried guards moved in to break up a fight between two men in the marketplace. A crowd started to gather around the group, and for a moment, it looked as if the scene might turn riotous before more soldiers appeared to try and restore order.

"So what do I do?" Jason asked as if talking to himself. "Do I surrender now, so all these people might have a chance to live?"

He thought of begging Ethan for mercy and his fists involuntarily clenched. Ethan had orchestrated this, had brought his army to their doorstep, had used E'mar to deceive them, had betrayed a truce and murdered Paeter – and had caused the death of his daughter. How Ethan must have been laughing at him this whole time, knowing what E'mar had planned to do, knowing that Jason would have to beg him for mercy in the end, no matter what.

He would have to beg the man who killed his daughter and ask him for favor.

"I'll never do it," he said aloud.

Kaler looked at him, seemingly reading his thoughts. "Jason, we may be able to evacuate the people. There are tunnels in Sanctuary designed for this purpose centuries ago. I used these the re-enter the city last night. They lead to many places far in the north. The entrances have lain hidden throughout the city, but the time for secrecy is clearly over. If we expose them, we should be able to able to evacuate the people within days. You could lead them to Marfort or maybe even to the Fareaches."

Jason considered the suggestion. It wouldn't save Fairhaven, but at least it would give his people a fighting chance.

"Won't E'mar know of this?" Jason asked.

Kaler shrugged. "There is very little he can do about it now. Perhaps your damage to the engines has delayed them more than they expected, or perhaps they do not care if people flee..."

"...because it's the *kai* they're after." Jason finished.

"Yes," Kaler said softly. "If that was Ethan's goal, then he has executed it brilliantly. All we can do now is ensure our people get to safety before the Helmsguard take this city."

Jason tasted bile. No matter which way he turned, Ethan would get what he wanted. He recalled the vision Veroulle had shown him. He remembered the fierce intensity of the flames as the city burned and the Temple flared like a beacon. He thought of the temple and of its searing light, and now he viewed it differently.

Had there been a hidden order in that vision? A suggestion to be heeded at the darkest of hours?

"Kaler," Jason said. "Do you want E'mar to take control of Maelene's *kai* and to wield it in Bythe's name while you and I cower in tunnels?"

"No," Kaler admitted quietly.

"Are you out of options completely?"

"No."

"Can you destroy the *kai*?"

Kaler looked at Jason and in that moment, two beings understood one another perfectly.

"Such an act would burn Fairhaven to the ground."

"And can you do it?"

Kaler did not hesitate.

"Yes."

BOOK 3
REVENGE

CHAPTER 1

"I built The Tower upon the Forge's Cradle. This was where all the gods were born, at least in a physical sense. The Render is where we first set foot on Kovalith, and it is where we harnessed our energies and took physical form. It was an umbilical cord to the nurturing kai, to the immortal energies beyond.

We stood on those grounds for an immeasurable time as we completed the art of creation itself. We combined our arts to weave the lands of the Render and then – once we perfected our art – we crafted the lands in the north and seeded them with life. The essence of all gods exists in this place, for this is where we were born. Centuries later, long after all the others had departed, I returned and constructed The Tower on the sacred ground. My skills knew no bounds, nor did my arrogance."

~Nishindra the Crafter

They were moving up a slight incline. Valeyn was now carrying Naya in her arms. She would have strength for this so long as the Faede didn't drain her to the point of exhaustion, but this was a concession that made Exedor unhappy, and Valeyn now found herself burdened with two watchful crimson escorts every minute of the day.

"How much longer?" Exedor growled to Maelene as they trudged up the slope.

"We are very close. I expect we will find it soon," Maelene replied in a voice edged with her own fatigue and irritation.

"What do you mean, *find it*? How can you not know where it is?"

"The Render is a strange place, Exedor. Things here do not have the same...permanence they do in the north. We were still learning how to mold this world, still trying to understand how it should work. Distance can be flexible here."

"Distance may be flexible, but my patience is not," Exedor spat.

Sensing danger, Valeyn gently placed Naya on the ground.

"Move back," Valeyn whispered, gesturing further up the ridge. Naya slowly obeyed.

"What would you have me do, Exedor?" Maelene asked patiently. "I promised you I would take you to The Tower. I could not promise to control the whims of the Render. We will arrive there when we are there."

"Don't lie to me!" Exedor snapped as he rounded on her. "I may not have eyes but I'm not blind. If The Tower was close, then we should be able to at least see it by now, but I sense nothing but open sky. Did you think you could fool me?"

"I am speaking the truth. I am not trying to deceive you," Maelene replied.

Exedor seemed to look at her for a moment before answering. "I don't believe you." He signaled to one of the Faedes, and it immediately stepped toward Ferehain. "I think I've indulged you long enough. I made a bargain with you in exchange for the lives of your followers. I've honored the deal, but I don't think you've been as honest with me."

"Exedor, please," Maelene called out, but Exedor refused to listen. The Faede stood before the weakened Ferehain, who glared up at it defiantly. Aleasea immediately stepped in between them, shielding Ferehain from the creature.

"Keep away from him!" she warned.

Exedor signaled, and three more approached them. Valeyn glanced at her two guards – looking for an opportunity – but they were both watching her as intently as ever.

"I wouldn't do that, Aleasea," Exedor warned in an almost bored tone. "I don't need them to kill you too, but I will if you force the issue. I really don't care that much."

Ferehain touched her on the shoulder. "No, please. There is no point," he said softly, but Aleasea remained where she was.

"How stupidly touching," Exedor said as he motioned for the Faede to continue.

Valeyn tensed herself to move when Naya spoke.

"There's something here."

She had moved herself to the crest of the rise and was now looking down the other side.

Everybody paused.

"And what is *something*, child?" Exedor asked.

"I don't know. There's a garden here, but it's...strange," Naya replied.

Exedor looked at Maelene, who was smiling with relief.

"I believe we may have found it," Maelene said.

"What are you talking about?" Exedor snapped and marched up the incline. He stopped, and his sightless eyes seemed to scan the landscape before him. A mask of puzzlement settled over his grotesque features. "What is this? Explain it!"

Valeyn hurried up the ridge to find herself peering over the lip of an immense crater. It ran hundreds of feet into the distance – a huge, circular footprint in the rocky ground. Valeyn saw that the inside of the crater sloped gently down toward a structure at its center.

"Is this supposed to be The Tower?" Exedor asked.

Valeyn quietly shared his surprise. From this distance, she could see a large circular network of hedges, intricately arranged at the center of the crater. They were speckled with brightly colored flowers, and even from this distance, she could see the hedges were enormous. She had not expected this.

"This is indeed our destination," Maelene replied as she crested the rise. A strange smile was on her face. "It seems someone has been busy."

"It's nothing more than a garden!" said Exedor.

"You, of all people, should know that appearances can be very misleading," Maelene answered. "This is The Tower. Within that *garden* lies power beyond your comprehension."

Exedor turned his scarred face to her then gestured again to his Faede. Two of them seized both Ferehain and Aleasea, and led them toward the ridge.

"Then take me down there," said Exedor. "And I warn you, whatever trap you're planning will cost you the lives of your followers. So be very, very careful, my dear mistress."

Maelene looked at the faces of her two Ageless, then turned and began the descent down the uneven surface of the crater. Valeyn took Naya in her arms and followed.

As they approached the first circular row of hedges, Valeyn started to understand the reason for their size. Beneath the green foliage – and invisible from a distance – lay a structure. A large curved complex that seemed to serve as a ringed perimeter to the garden within. It rose at least a hundred feet into the air and appeared to be carved out of one solid piece of dark blue rock. The sweeping, unnatural design reminded her of Anchorwatch somehow – a creation of the gods. The green hedges had grown across the structure over time, yet they were not wild. The hedge work seemed immaculately trimmed, with red and yellow flowers spread throughout the leaves like ribbons of color.

"This is The Tower, constructed by Nishindra the Crafter and also sealed by him before he left," said Maelene.

"Why is it covered with flowers? They're beautiful," asked Naya. Valeyn was suddenly reminded of Drela's flower stall back in Tiet.

"Yes, this I did not expect," Maelene answered as they came to a halt before the circular wall. She looked around for a moment then smiled. Valeyn followed her gaze to see a short, elderly man in the distance. He appeared to be trimming the hedge with simple tools, a small basket of green offcuts at his feet.

"Who is that?" Exedor asked.

"I believe he is the caretaker of this place, or at least that is his role now," answered Maelene. Exedor motioned to his Faede, but Maelene only laughed. "Oh please, Exedor. Do you intend to threaten everyone you meet? He may be our only way into The Tower. If your plan is to kill everyone who upsets you, then it is going to be a very long walk back for us."

She began walking toward the old man, who continued his pruning, seemingly oblivious to their presence. "Come, this is almost at an end," Maelene called over her shoulder.

They approached the man, who still did not so much as glance at them. He was dressed in simple, green gardener's clothes, with a wide-brimmed hat atop a round face that was lined with a silver beard. Maelene paused a short distance from him and watched as he clipped a long, thorny cutting from the hedge and gingerly placed it in the basket.

"Hello, Shin," Maelene said with a smile. "Were you not supposed to have left?"

The old man grunted as he straightened and stretched his back in relief from the work. "The same applies to you, doesn't it? Aren't you supposed to be dead?"

"I feel I was dead for a time. Now I have returned," she replied, staring up at the soaring greenery above them. "Shin, this is beautiful. I had no idea you were capable of such makings."

Nishindra shrugged and looked at her directly for the first time. Bright blue eyes peered out from under the broad hat. "Yeah, well, I got tired of my other creations, they all seemed to be getting a little...complicated. I wanted to try something straightforward."

"Did you take this from me?" Maelene's question sounded almost as if she were flattered.

"I used some of your *kai*. Just a little, mind you. It's all I could handle. I thought I might try to create something a little simpler to follow your work and to remember you."

"You have created something wonderful here, Shin. I doubt even I could have done much better," Maelene said.

Shin nodded curtly, then turned to look at the others, his eyes resting on Exedor. "So, you gonna introduce me to your travelling partners? Some of them don't look too friendly, do they?"

"I fear Exedor and his Faedes are not our friends, Shin. They have come to gain entry to The Tower," Maelene continued, but Shin was no longer listening to her. He was staring fixedly at Valeyn.

"Maelene..." he said slowly, "...is this...?"

"Yes, Shin. This is Valeyn, my daughter, and the first of the new gods."

Shin looked at her from head to foot, and Valeyn felt as if she were a piece of equipment.

"Incredible," Shin muttered. "I didn't think it'd ever be possible."

"Of course, it was possible. It was prophesied by your own constructs. I saw it here within the Oraculate. Did you not believe it?" Maelene asked.

Shin grunted and shook his head sadly. "She's Bythe's daughter then?"

"Yes, Bythe is her father," Maelene replied coldly.

"So where is he?" Shin asked.

"That's an excellent question, isn't it?" Exedor interrupted. "The short story is that Maelene stole his own daughter from him and has now fled here. Father is very unhappy, and I was charged with bringing these little troublemakers back to him for a reunion. But after I caught up with these two, we got to talking about your weapon contained within this place, and I thought it might be a good idea for a little detour into the Render."

"Who are you meant to be?" Shin asked.

"I am the Royal Inquisitor Exedor of the Iron Union," he said with a mock bow. Shin looked at him and crinkled his nose as if Exedor reeked of something the others couldn't smell. "What have you done to yourself? You're corrupted. You're filthy."

Exedor's face fell into a mockery of offense. "Oh, that's more than a little hypocritical coming from you, isn't it?" He walked over and placed his arm over Shin's shoulders. "What I've done is continue the work you started with Romona. I've been spending time in Kardak. You remember Kardak and Romona's Faedes, don't you?"

Shin shrugged himself free of Exedor's sarcastic embrace. "Get away from me. I want nothing more to do with that place. It's evil. You're evil."

Exedor laughed. The laughter fed on itself until it escalated into a cackle with a slight tinge of madness. "Evil? What is evil, Shin? You gods created the world as you saw fit. There were no rules, no laws of good or evil. The only laws were you could all do as you pleased. As I said, I'm just following your example."

"Exedor, please," Maelene said. "There is no need to antagonize anyone. The glory of The Tower is here before you. Is this not what you wanted?"

"No, I want to be *within* The Tower, not standing outside admiring its flowers!" Exedor snapped.

"No," said Shin. "I've spent my whole mortal life in the Forge creating things that wound up being twisted and perverted into evil. I'm sick of it. I sealed this place precisely so people like you couldn't get to it. You're not getting in."

"Nishindra the Crafter," Exedor smirked. "You've abandoned everything you've ever created, everything that makes you powerful. You've even locked yourself out of your own tower in an act of spite against the world. You can't stand here before me making demands when I'm the only one in control." He gestured to one of the Faedes, and it lurched up beside him, the rasping sound of its breath emanating from within the helm. "I've never used one of these to kill a god before. I wonder what it'll do to you?"

"Go to the hells, you little bastard," Shin spat.

Valeyn glanced at Aleasea and Ferehain, but they were all locked in by the remaining five creatures. Only Maelene seemed unconcerned. She ran her delicate fingers across the leaves of the carefully trimmed hedges as if considering something.

"One moment, Exedor," she said casually. "I need to ask him one final question before he leaves us." She turned to Shin without waiting for permission. "How did you manage to nurture the growth out here in the Render? I could never have achieved such a thing. Please, I must know the secret before you go."

The seemingly frivolous question surprised everyone into silence.

Shin looked at her with an unreadable expression. "I always crafted machines and objects, but they had a tendency to become corrupted. So I've spent my last years trying to understand something simple, something pure. I didn't have your gift of sustaining wildlife, but I had enough of it to seed one. I thought if I could design a self-sustaining cycle to fuel the life, then it might work, and it did."

"Incredible," Maelene whispered. "You truly are wise."

"I think you're overestimating the intelligence of any god who is stupid enough to accept such a pointless death," Exedor muttered.

"No, Exedor, you are the fool," Maelene's voice cracked like a whip. "Do you not hear what he has just told you?"

"I don't care how he grows his roses!" Exedor snarled back.

"You should. If you did, then you might have avoided this." Maelene closed her eyes and continued "He has created a perfect, self-sustaining system. I can feel it now. Oh, this is beautiful. Thank you, Shin."

Valeyn felt something hit her forehead. It was cold and wet. Then another one hit her cheek. She reached up to touch the side of her face, then examined her fingers. *Water?*

The drops came more frequently, and within seconds, a curtain of water was falling from the sky. Valeyn was stunned. She had never seen water falling from clouds. *Rain.* She had never thought it was possible. All water and plant life on Kovalith had been a gift from the gods. To feed life naturally seemed incredible. A smile involuntarily brightened her face and she began to laugh. Aleasea also grinned broadly, and even Ferehain looked amused. There was a childlike quality to that moment, as they all stood fascinated by the miracle of rain.

A shriek broke the silence and Valeyn swung her attention back to the Faede standing before Shin, but her trepidation turned back to joy as she saw the red cloaked figure thrashing about in the downpour of clean water.

"No!" cried Exedor, but it was too late. All of the Faede were now writhing in agony as the unrelenting water gave them no hiding place. They each staggered a few feet – trying in vain to find shelter – before collapsing to their knees under the pressure of the rain. Slowly they began to dissolve – just as Valeyn remembered from the river. Red chunks started to fall from their robes and melt within the downpour. Within seconds, only their crimson helms were left discarded on the ground, and the wretched creatures who once wore them were now freed from their servitude. As soon as the last of the Faede ceased moving, the rain stopped and Maelene opened her eyes.

Exedor immediately leapt clear of the group, watching all of them as if he were a rodent cornered by cats. "Stay back. I still have enough power to match you. Do not test me!" His voice was still strong, but there was a noticeable quaver in it now.

Ferehain and Aleasea immediately moved toward him but were stopped by Maelene.

"No, children. That's enough violence. I have no wish to see any more of you hurt," she called out in a clear voice.

"Mother, we cannot allow him to live," Ferehain said. It was the first time Valeyn had head him address Maelene as *mother*, and she wondered if he even knew he'd said it.

She walked over to Ferehain and placed a hand on his shoulder. "It is over, Ferehain," she said gently. "He cannot defeat us now, and every passing moment in this place only strengthens our position against him."

Exedor's face was twisted in frustration. "You planned to kill the Faede once we arrived here? How did you know? Tell me!"

Maelene shrugged and favored him with a beautiful smile. "Oh, I knew there were a dozen ways to disarm you once we reached The Tower, Exedor, but once I understood what Shin had created here, I simply thought this was the most fitting."

Exedor looked as if he were about to fly into a rage. Aleasea and Ferehain moved to stand on either side of him.

"Then we should guard him," Ferehain said, eyeing the grotesque device embedded within Exedor's stomach. "The power of Bythe should not be left unattended in this place. And we may yet have use of it."

Exedor spat at Ferehain's feet. "You will never take it from me!" he hissed.

Ferehain only smiled.

"If you wish it, Mother, then we will watch him," Aleasea said.

Valeyn stepped forward. It was as if they had all forgotten she was there – all but Shin. He was staring at her with a look that made her uncomfortable – as if her presence frightened him.

"So now what?" she asked the group.

Maelene turned to Valeyn and gave her the same radiant look. "Now, your destiny awaits, Daughter."

"No," Shin interrupted. "Walk away, Maelene. Please."

Maelene looked at him with mild surprise. "My friend, why should we leave? This is a wonderful moment. We can end this war and unify this world. Is that not what you wanted for so long? How many times did you plead with me and with Bythe for us to lay down our arms? Now I can see that you were right. I should have accepted this long ago."

"Maelene, I sealed this place for a reason. We all lost our way, you know that. I built terrible things, things that should never see the light of day. The power that's in there is too much. Please don't open it. Walk away, I'm begging you."

Maelene gently placed her palms on the shoulders of her old friend and looked down into his face. "But Valeyn will end this now. Do you see? There is no longer anything to fear. The fighting will end with her."

Shin seemed to slump as if defeated. "Very well. If this is what you want, then you'll have it," he muttered then turned and walked toward the hedges. Maelene motioned for them to follow. The two Ageless walked behind Exedor as they all followed Shin until he paused before an arched gap in the green wall. Valeyn could see it was a large door made of brass. She wondered what sort of man could ever open it before remembering this place was not designed for mortals.

"I sealed this a long time ago," Shin said as if talking to himself. "I can't even open it myself. I rigged it so only the energies of Bythe and Maelene combined could open it. I'd hoped that meant you'd come here together – in peace. Now this changes things."

"The prophecy of the Oraculate has been fulfilled through Valeyn. This is a far better way," Maelene answered. She looked at Valeyn and gestured to the door. "It is up to you now."

Valeyn glanced at Aleasea then stepped toward the massive brass doors. They were intricately crafted, with figures and scenes set in bas-relief within the metal. As she moved closer, she could see the figures of Dahz and Narak wrestling in one brass panel. In another she could clearly see Anchorwatch crafted into the metal in exquisite detail. All of the gods must have been captured on here by Shin. She took another step forward but before she could see any more, a strange feeling welled within her. The warm emerald *kai* of Maelene reached out to her from within the tower – as did the cold red *kai* of Bythe. A surge of panic filled Valeyn and she stepped backward, almost ready to run at the thought of Bythe's essence touching her. But before she could, the doors clicked and silently swung inward. Maelene's warm laughter was like the wind chimes Valeyn remembered from the Arcadia, but Shin's quiet sigh was cold by contrast. A breath of frigid air washed over them as The Tower opened its secrets.

"Lead the way," Maelene said to Valeyn.

Valeyn hesitated for a moment, but the energy of both her mother and father seemed to have retreated into the darkness of the ancient structure. She stared thoughtfully down the long pathway before her, then stepped across the threshold.

CHAPTER 2

"After the betrayal of Maelene, the legends she taught the Ageless were called into question. We know for certain that the gods tired of their life in the Forge. Many of them wished to return to their existence beyond Kovalith and to retrieve their kai from the land – destroying their creations. A handful of gods disagreed and petitioned the other gods to allow them to prove Kovalith worthy of existence. Eventually it was agreed to permit our survival for a time, in order to prove our worth and the value of the land they had created. We believe the gods will return to us in the coming of the Etherian – and our very existence will be judged by them.

We know that Maelene, Bythe, and Nishindra postponed the destruction of this world; however, their motives for doing so remain unclear."

~Aleasea of the Ageless

The tunnels were far larger than Jason had expected. They were incredible feats of architecture. Massive archways soared twenty feet high over the heads of the thousands of people shuffling under them, slowly making their way into the strange glow of the Ageless tunnels. The lucky families dragged small carts to carry the few possessions they had been permitted to take. The livestock had been set free to the western plains. There was no room for them in the tunnels, and Jason had no intention of letting them die in the upcoming assault.

Jason finished giving the final orders to the two soldiers assigned to Nadine's cart. He knew it had been an indulgence to assign two guards to watch over his family, but he didn't care. They were not to leave her side.

He looked over and caught sight of Sedren making preparations with a team of young men. Sedren had wanted to remain behind, but Jason wouldn't hear of it. The engineer had already completed his part of the destruction to come, and Jason's soldiers could now do the rest. The survivors were going to need engineers to rebuild, and Jason would not waste Sedren's life. He felt a small measure of hope that at least one good man would survive this.

Eventually, Jason ran out of excuses and mounted the cart. Nadine was resting on a makeshift pile of cushions with Raelle seated beside her. When she saw Jason, she whispered something to her daughter and gently rose, touching his arm affectionately as she left them alone. Nadine looked up at him with a wan smile on her drawn face, and Jason almost felt his heart break. She'd recovered physically from the birth, but he knew the emotional toll might never lift. He sat down next to her, unsure what to say. Without a word, she clung to him and he clung back. They sat gripped in each other arms for minutes while, all about them, people moved and spoke and bustled. He gritted his teeth and refused to let the tears come.

He glared down at the soldiers. "Keep her safe." His tone made it clear they now had but one purpose in life and that all other needs were dispensable. The seasoned soldiers saluted like cadets.

There was much that had been left unsaid between them, and her silent tears told him there was much that had no need to be said. She knew what awaited him.

Kissing her on the head, he forced himself to pull away – knowing if he didn't do so then, he would never leave her. She looked at him with red eyes and he looked back.

"I will always love you," he grated with a thick voice then hurried from the cart before his emotions seized him and he broke down completely.

He landed on the ground and took a few deep breaths to steady himself. Caydyn rounded the cart, cradling in his arms a familiar silver cat that looked around at the commotion with vague interest. "We almost left your personal guard behind. Captain Lewis would never approve, y'know."

Jason laughed at the sight and gently ran his hand over the smooth fur. The cat purred in reply, and Jason was grateful for the moment of unexpected affection. "No, we could never do that. We need all the protection we can get."

Caydyn placed the cat in the cart where she immediately began sniffing out the strange scents buried in the straw.

"Take care of them, please," Jason asked his father.

"Of course I will, but only until you come to take care of all of us."

Jason tried to say something, but he couldn't form the words.

"Tell me you're coming after us, Jason," Caydyn looked his son in the eye as if he were a child again.

Jason embraced his father, as much to avoid his gaze as to say goodbye. "Of course. Someone's got to show you the directions to Marfort. Gods know I can't leave it to my senile old father. You'll lead them right back here."

Caydyn laughed and clapped his son firmly across the shoulders. When they broke the embrace, Jason pretended not to see his father wipe the tears from his face.

"Now go. I'll be right behind you," Jason said.

"See you soon, Son." Caydyn smiled and turned away.

Seconds later he nodded to the guards and the cart lurched forward, joining the grim procession out of Fairhaven. He stood there as they left. He made himself watch, and he hoped the gods would forgive him for lying.

.   .   .

As soon as she entered The Tower, Valeyn could feel her senses distort. It was as if a surreal curtain had descended over her mind and she felt as if she were in a dream. She looked around slowly.

"Don't worry, you'll get used to it," Shin said as he walked alongside her. He shook his head ruefully. "It's been so damned long; I've forgotten how it feels in here."

Valeyn tried to focus on his words, but it felt as if her mind were drifting. The scene before her was hard to comprehend. She was looking down a corridor that seemed impossibly large; it was far too big to be contained within the building she had entered. The walls of the hallway seemed to be crafted of clouded glass, and the tiles before her were as black as obsidian. Valeyn stared about in wonder. Even Aleasea and Ferehain seemed to be unprepared for the sight. Exedor stood silently, no doubt trying to use his twisted gifts to probe The Tower for his own advantage, but Maelene did not seem concerned.

"The Tower is still sleeping, Exedor," she said calmly. "You will not find your weapon just yet."

Maelene led them down the corridor, her boots sounding crisp on the strange tiles. There were no lamps, yet the corridor seemed illuminated as if it were daylight. Valeyn could sense the *kai* of all the gods swimming within The Tower. The deep red pull of Bythe's *kai* was now almost impossible to resist, but her fear of it was greater. She clenched her jaw and tried to ignore both feelings.

"Shin built The Tower, but he chose its location specifically," Maelene explained as she led them down the massive hallway. "We are within the Forge, but also without it. What exists in here is only tangentially linked to what exists in the Render."

"This place is a bridge," Valeyn said almost involuntarily.

Maelene nodded with approval. "Very good, Daughter. You can feel it too. Yes, it is a bridge, or rather it was built upon one."

They walked a short distance before the passage led out into a darkened circular space. The darkness fled as soon as Valeyn entered and a vast arena lit up before her. Archways made of the same clouded glass surrounded the space on all sides, and balconies towered above her in tiers, glowing with a soft luminescence. It was immense. Valeyn estimated that it must have been large enough to cover the entire crater, had they still been outside.

"What happened to the garden?" Valeyn asked.

"It's still there, for now," Shin said, "but you won't be able to see it from here. We're not exactly within Kovalith anymore."

"We are existing in another plane of reality?" Aleasea asked.

"Yes," Maelene answered. "I tried to recreate something like this with the Arcadia, but I have not the skill of Nishindra. As you can see, my efforts pale in comparison to his work."

They all moved around the space, some remembering the wonders, others discovering them for the first time. Ferehain looked captivated and Aleasea slowly bent to one knee, muttering a silent prayer.

"Stop it," Exedor snapped at her. "Don't you see, even now? There's nothing sacred about this! This is just power that they possess and we do not."

"You're right, and you're also wrong," Shin replied. "Isn't power the essence of divinity? Isn't that what separates us from you? Isn't that the sort of divinity you're chasing by doing," he made a vague gesture toward Exedor, "whatever it is you think you're doing to yourself?"

"I am imitating you, Nishindra," Exedor replied with his mocking grin. "I'm crafting powerful wonders like you did. Does it upset you that a mortal can do the things you've done simply by following your own example?"

"No, it upsets me that you've missed the point entirely!" Shin snapped. "You're no different from the rest of them. It was never about power. It was about creation. Everything I ever did was out of the need to create something."

Valeyn looked at Shin and understood. "This was all your idea, wasn't it? You were the god who created the concept of Kovalith. You convinced the others to come here."

Shin met her eyes, and Valeyn saw the fear still lingering within him.

"You already see so much. Of all the things I tried to create, I would never have thought a new god would be one of them," Shin replied. "Yes, the creation of Kovalith was my idea. What's the point of being a god if not to create? Or to be worshipped?" He barked a short, bitter laugh. "That was how I managed to convince the others, of course, with *worship*. We could create a place where we would be adored. We would create life, then enslave that life. Bind it to serve us and praise us. Shallow praise, as it turns out."

"But you weren't interested in worship?" Valeyn asked.

"I only wanted to build beautiful things that people would adore. I guess that's a form of worship, isn't it?" Shin laughed again. "Maybe I wasn't as different from my brethren as I thought."

"Do not condescend to me, Shin. You were not so virtuous," Maelene said.

"No, you're right. I've got my own flaws, just like you. That's the thing about a mortal existence. That's what it does to you – it makes you lose sight of things."

Valeyn stepped toward him and felt a tendril of genuine remorse from the old god.

"You became so obsessed with your creations, you forgot why you were doing it, didn't you? You wanted to test the boundaries of who you were and who you weren't?" Valeyn asked carefully.

"Yeah," Shin replied as he forced himself to meet her eyes. "I didn't stop to think why I was doing it, or even if I should've been doing it. I just dived in and did the work as quickly as I could. I didn't want to think. By the end I was just outrunning my conscience."

Valeyn nodded slowly as the two gods understood one another.

"Ah!" Exedor's scornful voice cut over Shin's words. "And now it's time for you to reckon with that conscience, you old hypocrite. What were you doing with Romona in Kardak? What horrors did you visit upon innocents there in your pursuit of creation?"

Shin's face darkened and he fixed Exedor with a stare of pure hatred. For a moment, Valeyn thought he was about to strike out at Exedor, but instead, he turned to her and spoke in a voice filled with restraint. "The little man has a point. Would you like to see your birthright, Valeyn? Would you like to see the fruits of our labor? Why don't I give you a taste of some of the answers your mother is seeking?"

Shin didn't wait for her to reply. He turned from them all and marched toward a darkened archway on the far side of the arena.

They followed Shin across the enormous space as he vanished into the darkness of the tunnel. As Valeyn approached, she noticed the archway begin to glow and a dim light pulsed within the passageway beyond. She could sense the light somehow, and for a moment, she was reminded of the rooms beneath Kardak.

"I thought The Tower was sleeping?" Valeyn asked as they stood before the darkened archway.

"It is," Maelene answered. "The Tower is stirred by your presence and the power you bring, but you have not yet witnessed its glory. Come, this is something you must understand. You need to see what will be asked of you."

Maelene walked away abruptly and Valeyn followed. She passed under the archway and found herself in a cavernous room. The air inside was cold, and mist formed on her breath as she looked about her in the dim light. A central path split the area into two equal halves, and on either side of the path – carefully arranged in ordered rows – were dozens of caskets. A long pipe running the length of the arched ceiling glowed and pulsed as Valeyn entered. Shin was waiting for them at the center of the room, fixing Maelene with a cold stare.

"Is this what you came for?" Shin asked.

Maelene sighed and looked about her at the metal caskets. "I will not deny I once wanted to claim these, that is true." She glanced at Valeyn before continuing. "But I am no longer that person, Shin. I only wish to find a peaceful end to this, with my daughter."

"What are these things?" Valeyn asked.

Exedor walked over to one of the caskets. "And you dare to judge me?" he asked, shaking his head. "This is far beyond anything I have done."

Aleasea suddenly stepped beside Valeyn and took her by the arm. "Come away, please. This is a not a good idea." There was a look of comprehension on her face and a note of fear in her voice. Valeyn had never heard her speak in such a way.

She gently pulled herself free of Aleasea's grip and walked over to one of the caskets. It was made of metal and shaped like a tomb. Valeyn could see that each had a tube of that same clouded glass connected at the head of each box. The tube started to glow and pulse as she approached it – as if sensing her power and feeding off it. The overhead pipe also started to pulse, and a rhythmic beat started to sound throughout the chamber. It was a familiar sound, like a heartbeat, or a clock.

Valeyn involuntarily screamed as the casket shot upright. The metal door flung open and the towering form of Imbatal stepped forward.

.   .   .

Jason had lived in Fairhaven his entire life. He'd never even seen any other place until he joined the army. And while places like Bonehall might have been more imposing and more exciting, Fairhaven had always been his home. Jason looked up at the moon. It must have been approaching midnight. He stood before his house – his father's house, the home where he'd been born – and looked at its faded blue paint for the last time. He could remember playing with a wooden sword in the dirt road that ran past his father's workshop. It was probably his earliest memory. It made him smile.

He turned and walked back along the cobblestone streets. They were deserted now. The only people remaining were soldiers and a handful of Violari, all of whom had volunteered to remain behind. He could hear them at work, spread throughout houses and shops he passed by. As he walked toward the marketplace, he forced himself to look at every building he passed. He tried to commit every old brick, every shingled tile to memory. It felt like he owed these old structures that much.

He glanced to the south and saw the glow of the war engine polluting the night sky. He wondered if Ethan was planning to attack at dawn. Maybe he'd intentionally given them time to evacuate the population just to make things easier? It hardly mattered now. By morning Fairhaven would be a ruin, and soon after, he would be dead.

His only burning wish was that he could take Ethan to the afterlife with him. Perhaps the gods would grant him this chance? Perhaps he'd get the chance to prove that Ethan hadn't won everything? It was the only slim hope that kept him alive.

Jason glanced skyward again and reckoned it must be time. Kaler had retreated into Sanctuary with a small number of his Violari a few hours earlier. The work Jason had asked them to do was terrible, but necessary. It was no different for any of the soldiers who had stayed behind, least of all for him. He rounded a corner and came into view of the marketplace. There were soldiers readying the space with makeshift barricades – this was going to be the location of their final stand. He approached the market and saw the bridge leading over the river toward the Temple. For some reason, he remembered the day all three of them had sat there – Jason, Nadine, and Elyn – discussing their future. He paused and looked at the spot where they'd sat on the stone wall, idly discussing tomorrow as if it were theirs to own. Nadine later admitted that was the day she'd first started to fall in love with him. Now he knew he'd never see that look in her eyes again. It seemed like such a long time ago. It seemed like that cocky, happy young man had been someone else. And Elyn. Gods, if they'd only known what the future held for her. He wondered where she'd gone and hoped she'd found the happiness she sought.

"Well, you sure made the right decision to leave when you did," Jason quietly spoke to the night.

The night flashed green, and a mighty crack pierced the silence. Jason turned to watch the Temple. It started to tremble, then a gush of fire burst through the roof and spun into the night sky. Flaming debris fell to the city as the Temple was quickly consumed with the roar of an orange blaze. The Temple groaned and heaved with the eruption, and one of its ancient walls fell inward. It was a picturesque destruction.

Jason turned to look at the city rooftops around him. One by one, spotfires of light began to flare as his men set fire to their assigned buildings throughout the city. Sedren had identified the city buildings most susceptible to fire, and Jason had assigned soldiers accordingly. Within minutes, the southern glow of the war engine had become eclipsed by the roaring inferno growing within Fairhaven's walls. It was the scene of burning desolation that Jason recalled. His eyes stung from the thick smoke that clogged the air, and grime now covered his blue uniform. He walked over to the low wall along the river as he looked at the Temple of Fairhaven burning with the ferocity of the sun. Jason understood he was witnessing the immolation of the reserves of *kai* within the Arcadia. Like a plant burned at the roots, it would never grow back. Fairhaven was truly dead.

He turned from the funeral pyre and walked back to the marketplace. It was surrounded by wooden barricades, hastily constructed from carts and timber crates. Less than fifty soldiers waited there. They were all who remained. They were all he would allow. They stood, most of them with soot-covered faces, all of them grave. They knew what they had chosen to do.

Jason flashed them a smile as he entered the square. "One hell of a show, isn't it? Do you think those Helmsguard bastards have noticed yet?"

"I reckon they can't see crap with those metal cans on their heads, sir," said Lieutenant Shane. "I might have to go out there and point it out to them."

Laughter rippled among the group. Jason smiled, and he found it was genuine. He looked at the small group of men – men he was going to die with tomorrow. He looked at Lieutenant Shane, a man who had somehow escaped death and had now volunteered to face it again. Jason looked at them all and felt humbled.

"Boys, I don't know what tomorrow is going to bring, but the fact that you stayed—"

Shane stood to interrupt him. "We know what's going to happen, sir. We're going fight, sir. We're going to fight with you."

Shane gave him a meaningful look and in that moment Jason understood. This was not the time for a self-indulgent outpouring of emotion. He knew what his men needed to hear and who they needed him to be.

"No, Lieutenant," Jason smiled and continued in a loud and clear voice that rang across the square. "That's not what's going to happen tomorrow. Tomorrow morning, those iron bastards are going to strut though that gate with their polished armor and their fancy machine, and they think they're just going to walk in here and take our city from us. Well, sorry, Bythe. You can't have it!" He roared the last sentence and a cheer erupted from his men. "They're not taking a thing from us! They can have the ashes we *choose* to leave behind. They can taste the bitter disappointment of coming all this way for absolutely nothing. But most important of all, they can have one parting gift from every man here. We'll remind them one last time what sort of welcome Fairhaveners give to murdering bastards who knock on our door. Tomorrow, we'll give them one final punch in their smug faces!"

The roar was like a crowd ten times its number. Jason roared with them. He screamed into the night and hugged his men as he waded through them. As he looked into the eyes of each soldier, he witnessed the same resolution mirrored in every look. If he was to die tomorrow, then he was determined to die damned well.

CHAPTER 3

"Their lights go out...one by one. It is all I can think of now, sister. Every day I watch them fade and I envy them. I want to follow them into the darkness and see what lies in wait there for us. I will follow them soon. It is all that matters now. They pass out of my sight and I find it is not enough. I need to understand where they go. I need to watch their lights struggle and fade into the night we have made for them. I hope you are still there, sister. It seems there are so few of us left. The madness seems to take us all in the end, and there is little I can now do to stop it. There is such little point now. I want to follow the lights. I will follow them and see where they lead. Please remember me. Please remember what we have done here. Please forgive it."

~Romona – Goddess of Death and Regeneration

Aleasea was pulling Valeyn away as Imbatal towered above them, its impassive face staring down at their retreat. Across the room, the remaining caskets violently upended themselves and their doors snapped open with a deafening clatter. Tall figures stepped out of metal cases with a stiff, unnatural gait. They all stood like the figure Valeyn remembered – dressed head to foot in pure white. Their faces unreadable behind plain, white masks, with only the eye-slits giving any indication there was a living creature beneath. Naya screamed, and Ferehain pressed the girl behind him as he readied himself to attack.

"Wait!" Shin's voice boomed across the chamber. "They are harmless."

"Harmless?" Aleasea gasped in disbelief. "We know these creatures! Imbatal served Yvorre for decades. He killed hundreds in Fairhaven. He took my arm!"

Valeyn had never heard Aleasea acknowledge her injury before this. The words brought back her own memories – the sickening feeling of Imbatal's blade digging into Vale's body, crippling her mercilessly. Maelene looked at the floor as if deeply ashamed but said nothing.

Shin moved himself to stand between Ferehain and the creatures. "That was Yvorre's work. That one was her demon," he said. "These are dormant. They do not have the power to do anything without The Tower."

Valeyn looked about the space. "There're dozens of them," she whispered.

"One hundred and five," Shin corrected.

"My gods," Valeyn whispered. A terrifying comprehension dawned upon her. Just one of these clockwork demons had the power to kill untold numbers of the Ageless and to bring Fairhaven to its knees. If Elyn and Vale had not reconciled into Valeyn, then Fairhaven would almost certainly have been destroyed. The thought of over a hundred beings with the strength and dispassionate ferocity of Imbatal filled her with fear.

"Where did they come from?" Valeyn asked.

"They came from Kardak, didn't they? This is your great weapon," Exedor answered.

Shin continued to ignore Exedor and instead, turned his attention to Valeyn.

"This is your birthright, girl. This is the culmination of the labor of the gods on Kovalith. The perfect union of mortal life with the finest crafts of the gods. Take it and be proud!" Shin threw the words at Valeyn as if they were filthy.

Valeyn slowly approached the nearest towering figure and stared at its unmoving form.

"You built these with Romona. These are her patients."

"That's not how it started," Shin sighed. "At first I was helping her bring people back from the brink of death. I wanted to do good. But over time, I wasn't happy with just healing people, I wanted to improve them. I wanted to make them stronger so they wouldn't get sick again. I had already created clockwork engines to generate something similar to our *kai*. I began to craft this onto her patients. I think I wanted to see if I could be better than the other gods – create a better race than they could."

Valeyn could hear Aleasea's sudden intake of breath at the horrors of Shin's confession.

Shin turned and fixed Maelene with a baleful glare. "Once your mother found out what we were doing, she saw an opportunity for her escalating war with your father. She encouraged us relentlessly. We kept pushing the boundaries of what we could do, and it drove Romona to kill herself."

"That is not fair, Shin," Maelene objected. "I did not intend for that to happen. I certainly did not want Romona to harm herself."

"Rubbish!" Shin snarled. "You didn't care! Neither did I and in the end, neither did she. We were all so obsessed, we never stopped to think about what could happen. I had no idea how much her sanity was slipping or what she'd started doing to her patients, or maybe I just didn't want to know." He looked at Valeyn as if she were the only person who could understand. Pain was etched deep into his face along with the lines of mortal age. "She'd betrayed the people who came to her for help. She'd stopped healing them and started twisting them. She twisted their minds, their dreams...then when she was through, she twisted their bodies. They weren't even human by the time she gave them to me, but that's no excuse. I still didn't stop until madness took hold of her and she cut her own throat."

Shin walked over to one of the machines, stared up into its impassive white mask, and grunted a deeply cynical laugh.

"But how about this? Even then, after all that horror, I still couldn't bring myself to destroy these things. Too proud, I suppose. I brought them here instead, where I told myself they'd be kept safe."

Anger flashed in Maelene's eyes. "And by doing so, you denied me the very weapons I needed to bring peace. You could have helped me. You could have made Romona's death mean something, but you chose to hide instead."

"You didn't want *peace*, you wanted *victory*. Of course I kept them from you. These poor souls had suffered enough at our hands, at *my* hands."

Maelene held up her hands as an offering of goodwill. "Either way, what is done is done. We are here now."

Shin shook his head at her and turned away with a look of distress. Valeyn could sense something else was wrong, but her mind was still trying to process everything she had learned.

"So, is this the reason we're here, Mother?" Valeyn asked. "Do you expect me to take control of this army of monsters and lead them against my father?"

Maelene walked over to her daughter and looked at her for a long moment. "You were right about me in Tiet. You were wise not to trust me. When I came to you, I wanted to gain access to the power within this place. I wanted to take control of this army and use it, but I knew Shin had sealed The Tower against me. So I needed you, but your instincts were right. My motivations were selfish."

"And now?" Valeyn asked warily.

"Now, I feel differently, Valeyn. You have taught me that I must leave that decision to you," Maelene replied. She pointed a delicate hand at the creatures lined up across the room. "These could all be yours now. They could follow your commands if you wish it. The Tower is dormant. Shin has sealed it so only you can reawaken the power within, and if you do, The Tower will be yours to command."

Valeyn shook her head in disbelief. "I never asked for this. I don't know how to unify this world."

She turned from the creatures. She couldn't bear to look into those impassively murderous faces any longer. They seemed all too familiar somehow. The vaulted ceilings and the strange columns of The Tower seemed to be singing to her with a chorus of voices.

"I can feel him here, like I can feel you. You're all in this place," Valeyn whispered.

Bythe's terrifying energies lingered along with those of the other gods – like an instrument within an ensemble. Maelene walked up alongside her and together they looked around at the tiered archways above them. "We all built Kovalith together on this ground. It was so long ago. It was a different time back then. As we crafted the Forge, we all left elements of our energies throughout the land, but this is where it is most powerful."

"Tell me I can trust you, Mother."

Maelene paused and seemed to consider her words very carefully. "I want this to be over, Valeyn. We have all fallen so far from who we used to be. Even standing here reminds me of this."

"What do you want me to do?"

"When I used the Oraculate, I was able to see the vision of you on the throne of the Ironhelm, but no more than that. You will be able to reveal more. You can awaken The Tower, then we can unlock the secrets of the Oraculate together. We can unlock the mystery of your destiny and end this war."

Valeyn grimaced. She remembered the vision in the Arcadia very clearly. "So I can take possession of everything I find here? I can use it to do...whatever I want?"

"You can access our *kai*, Valeyn. I can help you," said Maelene.

"No!" shouted Shin. "Don't do this. This isn't what I wanted. I wanted you and Bythe to make peace and come here together. Then we could finally end it."

"What do you mean by *end* it?" Valeyn asked.

Shin looked at her and the fear was back in his eyes. He ran his eyes over her as if he couldn't believe she existed before turning to Maelene.

"It's over, don't you all see that? We failed. We promised our brethren we'd find a way to justify the existence of Kovalith, but we did the very opposite. You and Bythe split the world in two over your petty squabbles, and I was too impotent to stop it."

"But Valeyn can stop this now."

"No, she can't. You can't trust her judgment. She's no different from the rest of us."

Surprise shot across Maelene's face, but before she could speak Ferehain stepped forward.

"Then help us destroy Bythe. If you feel guilt, then you surely must help undo the damage you have wrought. Aid us."

"Do not judge me, Ageless," Shin's voice was suddenly without weakness or contrition. "I don't answer to you. You're the servants of my guests. Remember your place."

"But this isn't your decision to make for the rest of the world," said Exedor. "You've admitted as much yourselves. You've all gone mad. You don't have the right to make decisions for the rest of us."

"And you think that you do?" Ferehain answered, walking up to face him.

"I'm mortal. Kovalith is my home. I have more of a right than she does. Even you, Ferehain, have more of a right than them. What has Maelene done for you? She's acted only for herself. She even betrayed her own Ageless when she thought they were of no use to her. They don't deserve to rule over us, Ferehain. I know you agree with me."

"Enough!" Valeyn shouted. Everyone fell silent as her voice echoed around the cavernous space. Again, everyone demanding something from her. She needed to think, she needed a clear voice. A pure voice. She pushed her way through the group and found who she was searching for. Naya stood quietly in her crude walking irons. Valeyn knelt down before her.

"What do you think I should do?" Valeyn asked.

Naya smiled nervously. "Me? I don't know anything about this."

Valeyn returned the smile. For a moment, it felt like they were back at Tiet. "I want to know if you think I'm being selfish if I take all this power. Can I be trusted?"

"I don't know," Naya shrugged and looked down at her own ruined body. "But I know you're a good person. I guess if you can stop what happened to me from happening to other people, then yes, you should do it. You don't want to hurt anyone, Valeyn. I trust you."

Valeyn kissed Naya on her forehead then stood up and turned back to Shin.

"Show me what to do," she said.

Shin shook his head. "I'll have no further part in this. Every time I try to help, I make things worse. I've tried to advise you against this, so whatever you do next is on your own head."

"Come, Valeyn, I can help you. I have done this before," said Maelene. She took Valeyn's hand and led her out of the mausoleum.

Valeyn heard the footfalls behind her and knew the others were following. They walked back into the massive arena and halted in the center. Maelene turned to address Aleasea.

"Take Naya and stand well clear," she commanded. Aleasea gently guided the young girl into the protection of the archways. Exedor and Ferehain reluctantly followed.

"The Tower is built upon a foundation of *kai*," Maelene said to Valeyn. "You must reach out and sense the flows as they run through this space."

"The flows from both you and Bythe?" Valeyn asked.

"Yes, but only you can awaken both of them."

Fear bubbled within her, but she forced it down. "Will Bythe be able to find me?"

"He will know what you are doing, but it is far too late for him to act. Do not be afraid."

Valeyn nodded and closed her eyes, opening herself to the swirls of energy around her. She could sense the presence of so many different flows. All of them. All twenty-six. Swirls of violet, yellow, and blue stretched around her like ribbons. Spine-tingling notes of music seemed to drift around her. It was a wonderous symphony of light and sound. She concentrated, and a strong band of dark green came into focus – Maelene's *kai*. Reaching out with her hand, she gently wrapped it around her wrist. Then she drew in a deep breath and reached into herself, indulging the dark side of her soul that came from her father. A deep band of red flared in front of her. It seemed to stretch into the sky like a beacon. In that instant, Valeyn could feel a gentle pull, a distant connection with something dark – something very, very powerful. It seemed to be calling to her and for a moment she felt regret. It seemed to her that she needed to reach back along that thread and find the source. To find Bythe.

No!

She snapped herself back into focus and gripped the red strand of energy before her. The moment she touched it she felt the fabric of reality open. There was a hum, and Valeyn's entire body tingled. She opened her eyes and saw The Tower rising above her. It stretched – white and brilliant – toward the sky with a reach that appeared infinite.

The Tower was alive, and the deception of its name was now apparent. The Tower was never a solid construct. It was a shimmering tunnel of white energy spiraling to the heavens.

Only, it wasn't white. When her eyes adjusted to the dazzling display, she could see the spectrum of colors blending together in the whirlpool above. It was a unity of *kai*.

"Shin! What is this?" Maelene wore a look of concern as she called out to him.

Sprites of color floated down to them like the rain Valeyn had seen outside. She stared at a teardrop of bright orange slowly descending before it broke on her hand.

"It's what I told you." Shin's voice sounded hard and bitter. "I never intended Valeyn to be here. I wanted you and Bythe together. I rigged The Tower so when you came, it'd open to the *Etherian*, even if I wasn't here – *especially* if I wasn't here."

"You are summoning them?" Maelene asked.

"That's up to you. We can leave here – you, me, even the girl." Shin nodded at Valeyn. "We can go to them right now. But no matter what, this is ending. Our time here is done."

"No," whispered Maelene. "This is not how it will be. I will bring peace to this place. I need to prevail."

Valeyn looked up into the swirling vortex. She thought she could hear something. It felt like music – hovering somewhere within her mind. It was the call of home.

"We can go there?" Valeyn asked.

"No," Maelene snapped. "That is not why we are here." She reached upward, and strands of color broke free of the swirling tower of light and drifted down to her, wrapping themselves around her hands like elegant tendrils. When all the beautiful colors fluttered from her hands like banners in a breeze, she rotated her wrists in an intricate pattern of movements. The colors weaved together as one, forming a dazzling white band of light.

Valeyn could sense the new connection. It wrenched the two threads from her hands, and they joined the flow of power rushing into her mother. She yelped at the surprise jolt of pain that ran through her hands as the energies were snatched from her.

"You told me that you couldn't use another god's energies," Valeyn said, rubbing her tender palms as if they were bruised.

"Outside this place, that is true, but in the Render we all shared our *kai* together. It was necessary for us to build Kovalith. Here, the barriers do not exist."

Valeyn eyed her mother with a growing feeling of suspicion. "So, you only needed me to break Shin's lock on the *kai*?"

"Every fire is ignited by a spark, child. This fire needed two sparks which I could not provide alone. Now that the fire burns, I can lead us from here." She turned her face to Valeyn as a fierce passion flared in her eyes. "Do not worry. The Oraculate will guide us now. It will show us the path to unseat Bythe and place you on his throne. We will prevail, after all these years."

Maelene closed her eyes and an aura of glowing light appeared around her small body. She made a movement with her hands and a flare shot toward the tier above them. The archways surrounding them distorted like water droplets. These twisting forms reached out to each other and coalesced into a larger shimmering window, eventually enveloping the entire arena in a complete circle.

Valeyn recognized the Oraculate.

Maelene furrowed her brow in concentration and images began to flash through the window. The figures of twenty-six men and women stood in a crater, hands linked as a nimbus of colors weaved around them. The image was gone and replaced with mountains, bright red and impossibly high – growing like weeds and stretching toward the horizon. Dozens more images flashed before them, strange races Valeyn didn't recognize. There was a flash of the black towers of the Ironhelm – partly constructed – but then they were gone. More images passed, and Valeyn understood that Maelene was searching through the passages of time the gods had imposed upon Kovalith. The images were not random. They seemed to be significant, maybe even pivotal moments within Fairhaven's destiny.

"Wait!" Valeyn shouted.

The image had stopped on a landscape Valeyn recognized, albeit barely. Fairhaven. Valeyn took an involuntary step forward and her face fell in dismay. Fairhaven was ravaged. The walls had caved inward, and coils of black smoke rose from the charred remains of the city. Black-armored Helmsguard crawled through the wreckage like ants, and a massive tower of black metal lurched outside the remains of the Old City walls.

Valeyn felt Aleasea and Ferehain standing beside her, her horror shared.

"We must do something," Aleasea pleaded.

"It is too late. These events are about to unfold. You cannot stop them," Maelene murmured.

"Our people are still there!" said Ferehain. Valeyn saw he was right; a small ring of blue-garbed defenders were gathered around the ruins of the Temple.

"No, Ferehain. That is not why we are here. You must let go of the past, as I have. There are far greater concerns before us."

Valeyn took another step forward and stared at the image. Jason was there. He was clearly visible in the middle of the ruined marketplace, and his own appearance mirrored the devastation surrounding him. Before she could speak, a bright stream of blue fire shot up from the ground next to Jason and surged skyward, knocking him from his feet.

"The *Etherian*," whispered Aleasea. "Mother, it is the end of all there is!"

Valeyn watched in horror as more streams of color ripped from the ground under the helpless people, their forms obliterated as the color swept through them leaving behind no trace they had ever lived. The land started to tremble, and the few remaining buildings in the ruined city started to collapse.

"Jason!" Valeyn screamed as a red stream of energy surged from the ground and erased his image from existence. "Mother, please! We have to do something!"

"We have far greater problems, child. I am sorry."

Maelene tensed and again the image vanished. This time it was replaced by another familiar scene – sandy plains littered with rent bodies. Valeyn had witnessed this vision before. This was one of the many possible futures that resulted from the war between Maelene and Bythe. The image shifted again, and Valeyn recognized a prophesied vision of city streets lined with rotting carcasses no longer recognizable as human. Again and again the images shifted, but the vision of Valeyn atop Bythe's black throne was nowhere to be found.

Maelene grunted in frustration as the images spun faster and faster. Every scene a landscape of carnage and death. Valeyn was not among them.

"Where is it, Shin?" Maelene called. "What have you done?"

The images whirled with increasing speed, and Valeyn began to feel dizzy. Naya fell to the ground, clutching her stomach with nausea.

"Enough!" Shin yelled, and the images stopped. He walked into the center of the room and stood erect with his hands clasped behind his back. There was a strange sense of finality in his posture as he met Maelene's eyes. "There is no prophecy, Maelene. It was a lie. I seeded the vision into the Oraculate, knowing you would find it."

There was no sound in the chamber but for the faint moaning of Naya.

"This doesn't make any sense." Valeyn said. "Are you saying you made it up?" Valeyn looked from Shin to Maelene. Her mother was staring at Shin as if she were carved from stone.

"It was manipulation," said Ferehain. "He only wanted to bring both Bythe and Maelene here."

"You were both tearing the Forge apart. You still are. Look at the future! Every path still leads to death, even now. I knew that you and Bythe would keep coming to me for more weapons to use against each other. You'd never stop your mad games until everyone was dead. So I shut down The Tower. Everything but the Oraculate was sealed. When you came here searching for me, as I knew you would, you saw a prophecy I'd created."

"I don't believe you," Valeyn said. "We all saw the vision of me. How could you possibly know what I was going to look like?"

Shin laughed. "It wasn't you, girl. I admit I came pretty close to the finished product, but the woman in the vision looked very different to you."

Valeyn recalled that the woman in the vision had looked different to both Vale and Elyn. That hadn't been surprising at the time, but did she look like *Valeyn*? She couldn't recall. In fact, she'd never even thought about it.

"You saw my vision before you saw Valeyn, then you just chose to remember it the way you wanted to – or to *not* remember it," said Shin.

Valeyn realized he was right. Once events had been set in motion, none of them had questioned the details of the prophecy. Valeyn was stunned at her own naïveté.

"Once Maelene had left, I sealed The Tower completely," Shin continued. "I made sure it could only be opened if both she and Bythe returned together. I hoped they wouldn't – I hoped my lie would make them reconcile – but if they came back looking for more answers, then The

Tower would open the *Etherian* and the gods would return. They would pass judgment, and we could finally end this mistake.

"That's horrible. What's wrong with you? What were you trying to achieve?" Valeyn whispered.

"An end to all this!" Shin shouted. "Don't you dare denounce me as a villain when you can see with your own eyes what they're going to do to this world. Everyone is going to die because of their madness." He waved wildly at the images of desolation around them. "I tried reasoning with them both after Romona killed herself. Nothing worked. So I hoped I could reach them through sympathy, or maybe even through pride. If they both believed their daughter could unite Kovalith, then maybe they'd finally stop fighting. Maybe this future could be avoided."

Silence hung in the air as everyone slowly understood the implications of his words.

Shin grunted a cynical laugh. "It almost worked. I managed to convince Maelene, and for a moment I thought I'd saved the world." His face darkened and all humor vanished from his eyes. "But I had no idea Bythe would react the way he did. When I thought he'd killed Maelene...I gave up. I thought it was over."

Valeyn looked at Shin as if he still held the answers. She still could not fathom the implications of what she was hearing. "But I exist now. Surely that means something. I can still do something?"

Shin shrugged. "It means whatever you want it to mean. I'm sorry, kid, but there's no special purpose to your existence. You're no different from the rest of us. You're just another god who's probably going to go mad."

Maelene stepped away from them. Her face was impassive, yet Valeyn could sense emotion roiling within her.

"Maelene," Aleasea called out. "Are you alright?"

"Everything I did – all I sacrificed – it was all for nothing." Maelene's voice was barely audible.

"I didn't know what Bythe would do to you," Shin countered.

"All those years I spent in the Ironhelm resisting him, then the..." It was as if Maelene couldn't force herself to give voice to the memory. "I went through so much pain...I became so twisted...and it was all for nothing?"

Valeyn could sense something familiar. A greasy blackness seeping through the presence of Maelene. "Mother, please—" she began but Maelene cut her off.

"Do not call me that. I am not your mother. I wish I'd never given birth to you." Maelene turned back, and her eyes were again the sunken pits that Valeyn remembered from Vale's childhood.

Aleasea had moved up alongside Valeyn and stood ready. "Dear gods, Maelene, do not do this to us again," she warned.

Maelene looked at Aleasea, and the malice of Yvorre crept deeper across her features. "To you? What about what has been done to me? What about the pain he put me through? All for nothing!"

"It's too late. What's done is done," Shin answered. "The Tower's signaled the *Etherian*. They will be coming to judge us. It's over now, Maelene."

The aura of light flared around Maelene. Fury gripped her as she looked about the space like an animal trying to understand a trap it had stumbled into.

"Fine..." she muttered and extended her hand. A torrent of white energy crackled across the room and seared through Shin's chest. Naya screamed as he fell dead without a sound.

Ferehain moved to stand alongside Aleasea and shot them both a look of warning.

"Mother, please don't do this. Remember everything we shared, everything you told me. You didn't want to be like this." Valeyn tried to meet Maelene eyes, but it was like trying to stare into the heart of the sun.

Maelene flung her hands toward the tunnel of light above her. The spinning vortex of white began to slow, causing each of the colors to become more discernable. "You cannot know how I feel. I will not allow your father to win. I cannot. If Shin wants an end to this, then that is fine. I will give him an end. There is no one to stop me."

"At last!" Exedor shouted almost triumphantly. "The gods truly reveal themselves to us. I was right about you. In the end, you're nothing more than a vengeful old woman!"

Piece by piece, the mosaic of light began to break apart. Beams of blue, indigo, scarlet, and bright green cascaded around them haphazardly. The spectacle was unlike anything Valeyn had ever seen. It was captivating. It was a display that could have been beautiful had Valeyn not sensed a penetrating danger behind it.

Slowly the light rainfall of energy paused, and for a moment, filaments of color hung suspended around them. Maelene stretched her arms wider and grunted with effort. Words Valeyn did not understand rumbled deep in her throat, and the fragments of color began to float skyward as if caught on a breeze.

The Ageless seemed to sense it first.

"Maelene, what are you doing?" Ferehain's voice was grave.

Maelene didn't answer. Instead, the beams of light began to spiral upward like a wind funnel. The Tower trembled.

"Maelene! Stop this!" Aleasea cried. "Remember the vision in the Oraculate. You saw what this will do to Fairhaven."

"No," Maelene answered. "I will not let him win. I will not let him laugh at me. Not after everything I endured. I'll see the world burn before I let him take it."

"What's she doing?" Valeyn asked.

"Can't you feel it, girl?" Exedor answered. "She's using The Tower to pull the *kai* out of Kovalith. Even I can sense it! She's bringing about the *Etherian*."

"Mother, that's going to kill everyone. You're going to kill Jason! Mother!" Valeyn shouted.

"I told you not to call me that!" Maelene motioned violently with her hand and a spear of deep red light washed over Valeyn. She felt a flood of wild emotions and fell to her knees screaming. "Here, revel in your father's power. Is this not what you have resisted all this time?" Yvorre mocked.

Naya called out and awkwardly limped over to where Valeyn lay. The Tower shook again, and a crack appeared in the terrace above.

"Look at the gods you've chosen to serve," Exedor shouted over the rising din. "See them for what they really are. Nothing more than selfish madmen."

"Shut up!" snapped Aleasea.

Ferehain looked at Exedor. "Will you help us?"

Exedor's ruined face twisted into a smile. "To overthrow the gods of Kovalith? The question is, will you help me?"

Ferehain didn't answer. He nodded to Aleasea, and the two of them moved in opposite directions as if to flank Maelene. The black and green cloaked figures moved like cats circling prey. She glanced at them both and shook her head slightly.

"My students, what do you think you are trying to do."

The Ageless said nothing. Instead, they both extended their arms, and Valeyn could see the bright green glow of *kai* flare around them.

But Maelene was quicker. Without so much as a gesture from her, the green energy began to bleed away from both Aleasea and Ferehain and joined the nimbus of color floating skyward. Both of them wilted as Maelene began draining them of power. Exploiting the distraction, Exedor stepped forward to stare at Maelene. The colors Valeyn could see flaring around Exedor were strange – the deep red of Bythe mixed with an inky corruption. It felt unclean to look at.

Maelene cried out and The Tower shook again. She reached out as if trying to snatch the power from Exedor, but the black contamination seemed to slip from her grasp. The putrid aura around Exedor flared again as he launched another attack on Maelene's fragile mind. She lurched back a step, and the myriad colors broke loose of her hands, thrashing errantly about the shaft like a whirlwind.

"No!" Maelene screamed as the energy of The Tower was ripped from her.

Valeyn staggered back to her feet. She could feel the *kai* thrashing about her. She could sense the dark red and bright green trails of light as they began to surge upward in a growing tide. She closed her eyes and opened herself to them, to the souls of both her mother and father, and of Elyn and Vale. Streams of green and red surged toward her from out of the maelstrom and flowed into each hand. She could feel a fire welling within her, an indescribable sense of potency.

Maelene shouted an ancient curse as a mighty cloud of green flared around her. The Tower heaved violently, and the ground seemed to shift underfoot. A crack opened within the black glass of the floor, and Exedor leaped sideways to avoid falling. The terraces above splintered, and broken bricks of glass crashed to the floor about them. Exedor cried out as the avalanche devoured him.

Freed from his assault, Maelene flung out her hands and again called the spectrum back to her – twenty four colors snapped to her waiting hands, yet the deep red of Bythe and Maelene's own bright green energies remained with Valeyn.

"Give it back!" Maelene screamed. Her burning eyes now sat in sunken pits of a long and heavily wrinkled face. She again looked like the woman from Vale's youth, a woman who had lived far past her natural time. "It's not yours. Give it back to me!"

"You're wrong, Mother," Valeyn shouted and her voice matched Maelene's. "You've told me this is my birthright. You told me to stop running from it. I won't let you destroy this world, and I don't believe you want to do this."

Maelene reached out, and Valeyn could feel her pulling at the energies, trying to drag them out of her grip. Valeyn closed her eyes and latched onto them with her mind. She pictured a trap snapping shut around the two threads. Maelene tugged at them both, but they held firm.

"What do you think you're doing?" Maelene's voice held a note of panic.

"I've stopped hiding, Mother. It's time you did the same. Stop this martyrdom. Stop pretending to be someone you're not. Who do you want to be? Maelene or Yvorre?"

"Stop it," she growled.

"Or perhaps you're like me. Perhaps you're two different people?"

"Stop!" A flare of bright blue fire leapt from Maelene's hands and slammed into Valeyn's chest. She was flung back to the floor, the breath exploding from her lungs as she hit the hard, black surface, but she seemed to be otherwise unharmed. She kept her mind focused on the two strands of energy trapped in her mind and got back to her feet. Maelene was walking toward her like a vengeful specter. Her spine was bent, and her arms had grown too long for her body. Maelene seemed to be almost completely gone, subsumed by the worst parts of her nature – by Yvorre. Valeyn steadied herself. She didn't want to kill her own mother, but there seemed to be no other choice. Yvorre seemed to sense this hesitation, and a black smile darkened her face.

"You're going to have to kill me, Daughter, or give me what I want – or I will kill you. No matter the choice, you cannot win. Decide who you are going to be: the pathetic Elyn or the heartless Vale."

Valeyn felt her tendril of feeling creeping out toward Yvorre but she didn't stop it. She closed her eyes as she made contact and sensed a familiar conflict within her mother – and in that moment, finally understood her.

"I'm neither of those girls anymore, Mother. I'm Valeyn." Although she'd said those words before, she knew this was the first time she truly believed them. "I've made mistakes and bad choices, just like you have. You don't have to try and make it all mean something. You're not right; neither is Bythe. You're both as flawed as I am. Don't you see?" Valeyn looked into the sunken eyes of her conflicted mother. "We're the same. Two broken halves each trying to contend with the other. The more you try to be Maelene, the further you retreat into Yvorre when you fail. Just accept who you are, accept who you aren't, accept *what* you aren't."

A flash of indigo blinded Valeyn's vision, and she was hurled back again. This time there was pain. A terrible cry rent the air, but it was not hers. Valeyn opened her eyes to see Yvorre thrashing aimlessly in rage.

"Quiet, all of you. Just stop!" she snarled.

Valeyn started to rise but Yvorre roared something unintelligible and an orange flame washed over her. The Tower shuddered again, and more glass rocks fell from the terraces above. There was a scream, and Yvorre spun to her left – blue fire flaring ready in her hands.

The old woman looked down into the terrified eyes of Naya. She lay broken and helpless. Her crude leg irons had been shattered from the falling rocks and from Yvorre's indiscriminate hate.

"Please don't hurt me." Naya's voice was a whimper. The plea of a child without any hope of protection. It was nothing less than a pure and desperate plea to live, like another child might have once begged to live.

Yvorre's face fell from anger to surprise to dismay. A wail of grief rose from her throat, and she sank to her knees. The whirlwind of light paused, and the room was suddenly quiet but for Yvorre's muffled sobs. Aleasea and Ferehain were slowly rising to their feet, relieved of whatever trap Yvorre had placed them in. The room was littered with the fallen rubble from the broken archways, and a crack had lifted one half of the room several feet higher than the other. Exedor's body lay partially covered by the glass rocks. Valeyn stood and watched Yvorre cautiously. The older woman rubbed her eyes and bent over, gently cradling Naya as she lifted her from the floor. She looked down at Naya, Maelene's warmth shining on Yvorre's twisted face.

"Shin was right, child. I have lived for far too long."

Valeyn took a careful step forward. "Mother?" she asked.

Yvorre looked at her daughter, and Valeyn could see a fragile peace restored to her eyes. "I do not belong here, Valeyn. No matter what I try to do, I will cause pain and suffering. I have lingered in this place for too long, and I have permitted it to poison me. My every waking thought has been obsession, a need to triumph – and for what? What have I gained? What has it cost us?" She looked around, as if viewing the world for the first time. "I have to leave. I do not want to...but I must."

Valeyn didn't know what to say. She was unprepared for the mixed emotions evoked by Maelene's confession.

"There's no place for me here – no place for people like us." She sighed and looked down at Naya. "What would you do, child? What do you want?"

Naya looked from Maelene to Valeyn as if unsure what to say. "I just want to live. I want to be happy, and I want to be normal."

Maelene smiled and tears filled her tired eyes. "And these are the only ambitions we should have pursued, the only ones that should satisfy us." She turned to look at the destruction around her, at the bodies of Shin and Exedor, and then finally at her children – Valeyn, Aleasea, and Ferehain. She shook her head in remorse. "Shin was right. I cannot stay. We do not belong here. I am so sorry for what I have done, for everything I have done. You will need to follow your own path now. I am not the one to mold your future."

Aleasea nodded and bowed her head. Ferehain simply watched her expressionlessly. After centuries of guidance, of ideology and dogmatic purpose, there were now no final instructions, no parting advice – only the pragmatic reality of what had to be done. In that moment, Maelene seemed diminished somehow. As if the lies of all the gods were now recognized and the falsehood of their existence exposed.

Maelene's eyes met Valeyn's. "Daughter, please trust me with the *kai*. We need to leave Kovalith. Quickly, please."

Valeyn reluctantly relaxed her mental grip, and the two tendrils of green and red drifted from her. Maelene gently snatched them out of the air, and the nimbus of color reignited above them.

Maelene looked down at Naya as if she were a newborn. "I will take you to a place where you will never feel pain. Where you will walk again and live forever. Where I can show you wonders that nobody on this world has ever seen. Would you like that?"

Tears welled in Naya's blue eyes. "I'd like that very much."

Maelene smiled and looked at Valeyn. "Come with us, please. This place is also not for you."

Valeyn felt an urge to say yes. It would be so easy to go with them and to never feel the burden of pain or responsibility again. She wondered if anyone would begrudge her this reward? Hadn't she earned it?

But there was another opportunity before her that she could not ignore. The fires of the *kai* called to her, and she knew this bridge could take her anywhere within Kovalith. The images of Fairhaven's ruin clung to her mind. She had to know if Jason survived. Had she changed the future she'd witnessed in the Oraculate? She couldn't abandon Jason to whatever fate awaited him, not when she might yet prevent it.

"I can't follow you, not yet," Valeyn admitted. "I need to go to Fairhaven."

"Think on this carefully. You might never regain entry to The Tower once you leave. This may be your only chance."

Naya looked at her imploringly. "Please come with me, Valeyn. I'm going to walk again. I want to you see."

Valeyn smiled down at her. "Soon, Naya. I'll join you soon. There's something I need to do first – a couple of things."

Maelene nodded as if she understood. "Come to us as soon as you can, child. Shin was right. There is nothing but madness for you within the Forge."

The whirlpool of color swum above them all, only this time it had reverted to a beautiful conduit to the sky. It began to descend, focusing like a funnel to the center of the damaged room.

Aleasea touched Valeyn's arm. "Take us with you. We will help."

"No, her journey is too dangerous for us," Ferehain snapped. "Valeyn can do what must be done. We can travel to her later."

Aleasea looked at Ferehain in confusion for a moment but relented. "Very well. We will join you as soon as we can, Valeyn. Please take care of yourself."

Valeyn took Aleasea's hand and smiled. "I'll be fine. I'll see you both again."

Ferehain nodded – which Valeyn realized was probably the most affection he had ever displayed toward her. For a moment, Valeyn considered hugging him simply to see how he'd react. Instead, she pushed the thought away with a smile and nodded in return. She turned and walked into the spiral of energy that had already enveloped Maelene and Naya. An array of color and light immediately assailed her. It was as if her body no longer existed and her mind floated within a storm of light and delicate music. Music that was calling her home. She steeled herself against the temptation and focused on Fairhaven.

Come to us, child.

A chorus of voices seemed to echo within the colors. Voices from a family she never knew. She turned away.

Fairhaven. She fixed the image firmly in her mind.

"Come to us soon, Daughter." Maelene's words were so faint they were almost a whisper.

"Goodbye, Valeyn. I love you." Naya's voice drifted to her, and Valeyn clung to every word, knowing she would never hear them again.

The two forms vanished into the spectrum of light, and Valeyn felt her own consciousness start to fade.

Fairhaven.

She fixed the image of her burning home into her mind as it dissolved into the colors of the *kai.*

There were two more things she needed to do.

And she was tired of hiding.

CHAPTER 4

"Do not become distracted by the petty goals of war.
Do not become distracted by Fairhaven, nor the Ageless, nor even by
the seduction of victory.
These things mean little to me.
There is but one command you must follow.
There is but one order you must see done above all others.
Bring my daughter before me."

~Imperial Orders of Lord Bythe the Immortal
to Commander Ethan of Mac-Soldai

A haze lay thick in the air as Ethan stepped through the blackened rubble of Fairhaven. Curls of smoke rose like vines from fires smoldering within charred piles of rocks and timber. He still struggled to understand how this had happened, *why* this had happened. He picked up something lying in the rubble – a blackened bronze sign covered in soot. He brushed the grime away with his gloved hand to reveal the words *The Last Jar* stenciled into the metal. This had been a tavern once. Now it was nothing, erased as though it had never existed. The sign clattered as he threw it back into the wreckage like rubbish. Most of the city was gone, burned out of existence through the early hours of the morning while his men could only stand and watch from a distance. They had moved into the city at first light, but it was as they had feared; Fairhaven had been gutted. The outer wall had withstood the blaze, as had the inner wall around the Old City, but in between the two structures there lay nothing but ruins. Here and there stood a half-collapsed warehouse or stone building that had somehow been spared from the blaze, but those surviving structures were the lucky few.

This was not happening the way he had planned it. He was supposed to subdue Fairhaven with terror and claim the Temple in the name of Bythe. Once word had spread that the Iron Union now controlled the power of Maelene, the will of the Outer Wild would collapse. Bythe had entrusted him with this mission. The desecration of Maelene's creation would almost certainly draw Valeyn out of hiding – perhaps even Yvorre – then Exedor would find her and bring her home to the Ironhelm. But Jason – that *madman* – had destroyed everything.

Fairhaven had been defeated; this was evident. He had even given Jason enough time to evacuate his people – a clear concession between commanders, if an unspoken one. There had been no cause for this. What sort of nihilistic rage had fueled these flames?

"Gone, I tell you, it is gone!" E'mar's voice rose in a shrill pitch as he hurried toward Ethan through the rubble.

Ethan rubbed the bridge of his nose. E'mar's fragile temperament was not what he would have expected from the fabled Ageless, but then he should have expected that E'mar would not behave like his brethren. E'mar had reached out to Bythe of his own accord – had made a deal with a sworn enemy.

A traitor. There was no greater sin in Ethan's eyes. Even Jason's destructive sabotage was worthy of a measure of respect, but E'mar's treachery was contemptable on every level.

"Calm yourself, Ageless. What is gone?" Ethan asked.

E'mar reached into his robes and brought forth the Cour. Its pulsing green light seemed to be weaker. "The source of *kai*. They have destroyed it."

Ethan closed his eyes in a vain attempt to restrain his mounting anger. "We need to get you to the Temple. You won't know for sure until—"

"Do not lecture me on this! You know nothing of these things. I have been one with the *kai* for hundreds of years. I can feel it."

"Then how could you let this happen?" Ethan shouted. "You were supposed to control your Ageless and prevent them from using the power. How did they do this?"

E'mar shook his head frantically. "I do not know. I sealed the Arcadia from them all. I understand the Entarion, but the ways of the Violari can be foreign to me. Who knows what black tricks that coward Ferehain taught his followers?"

Coward? Ethan figured there had been but one coward among the Ageless – the one standing before him. The one who had reached out to Bythe, who had become disillusioned by the betrayal of Maelene and by his own lack of importance within the Ageless. A man who had been promised lordship over Fairhaven and the Temple once it was occupied by the Iron Union. A man who – like so many others – had simply craved power and recognition as a hopeful end to the insecurities that plagued him. It seemed that immortality was no barrier to vanity after all.

"Then let's find out what they've done," said Ethan as he walked past E'mar toward the center of Fairhaven. His men had reported the barricades as soon as they had penetrated the Old City. Ethan had to admit he'd been surprised. He'd been ready for the possibility of a rear guard, but he hadn't expected Jason to remain in a defensible position. What was he hoping to achieve? Everything the man had done was completely irrational, and now he was going to get more of his men killed through his own reckless spite. E'mar followed as they cleared the inner wall and approached the marketplace.

Salus saw Ethan approaching and gave him a rough salute.

"What are we looking at, Salus?" Ethan asked.

"We've got the square surrounded on three sides, but the side by the river leading up to the Temple is cut off from us."

"Can't we approach the Temple from the other side?"

"We tried, but it's a mess over there from all the burning wreckage. It'll take days to clear."

"So, we have to go through these men if we want to get to the Temple," Ethan mused.

"I'm certain it's intentional, sir," Salus answered.

Ethan removed his helmet and ran a gloved hand through his red hair; he was tired. He scanned the barricades dotted with men in blue. "Is he there?"

Salus didn't need to ask who Ethan was referring to. "Yes, he's in command."

"Well, at least he has enough integrity to stay with his men." Ethan glanced at E'mar. "Well, what do you say, Ageless? Should we go and talk to him?"

"Sir!" Salus started to object, but Ethan held up his hand.

"It's alright. I won't get too close. Besides, I'll have E'mar protecting me."

E'mar glared at him and held up the pulsing glass ball. "If I do not restore access to the *kai*, then there will soon be little protection I can offer."

Ethan ordered a squire to bring him a blue cloth then walked out toward the marketplace with it held aloft. He could see the blue-clad soldiers with their arrows at the ready and made sure he stayed back far enough to make himself a difficult target. Still, he hoped there were no fine marksmen left among that group. He waited with the blue cloth held in the air, unsure if this would even work. After several minutes, Ethan was about to return when he saw one of the barricade carts move and a figure in blue wedged himself through. Jason's blonde hair identified him as he stopped some distance away.

"I'm here to talk, Captain," Ethan called out over the space between them.

"The last time you offered to talk, you murdered innocent people like a coward." Jason's voice carried clearly through the morning air. "And him," Jason pointed at E'mar, "he betrayed his own kind. The men of Fairhaven don't meet with cowards and traitors."

The roar of a cheer rose up from behind the barricades. Ethan gritted his teeth. Jason's words were the worst kind of weapon – the truth. A truth that could cut through your pride and your conscience. A truth that could tarnish his victory, possibly even disgrace it, especially if his victory was as Pyrrhic as he feared.

"You are beaten, Captain," Ethan retorted. "I offer you the same courtesy I offered you before. Surrender to us now and I will spare the lives of your men. You know you cannot win."

"And neither can you!" Jason shouted. At these words, Kaler emerged from behind the barricades and stood alongside Jason.

"I have burned the Arcadia, traitor," Kaler said to E'mar. "The *kai* within is no more. You will not take the power. None of us will have it. We have ensured your betrayal has been for nothing. Consider it our final gift to you."

"You've come here for nothing, Ethan," Jason shouted. "You've taken everything from us. You've taken everything from me. We're leaving you with nothing in return."

E'mar moaned and Ethan felt fury begin to mount. His mission was a failure. Fairhaven's only real value had been the secrets within the Temple. Now they were gone. He wanted to strike out at the useless sorcerer next to him, but he curtailed his anger instead. He took a step forward, choosing his words carefully, hoping to turn the balance in his favor.

"What are you hoping to achieve, Jason? This is childish now. You will not accomplish anything by leading your men to their death over your own hurt pride. Surrender for their sake!"

Jason stormed forward recklessly and halted in the middle of the open space, in full view of the Helmsguard archers. Ethan raised a hand to hold them off. If the Helmsguard cut Jason down during this show of defiance, the Fairhaven army would fight to the last man.

"This is not hurt pride!" Jason shouted. "You betrayed and murdered my family. You killed my child. I will see you pay for your crimes before I die."

Ethan closed his eyes as a grim understanding settled upon him. He wasn't facing a man ready to die – he was facing a man *looking* to die. How had things come to this? He had never intended to push Jason this far.

"I'll make you a deal, Ethan," Jason continued. "Prove to me you're not a coward who murders old men and women under the flag of peace. Face me now, and I will order my men to surrender, no matter the outcome of our duel. Reclaim your honor. Or are you nothing more than a coward who would rather hide behind the green robes of a traitor?"

The words stung and Ethan bristled at them; they were made all the worse for their honesty. Everything Jason accused him of was true, and Ethan's men knew it. Of course, the Helmsguard would never question him publicly, but the courts of the Iron Union were a very different matter. A failed mission was bad enough, but to fail and wear this disgrace to his family would be unthinkable.

Jason had managed to turn the trap of pride against his captor.

"Fine!" Ethan snarled and drew his sabre. Somewhere behind him, Salus shouted a warning but he ignored it. Ethan began walking to the middle of the space where Jason stood. Both sets of eyes were fixed on their enemy.

The ground trembled. It was slight at first, but quickly intensified as Ethan closed in on Jason. He stopped warily.

"What is this? You bait me with honor then you deceive me with a trap?" Ethan called out.

Jason's face betrayed his own confusion. He looked at E'mar then back to Ethan. "You coward! Don't try to blame your tricks on me! Are you that scared of me that you have to—"

Jason's words were cut off by a torrent of deep blue light streaming from the ground. It shot high into the sky like a comet, then turned and flew southward, leaving a streaming blue tail in its wake. A moment later, another sheet of light erupted from somewhere outside the walls and launched skyward in a crimson blaze. The trembling of the ground intensified, and Ethan struggled to maintain his balance. The stone wall along the Claiream River cracked, and rocks tumbled into the water with a splash. All around them, more shafts of light were erupting from the ground and streaming southward. Ethan gave Jason a cold smile.

"I commend you. It almost worked, but you launched your trap too soon."

Jason's face was a mask of rage. "Stop lying! This is your doing!"

Ethan hesitated. The fury in Jason's face was too genuine. Perhaps this wasn't his plan. The sheer power certainly seemed to be beyond him. Either way, this wasn't worth the risk, and he decided to be grateful for the opportunity to retreat with his honor intact, especially when he had more efficient ways of dealing with Jason. He saluted Jason with his sabre then walked backward toward his men, careful to never turn his back on his adversary.

"Coward!" Jason screamed. For a moment it seemed he would run after Ethan, but he looked at the Helmsguard poised with their loaded bows and decided against it – the difference between an honorable death and a stupid act of suicide restraining him. "Come back and face me!"

The ground shook again, and this time Ethan lost his footing briefly before regaining his balance. "What's going on?" he growled at E'mar once he was within earshot.

The Ageless was looking about him with an expression of awe and terror. "It is the *kai*, all of it. It is all breaking loose from the Forge and returning to the Render."

"What does that mean?" Ethan snapped.

"The *kai* of all gods binds the world together. Without it, Kovalith will be no more!"

Ethan's head snapped back to where Jason stood. *This can't be* his *doing.*

There was another shudder and the trembling stopped. Ethan looked over his men to satisfy himself they were unharmed.

"Ethan! Face me!" Jason screamed again. Ethan turned to Salus and gave him a signal. The order was passed to a messenger who sprinted toward the city gates. Ethan then turned back to Jason.

"No, I don't think so, Captain. I don't think I can trust you to fight with honor," Ethan called out.

Jason spat on the ground. "Then come and take us when you work up the courage, bastards. We're ready to take you to our graves."

Ethan smiled. "No, I don't think we'll be doing that either. Now that you've destroyed the Temple, well, we really don't need to be that cautious anymore."

A terrible shriek filled the air, and the wall to the south vanished in a torrent of flame. Bricks flew in all directions as a gaping hole was ripped in the ancient fortification. As the smoke cleared, the silhouette of the last war engine slowly began to materialize. It lurched toward the gap with its awkward gait. The team of Cremators scurried around the base, pouring the liquid Godfire into the belly of the engine as it moved.

Jason stared at the machine and a grim realization settled across his face. Ethan could almost read his thoughts. He shouted a command to the Helmsguard, and two hundred men drew sabers and nocked arrows into longbows. For Jason, it was now a choice between death by fire or death by suicidal charge. They both knew which Jason would choose.

"Stop!"

The voice rang impossibly clear over the marketplace. Ethan turned in the direction of the voice, toward the bridge. There was a woman, tall and proud with long, sandy-colored hair tied behind her head. She was unarmed, but she walked with a sense of power and purpose that suggested she had an army of followers at her side. Ethan looked at her, and in that moment, he realized Bythe's prediction had been right. His efforts had not been in vain. Valeyn had returned.

·   ·   ·

She had emerged from the smoldering ruin of the Temple, shocked by the sheer devastation around her. It was far worse than the brief view from the Oraculate. There was nothing left of the city she had once called home. A smoking gap lay in the wall to the Old City, and a massive black tower was lurching through it. Even Vale had never seen a machine like this in all her years at the Ironhelm, but she now understood this could only be the product of the unholy work between Shin and Bythe. She looked toward the marketplace and saw what she hoped to find – a small group of Fairhaveners were assembled against the surrounding Helmsguard. Valeyn wasn't sure what she could do, but she knew she had to try something. The steps of the Temple shifted as she hurried down them and over to the stone bridge; there she paused. Among the Helmsguard figures, Ethan's red hair was visible and unmistakable to her. A wave of relief flooded her at seeing the familiar face and she prayed to the gods that she wasn't too late, that Jason was still alive.

"Stop!"

Everyone turned at her shout. She crested the bridge and took in the scene before her. The Helmsguard were clearly victorious. Vale's military training came to the fore of her mind, and she recognized the Ringed Fortress formation used by the Ironhelm – a battlefield tactic to enforce surrender or to ensure an efficient victory. What surprised her was the figure of E'mar standing alongside Ethan. The Ageless look like a mockery of his name, now tired and weary as he stood regarding Valeyn as if she were a viper. She could sense deep fear emanating from him – fear and regret.

"Elyn?" Jason's disbelieving voice took her by surprise. Valeyn looked at the strange man who spoke and saw through the grief-stained face to recognize the eyes of her friend.

"Jason!" It was an exclamation of equal parts horror and relief.

Within seconds she had crossed the market and wrapped him in her arms. It felt odd to be taller than him, but at that moment it didn't matter. The sorrow radiating from him was like a black pit of despair, and she gripped him tightly as if willing him to hold together.

"Jason, what's happened here?" she whispered.

Jason couldn't reply. He thumped his fists against her back in a futile gesture of rage. He didn't need words. Valeyn could feel his grief. The images of the past few months swirled through her head and almost knocked her down.

"Oh my gods, Jason. I'm so sorry." It was all she could say in the face of such despair.

"He betrayed us, Elyn. I couldn't stop them. I had to burn it all." Jason was raving like a man deranged, and it seemed Valeyn was the only force holding him upright.

"Commander Vale, you have returned to us." Ethan's voice rang out across the marketplace.

Valeyn gripped Jason firmly. "Let me handle this. Stay here."

She turned from Jason and walked out into the open space where Ethan was waiting. "You murdered Paeter?" Valeyn's voice was cold.

The confidence in Ethan's eyes faltered for a moment, then a fire returned to them. "This is war, Vale. You understand that, or at least you used to understand.

"No, I never did anything like that. I never betrayed trust, I never betrayed honor, and neither did you."

"You betrayed us!" Ethan cried. "You left us and sided with them." He pointed to Jason and Kaler.

"I sided with no one. I left Fairhaven the same day I left you. I would not be used as a piece in anyone's game – not by them, not by you."

"I had to face Bythe after you left us. Don't you dare judge me for what I've had to do since. If you condemn me for my actions, then you should have remained behind to prevent them. Don't you understand? You were our leader, Vale. Your *absence* brought this about."

Valeyn sighed and looked over at the Helmsguard assembled behind him – obedient and loyal. "You're right about that, and that's something I intend to fix."

Ethan's face lit with faint hope. "Are you surrendering to us?"

She shook her head. "No. I'm not going to be your prisoner. I'll return to my place as your commander, and together we'll return to my father."

Ethan's stare was disbelieving. "You cannot be serious. I won't hand over my command to you simply because you've *chosen* to return."

E'mar surged forward. "You arrogant little bitch. You destroyed us. You brought a disease into our Sanctuary that rotted us from the inside. It was all you. And now you want to come back and claim the glory? You're too late. I control the power now." E'mar thrust the Cour forward and a lance of green energy flew at Valeyn. Ethan shouted something but it was too late – the green fire tore through the air toward her. She raised her hand and caught the *kai*. It stretched like a rope between them. E'mar's eyes widened in surprise.

"No, this isn't possible," he muttered. "I control it. It's mine!" He extended his other hand in an attempt to launch a second attack, but nothing happened.

"It was never yours. It was my mother's, and now it belongs to me." Valeyn gestured slightly with her own spare hand, and the glass orb in E'mar's hand flared and then shattered, causing him to scream. Green light swirled around him for a moment then trickled across the space to Valeyn, like water naturally seeking a path down a hill.

"No!" screamed E'mar as he felt the energies of the Ageless stolen from him. He gripped onto the green fire between them both, but Valeyn gripped also, and with a flick of her arm she sent E'mar flying through the air to crash unceremoniously several feet behind her.

E'mar tried to get up, searching for his bearings. "Oh gods," he said as he looked up into the face of the man standing above him. Jason stared back at the man who had betrayed Nadine's father to his death. The man who had caused Nadine so much pain. Perhaps even the man who had cost him his daughter? Jason would never know the truth.

But today he decided E'mar would be a good enough proxy. He rained blows as savagely as he ever had. With every jolt, he thought of his cold baby lying on the bench. Elyn. He screamed in fury as he pummeled his fists on the Ageless, and when he felt his hand break against the wet ruin of E'mar's face, he began kicking him. Jason kicked E'mar until he felt bones break, and he finally fell to the ground in exhaustion. He remembered the guilt and nausea he'd felt the first time he'd killed a man. Now he felt nothing. Tears left tracks through the grime on his face, and he stared vacantly through the body of E'mar – the brutal result of his work.

Ethan backed away from them. "No, I won't let you win this time. Not again." He signaled to the Cremators, and the war engine began to shudder with its shrill whine.

"And I'm no longer giving you a choice," Valeyn answered.

The war engine pulsed to her eyes – the Godfire within flared red with the energy of Bythe. The energy of her father, that she now understood, and that she no longer feared.

Valeyn tensed her legs and launched herself at the machine. Her body flung through the air, and she landed before the engine in one leap, causing the Cremators to scurry backward in fear. She righted herself and stared up at the twisted tower of Iron. The red energy of the Godfire surged throughout the construct. She could sense it as if it were calling to her. Vale closed her eyes and drew on the power. There was a groan of metal as the tower began to tilt toward her in response. The Cremators began screaming as they ran away from the engine. Behind her, Valeyn could hear shouts from men, orders to stop her – she concentrated harder and called to Bythe's *kai* with all her will. The war engine simply ripped apart, and a molten flame enveloped everything around her. She briefly heard screams of horror before the sounds were eclipsed by the roar of the red fire. It burned her clothes and seared her flesh, but within that inferno she was unharmed. The Godfire couldn't hurt her. It was only another form of the essence of her father, and now it was hers to command.

She let the fire wash over her, through her, cleansing her and forging her in its fury. Then she called the blaze to her breast, drawing it into herself as if it were nothing more than air. The bulk of the ruined war engine was still toppling toward her and she let it come. With her arms outstretched, she smashed her fists against the black iron of the weapon as it fell against her, splitting the metal with her hands and sending it flying in shards.

Valeyn turned back to the Helmsguard and stepped forward. She was burning bright with a red fire that danced over her naked body and set her hair alight as if it were pure flame. She walked toward Ethan, ignoring the Cremators who all prostrated themselves in her wake. Even Ethan looked awed. She stood before the assembled might of the Helmsguard – a beautiful naked fire – and spoke in that same terrible voice.

"I am Valeyn, daughter of Bythe the Immortal. You will kneel before me."

One of the Helmsguard instantly saluted and kneeled with his head bowed in the appropriate show of respect to Bythe. The man standing behind him quickly did the same. One by one, the entire Helmsguard army dropped to a knee and saluted her. Valeyn did not react. In that moment she expected nothing less – she commanded nothing less.

Ethan refused to bow. Instead, he stepped before her. "You're not our leader anymore, Vale."

"Yes, I am, Ethan. I am the daughter of your god. You will follow me because you owe me that respect, and also because I will give you what you want. I will return to the Ironhelm with you."

He looked at her and seemed unsure what to say. She interrupted his thoughts, keen to speak before he had a chance to wrestle with his pride. "I will lead you back to the Ironhelm, Ethan. I will lead my men. I was Vale, Commander of the Iron Union. I am Valeyn, daughter of Bythe. My claim to command is sound. My father will welcome my return, and you can be at my side when I do." She fixed him with a glare that burned even more intently through the fire. "Or you can try to fight me, and I will make sure you return to the Ironhelm without me – again."

Their eyes remained locked. Then Ethan placed his closed fist across his chest and – never breaking their gaze – kneeled before her.

Valeyn let the red fire cool on her skin and stood before them all – naked and powerful. She felt no shame or sense of modesty as she commanded Ethan to send his men beyond the city walls. They obeyed without question. Only Ethan lingered behind. Ignoring him, she walked over to where Jason sat beside the ruined corpse of E'mar. There was a sense of complete emptiness from him. Wishing to spare him any further discomfort, she took E'mar's green robe from where it had ripped free and fallen in the dirt, and she covered her naked body with it.

Kaler nodded respectfully toward her. She remembered him and his treatment of her in the Arcadia, but her childhood grievances seemed petty now.

"Leave us," she commanded curtly, and he obeyed without a word. "Jason, you need to get up."

He looked up at her with hollow eyes as if he hadn't heard her. She leaned over and gently pulled him to his feet. "On your feet, Captain. These men still need you."

He glanced back at them, and Valeyn realized he'd forgotten they were there. "We were going to die. We were supposed to die here."

"You're not going to die today. I won't allow it. The Helmsguard are going to let you leave. You're going to take your men and find the others. You're going to protect them and lead them. You're all they have now."

He shook his head and looked away. "I don't want to."

"I know, and that's why you need to." Valeyn touched his cheek and turned his face toward her. She looked into Jason's eyes and connected with his feelings effortlessly. She could sense the turmoil of a thousand conflicts within.

He glanced at Ethan and his eyes hardened. "Let me face him."

"No!" Valeyn's voice was commanding again. A conversation came unbidden to her mind as a memory from Jason reached out to her across their connection. Captain Lewis's last words to Jason from a lifetime ago. "Will you pick a fight to prove something to yourself, so others can pay the price your pride demands? Is that the sort of man you want to be?" she said.

Jason looked at her in shock. He opened his mouth as if to answer but closed it again.

"There's been enough killing," Valeyn continued. "Leave him to me. I'll make sure the Iron Union pays for what they've done today."

Jason shook his head. "I don't know, Elyn. Everything's different now. I don't know if I can keep leading these people. I don't think I can go back to the man I was."

"Jason, look at me." Valeyn asserted herself in front of him. "You've faced things I can't imagine. You're the strongest and bravest man I've ever known. I know you can overcome this. You're not going to be the same person anymore, but if there's anyone who can come back from something like this, it's you."

Jason signed and nodded vaguely. "What are you going to do?"

Jason had asked her that same question a long time ago. This time Valeyn was ready to give him a different answer.

"I'm going to Bythe. I need to confront my father. I need to stop this pointless war. It's cost us all far too much. I need to make sure that what happened here never happens again, but I can't do that and protect our people at the same time. I need you to defend them for me, please."

Jason looked from Ethan to Valeyn, then finally nodded.

"Elyn..." he said softly. "I called my daughter Elyn."

Valeyn pulled Jason to her and hugged him fiercely. "I love you so much, Jason. Please stay alive for me. I can't lose you too."

Jason nodded and she felt his tears against her neck. She held back her own grief. She would have to find time for it later. She needed to be strong in this moment. She pulled back and looked into Jason's eyes. "Find Nadine. Tell her I love her. Watch over her, and I promise I'll find you again." She kissed him on the forehead like he was a brother then stepped away. "Now go, quickly."

Jason took a few steps back and roughly wiped the tears from his eyes as if to hide them from his men. "Take care of yourself, Elyn," he said.

Valeyn smiled at him in a playful way. "Have you forgotten who defeated Imbatal? You really need to stop treating me like I can't swing a sword."

He smiled back at her then turned and walked toward his men. Kaler again respected her with a formal bow before following Jason.

Valeyn knew it was time for her to go. She turned her back to the ruins of Fairhaven and walked to where Ethan waited. "Still here? Are you afraid I'll run again?" she asked as she approached.

"No, Vale. I didn't think it would be appropriate for you to return to the Ironhelm wearing the robes of our enemy, and since you're technically back in command now…"

Ethan had unstrapped his breastplate while he spoke and handed it to her. It was beautifully crafted, like all ironwork from the Union, plates of black iron with gold trimming on the edges.

"Thank you, Ethan," she replied as she took the armor in one hand. "But I'm not sure this is appropriate either." She looked between the black armor and the Ageless cloak before letting the green cloth fall to the ground. Her gaze turned to the breastplate and she gripped it firmly with both hands. The metal began to shift as if it were clay. Molding it with her thoughts as much as with her hands, she pulled it to her body and let the metal wrap itself around her form. It grew over her figure wherever she willed it, iron plates overlapping over her form like an insect's shell, and within moments it covered her completely – a suit of iron, colored with the bright, emerald hues of Maelene.

Ethan nodded. "Well, that is sure to make an impression."

Valeyn took a last look at the ruins of the Temple and hoped her Mother could see her. She almost said a prayer.

"I'm ready," she announced.

Ethan extended his arm toward the western gates. Valeyn walked toward them, leaving the ruins of Fairhaven behind her, knowing she would never return.

EPILOGUE

Ferehain watched as Valeyn vanished into the brilliant spectrum of light. Once she had disappeared, the funnel of power died and The Tower fell silent.

"Then it is done. The Tower is dormant once more," Aleasea said as she looked about the ruined chamber.

"It would appear so," Ferehain answered, walking over to where the body of Shin lay. He looked down at him thoughtfully. "Just another old man in the end."

"What do you mean?" Aleasea asked but Ferehain didn't answer. Instead, he continued his tour of the rubble, talking almost to himself. "It would seem that our *betters* have taken the keys to The Tower with them."

"They will always leave you behind. They do not care." The weak voice of Exedor drifted from within the rubble and Ferehain smiled. Aleasea was immediately on guard, but Ferehain waved at her casually.

"Please, Aleasea, he is certainly no threat to us in his current condition." Ferehain found what he was looking for in the rubble and collected it before turning to where Exedor lay. He was coughing under the rubble. A giant chunk of glass rock had crushed his legs, and blood trickled from his mouth.

"You see it, don't you?" Exedor rasped as the two Ageless approached. "These gods have never been fit to rule over us. We were mad to ever worship them...mad or weak."

"I cannot deny the truth of that," Ferehain said as he stood over him.

"Then work with me. With my knowledge of Bythe's workings and your experiences with Maelene, we could be unstoppable. There is only one god left in the world now, and the Prodigals are ready to act against him."

Ferehain nodded slowly, and Aleasea looked at him with shock on her porcelain face. "You cannot form an alliance with this creature, not after all he has done," she said.

"He makes an argument I cannot deny. The time of the gods is over. There is now only one left, and it is time he finally meets my justice." He looked down at Exedor and smiled. "But you are wrong about one thing. I have no need of you."

Ferehain revealed the metal bar he had taken from Naya's leg irons in the rubble and brought it down onto Exedor's body. Over and over, he smashed the pole onto the broken arms, legs, and ribs of the screaming Inquisitor.

A crack of laughter broke from Ferehain's lips as he threw the bloodstained bar aside with the clatter of metal. "Perhaps the gods are not all bad, Exedor. They do seem to have an ironic sense of justice from time to time."

He reached down and ripped the shirt away from Exedor's bloodied frame. Gripping the metal device that was stitched into his stomach, Ferehain wrenched it free as Exedor unleashed a sickening scream of primal desperation before passing out.

"Ferehain, what are you doing?" Aleasea gasped.

"The key to opening The Tower lies with the essence of Bythe and Maelene together. The metals of the Iron Union hold little mystery to me." He concentrated on the bloodied piece of machinery, and it began to glow a lurid shade of red. A smile lit up his face along with the scarlet light. He reached out with one hand and called the green *kai* of Maelene to him. As soon as the green light shone in his hands alongside the red, the swirling vortex of The Tower snapped back to life above them.

"Ferehain, my gods," Aleasea whispered.

"He was right about one thing, Aleasea. They are not worthy of worship; they have never been. I do not expect you to understand this, you have always been an idealist. Perhaps that is why I once loved you." Ferehain shrugged as he walked to the archway at the far side of the room.

"Ferehain, please wait," Aleasea called as she followed him. "What do you hope to achieve with this—"

Her words died as she entered the chamber. The rhythmic ticking of a hundred mechanical hearts stopped her. They had awoken with The Tower, and they now stood ready.

"No, Ferehain. You cannot do this, please. They are monsters!"

Ferehain's blow was as surprising as it was brutal. It struck her on the side of the head, and she crumpled to the cold floor without a sound. He looked at her prone body and felt a twinge of remembered pain. He paused and chose to remember tender moments with her from a long time ago. He relished them for the last time, then closed his eyes and, with a conscious act of will, he burned them from his mind forever.

"They are not monsters. They are soldiers. They will never grow old, never die."

The creatures turned their heads to greet the master of The Tower. One hundred and five clockwork horrors snapped to mechanical attention and awaited orders. Ferehain looked over them and smiled.

"They are ageless."

TO BE CONCLUDED...

ACKNOWLEDGEMENTS

Again, another book has been painstakingly produced and again there are so many people who have helped bring this creation to life. I sincerely thank you all.

To Pamela Taylor – a great editor and author - who has helped polish my rough words into something resembling the English language.

To Richard A.A. Larraga who took beta reading to the next level. You've been an amazing help and I thank you for all of your efforts. Your attention to detail is exceptional. Thanks to the others who also helped me add the finishing touches – Ally Burnham, Mel King, AK Alliss, Tash Austin Brown and Adalaide Hyde.

To my brother Andrew, for once again reading my rough ideas and giving me the early feedback I needed to shape this story. This trilogy would not be the same without you.

To my beautiful wife Anya, who has supported me while I sat in my writing chair day after day and unquestioningly volunteered to read everything I write. You've been an inspiration and an anchor. Again, this book just would not have existed without you.

And finally, thanks to the readers – that's you - who are taking this journey with me. I'm very grateful for your time and I hope you're enjoying the ride

About the Author

Christopher Monteagle is a lifelong fantasy reader and writer of fiction in various forms. Growing up in outback Australia with no running water, electricity, or - needless to say – television, Christopher was introduced to books by Tolkien and Herbert to pass the time. He soon began writing his own stories and became immersed in the worlds of fantasy and fiction. *The Union of Lies* is Christopher's second novel.

NOTE FROM THE AUTHOR

Word-of-mouth is crucial for any author to succeed. If you enjoyed *The Union of Lies*, please leave a review online—anywhere you are able. Even if it's just a sentence or two. It would make all the difference and would be very much appreciated.

Thanks!
Christopher Monteagle

For fans of **Christopher Monteagle**, please check out our recommended title for your next great read!

In the Wake of Gods
The Godless Trilogy: Book One

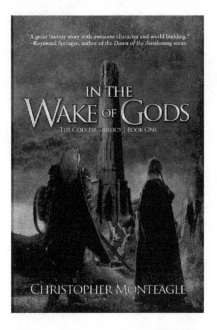

"Loved it! A thought-provoking fantasy novel with intriguing and empathetic female protagonists."
-*REEDSY DISCOVERY*

View other **Black Rose Writing** titles at
www.blackrosewriting.com/books and use promo code
PRINT to receive a **20% discount** when purchasing.